children of chaos

books by dave duncan

Please see www.daveduncan.com for more information.

children
of chaos

◆

dave duncan

◆

a tom doherty associates book  new york

CHILDREN OF CHAOS

Copyright © 2006 by Dave Duncan

Edited by Liz Gorinsky

A Tor Book
Published by Tom Doherty Associates, LLC
175 Fifth Avenue
New York, NY 10010

www.tor.com

Tor® is a registered trademark of Tom Doherty Associates, LLC.

Library of Congress Cataloging-in-Publication Data

Duncan, Dave, 1933–
    Children of chaos / Dave Duncan.—1st ed.
        p. cm.
    "A Tom Doherty Associates Book."
    ISBN 0-765-31483-5 (acid-free paper)
    EAN 978-0-765-31483-3
    I. Title.
    PR9199.3.D847C48 2006
    813'.54—dc22

                                    2005033423

First Edition: June 2006

Printed in the United States of America

0 9 8 7 6 5 4 3 2 1

This book is dedicated to the memory of
Robyn Meta Herrington
1961–2004
who loved it and helped make it.

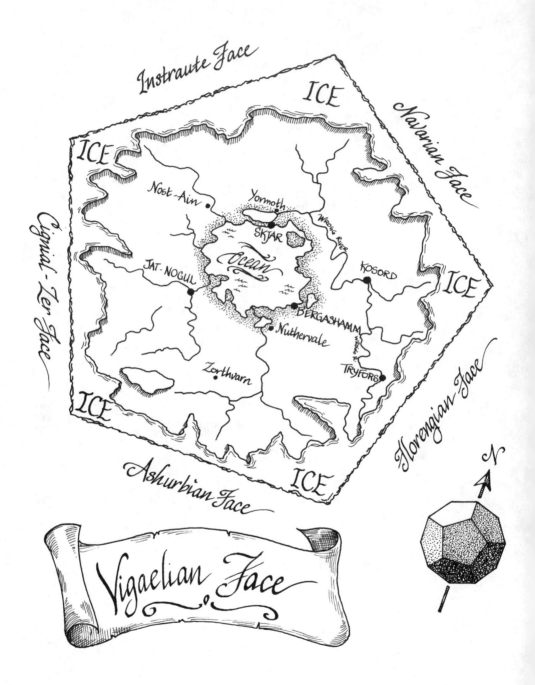

Instraute Face

ICE

Navarian Face

ICE

Cignal-Zer Face

ICE

Nost-Ain

Yormoth

SKJAR

Ocean

Wrong River

KOSORD

ICE

JAT-NOGUL

DERGASHAMM

Nuthervale

Wrong R.

Zorthvarn

TRYFORS

ICE

Florengian Face

Ashurbian Face

ICE

Vigaelian Face

N

Navarian Face

Vigoelian Face

ICE

ICE

Veritano • UMSINA
Piaregga
• Napora
CELEBRE • • Reggoni

Ocean

Miona
Ravima

Boluzzi

Merilan

ICE

ICE

Piandese Face

ICE

Ashurbian Face

Sien-Vesp Face

N

Florengian Face

Preface

THE GODS

The true rulers of the world are the Bright Ones:
Anziel, goddess of beauty
Cienu, god of mirth and chance
Demern, god of law and justice
Eriander, god-goddess of sex and madness
Hrada, goddess of crafts and skill
Mayn, goddess of wisdom
Nastrar, god of animals and nature
Nula, goddess of pity
Sinura, goddess of health
Ucr, god of prosperity and abundance
Veslih, goddess of the hearth and home
Weru, god of storm and battle
(There is also **Xaran,** goddess of death and evil,
    whose name is not spoken.)

IMPORTANT MORTALS

Hrag Hragson begat a daughter, **Saltaja,** and four sons, **Therek, Karvak, Stralg,** and **Horold.**

Piero, the doge of Celebre, had three sons, **Dantio, Benard,** and **Orlando,** and a daughter, **Fabia.**

Karvak died in Jat-Nogul and Dantio in Skjar.

HELPFUL NOTES

12 Werists make a flank.
4 flanks and a packleader make a pack.

5 packs and a huntleader make a hunt.

5 hunts and a hostleader make a host, 1,231 men.

A **pot-boiling** is the time needed for a crock of cold water to come to the boil on an open fire, roughly one hour.

The unit of counting is one **sixty**, which therefore takes a singular-form plural: e.g., "four sixty," as we say "four hundred" or "four dozen."

SOME OBSCURE VOCABULARY

Chthonian: Related to the underworld

Corban: An offering sworn to God

Menzil: The distance a caravan travels in one day

Henotheist: A person who worships a single god without denying the existence of others (on Dodec, usually a member of a mystery cult)

Polytheist: A person who worships many gods (as most people on Dodec do)

Extrinsic: An outsider (used by members of a mystery to indicate a non-member, either a polytheist or a member of another cult)

THE WORLD

The Dodecians' image of their world is a physical impossibility. I have summarized the logic in an appendix at the end of the sequel volume, *Mother of Lies*. Until you have a chance to read that, please be charitable. It is not so very long ago that most people thought the Earth was a flat disk. The Dodecians may be mistaken, but they are not crazy enough to believe anything as absurd as that.

Prologue

LORD DANTIO

was very frightened, clutching the rail as tightly as he could—much tighter than he needed to, because the chariot ran smoothly on the paving and Papa was not going fast. The axle squealed, the guanacos' little hooves clip-clopped, wheels rumbled, the leather straps of the floor creaked, but that was all. No other sound.

When news of the massacre at Two Fords reached Celebre, the city went mad. For three days and nights the people mourned, clamoring and wailing, blowing trumpets, beating on drums or pots. Panic-stricken crowds packed into the temples until worshipers were being trampled or suffocated. But then, suddenly, the enemy was at the gates and the noise stopped. The city fell silent—completely, appallingly, silent.

Yet everywhere there were faces, thousands and thousands of faces—massed on balconies and roofs, in every window, and ten or twelve deep along both sides of the wide avenue—and they were all staring at him. All silent. Could they not even call out just one farewell, sing a dirge for him, shout a blessing? The entire city seemed to have turned out to watch his departure. He stared straight ahead, trying to ignore all the faces and keep his eyes fixed on the great gates drawing closer up ahead. He was horribly afraid that he was going to weep, or throw up, or piddle, or do something even more terrible to shame himself and Papa.

"Almost there," Papa said. "You are doing wonderfully! I am enormously proud of you."

Dantio looked up, feeling his lip quiver. Despite all the promises he had made to himself, he had to say it: "Papa, I'm scared!"

His father winced, as if he'd stubbed a toe. "You don't look it! I told you—courage is simply doing your duty even if you are frightened. By all the gods, son, you are a very brave boy doing his duty."

Brave people did not tremble. Their mouths were not drier than salt.

"Don't let the crowds worry you," his father said. "They're counting on you, son. The whole city is counting on you. And so am I. I am so proud of you I want to weep. Celebre is proud of you."

At last the chariot rumbled under the great arch into the narrow barbican, out of blazing sunlight into the shadow of high battlements. There were no soldiers up there manning the walls, because Celebre's city guard had died with the militia at Two Fords. The noise of hooves and axle redoubled, echoing. Papa slowed down to take the curve through the outer gate.

Dantio took a quick look back. The second chariot was bringing Mama and the baby, driven by a Nastrarian in his green robe. Witness Fiorella, wearing her seer's blindfold, was driving the third, bringing Benard and Orlando. Benard's face was only just visible over the rail; he looked scared, although he had nothing to worry about—he would be coming back. Orlando was too small to see over the sides of the car at all. He would be peering out through the wicker and probably throwing a temper tantrum because he had been strapped in.

One flap of the outer gate stood open and unguarded as the doge and his eldest son rolled past them, out into the menacing world beyond, into the noontide glare. *Goodbye, Celebre!* The open expanse around the city served variously as fairground, playing fields, and farmers' market, but that day it was deserted, just abandoned animal paddocks and grassland already burned brown by the dry-season heat. The Sturia road was a stripe of baked red clay weaving across it to disappear into olive groves and vineyards.

Papa drove at a walking pace on the rutted surface. There was no sign of the ice devils, but they would be waiting in the shade, staying out of bowshot of the walls.

Holy Demern, the Lawgiver, had decreed in ancient times that a boy of ten was old enough to understand oaths and laws. At ten he could be sentenced to men's punishments, like flogging or even hanging. He could be taken hostage.

Dantio was eleven.

He did not know where he would sleep tonight. He could not shake off the terrible fear that he might never see his home and family again. At his feet lay a bag of clothes Mama had packed for him. The ice devils had spared the little town of Sturia when it opened its gates and yesterday had promised to spare Celebre too, but they had warned they would demand hostages.

A chariot emerged from the trees, being driven much faster than Papa was going. The two men in it were obviously not Florengians, so they must be ice devils. Another followed it, more slowly. Dantio's knees began to shake even harder, and not just from the bouncing of the webbed floor.

"That's far enough." Papa reined in alongside a corral fence and dropped the brake. He went down on one knee and clasped his son in a fierce hug. "Well done, well done! That was the worst bit, I'm sure—all those people watching you."

Dantio did not think the worst bit had even started. He nodded and tried not to cry, biting his lip. His father's mourning robe smelled of lavender. It was the one he wore to funerals.

"Even if the Vigaelians do insist on taking you as hostage for my good faith, son, they will have to look after you well. Holy Demern gives very strict rules in His Arcana about hostages being well treated. Oh, Dantio, Dantio! We Celebrians are peace-lovers, not cowards. If we had any chance at all of defending the city, we would do it. If the bloodlord will take me instead of you, I will go gladly, but that was not what his messenger demanded.

"And I swear to you again, son, that I will do nothing to break the terms we agree on. I will give them no cause to harm you. And in a year or so, when they have learned that they can trust me, I will try to get them to send you home and take some other hostages in exchange—young men, not a child."

Dantio sniffed a few times and whispered, "Yes, Papa."

His father squeezed again and then released him. "You aren't behaving like a child. Keep being brave, always be polite, and no harm will come to you. Come along, let us go and see these Vigaelians."

Dantio jumped down, onto his shadow on the clay, and Papa followed. The other two chariots had halted alongside, and the Nastrarian was already in control of all three teams, stroking the guanacos' necks and murmuring as if he were talking to them. Being an initiate of the cult of holy Nastrar, he probably *was* talking to them; he would keep them standing there happily for hours, and be quite happy himself just doing so. Nastrarians never cared for people much.

Papa lifted Mama down, with Fabia still in her arms. Benard ran at once to his mother. Witness Fiorella unstrapped Orlando and set him down without letting go of him—she had no need to call on the wisdom of her goddess to know he would try to run away. He screamed and kicked. She would be needed in the parley, so Dantio went to take charge of Orlando. It would be for the last time.

"Come," he said. "Come and see the ice devils. They're very fierce."

The family terror decided that this sounded promising and went quietly. He even let Dantio hold his chubby little hand, although that would not last long.

The first ice devil chariot had stopped at a distance. One man had stayed aboard to control the team and the other was striding forward to meet the Celebrians. He was unarmed and very big. Some of the wilder stories had described the Vigaelians as monsters, but this one seemed quite human, apart from his bizarre coloring. He wore what seemed to be a black woolen blanket wrapped around his body, leaving his arms and legs bare. His head and face glinted with golden stubble; sunlight flashed on a golden collar around his neck. His eyes were a sickly blue. He stopped and looked around, waving angrily for the other chariot to hurry.

He had bigger muscles than even Markeo, the palace wheelwright.

Markeo had died at Two Fords.

"Why is that man red?" Orlando demanded.

"The sun burned him," Dantio said.

"Why?"

"Because." Dantio had heard that the ice devils' skin was pink instead of brown, and he could see that some parts of the man were pale, but most of him was blistered and peeling. He glanced back and saw the roofs and walls of Celebre packed with people, watching to see what would happen, waiting to learn their fate.

The second ice devil chariot arrived, and stayed just long enough to deliver a very oddly dressed person, draped from top to toe in cloth that had once been white. Since even her face was completely covered, she must be a seer. She scrambled down awkwardly, but more as if hampered by her long skirts than as if she were blind. How could she stand such clothes on such a hot day? Her driver drove the chariot away and she minced forward to stand at the big man's side. Only her hands showed; they were pink.

"'Anto, is that man hurt?" Orlando demanded. He must think she was bandaged.

"No, she's a seer, like Fiorella," Dantio said.

Orlando turned to frown up at Fiorella, who wore a respectable ladylike gown of dark brown and a blindfold to show she was on duty. Witnesses saw with the eyes of their goddess.

Papa bowed. "I am Doge Piero, ruler of this city. I have come to parley, as we agreed, and have brought all my children, as you requested."

The white-shrouded woman spoke. She would not be able to speak Florengian, or even properly know the words, but seers could always tell meaning, just as they could hear lies or recognize poison in a glass of wine. The man in black scowled and replied in a deep, rumbling voice, as if he were gargling rocks. When he had finished, Fiorella translated.

"He says he is Stralg Hragson, bloodlord of the Heroes of Weru, and he did not come to parley. He never requests, he gives orders. He is here to accept your submission and oath of allegiance."

Papa said, "I have agreed to give them. And he promised he would swear to respect our lives, property, and laws."

The Vigaelian seer interpreted. The bloodlord rumbled again.

"He says you already have his word."

That was not fair! If Papa had to take a solemn oath, then the murderous Vigaelian should certainly do the same, not just quote a promise sent through a messenger. More rumble.

"He asks who the woman is." Fiorella added softly, "Be careful, lord!"

Papa hesitated, but no one could deceive a Witness, so he had to tell the truth. "Oliva, my wife." He did not say that he had refused to bring Mama at first, but she had insisted she would not trust Fabia to a nurse. Dantio had overheard the argument yesterday.

Rumble. "The bloodlord also says that if you do not immediately kneel and kiss his feet in submission, she will be first to die."

Orlando let go of Dantio's hand. Dantio caught his arm instead. Orlando opened his mouth to scream and Dantio said "Shush!" so fiercely that he actually obeyed. Benard was hiding behind Mama, who was having trouble with Fabia. The baby could smell her milk and wanted to suck.

Horrible! Papa walked forward and sank to his knees in front of the hateful monster in his black shroud. Dantio looked away, unable to watch this humiliation of the father he loved.

Far to the northwest, under a sky of indigo, sharp young eyes could just make out the glimmer of white that marked the Ice, where no one normally went. Only a few brave traders ever ventured over the Edge to the Vigaelian Face. Even fewer returned, and the goods they brought back were always small items, valued mostly as curiosities. Mama had shown Dantio a rather ugly little jade pot in the ducal collection and told him that it came from Vigaelia.

But this year, soon after the end of the rainy season, a horde of starving, sickly-pale men had streamed in from the Edge and started rounding up herds on the Altiplano, eating them raw and killing any herders who objected. They had converged eventually on the little hill town of Nelina. Seeing that the invaders had no siege equipment and seemed to have no weapons at all, Nelina had closed its gates on them. The ice devils had swarmed straight up the cliffs and the sheer walls above. They had killed every living thing in Nelina, even the cats and the birds in the trees, it was said.

Most Florengians were polytheists, but some belonged to mystery cults, secretive orders of henotheists sworn to the worship of a single god. There were Witnesses of Mayn, like Fiorella. There were Sinura's Healers who cured sick people, Speakers of Demern to quote the laws, and many others. But, as Papa had sadly explained to Dantio, Florengia had no Werists—men who, like these Vigaelians, had sworn to the god of war—and that lack was clearly going to be Florengia's downfall.

After decimating Nelina, the Vigaelians had moved on to Sturia. They spared Sturia when it submitted, though they claimed the small fee of looting its food stocks. Papa, as ruler of the largest and richest city in the northwest, had hastily organized an army of all the able-bodied men within marching distance. They had met the enemy at Two Fords. Although they had outnumbered the invaders by at least three to one and been well armed with bronze swords and spears, the Werists had slaughtered them all, sparing only two wounded boys, whom they had sent back with news of the massacre. And now they were at the gates of Celebre, which had no way to resist them.

When Papa finished repeating the oath the Stralg monster dictated, he was told to rise. He backed away from the bloodlord, bowing repeatedly.

Now, Dantio supposed, he would be taken as hostage for Papa's good faith. He was so full of rage and hate that he no longer felt afraid. They were subhuman brutes! Soon the gods would destroy them.

"Noble Stralg says that he requires three sixty strong youths to begin training as Werists. His men will choose them."

"As the bloodlord commands. I beg him to allow me a day or two to warn my people of this."

"He gives you until tomorrow. And he requires food for three sixty sixty men, delivered to these gates before sundown, every day until you are told to stop."

"So shall it be, as long as our stocks last. Ask Bloodlord Stralg why he is doing this. What does he hope to gain by bringing his horde over the Edge and slaying so many people? Does he expect to move great trains of loot over the Ice? Does he not fear the wrath of the Bright Ones?"

A translation, then the Vigaelian sneered and replied at length.

Fiorella said, "He says the only god he fears is Weru and warfare is His worship. We Florengians are timid and neglect the Terrible One, so we must be taught . . . to fear Weru until we wet our legs at the mere mention of His name. You and your wife may return to the city. He will keep your children as hostages for your continued obedience."

Papa flushed scarlet. "No! This is my eldest son, Lord Dantio. He is eleven years old. I brought the others only to show that they are too young."

"He says all of them."

"Benard is eight and Orlando only *three*, in the holy names! The Lawgiver wrote that only males over the age of ten may be taken as hostages."

Stralg turned and waved a signal. Men started walking out of the woods behind him. They stopped as soon as they came into view, but then more appeared, a line of them standing about an arm's length apart, a line growing longer and longer until it stretched off into the distance in both directions. They were unarmed, and yet that was how they had slaughtered every man sent against them at Two Fords. A great moan went up from the city, as if the stones themselves grieved.

"The bloodlord says that he gives the laws here."

Orlando squirmed free of Dantio's grasp and made a break for freedom.

Stralg held out his hands. Orlando, always wayward, went to him, trotting on stubby legs. The Werist lifted the toddler high overhead. Orlando laughed at being so high above the world. The ice devil stepped over to the fence.

"The bloodlord asks if you want to see the inside of your son's head, lord." Fiorella's voice turned shrill. "He means what he says! He will kill the child."

"My sons, then!" Papa shouted. "Let him take the boys, but my daughter is a babe at suck. Holy Demern has written—"

The big man roared, not even waiting to have Papa's words translated.

"The bloodlord says he will take the cow too, so the calf can feed. He says you must give them all up or watch them all die, and then he will put out your eyes."

Benard was sobbing and gasping with terror. Mama knelt to put an arm around him and Fabia began to cry too. Dantio felt cold drops of sweat race down his ribs. Terrible, terrible man!

Papa fell on his knees. "I beg him to show mercy to a mother and her babe! Does holy law mean nothing to him? Has he no pity?"

"He says no, he has no pity. He has never had pity. You must decide."

Time stopped. Dantio realized he had forgotten to breathe and took a deep gulp of air.

Fiorella said, "I sense great greed, lord, and regret. He regrets his promise not to loot the city, now he sees how big and rich it is. He is not trustworthy and his intentions toward your lady are not honorable."

Mama said, "What happens to us does not matter, Piero. Remember what you told Dantio about courage. You must not give the monster any excuse to sack Celebre!"

Papa said, "I will yield my children."

The Vigaelian seer had translated it all. The bloodlord sneered and set Orlando down. Orlando decided he did not like Vigaelians after all and ran to join the others mobbing Mama, wanting his share of attention.

Dantio was not going to be alone! He would have Mama and the others for company. He felt a wonderful rush of happiness at that and hated himself for it. What sort of slimy worm was he, to enjoy having his family share his misfortune? But he would not be alone.

He ran to help. He picked up Orlando. "We are going for another ride in a chariot—won't that be fun?" He took Benard's hand. "Come, Bena! Say goodbye to Papa. We have to go with the nasty man. Don't be afraid. Mama is coming with us, and I will help her look after you."

Part I

Spring

ᴜᴨᴇ

BENARD CELEBRE

was not looking for trouble, far from it. But a woman screamed.

Benard spun right around and headed back along the alley. Nils, who had been shambling unsteadily beside him, took a moment to realize that he was now alone. He hurried back to wrap both hands around his friend's thick arm and pull. "No!" he said. "Not at all. No trouble, Benard. Benard, they are *warriors!* There are three of them! They will *shred* you." As Nils was not only slighter, but even drunker, he found himself being towed along the alley willy-nilly. They and some friends had set out at sunset to celebrate Nils's betrothal to the palace's head cook's daughter and had done so most thoroughly. Benard was hoarse from singing and the world had been awash in beery good cheer—until that scream.

Despite predawn weariness and the somber shadow filling the alley, the air was still as muggy as a sweat house; birds darted after insects and crickets chirped in the thatch. Already a lurid red filled the eastern sky. Most people slept, true, but there was enough light for Benard to know that the raucous thugs he had passed a moment before at a tavern door were warriors. He had not realized that they had a woman with them. And she had not screamed until now.

"Benard!" Nils pleaded. "They are Werists. They are initiates. They are *armed,* Benard! They will *smash* you!"

There might be something in what the carpenter said. A gentle, peace-loving artist really ought not pick a quarrel with brass-collar Werists. Benard was not in the habit of getting into fights, although he had a notable flair for finding trouble. *Three* warriors? That seemed a lot, even in his present liquaceous condition, when he could barely find his fingers, let alone count on them.

Then the woman screamed again and the men laughed louder. Benard sped up.

Clinging like a vine to a tree, Nils bleated shrilly. "Benard! At this time of night there's only one sort of woman in the streets. She knows what she's doing. And you can't help anyway."

Reluctantly, Benard decided that his small friend was right. He really ought to head back to his shed and get some sleep. Unfortunately, he reached that decision just as he turned the corner and saw her. He could never refuse beauty, and this girl was lovely. Gorgeous, breathtaking, spectacular—young and lithe, struggling in the grip of a hulking lout twice her size. The brute was behind her, clutching her to his chest with one arm and reaching inside her wrap to play with her breasts. His equally large friends stood around laughing at the sport.

Their flaxen hair and beards were cropped short to deny handholds to enemies. They wore the brass collars of Weru and the absurd garments called palls, which were merely lengths of cloth wound around their torsos and over their shoulders, leaving their limbs bare. Werists' palls were striped in colors that proclaimed the wearers' ranks and allegiances. Benard recognized only the purple of Satrap Horold Hragson, who ruled both the city and its garrison—officially for his brother, Stralg, but in reality for his sister, Saltaja Hragsdor.

Had he been granted a little longer to think—say, a pot-boiling, in his present condition—Benard might have come up with some witty or original opening remark, but instead he bawled out the first cliché that came into his head.

"Take your filthy hands off her!"

Nils disappeared like a shooting star.

Drunk or not, the three warriors surrounded Benard instantly. He realized that the one tormenting the girl was Cutrath Horoldson, and things could get no worse after that. Last sixday all Kosord had celebrated the coming-of-age and initiation of the satrap's son, because Horold Hragson had made it known that he would look with disfavor on anyone who chose not to. Apparently Cutrath and his cronies were still celebrating. Drunk or sober, they were equally dangerous.

Ever since Benard's arrival in Kosord fifteen years ago, Cutrath had been his personal plague. Although several years Benard's junior, Cutrath had been protected by his high birth and supported by a pack of eager followers, whose mission it was to make the despised Florengian hostage's life eternal torment. Only when Benard had escaped into apprenticeship and Master Odok's house had he been relatively free of his persecutor. Even then, Cutrath and his mob had known that Benard must report to the palace at least once each day, and had often lain in wait for him.

Now the little shit had become an enormous shit, initiated into the Heroes of Weru at minimum age because his father was the satrap and his uncle was Bloodlord Stralg. Now he could be a lot worse than just obnoxious. His pall was of finer weave than his companions', the shoulder straps of his scabbard were decorated with faience plaques, and he wore tooled leather ankle boots instead of regulation sandals. He clutched the woman's arm with one hand, ignoring her struggles. He was not too drunk to recognize his longtime favorite victim.

"What did you say, Florengian scum?"

Benard was sobering rapidly, if too late. Only his goddess could save him now. Alas, what could the lady of art do against the god of battle? He stole another wondering glance at the girl and hastily began the major invocation—praying in silence, of course, for pleas to one's god were part of the mysteries. . . . *great Her majesty and in infinity the realm of Her blessing . . . She is star of the horizon and fair path amid the storm . . .*

Aloud, he said, "I said you've got my girl. You all right, Hilde?" He had no idea if that was her name. It was just a sweet-sounding name for a beautiful girl. Everything looked red in the predawn glare, but he, of all people, should have realized sooner that her wrap was scarlet, which meant that Nils had been right—he was about to be massacred for trying to save a harlot from a rambunctious customer. But her loveliness ought to attract the pity of holy Anziel, even if his own merit did not. He hurried through the intercession . . . *brandish the rainbow and shape the wind . . . She hears his appeal and bends Her sight as the hawk rides the morning . . .*

"No," Cutrath said, "she is not all right. She will shortly be even less right. And you shall be much worse. She is not your girl and when I have done with you, you won't have any use for a girl anyway."

"He never did," said one of the others, and they all guffawed.

Now open the door that thy servant configures, by the eyes of a serpent, the plumage of kingfishers . . .

"On your knees, Celebrian slug." Cutrath was almost a head taller than Benard, although no wider. His hair and downy beard were the color of campfire flames; he had been a beautiful child before his nose and ears were smashed for the sixtieth time.

"Run away, man!" the girl shouted. "You can't help me."

Running away from Werists was not an option. Holy Anziel had always been generous with Her aid to Benard. Could She help him, now, though? Dare he appeal to Her in such a cause, and in such a state of drunkenness? If he didn't, he was about to be mashed or diced. Forcing himself to concentrate, he planned a rogation.

"I say she's my girl," he proclaimed aloud. "You want to fight me for her?"

"Do we *what?*"

The thugs exploded in helpless mirth. They leaned against the walls or clutched one another's shoulders while their laughter echoed raucously along the alley, momentarily silencing even the crickets; but their eyes never left the prisoner and Cutrath did not release the girl. It was understood, of course, that a Hero must die rather than lose a fight, so fairness was sacrilege. Benard had automatically challenged all three of them, one at a time or all together as they chose.

"Fight me for her." Having established a calm silence in one corner of his mind and furnished it with the images he needed, he silently sent the rogation to his goddess: thongs dangling, strips of leather rising, a dance of beauty, for this innermost prayer was written in pictures. He dared not look at the reality, but he did not need eyes to find figures in stone or see the face he would draw out from clay and glaze, and he did not need his eyes for this. Everything was shape, symmetry, pattern. Beauty.

Meanwhile he said, "Tell your friends to stay out and I'll beat all the crap out of you, you baby barbarian. It's time somebody did. There's mush too . . . I mean *much*. Much too mush of it in there."

Cutrath seemed truly unable to believe his ears. "You speak to *me* like that, you southern trash? Dauber! Muck-dabbling, muddy-fingered, cowardly follower of female gods—you think you can fight *me?*"

It was fortunate that the satrap's son always needed time to work up his fury before a fight, because Benard needed time to move and shape and pattern. He felt the blessing of his goddess fill him like a holy fire, but he must do his tampering without alerting his foe to what was happening. Nor must he provoke the warrior so far that he would battleform into some fearsome carnivore, an abuse of Weru's powers that Cutrath would not regard as in any way unfair. . . . *justice is beauty . . . knot is beauty, curves and loops . . . double knot, triple knot . . . all beauty . . .*

"Coward, you call me? I'm the one who's offering to fight. You're all big talk and bad breath. Put up your fists, stinkard!"

"What are you waiting for, Hero?" asked one of the others. "You don't need *help,* do you?"

"Hold this!" Cutrath yelled, hurling the woman at his friends, "while I murder the mudface." He spat on his hands.

The woman redoubled her screaming and struggling until the third man joined in and clapped a hand over her mouth.

"Prepare for maiming, scum!" Cutrath's eyes gleamed.

"Come and try!" Benard raised his fists with very little idea of how they were supposed to be used.

Veteran of innumerable brawls, Cutrath knew exactly what to do, and would undoubtedly have done it with style and murderous grace had he been fully cognizant of the situation. He chose a judicious opening by lashing out with a kick at his opponent's kneecap, no doubt planning to stamp him to mud as soon as he was on the ground. In fact, that one move would have settled the fight right away had the laces of Cutrath's fancy ankle boots not been tied together. He reeled off-balance, bewildered, wheeling his arms wildly. Benard slid into the gap and planted two punches so hard he thought he'd broken every knuckle. The kid's belly was as solid as a block of marble and his chin even harder, so Benard added two more hits, and the Werist fell. Given room, he would probably have just sat down very heavily and then come back up screaming mad without his boots; alas, his head struck the wall, solid adobe. He slithered down it and crumpled into a heap, feet together, knees apart, mouth open.

Benard applied more blessing, untying the knots without a glance at them. His heart was pounding faster than the crickets chirped, his hands trembled with reaction. He could not hope to work such a trick on the other two brutes, so he must bluff.

"Mine!" he said firmly, pulling the girl away from them. "I won. My prize. Come, darling, ish bedtime. You boys get your buddy home before anyone else sheesh him."

To his astonishment they not only released her, they let him walk away with her. That was unheard-of leniency from Werists. It was a reasonable assumption that Hero Cutrath, when he awoke, would not be so forgiving.

✦

The only real street in Kosord was the riverbank. All other paths were merely gaps between houses—dust baths in summer, mud wallows in winter. They widened and narrowed, bent and divided, went up and down at random, and ended unexpectedly. In some places a man had to turn sideways to get through. With rare exceptions, buildings were made of sun-dried mud brick, cool in summer and relatively draft-free in winter. Outer walls showed no windows, because even the humblest homes enclosed a court for vines, bean shrubs, vegetables, a few pigs and ducks, and the privy. Roofs were thatched with reeds.

Benard paid no heed to where his new friend was taking him. Never before had he registered his upper arm as an erogenous zone, but it was rapidly becoming one as she stroked and fondled it. In the summer heat he wore only sandals of plaited reeds and a work smock—a sheath of clay-smeared canvas hung on shoulder straps, well furnished with pockets of various useful shapes.

She wore a red wrap that reached from her armpits down to her thighs, just, but so flimsy that her breasts were clearly visible through it. Even in the dim light, he could see that her beauty was stunning, her proportions classical. He needed models—would it be blasphemous to use a harlot as a model for a goddess?

"Call me Hiddi."

"Benard Celebre," he said.

"You are so brave!"

So drunk, lady . . . He had been *crazy!* "Any man would want to rescue a woman as beautiful as you."

"To challenge Werists!" She squeezed his biceps admiringly. "So strong! A potter?"

"An artist. Sculptor, mostly."

"What's that?"

"A stonemason." Near enough.

"You don't talk like a stonemason." She was probably trying to calculate what sort of fee she could extract from him. "You talk like palace folk."

"I was brought up in the palace."

She laughed excitedly. "That explains it, then. Oh! You're not a slave?" Her busy hands had found the seal tied to his wrist, the mark of a reputable freeman.

"No."

"You look like a Florengian!" Meaning he had black hair and skin browner than any Vigaelian would achieve in the height of summer.

"Not all Florengians are slaves. I'm a hostage."

"What's a hostage?" Obviously Hiddi's education had been limited. Her lovely mouth produced an ugly peasant growl, fresh from the irrigation ditch.

"Well, when I was eight years old . . . *Oh, pig litter!*" What was he wasting time on that for? "Ask me when I'm sober." He kissed her. Her lips tipped fire into him, a thrill of passion pouring downward to explode in his loins. He felt sweat break out all over his skin. He almost walked her into a wall.

"Not far now, lover," she whispered. "Oh, I can't wait . . ."

"Did Horoldson hurt you much?"

"Him? Naw, he's one of those men who like to think they're hard and cruel. If I cry and squirm that excites them."

"You know him well?" Benard asked glumly.

"A few times. He thinks he's good, but he's very clumsy and obvious. Here we are!"

They had arrived at a flight of steps, the entrance to a large building clad in painted tiles. Wall lamps cast a flickering light on a welcoming image, one Benard both knew and detested, a life-size nude combining female breasts and vulva with male beard and phallus. That was Eriander, androgynous divinity of coitus and madness, and the ugliest image Benard could imagine, an offense against all laws of beauty.

He stopped dead. "No! I can't go in there, Hiddi!" An initiate of the Hands of Anziel could not worship Eriander in Her temple.

Hiddi laughed as if she'd met such scruples before and knew exactly what to do about them. "Darling, you're sweating like a stallion. What's that bulge, Benard, mm?" Her wrap dropped around her ankles, leaving her wearing sandals and a quizzical expression.

There should have been smoke rising from Benard's smock, but his thumping animal lust suddenly lost out to another form of excitement. In the soft lamplight she was as close to feminine perfection as he could recall ever seeing, a typical Vigaelian with cream-pale skin and almost invisible golden fuzz at groin and armpits; her limbs were straight and slender, belly barely curved, hips wide but well shaped, breasts high and firm. Her hair was a foam of golden curls. How much of that was real and how much illusion, a gift granted by her goddess?

"You come along with me, Benard!" She held out a hand to lead him, and the whole world seemed to tilt toward her.

The beer fog had lifted. He hardly heard her. "No!" he muttered. "I cannot. Not in there."

"Is chastity your corban?" She smiled in disbelief.

"No, but I can't . . . can't go in there."

"Married? Most men can pee across that ditch."

"Not married."

"But you want me very much. *Very* much! And I want you! Don't you ever hammer on something softer than nasty old rock sometimes?"

"Turn around."

Amused, Hiddi undulated in a slow turn. There was not a mole or freckle on her anywhere. She was very young and quite beautiful enough to have suitors by the score. The Nymphs of Eriander claimed to be a holy mystery and were often spoken of as dangerous. Benard suspected they were merely a prostitutes' guild, with no more ability to turn men into slobbering idiots than all women had. He had never availed himself of their services—not because he feared their supposed god-given powers to enslave, but because he found other women quite alluring enough and frequently available.

"Stand up there," he said, and Hiddi obediently went up two steps. "Don't wiggle. Put that hand on your hip, hold the other one like this. Tip your head." He gazed in rapture at the miraculous breasts, the pink softness around the nipples.

"Benard! Most men do more than look. Much more. You're not going to kiss me again?" She fluttered kohl-darkened lashes at him.

"No," he said hoarsely. "I must not. But listen. I am carving statues of the Bright Ones for the Pantheon. It is my first big hire, a very big one . . . I needed a model for holy Anziel Herself, my lady of beauty. She sent me to you. I will use you as the model and carve a statue that looks just like you."

Hiddi frowned, suspecting mockery. "Doing what?" She must meet many strange men in her trade, but perhaps none stranger than this.

"Just standing. I will preserve your beauty in marble forever. Your great-grandchildren will see your likeness and marvel at how beautiful you were."

With a sudden switch to laughter, she ran down the steps and tried to embrace him. "Do that tomorrow! Tonight is for *fun!*" She struggled to kiss him. "You talk pretty, Benard! Show me what you can *do!* I want you! I want you to *enjoy* me."

He pushed her away and held her at arm's length. "Your goddess will not mind you being a model, will She?"

Hiddi pouted. Unable to reach anything else, she began stroking his arms again, and even that sent tremors of excitement through him. "Why should He mind? He gives joy to everyone."

"Then come and see me in daylight. I live . . . work . . . in a shed in the yard behind the Pantheon. I will make a few models. In clay. I need to see you in daylight, but mostly I work from memory." He was never going to forget her as she was now.

"But I owe you—"

"Nothing. Thank you, Hiddi. Now I have seen the perfect woman, which is reward enough. Twelve blessings on you."

"You spurn me? You treat me like trash!"

She sounded close to tears. To a careful eye, though, she did not quite look it. His resolution wavered. Then the careful eye came to his rescue.

"No bruises! None anywhere? You're not hurt!" No red fingermarks where Cutrath had gripped her arm; no signs where she had been squeezed or pinched or slapped. "So it's true what they say? You *did* use a blessing on him! And on me!" He pushed her away so hard that she staggered.

"True what who say?" She came for him again and he struck down her hands in sudden anger.

"Everyone."

According to the wilder legends, a Nymph could enslave a man with a single touch. *Pigballs!* No wonder he had been reduced to a slobbering idiot! She had used her powers on Cutrath's friends to stop them joining in the fight, so she had saved Benard more than he had saved her. She had never *needed* saving.

"Goodbye, Hiddi!" He turned and ran away toward the dawn.

t w o

ORLAD ORLADSON

was Attending the God, which was the fourth test of the second level. He stood blindfolded before the image, clasping a bronze sword in his right hand and an ax in his left. He wore nothing except the rope collar that had encircled his neck since he won probation three years ago. Hostleader Gzurg had pointed out that the candidates could reasonably beg for clothing for this test, up here in icy Nardalborg, but of course they had all spurned any such display of weakness.

They must attend holy Weru until He dismissed them. They were not allowed to move at all, although as a special mercy, they could wriggle their toes to keep blood moving. Any candidate who dropped his sword or ax before his dismissal would be punished, which probably meant a beating sharp enough to ruin his chances of passing the tests still to come.

Nardalborg was an indomitable stronghold, controlling the supply lines of Bloodlord Stralg, over in Florengia. Set on bleak and rocky moors, it dominated the trail from Tryfors to the Ice, which began only five menzils away, and whose sinister glint haunted the eastern sky. Bitter winds ruled this pitiless land, driving gray showers over its treacherous bogs, its bottomless black tarns and white frothing torrents; here roamed catbears and even more savage rock boars. There was a gale blowing now, wailing in the eaves and also thumping a loose shutter: *thud! thud! thud!* to drive a man mad.

Orlad could smell the bitter peaty scents; he could certainly feel the wind on his bare skin, but he could not see. The mammoths in the paddocks trumpeted sometimes. The waterfall's deep rumble was a constant in Nardalborg, but it was the accursed shutter that Orlad noticed.

Thud! thud! thud! . . .

Sixteen probationers had come into the shrine for this test—when? Yesterday? It might have been days ago; there was no way of telling except by hunger and thirst and pain. And the thumping of that damnable shutter. Sometimes the sound of rain or sleet on the roof. Strange lights moved in the darkness, and Orlad knew he was close to hallucinating. The god had been known to reject candidates in this test by driving them permanently mad.

Naked and blindfolded, a man was defenseless, utterly vulnerable—this tested trust and courage and humility. There were watchers. No doubt Hostleader Therek Hragson came by sometimes to see how his lads were faring, but testing was done by outside examiners and the hostleader was not supposed to interfere. In practice, though, he probably made sure his favorites were not treated too harshly, because Therek was satrap of Tryfors, brother of Bloodlord Stralg, and nobody was going to argue with him.

But this time the examiner was Hostleader Gzurg Hrothgatson, one of the finest warriors in all the Heroes of Weru. He was old now, but he had been at the bloodlord's side on the first crossing of the Edge, that magnificent epic of will and endurance when men had climbed on ladders built from the frozen bodies of their fallen—and fed on those bodies, too. Only a third of the horde had survived that journey. It made Orlad very humble to think he might one day follow in such footsteps; he could not imagine what feats his generation could ever perform to equal those of Stralg's Heroes.

Gzurg undoubtedly kept an eye on the candidates. Only he was allowed to speak to them. They could answer his questions, that was all. A couple of times he had barked out orders unexpectedly, but the candidates must ignore them, because they were under the command of the god alone. It was a great honor to have been trained by taskmasters as hard as Satrap Therek and Huntleader Heth Hethson; an even greater one to be tested by the magnificent Gzurg.

Thud! thud! thud! . . . When this was over, Orlad was going to find that shutter and tear it to pieces with his bare hands.

A few times he had thought he heard quiet sniggers. As a child he had been brought to watch men Attending the God, so it was only fair that others be allowed to see him and his companions standing here naked and wet-footed. Yes, they would laugh, but he would set an example for them to follow when their time came.

He was the last now. Weru had already dismissed fifteen of the sixteen. Fifteen times the crash of ax, sword, and body falling simultaneously to the flags had announced that another had fainted. Sometimes there had been a groan or two later as the candidate recovered and dragged himself and his weapons away. In one sense Orlad had won, in that he had proved himself the strongest, but that victory was tempered by knowing that he was the oldest of the current candidates and should be able to endure more. In another sense he had lost, in that the god clearly expected more from him; he would receive no credit for his longer ordeal when the next trial began. It seemed a long time since that last crash.

He *would* be worthy, though! Satrap Therek did not approve of a Florengian aspiring to join the Heroes. His attitude was understandable, because his brother the bloodlord had trained and initiated youths in Florengia itself, only to find that they no sooner won their brass collars than they broke faith and joined the cowardly guerrilla rebels. As retribution, Satrap Therek had held Orlad back until now from trying for promotion to cadet.

Orlad was determined to pass. He had always been different, as long as he could remember, but he had never conceded that he was inferior, no matter what they did to him. He could hardly recall a day in his life when he had not had to fight someone. He had been born on the Florengian Face, but he had been only three when he came to Nardalborg and he remembered nothing of his life before that.

Thud! thud! Pause . . . *thud!* . . .

The floor began to move; waves pounded in his head. He wriggled toes frantically until the weakness passed. He wondered if anyone ever died of thirst during this test. There were gruesome tales of men cracking their heads open when they fainted, or falling on their swords. His belly emitted a plaintive rumble.

"Hungry?" asked a voice right behind him.

He twitched, naturally, but he did not think that would count. He did *not* drop the sword or ax. His mouth was so dry he could hardly make the words.

"My lord is kind to ask."

"The god is testing you hard," Gzurg said. "Do you think He refuses to have a Florengian in His cult?"

"My lord is kind."

"Answer the question."

"Lord, He shows favor by letting me prove my dedication."

"Bravely rationalized," said the low voice. Gzurg had trouble speaking softly because his muzzle now resembled a crocodile's. The word passed around the candidates was that he had sixty-four teeth, and obviously some of them were as big as thumbs. Each of his thighs was as thick as a normal man's chest. Even in his human aspect he was magnificent; Orlad wished he could see him in full battleform.

"What sort of a name is 'Orlad'? You know what it means?"

"Lord, it means a small rodent with very sharp teeth. My lord."

"Is it your real name?"

"I think my original name was something hard to say, like 'Orlindio,' my lord. I have forgotten."

"You are old to be still a probationer. Or does your coloring make you seem older?"

"My lord is kind."

"Your lord wants an answer."

"I am obedient to the satrap, my lord."

The warrior grunted. "We are all waiting for you to be dismissed so we can begin the run."

"My lord is kind."

Chuckle. "Nothing rattles you, does it? You have outclassed all the others so far. If you continue to perform at this standard, I shall not only award you the chain, I shall insist that you try for brass as soon as possible."

Joy! Joy! Joy! "My lord is very kind!" The praise brought a painful lump to Orlad's throat. To prove himself! To hold up his head among the Vigaelians! To be *equal!*

Thud!

Thud!

Thud! . . . Had the packleader gone?

No. "There is one small problem," said the deadly whisper, barely louder than the wail of the wind. It was in front of him now. "You know the last test."

"Anger, my lord."

"Of course. We must be sure that you can feel true rage. It is by anger that the warrior calls on the god to give him his battleform. It is anger that makes him fearless in the service of his lord. Do you know why Florengians and Vigaelians hate one another so much?"

"No, my lord."

"Because we have been fighting for fifteen years, that's why! The longer the war lasts, the more we hate. But can a man with black hairs on his belly hate like one with gold?"

Never a day without a fight, often two. Could Gzurg not see his scars? "I am confident, if it please my lord."

"Mm." The warrior sounded doubtful. "And who shall I give you to demonstrate your anger? If I give you a Florengian prisoner, men may whisper that they are contemptible and easy to hate, or that they are weak and easy to hurt. If I give you a Vigaelian, they may ask if you are truly loyal, or are in fact a secret Florengian supporter. Mm? You see my problem? Which should it be?"

"As it please my lord."

"One of each, then? Can you muster enough anger for two?"

"My lord is kind."

"Mm," Gzurg said again, only this time it seemed a sound of approval. "And what means would you prefer? The lash? The armored glove? The club?"

"As it please my lord." Orlad knew that this was the right answer from the sudden roaring in his ears and the tilting of the floor as the god released him. He heard his sword and ax fall, a long way away.

three

SALTAJA HRAGSDOR

was known as the Queen of Shadows, among other less flattering things. Her origins were a mystery, her age unknown. She was greatly feared, for it was universally believed that she was a Chosen of Xaran and the Ancient One gave her many terrible powers. There was no doubt that anyone who opposed her usually died, one way or another.

Queen of Shadows . . . and shadow queen. For fifteen years she had ruled the entire Vigaelian Face as regent for her brother, Bloodlord Stralg, waiting for him to return from Florengia. For the fifteenth time spring had opened the pass and Stralg's dispatches had been rushed by relays of chariots from Tryfors to Bergashamm and then by fast ship to Skjar. Now Saltaja was forwarding his orders, maintaining the usual pretense that they came from her husband, Satrap Eide.

She felt most at home in darkness, but many people shunned daylight in Skjar. Already the days were becoming unbearable, the air in the canyon like a huge argali-wool blanket, unbreathable and motionless, even on her favorite terrace high above the river. Her wrap of black linen clung clammily to her skin; she had thrown off her head cloth. In the room behind her, two scribes sat cross-legged on the floor under a single lamp apiece, busily poking their styli into slabs of wet clay and dribbling sweat onto the tiled floor. Heavy drapes in the doorway kept the light from reaching her.

"Write," she said. "From Satrap Eide to Hostleader Landar, governor of Salnorn. Usual titles, usual greetings." She waited, staring out at the darkness. "Write: 'You have custody of the hostage Mardo Stighetto, from the city of Ravima.'" She sounded the outlandish names carefully. "'Inform the—'" She prided herself on her memory, but it had been many years and there had been very many hostages. Also, she needed to calculate. About a dozen years ago; a pudgy, rather stupid child, he had been four or five . . .

"'Inform the youth that his city has played false and surrendered to the rebels. His father the king and the rest of the royal family were then torn to pieces by the mob. Make it known that this is why he has lost his rights as a hostage and is of no further value.'" She paused to let the scribes catch up. "'Put him to death by whatever means please you. Report your compliance.'" Usual closing.

"Larth, read back," she said, and listened as an unpleasantly nasal voice repeated what she had said, decorated with flowery scribal frills. "Nerkurtu?"

"I have the same," said the younger scribe.

"Bring them." Light flared briefly as the boy apprentice backed out through the drapes. When they fell back behind him, he turned in her direction and stood blind, holding out the tablets on a tray. She could read very little of the complex cuneiform script, but she saw well enough in the dark to stamp the clay with her husband's seal. When they had been baked, she would have other scribes read both letters to her again—separately—before one was dispatched and the other placed in the palace archives. To trust anyone was folly. The apprentice went back inside to carry the letters to the ovens and roll out more clay.

Overhead the spangled heavens were framed between the twin blacks of the canyon walls. Skjar was a city of islands, among which the river murmured unceasingly. Here and there she could see scattered pinpricks of light from lamps or candles. Below her lay ghostly white rapids and reflections of stars fallen in still pools.

"Next," she said. After having had the tablets read to her several times, she almost knew them by heart.

Larth's thin voice began to squeak to the bats flittering by overhead: "The noble bloodlord writes, 'The cities of Nianoma and Piaregga waver in their loyalty. Return their hostages to me that I may stiffen the rulers' resolve.' May these words please my lady."

They didn't, much. Stralg meant something like "So I can call their fathers in to watch their children being battered." At times her brother was a fool. Because frightfulness inspired terror at first, he thought it always would, but it didn't. Repeated brutality provoked numbness, then fury, and finally retaliation. Besides, he needed fresh troops far more than he needed prisoners to torture; the number of live bodies Therek could run over the Edge in a season was limited.

"Never mind that one," she said. "What's next?"

As she waited, she paced the terrace, which was only a niche chiseled out of the living rock of the cliff. She liked the feel of cool bedrock under her bare feet and the curious contrast of temperature when she rested forearms on the sun-warmed stone of the balustrade. She was a large woman, and the heat was still murderous. Somewhere she heard a faint rumble of wagon wheels. Soon overeager roosters would start crowing.

Larth said, "The noble bloodlord writes, 'The doge of Celebre has always been true to his oaths, but his health ebbs. If I decide to withdraw from Miona, Celebre may become important again. Send one of the hostages to rule when the doge dies.' May these words please my lady."

Typically, Stralg could never be perfectly honest, even with her. "If I decide to withdraw from Miona" meant "If I get driven out of Miona." Or even *When* I get driven out of Miona." By conceding the possibility, he was virtually predicting it. Wherever Miona was.

It was no secret now that the war went badly. At first his Werists had met no divinely inspired resistance, and slaughtering extrinsics was child's play to warbeasts. He had subdued all of Florengia faster and more easily than he had previously conquered Vigaelia. Then he had made an error—just one, but one scratch can kill a man, and that single miscalculation had festered like a belly wound. If he now foresaw Celebre becoming important, he must be contemplating defeat. At Celebre, he would be back where he started, with his heels on the Edge. Celebre controlled the way home to Vigaelia, so the dying doge must be replaced by an equally reliable puppet.

Saltaja had no trouble remembering the Celebre children, because they had been the first hostages to arrive, and they had caught her attention several times since, notably when Karvak Hragson died in strange circumstances. One boy was certainly dead, and the others would no longer be children.

Young males being notoriously unreliable, the girl was the obvious choice. She was nubile and could be sent home with a suitable husband to do the actual ruling while keeping her busy with babies. The two surviving brothers would be potential rival claimants and must be eliminated, but it would be prudent to see her on her way over the Edge before disposing of them.

"Write. From me to Satrap Horold Hragson of Kosord. Usual titles. 'To her valiant brother, twelve blessings and her deepest love. You have custody of the hostage . . .' "

Wait!

The Celebre girl was right here in Skjar. Her route to the Florengian Face would take her past both Horold in Kosord and Therek in Tryfors. Saltaja had been thinking for some time that she ought to investigate what was going on in the family. Therek, especially, was becoming worrisomely erratic. She need not go right to the Edge itself, but certainly as far as Tryfors, the jumping-off place for crossings. Yes, a personal inspection felt like a very good idea. She could deliver her instructions face-to-face and also escape the steam-bath horrors of another summer in Skjar.

"Cancel that letter. Send for my husband! Tell him to bring a Witness."

She wiped her streaming forehead. Why did she ever put up with this stew pot of a town anyway? Originally, she supposed, because it was where Therek, eldest of the brothers, had been initiated into the Heroes, the mystery cult of Weru. *Xaran's tits!* That had been thirty-five years ago! Therek had helped the others to become Werists also, still here in Skjar. And it had been in Skjar that Stralg had won the title of bloodlord, the Fist of Weru. Before his reign that had always been a meaningless title, but from the first Stralg had intended to claim his right to rule all the Werists of Vigaelia. His wounds had barely healed before he overthrew Skjar's city elders and began using the city's wealth to finance his campaign. In a mere ten years he ruled the entire Face, Werists and extrinsics both. He had kept Skjar as his capital mostly because it was central and had good communications. It was convenient. Insufferable, but convenient. Also, it was rich, able to support a standing army and the cumbersome machinery of government.

When Stralg went off to conquer Florengia, he had officially left his brothers and brother-in-law to rule Vigaelia for him, and in practice left Saltaja to rule them. Karvak had died when Jat-Nogul rose in rebellion. Therek, Horold, and Eide had promptly crushed the rebellion and sacked the city in reprisal. Otherwise nothing much had changed in fifteen years.

She began pacing again, horny feet scuffing on the tiles. "Next?"

The next item was another of Stralg's rants about the need for more men, and she ignored it. Recruitment was becoming harder and harder as the war dragged on with no sign of any Heroes returning, other than the few who were too badly maimed to continue fighting yet could still manage the return crossing. Training a Werist took years, so there were still as many men being initiated as Therek could ram over Nardalborg Pass in a season. The manpower problem could wait. "Next?"

Next was a demand for gold. That was new. At first Stralg's campaign had sent a torrent of loot and slaves back to Vigaelia. The flow had dwindled as resistance sprouted, and this new demand meant he must be having trouble feeding and housing his horde. She dictated a letter to be sent out to all the cities in Eide's satrapy and made a mental note to call in the bursar from the temple of Weru, where most of Skjar's wealth was stored. She would have to fleece the local Ucrists, also.

Whatever was keeping her moronic husband? She pushed through the drape into the lamplit room. The air was stifling. The two scribes and the boy looked up in alarm.

"Guard!" she barked.

A Werist materialized in the far doorway, practically filling it. "My lady?"

She noted with satisfaction that he was as frightened of her as the two clerks were, although he was twice her size and a fraction of her age.

"Where is the satrap?"

The boy gulped, looked behind him, and stepped aside with a gasp of relief. "Here he is, my lady!"

Eide lumbered in, unarmed and barefoot, wearing his pall wrapped around him like a towel instead of properly draped. Eide had always been a bull of a man, and now he was twice as big, three times as hairy, and much more bovine, with two stub horns and an animal smell. Obviously—obvious to Saltaja, if not to others—he had been fetched from some woman's bed, but that was normal for him. She had not let him touch her in years. He was out of breath, which was a satisfactory demonstration of obedience.

His entry made the room crowded. The scribes moved hastily into corners and tried not to stare at his feet, which he rarely left uncovered. The Witness of Mayn who followed him in was tiny, swathed completely in white, without even her hands showing. She looked like a discarded pillow alongside the giant.

Eide grunted a surly "?" and yawned.

"I want to know where the three Celebre hostages are. Ask her." Under the compact, the Witnesses would answer only Stralg himself and his three hostleaders, Eide, Therek, and Horold. Saltaja had to send all her queries through one of them.

Eide growled, "Answer the question."

Some Maynists would insist he repeat it. This one was either more obliging or anxious to go back to bed. "None of them is within my range."

"What is the Wisdom on them?" Saltaja asked. The Wisdom was the collective knowledge of the cult, but how it worked was part of the mystery, a secret known only within the Ivory Cloisters at Bergashamm.

"Answer," Eide said.

"The girl has gone inland, to her guardian's estate at Kyrn. We have no reason to believe that the hostage Benard Celebre is not still in Kosord or the hostage Orlando Celebre at Nardalborg."

"The Ucrist Wigson is here in Skjar?"

"He is. Working in his counting office." Witnesses rarely volunteered information. This one sounded young and might be showing off the range of her sight.

Satisfactory. Saltaja was about to dismiss the two of them, when her native caution stirred. "The first Celebre hostage, the eldest—tell me of him."

"He died," said the woman in the shroud.

"You confirm that he did physically die in the commonly understood sense of the word? You are not using the expression in some special cultish way?" She had caught them out in half-truths before now.

"The boy Dantio Celebre died fourteen years ago from shock and loss of blood, and his heart stopped beating. It is so recorded in the Wisdom. You have been informed of this three times."

"You may go." Saltaja nodded to the satrap. "And you also, my sweet. But send me Huntleader Perag Hrothgatson. I have a job for him."

"Send for him yourself." Eide turned to follow the seer out.

Saltaja said, "No. You will *go* and *bring* him to me."

He froze, and for a moment she thought she would have to discipline him. Then he snorted a surrender noise and left, his feet clopping like hooves on the tiles.

So it was decided. She would deliver the girl to Tryfors in person. Not by chariot, of course. Not for the Queen of Shadows that endless bouncing, the dust and heat and rain. They would travel by riverboat.

Four

THE ELDEST

awoke and saw that she was dying. Death was all through her, like ivy in a forest, spreading fast. Whatever the common folk might think, the Witnesses of Mayn did not prophesy; the word was a joke among them, a reminder that the gods could not be bound. The seers' blessing was knowledge, and the Eldest knew that she would not rise from her bed. That was not prophecy, it was accomplished fact. Already her feet and hands were cold, no longer hers or part of her.

She lay still, composing herself, calming that faltering, frail heart. Reproaching herself for feeling fear. Chiding herself for her sorrow. Many, many things she had wanted to finish, but death was no respecter of agendas. She should be grateful for these few last moments, a grace from holy Mayn. Always the Eldest of the Witnesses was granted a farewell, so that she might name her successor. Some were also permitted to pass on some special insight from the goddess.

She had been given so many years! She was Eldest of this, the mother lodge in the Ivory Cloisters at Bergashamm, and thus Eldest to all the Witnesses on the Vigaelian Face, and although "eldest" was her title, it was close to literal truth in her case. She had been already old when she was appointed vicar of the goddess, so many years ago. Her name then had been Raven, but she had not heard it used in all those years. Her reign had not been an easy one, perhaps the hardest ever, and she still could not be sure that she had made the right choice. She, who should be the wisest of all the gods' children must withhold judgment on her own life's work. But she need not worry about that now. Very soon the goddess would reveal the answers, solve all mysteries.

Sunlight on the wall showed that it was still very early. Taking her last farewell of the worn old stones and silvered beams, of the threadbare rugs she had knotted herself long years ago, the Eldest was reminded that she was blind. It had happened gradually as she aged, and she had barely noticed, still seeing the world with the goddess's eyes, which worked much better than her own ever had. Here on her deathbed, the Eldest saw into kitchens and laundry and larders; the refectory where novices were laying out bowls for the morning meal; the great weaving hall where the goddess's work was done. The fields beyond the walls she could no longer reach; her sight was dwindling.

Urgently she needed the members of her hand, but the blessings Mayn granted did not include summoning. Not that the Maynists' abilities were limited to sight. Their other senses were also blessed. The Witnesses took the sacred number to extremes: five edges of each Face of the world, five senses, five blessings, five fingers to a hand. The sisters themselves were grouped in hands—five reported directly to the Eldest, five to each of them, and so on. All five of the Eldest's hand were in residence at the moment. They would see her. The range of seeing depended on the importance of what was to be seen, and her passing would matter greatly to them.

Meanwhile she must consider her successor, because the name she spoke would control the course of the cult for years. Werists did not live to be old men. Even if they did not die at the hands of their own kind in battle or brawl, the gross demands their god's blessing made upon their bodies led to early death. They professed to glory in their choice of fame over long life, but they made that decision while still too young to comprehend the cost. Stralg would die; the evil would pass.

She needed to cough away pain, but the effort was unthinkable.

Stralg, Stralg! So the monster would outlive her? By one of holy Cienu's divine jests, the Witnesses of Mayn and the Heroes of Weru in Vigaelia had each received a new leader on the same day. She had been named in the dying words of her predecessor. How Weru revealed His choice was a secret of His mysteries, but the death toll suggested that mortal combat would be a reasonable guess.

About twenty sixdays later, Stralg had come calling at Bergashamm. It had been done on a whim, certainly, or else the seers would have felt his intention. Leading a host through the neighborhood, he had suddenly detoured and thrown a cordon around the Cloisters. He had entered alone—over a locked gate, ripping a door from its sockets, and marching into the innermost sanctum, the great hall, where none but Witnesses might come.

The vault was high and dim, for the Witnesses had no need of light and large windows would pass drafts to disturb the webs. From Bergashamm the seers went out into the world to Witness. When they returned, it was to the hall they brought the truths they had garnered, the threads they had spun, there to be woven into the great webs that were their records of the world and its ways. They sang as they worked among the high looms, weaving melody as they wove happenings, glorifying their goddess.

The Eldest was there when Stralg intruded. His coming had been seen by then, of course. The singing had faltered into cries of terror and the others had all fled. She stood alone, still and white-draped in the gloom, forcing herself not to shrink from the stench of evil.

He was still young then, powerful—wickedly handsome and arrogant to the point of insanity, daring to violate this house of peace. The scars on his limbs were visible to all. Her sight told her of worse hidden under his all-black pall, and traces of wound fever still lingered in his too-bright eyes, but his many jousts with death had given him no humility. He reeked of both cruelty and ruthlessness, but so much cruelty that the other hardly mattered. If he so chose, he could wield the fearsome blessing of his god to destroy everyone in the abbey single-handedly.

"You are in charge of this brothel?" He had a magnificent voice, she recalled, probably the most melodious male voice she had ever heard.

"I am the Eldest of the Witnesses, yes. You are the light of Weru on Vigaelia."

"I need your wisdom."

She could smell the bloodlust on him and fully expected to die. "The only wisdom I will give you, Fist, is that the best warriors never need to fight. Use your strength to keep peace, not make war. Holy Demern enjoins us that the weak should be protected, not oppressed."

"Demern? Weru is my god!" Stralg grabbed up a folded, completed web and ripped it in a fearsome demonstration of physical strength. "I came for wisdom, Eldest! Not platitudes. The Heroes of Weru are divided. They squabble over dogma, over personal ambition—even over political trivia, for when the merchants of a city covet the trade of another, they send their Werists to rend other Werists. I will unify the cult."

The Eldest remained silent, praying for courage to bear whatever might happen. There were very few men in Bergashamm, none of them fighters, and Stralg had sealed the abbey.

"All Werists will be loyal to me," he said. "I will appoint governors to rule the cities, and I will set my brothers as satraps over them. They will rule all Vigaelia in my name. Then we shall have peace, not war. You must approve. You will assist."

She spoke what she expected to be her epitaph. "Never. The world does not concern us. We renounce it, personally and collectively, to pursue knowledge for its own sake. We may neither meddle in events nor share our wisdom with others, and this has been our creed for more lifetimes than even we can number. Many a sister has perished in torment for refusing to advise a tyrant, knowing her death will be a sign to the people that their ruler is unworthy."

He met this defiance with a winsome, almost boyish smile. "And have not those same tyrants frequently discovered their enemies coming against them armed with perfect knowledge of their strengths and weaknesses?"

"Such has been recorded."

" 'Such has been recorded'! Is that the closest you can come to lying? You regularly testify for the Speakers."

"They are the only exception. Wisdom cannot flourish without peace and order. In criminal matters we provide evidence for those who judge in the name and by the laws of holy Demern."

"From now on, you and your seers will serve me instead."

"No." Fear swelled in her heart, for his mind was clotted blood and he planned worse than just her death.

Stralg smiled and departed.

Shortly thereafter he sent in some of his brutes and they took away five.

◆

The mangled bodies were returned the following morning, but of course every seer had seen what was being done in his camp during the night. He took away ten more. The Eldest knew by then that Stralg Hragson would wipe out the cult before he would yield.

Her only hope sprang from the blessing of her goddess, for she could feel the revulsion seething in the Werists who came each morning to return the corpses and drag away more victims. Twenty, then forty . . . None of the bloodlord's men was as ruthless as he was, but the mutiny she prayed for failed to appear. Their rage was directed against her, for forcing them to perform such atrocities, and their loyalty to Stralg grew stronger, not weaker. On the fifth day they drove away eighty victims, but they also broke into the storerooms and took bales of priceless weavings, which they burned. Next morning, when most of the Witnesses remaining had collapsed in shock, the Eldest went out to him.

They met in a rainstorm in a field of mud stinking with blood and death, while his sullen host watched from the distance. The corpses of the eighty were being loaded into carts.

"So you value cloth more than life?" he mocked. "I must try burning buildings, too."

"We shall yield," she said, "partway."

His laughter was not pretense. "You will yield utterly, or die. Do you think I cannot double eighty, or burn your abbey around your ears?"

"Then you destroy us, for we shall lack the numbers to gather the knowledge you require."

He showed her his wolfish teeth. "If I cannot have it, no one shall. I will torch your storerooms today. Yield or die, old woman."

"Hear my terms. We shall answer your questions, but yours only. You do not want every warrior to be omnipotent."

His eyes narrowed as the evil mind behind them calculated. "That is true wisdom. But it takes many sixdays to send a message across the Face. So you will answer my hostleaders also. I promote only whom I trust. Them and myself."

"You and no more than four hostleaders." She felt his surge of triumph.

"And no one else!"

"No one else," she agreed. "And we keep our anonymity, our habits and veils. Our persons will not be harmed."

He shrugged his indifference, well pleased with what he had won. "Where is Hostleader Snirson and how many Werists does he have with him?"

"Snirson died of wounds a sixday ago. His host has scattered."

Stralg laughed again; he had known that.

"One other thing," the Eldest said. "We shall never volunteer information. We give true answers and nothing more."

He liked that less, for he was a clever man. The balance of his mind swung back toward death and horror. "Then you can aid my foes."

"I have said we shall not."

"By remaining silent you can aid them."

"To tell everything that may be relevant would take forever. Do you want sixty-sixty sisters babbling in your ears all day long? Ask if a man is a traitor and we shall tell you, but we shall not warn. Only holy Mayn knows all. Those are my terms. Accept them or slay us."

Stralg had hesitated, angrily weighing compromise against massacre.

Then, impatient and flushed with victory, he had accepted her terms. He had never gotten around to imposing others, and while the concessions she had won were almost meaningless, she was probably the only person who had ever made that monster back up even a hairsbreadth.

So the vile bargain had been made. So an organization made up mostly of nosy old women had become the despot's sharpest weapon. Until Stralg, the Fist of Weru had been a figurehead with no practical authority over Werists outside his own city or district, and any previous bloodlord who had tried to widen his rule had died young. The seers had helped Stralg win supreme power over the whole Face, and they had helped him keep it, betraying countless rebels to his awful vengeance. Always the rationalization had been that they were biding their time until he could be overthrown, but that time had never come and never would until Stralg's black heart stopped beating.

The Eldest had made her decision long ago and to change it now would be to admit failure. She knew that mutiny smoldered under the ancient crust of obedience, but she must choose a successor who would follow the course she had mapped out, who would write the same story upon the next tablet. LeAmber, she decided, was the one. LeAmber was young, true, not even fifty yet, but she would do nothing foolish. She would wait out the bloodlord's death.

The alternative to LeAmber was Tranquility. Tranquility was older, but rash; she would raise up the Witnesses to defy Stralg and so risk everything. Tranquility's faction maintained that the evil was more than Stralg, that chthonic powers more dreadful than even Weru stood behind him, and the terrible thing he had built would live on even after he died. The Eldest had refused to accept that argument, for there was no evidence that the man's sister was a Chosen of Xaran. There never could be real evidence, and Maynists must deal in facts, not theories or pseudo-prophecy.

The sunlight had moved. Her hand must come soon or be too late. The refectory was a blur now, as the shadows closed in. Most of her was dead already.

And yet . . . when there were no facts? If the gods refused certainty, then must not mortals sometimes act on partial knowledge, weighing possibilities and calculating uncertainties? If the Witnesses were ever to renege on their pact, then now was the time, for Stralg was aging, he was far away on the Florengian Face, still striving to conquer it as he had conquered Vigaelia. After fifteen years, success was souring into defeat. If LeAmber was wrong and Tranquility right, then now was the time to abrogate the treaty. Was this an eldest's legendary dying insight, or only the maundering of a dying crone? Had she been *wrong* all these years? Must humanity ever be stretched upon the same rack, with a succession of different sandals on the levers?

Softly the five of her hand had come. They gathered around in silence, kneeling by the bed, hands joined with hers for comfort, and she knew them: Rose, Indigo, Carillon, Cinnamon, and Willowbark. Two of them were almost as old as herself, while Willowbark was barely forty. They were united in their grief. Sorrow poured through their union until the Eldest's blind old eyes filled with tears. They shared the pain, knowing that her essence now was death.

"Can you speak, mother?" Rose whispered. "Have you some special word for us? Will the lady of Wisdom speak with your final breath?"

Of course she would! The Eldest wondered how she could not have realized sooner that she had a message to pass on. "A weft," she said, "tonight, a weft!" She felt their dismay when they could not see what was so plain to her.

In any attempt to explain to extrinsics how they sensed the world, Maynists were forced to speak in metaphor. They spoke of weaving, of mosaics, of patterns. They talked of nodes, of cusps, of subtle touches on the tiller by which the gods steered the world—the single snowflake that could launch an avalanche, the sensual moment when a husband turned to his wife in the quiet of the night and sired a great teacher or a monster, while on some other night she might have conceived a different child for him. They took special delight in identifying what they termed a weft, by which they meant an important event, action, or decision that ultimately produced results contrary to its original intent. The analogy, of course, was to the weft thread in a weaving, which turns at the edge and goes back in the opposite direction to make the pattern.

Rose said, "Tonight? What is its nature?"

"She is leaving!" The Eldest struggled and found enough breath to whisper, "His sister . . . going to . . . Tryfors . . ."

"Sister? But where did this weft occur, mother? Tell us!"

Why could they not see for themselves? "Skjar."

Ripples of content . . . No matter how important this weft, Skjar was too distant for any Witness here in Bergashamm to scent it. But the local chapter would send in its report and the data would be woven into the history so that all could know. The incident must be great indeed if the lady of wisdom Herself deemed it worthy of mention.

The Eldest sensed another presence. The Ancient One had come for her, and it was time to go.

"We are humbled and will record it, mother." That was Cinnamon, pushing herself forward as usual. "But who will be Her voice to us from now on? Say the name, mother! Who will be our new Eldest?"

LeAmber, and keep the covenant? Wait for the tyrant to fall?

Or Tranquility? Warn them of the greater darkness behind Stralg? Tranquility's faction would provoke the tyrant's wrath. Must the Eldest admit that she had been wrong all her life? No, not that. That weft tonight would save her from that shame.

"LeAmber," she whispered.

She felt their anger and dismay like physical blows.

How dare they question her and delay her here when she must be gone? How could they not sense that the Old One was standing over them, waiting for her?

"Did you say 'LeAmber,' mother?"

Yes. They would feel her insistence. Of course it must be LeAmber! The compact must be preserved.

Now she could go. Now she had done. Relieved at last of her burdens, Witness Raven, the Eldest, sank into the gentle arms of the Mother.

Five

FRENA WIGSON

was driving her chariot down a long hillside, hooves drumming, wheels bouncing, axle squealing, leather floor squeaking. She clutched the reins in one hand and the rail in the other and let her knees absorb whatever jostling and bouncing was not stopped by the webbing. That was the theory; in practice she was going up and down like laundry in a water trough. The wheels leaped from ridge to ridge and the wind whirled her hair like a flag. Exhilaration!

"What village is that ahead?" She had to shout very loud.

Verk yelled back, "Bitterfeld, mistress. A very forgettable place."

There were few things more enjoyable in life than driving a pair of strong young onagers on a fine morning and letting the wind blow your hair around—assuming you had hair suitable for the purpose—but it was not the best situation for conversation. On a smooth track, yes, but there was no real track at all through these hills. Travel was very educational.

Her companion was Verk, her father's senior guard. His big hand grasped the rail without a single white knuckle and he held himself rock-steady with no visible effort except the rhythmic flexing of the muscle in his forearm.

"Tell her she's driving too fast!" Uls howled from the other chariot, close behind. If he remained farther back, he would not have to breathe Frena's dust, but Uls was not the sharpest sword in Skjar and he invariably stayed closer to Verk than his shadow. The brothers were so alike that nobody could tell them apart—as long as neither spoke. After that it was easy.

"Am I driving too fast?" she said.

"Dark and Night are enjoying the run," Verk said. "If you do not let them get overheated, they will come to no harm."

He was being tactful, because Frena had no practical way of reducing speed at the moment. Pulling back on the reins would frighten the onagers and hurt their mouths. She lacked the strength to do any good with the brake lever and would certainly not ask Verk for help. But Dark and Night were as sure-footed as ibexes, and the car had been specially made for her by the best wheelwright in Skjar.

Here the stony hills opened up to cup a valley, bottomed with scabby grain fields. She did not know this road at all. She usually traveled by the north trail, but Father's letter had said to come the south way, without saying why.

"Bitterfeld?" she said. "Father owns this land!" She had heard the name on the tribute list. "They are late planting." She should stop and talk with the headman. It never hurt to let them know that Horth Wigson was watching.

"The rains are late," Verk said.

She did not know Verk well. As chief household guard, he spent most of his time close to Father, but he was a pleasant companion, well-spoken and good-looking. Father had hired the twins not long before she left for Kyrn, to spend the summer in the hills as all sensible rich folk did.

The chariot was a tight fit for two people and necessarily intimate. Verk's long braids hung below his bronze helmet, jiggling and dancing as the car bounced, and the wind rippled the golden fuzz on his arms. His armor was a knee-length leather smock coated with bronze scales, the hot sun making it reek of the dozens of house guards who had worn it before him. That was not his fault, but it was another reminder of proximity. His free hand was supposedly steadying his scabbard against his thigh, but every few bounces Frena would be thrown against that arm, like it or not, and her wrap was sleeveless also—skin against skin.

Fortunately Frena always kept her emotions under tight control. She had no romantic interest in a mere swordsman, a slab of a man who would risk his life for the chance to live and eat in a mansion. Verk was intelligent enough to share a little mild flirting without getting illusions.

He glanced down at her with a gleam in his unusually dark blue eyes. "If you do lose a wheel or snap the axle, mistress, please make sure you break my neck as well as your own."

"You are feeling suicidal? Angry husbands after you?"

"Husbands never frighten me, but an angry employer would."

"My father is a gentle, loving person, and extremely generous to his staff."

"*Aee!* That's true, mistress, but they do say he's mean when his servants skimp their duty."

"That's not true. Give me one example! Just one!"

"Quera."

"Who?" Frena said uncertainly.

"Quera. He had her impaled, they do say."

"No! You've been listening to slander. Who says that? That horrible Master Pukar, I'll bet!"

Verk shrugged his bronze-clad shoulders, not looking at her. Not smiling.

"You weren't there and I was!" Frena said icily. "I was only thirteen, but I saw! That awful woman was brought in to be Mother's night nurse when she was injured. When Mother died, Father could have beaten her and then dismissed her, or he could have had her charged with negligence. He didn't do either. He threw her out in the street with his own hands. I saw it! She deserved much worse than that, but even a court would not have *impaled* her. Impaling is only for really terrible crimes."

"*Aee!* Gold clinks louder than thunder, they do say."

"That is treason! And blasphemy! Judges in Skjar are all Speakers of Demern. Witnesses of Mayn give testimony. You accuse initiates of those holy cults of accepting my father's bribes? Of being intimidated by him?"

"Who won't march to the beat of the golden drum?"

This was subversive talk, going beyond informal chat. No servant should speak of his employer like that. "If my father wins a judgment it is because he is in the right."

"Ah, I meant no affront to the master, dear lady! Forgive a poor swordsman's folly. Any man who wears a sword in Werist country is born stupid."

"Tell her to slow down!" Uls yelled again. He was falling farther behind, still enveloped in the red clouds raised by Frena's wild passage. Uls was stupid. Verk was not.

Horth Wigson enjoyed owning things in sets—strings of pearls, fleets of ships, streets of houses, and now a pair of identical house guards. Not to be outdone, his daughter had treated herself to a matched pair of black onagers, very rare and very costly. After all, onagers were useful, while swordsmen were only decorative—life-sized animated bronze ornaments. Verk and Uls attended Horth when he expected important visitors. They escorted him on the rare occasions when he went calling on someone. The rest of the time they did little except harass maidservants.

Yesterday he had sent them to Kyrn to fetch Frena back to the city. The tablet they brought had been cracked, but quite legible. The seal impressed on it had certainly been his, and the Kyrn house scribe had read the message as being what the swordsmen said it was, that Frena was to go home to Skjar as soon as possible and they were to escort her. It had not said why Father needed her, which was annoying.

She hoped her visit would be short. The city was a steam bath in summer. Kyrn, on the far side of the hills, was blissful. All her friends were there now—boating, swimming, hunting birds in the marshes, driving chariots. In groups, of course. Women must watch their reputations, and very rich youngsters must be well guarded. All her friends were rich, although no old family fortune could compare with Father's. Not that life was all play at Kyrn. Far from it! She supervised the lambing and planting. Today she should be directing the planned extensions to the threshing floor and oast house.

"What did you mean, if not what you said?"

Verk pummeled himself, as if trying to scratch an itch under the bronze smock. "If Quera had been bribed to harm your mother, would you just throw her out in the street?"

The chariot was slowing down as the ground flattened and the onagers tired. Frena was able to spare her companion a hard stare.

"Are you suggesting my mother was murdered in her own house?"

"Someone tried to murder her outside of it, mistress. They might have paid her to finish the job."

Frena had never thought of that. But she had *seen* Father throw the stupid woman out. What was Verk trying to tell her? He shielded his eyes from the sun as he studied the village ahead.

The track was barely visible, and Bitterfeld was only a scatter of mud hovels around a spring. No doubt one of those thatch roofs covered a shrine to the Bright Ones and some others cattle sheds. What a revolting prospect! How could anyone stand the lethal dullness of life in such a burrow, where the principal occupation would be keeping the livestock out of the crops? But Father owned these lands, as he owned so much around Skjar, and the residents would certainly make Frena welcome, offer confections of berry juice, honey, and cream; have the children sing and dance for her. She would inspect the village and tell Father's tallymen what was needed, if anything.

Except that there was nobody home. Some sort of ceremony was already in progress a couple of bowshots away from the village, at the base of a rocky knoll bedecked with a few straggly fruit trees. The crowd looked surprisingly big to have come from so few houses.

"What's happening? A midsummer festival?"

"Something," Verk muttered, frowning.

"Praying for rain, perhaps. Let us go and see." Frena worked the reins, easing Night back, flicking Dark's haunches. The chariot curved off across the fields, heading for the assembly.

The center of attention was a man standing under a tree with his arms raised, as if appealing to the Bright Ones. The crowd had gathered in an arc before him, children closest, adults on the outside. Voices surged like waves of Ocean beating on shingle, but in no song or chorus she knew.

"What in the world are they doing?"

Verk did not answer, his craggy features oddly tense as he studied the scene.

"Which god do farmers pray to?" Even a city girl ought to know that much. "Holy Weru, perhaps? He's god of storms."

Still concentrating on the crowd, Verk muttered, "Not Weru, mistress! Not farmers."

"Holy Ucr, then?"

Everyone knew Father was an initiate of the Ucrist mystery, for no one could acquire so much wealth without the god's blessing. As patron lord of prosperity and abundance, Ucr should support farmers as much as merchants.

"They might pray to Ucr to stay away," Verk muttered. "Holy Nula, more like. Turn away, mistress! This is not for you. Go back—now!"

"You do not give me orders!"

"Stop her!" howled Uls, who had caught up with them by cutting the corner of the curve.

The crowd had noticed her approach and turned to watch. So far the man under the tree was ignoring her . . . and was wearing nothing but a blindfold? The man under the tree was hung there by his wrists, feet barely touching the ground. He was bloody, as if he had been savagely beaten.

"What is this?" Frena cried.

"Drive on, mistress!" Verk barked. "This is not for you."

"I am not going anywhere until I understand what is going on here! And what are those men over there doing?" Three of them, digging a hole.

"Tell her that black hair is bad luck!" Uls yelled shrilly.

"And black onagers, too! Drive away, mistress, as you value your life. They think you're coming to rescue him."

"I *will* rescue him!" she shouted. "What crime has he committed? What Speaker has pronounced holy Demern's judgment? Is that hole meant to be a *grave*?"

"Of course it is," Verk howled. "Now, *drive on!*"

Some of the watchers shouted and started running forward.

"Remind her what happened to her mother!" Uls screamed.

"I will not drive on!" Frena bent and gripped the brake lever with both hands. She raised it to dig the claw into the ground; the chariot shuddered and slowed, throwing her against the wicker of the front and raising a cloud of red dust. "What they are doing is murder. Tell them who I am. I want to know what they're doing to that man and what he's done to deserve—"

"Missy!" Verk barked, in a tone she had not heard from him before. He jerked the brake lever from her grip by slamming it down with his sandal. "Your father swore by his god that he would have me impaled if I did not bring you home safely today. Now you must drive on or I will."

With his longer arms, he reached past her to tug on Dark's reins. He snatched the whip from the socket and expertly laid it on Night's back.

Braying in protest, the onager surged forward and the car began to turn away from the mob.

The mob howled and gave chase.

"What the man has done is use the evil eye, mistress. I expect he cursed the lambing or made the rain stay away." Something clinked off his helmet. "What they are doing, mistress, or are about to do, is send him back to the Old One who sent him, and whose thing he is." Gradually the chariot was gathering speed. "And good riddance for all such as he!"

The crowd was running. They were coming for her, like the mob that had killed her mother. Black hair was unlucky, the mark of the Old One. Nonsense, of course—Florengians had darker pigmentation than Vigaelians, that was all, and she had inherited it from her mother. Shouting and baying, the crowd streamed toward her. She could make out no words, but the hatred was obvious. The village dog pack had arrived already, yapping and snarling all around, making Dark and Night twitch and snap and try to kick.

The man under the tree had been a Vigaelian spattered with filth and blood, not a Florengian, so it was not his color that had provoked the lynching. Perhaps he really was a chthonian, a Chosen of the Old One.

Stones spun through the air, narrowly missing her. The mob's words were still incomprehensible, but there was no mistaking the rage and threat in that animal roaring. She cried out as a rock struck her shoulder.

"Uls!" Verk yelled. "Cover my left!" He thrust the whip into Frena's hand and drew his sword.

She thrashed the onagers and screamed at then to go faster. The stubborn brutes were distracted by the dogs, more inclined to kick and bite than run and draw the pack after them.

"I still don't understand!" she said as calmly as she could. The Old One, Mistress of Darkness, was named *Xaran,* but that name was never spoken except in holy rites, lest it summon Her. The Chosen were Her agents, supposedly workers of evil. Yet it was very hard to see evil in that helpless victim dangling under the tree, or holy Demern's justice in this brute horde.

"He belongs to the Evil One." The swordsman yelled more oaths at the onagers. He was trying to shield her as rocks and sticks rang on his metal scales and thumped against the sides of the chariot. "She sent him. They have covered his eyes lest he afflict them with evil, and gagged his mouth to stop his curses. They must send him back to Her who sent him, laying him facedown in the ground and covering him with good earth. Do you want to share his grave, mistress?" He goaded the onagers with his sword, but missiles were striking them, too. Braying with rage, they lurched into a full gallop.

Frena's arm was bleeding, and she'd have a nasty bruise there soon. If one sharp stone could hurt this much, what had the man under the tree endured already? Or her mother, who had been waylaid by an unknown mob of thugs outside her own front door, and beaten so badly that she had died a few days later? At least she hadn't been buried alive! *Blood and birth; death and the cold earth . . .*

Now a raging, screaming mob was pursuing her as the two chariots squealed and bounced away from accursed Bitterfeld. Nimble youths were closing the gap, and some were armed with poles. Although they were only skinny, near-naked shepherd boys with wild, shaggy hair, as they drew nearer Frena thought she would rather be chased by a pack of hungry cat-bears. Everyone knew that madness came from holy Eriander, not the Old One, but surely the bloodlust and hatred in those boys' eyes was pure evil? Fortunately the onagers, having decided to run and not fight, were going as fast as they could; now all the snarling and snapping just made them try harder.

Uls had pulled alongside them on the left, but the pursuers were not much interested in him. They wanted the girl with black hair, dark eyes, and brown skin. Many townsfolk in Skjar considered such coloring unlucky. Frena had been cursed in public more than once and out here people were even more superstitious.

Journey had become nightmare, a pleasant drive a flight for life. Again she lashed the onagers. Two youths were closing in at the back of the chariot, evidently intent on grabbing Frena. Another was running alongside, staying out of Verk's reach and trying to strike him with a pole. Verk parried repeatedly, but the bouncing of the car made both attack and defense matters more of luck than skill. If that pole caught Frena with a crack on the head, she would be sharing a stranger's grave.

She felt a tug on her fluttering robe, but Verk was not so distracted that he missed the move. He swung. The boy screamed and went down in blood. His companion tried to board in the confusion and met the same fate. A staff rang on Verk's helmet. Older men were arriving, carrying larger poles, and they were more dangerous, trying to spoke the wheels or break the onagers' legs while staying out of reach of the swords.

But even hardy hill folk could not outrun onagers for long. One by one they gave up and slumped to the ground. When the last of the dogs had disappeared, Frena glanced back along the trail of crushed grain she had left from the village, confirming that the chase had been abandoned. So she was safe, and could now take time to admit to a whirling heart and sick terror. The exhausted onagers dropped from a trot to a walk.

"It's all over," Verk said. He put an arm around her, and she realized that she was weeping. She was not sure which shocked her more—her weakness or his brazen presumption. But she let his arm stay there while she dribbled tears on his shiny scales.

The chariot stopped.

"I was a fool. It was my fault for not listening to you. I'm sorry. And I'm very grateful to you and Uls."

"*Aee!* Just doing our duty, mistress. Saving our own skins also. That's never hard."

She swallowed and wiped her eyes with the back of her hand. She was trembling quite disgustingly. "My mother . . . She had two swordsmen with her when she was attacked."

"Hadn't heard *that*," Verk growled. "What happened to them?"

"No one knows. They must have run away."

"All bark and no bite isn't worth table scraps."

She pulled free of his arm. "My father will reward you well."

Verk pouted. "Happy ending won't excuse bad start."

"You're right. It would be best if Father never heard about it."

"*Aee!* The onagers don't speak much, but Uls . . . Uls!?"

Uls was sagged limply over the rail of his chariot. His brother leaped down and ran to help.

✦

The hills dividing Lake Skjar from Ocean had once been famed for their forests of cloud-combing hemlocks. It was written in the Arcana that arrogant mortals had used the timber to build themselves houses fit for gods, and holy Demern had removed the trees until mankind learned humility. Apparently that had not happened yet, because the Bright Ones had not returned the trees. The sunburned slopes were barren, fit only for pasturing ibexes, and the only memorials to their former glory were a few fragments of giant roots wedged in the rock.

At a division in the trail, Verk reined in his chariot and waited for Frena to bring hers alongside. He had been driving Uls, whose arm had been shattered by a blow from a staff. Although Verk had bound it up with the strap of his scabbard, Uls was obviously in agony—his face ashen, the immobilized limb swollen and discolored against his mail vest.

One branch of the track wandered on along the hillside; the other headed down toward the shore, where a narrow strip of flat land showed a startling green. The lake spread out beyond, a bright expanse of blue that met a sharp horizon speckled with storm clouds like puffs of mold on week-old bread.

"Onager ranch down there, mistress—By-the-Canyon."

"Yes. Father owns it." She was weary from the journey and still depressed by the horrors she had seen at the village. She kept thinking about the ghouls and their victim, wondering if they had finished burying him yet. Had he truly been a Chosen, or as innocent as her mother?

"The bouncing is hard on poor Uls," Verk said. "And the teams are tired. If we leave them all down there, I can drive you home now and come back tomorrow with help."

Normally Uls protested loudly at any suggestion that he be parted from his brother. He was beyond even that now.

Frena said, "He will be missed. If we can go on to the city, we can take him to the House of Sinura." She could have the cut on her arm healed at the same time. Cost was no problem to Horth Wigson's daughter. "I would just as soon not worry my father by mentioning what happened." He had so many worries!

Verk said, "There is also the matter of the sword, mistress. It's a poor swordsman drops a precious bronze sword and forgets to pick it up."

"Can't we stop somewhere and buy a sword?"

Silence. Verk was staring at her, and for some reason she felt her face burn all the way up to the roots of her hair. How dare he look at her like that!

Finally he said, "*Aee!* I am a lucky swordsman today."

"What do you mean?"

"I mean that when your father hired us he made me swear on the Arcana that I would tell him when anyone offered me gifts. He swore on the shrine of Ucr that he would give me thrice. So now I get three swords I can sell?"

"Me? *Bribe* you? You *dare* accuse me of . . ."

But he *had* dared, and she *had* tried to bribe him. She looked away, unable to meet his cold stare. More furious at herself than at him, she said, "Let us get Uls down to the ranch house quickly."

◆

So it was that Uls was dosed with poppy and put to bed, the weary onagers led away to be fed and watered. Frena herself was granted refreshment with all the deference due Horth Wigson's daughter. Rested, she drove off along the trail with a fresh team and Verk as passenger once more.

"I was not trying to get you impaled, Verk." She studied the road ahead. "I just want to keep Father from being worried unnecessarily."

"My lady is kind." His tone was so flat she could not tell if he was mocking her. "I know of a swordsman who failed to save his master and the master's wife had the man skinned. *Aee!* It was sad."

"I am sure Father will not skin you. I would just as soon not tell him. He would be very upset." He would be devastated. Horth, who now rarely went anywhere, in his youth had made the arduous, hazardous trek over the Edge to the Florengian Face. This had been long before Stralg's invasion, when the trail was less used and even more difficult than it was nowadays. Horth had returned with precious trade goods that had formed the foundation of his fortune, but he had also brought a wife, Paola Apicella, the only love of his life. Rich men were expected to keep concubines, sometimes junior wives, but there had never been a hint of another woman for Horth, even after Paola's death three years ago; never a whisper among the servants. A brutal and senseless mob attack in the streets of Skjar had killed her. He must *not* learn that the same sort of mob had so nearly claimed his daughter.

Verk said, "I spoke in haste, mistress. How can we explain Uls's absence? My brother is a simple soul, yet I am fond of him. I do not wish to see him skinned."

"Stop ranting about skinning! No one skins anyone in Skjar. He fell out of his chariot when the axle pin broke and the wheel came off." A white lie, surely, told without malice, just to save her father needless anxiety?

"*Aee!* Then the wicked stableman who mounted the wheel must be beaten."

Frena opened her mouth indignantly and closed it again. That might be true. All this talk of punishment was strange to her. She had never considered a life where such things might happen. "It was my fault. I set too fast a pace and Uls's chariot overturned on a rock."

Verk's pale face twisted under its lawn of golden stubble as if wrestling against a smile. "And what sort of guard would let you be so foolish? *Aee!* I will be impaled most surely."

"Stop that! You know perfectly well that Father orders no punishment more than the law allows."

"Forty lashes for a man of my age," Verk said sadly. "But who counts? A court will surely judge a sturdy swordsman fit to bear more anyway. Who will employ him when he bears such scars?"

"Then a thunderbolt startled Uls's onagers and they ran away with him. That can happen to anyone."

Verk nodded judiciously. "The master might consider a broken arm punishment enough for that. But I should not have let you drive close to the villagers, so I must throw myself at his feet and beg for my life."

"It was my fault! I will not let him punish you."

Verk said, "My lady is kind," again, with very little conviction.

◆

When they came to the place where the Skjar River drained out of the lake, Frena yielded the reins to Verk. Soon walls rose on both sides to form the twisted gorge called the Gates of Weru. There, on uncounted rocky islands, stood the greatest trading city in all Vigaelia. When the stream divided into a dozen dancing torrents, the road left the bank and headed across First Bridge to Bell Song, uppermost island of Skjar. Soon the air was too wet and hot to breathe. Frena felt like a fish in chowder, already. Verk chose to go by way of High to Milk Yellow.

Skjar was a web of bridges. Some crept over the water from rock to rock, writhing and humping like snakes. Others were giddying, rope-bound catwalks strung between the summits of rocky spires. Some were mere planks too narrow for two pedestrians to pass, others had sprouted double rows of stores and houses along their length.

From Milk Yellow to Snakeskin and Egg . . .

Some islands were wide and relatively level, others were rocky spires with dwellings adhering to their sides like bizarre fungi and spreading out-ward from the summits in mushroom caps. Skjarans considered any rock above the waterline to be potential foundation for something, even if only the pier of a bridge, and any group of three or more was enough to support a building.

From Egg to Limpet Bend . . .

Skjar was people: carpenters, saddlers, weavers, scribes, brewers, merchants, porters, priests, brass workers, dye makers, and a myriad other crafts. Often among them could be seen Werists in their palls, white-shrouded Witnesses, green-clad Nastrarians, and other recognizable cultists. Mysteries that did not require their initiates to wear distinctive garb must certainly be represented also.

Skjar was incredibly ancient and yet forever new, because it was built of wood, following its ancient skill in boatbuilding. Year by year it was culled by rot, earthquakes, winter storms, or chance fires. Frena had not been gone a thirty and yet she could see changes—Triangle burned down to bedrock, the new bridge between Sheeplick and Honeycomb open at last.

The air was sticky and stale, reeking of food and garbage and close-packed people.

"What did you mean when you said farmers would pray to holy Ucr to stay away? He is their god also."

Verk chewed his lip while easing the onagers through a teeming little market, trying to keep moving without letting Dark and Night clear a path with their teeth. "I spoke out of turn, mistress."

"Continue doing so. Answer me!"

He flashed her a momentary glance, then went back to looking straight ahead. "I beg leave to remain silent. The master would disapprove of what I almost said."

So now they were to be confidants, were they, she and this metal-plated servant?

"I won't tell him, I promise."

Night flashed a hoof out sideways, sending a plump matron reeling into her companions. Curses and threats flew. Verk was remarkably adept with obscenities when he wanted to be. Surprisingly, when the incident was over and the chariot moved again, he returned to Frena's question.

"In hard times farmers see their children starve, mistress. In good times crops fetch bad prices. City mouse always eats better than country bull."

"What has that got to do with Ucr?"

"Ucr looks after his own, they do say."

"Meaning?"

He sighed. "Meaning, in hard times farmers must borrow food to live, mistress. Those that have lend to them that have not. And then the lender forecloses, so he ends up gaining land for a fraction of its worth. Farmer becomes serf, and his children less than that . . . so they do say," he added with another quick glance.

Frena shuddered. "Are you implying that *Father* does that?"

"Never, never, mistress! *Aee!* It would be a poor swordsman who said he guarded a monster, now wouldn't it? Who could trust him?"

She knew that the man was mocking her; she dared not comment in case she made even more of a fool of herself. No servant had ever dared speak to her so frankly. Verk was showing her a whole new way of looking at her father and, by implication, at herself.

Up the long sloping bridge to Grand, higher yet to Ossa's Leap, over the masts of a ship to Dead Ringer, then Live Ringer, and steeply down to Temple . . .

"And you really have no idea why Father has sent for me?" There had been no hint of the matter in the tablets he had sent her about the new stables less than a sixday ago.

"He did not confide, mistress. Mouths can hold converse but not secrets, they do say."

"You mean you heard rumors?"

"I did not," Verk said firmly. "Not a mouse squeaked."

So the decision had been sudden. The tablet Father had sent to Kyrn had been cracked, as if fired in haste.

"Yesterday—did anyone come to see Father yesterday?"

After a pause, Verk said, "None that he had me watch over, mistress."

The pause felt like a clue. He was coaching her, as if he had been sworn not to tell her something and wanted her to ask the right questions.

"Did you escort him anywhere yesterday?"

"Not I. Nor Uls."

Then who? "But he did go out?"

The next pause felt like a refusal. The wheels rumbled slowly the whole width of Eelfisher before the swordsman spoke again.

"They do say so, mistress."

Frena pondered her next move. How many questions did she have left? "Without his usual guards?"

"With no guards."

She thought *Aee!* It was catching. "But he never does that!"

Verk chewed his lip for a moment and eventually said, "Well, he did have the Werists."

"*Werists?* Did you say *Werists?*"

"Wearing satrap's stripes. Brought him back later, no harm done."

"I'm glad to hear it!" She could not recall the palace ever sending Werists to fetch her father. She doubted very much that Satrap Eide would have had anything to do with that outrage. She sensed the hand of his wife, Saltaja Hragsdor, the real ruler of Skjar and all Vigaelia. "Was Father expecting them?"

"At dawn? Tearing off shutters? Slaughtering watchdogs? Any other man would have been in bed, but you know the master, never sleeping . . ."

"There was a fight?" she cried.

"*Aee,* no! Swordsmen don't argue with Werists, mistress. It's part of the law—we don't even have to *try* to fight Werists!"

Verk was shamed, furious. He and the others had been made to look irrelevant. Her father admitted that a man had to be either stupid or very brave to join the guards' guild, for an extrinsic wearing a sword was a red rag to a Werist. And if the Werist turned on the man, a red rag was all he would be.

What had provoked Father's unexpected summons to the palace yesterday and why had it caused him to send for her?

Eelfisher to Chatter Place and then to Blueflower. There Frena was on home ground, amid familiar smells of tar and fish and saltwater, hearing the sounds of rattling oxcarts, wailing seabirds, creaking windlasses. Masts and sails moved between houses. The sparkling crystal freshets that drained the lake had divided and merged, widened and grown brackish, and finally spread out into shipping channels, salt and foul; greasy outlets to Ocean.

Her earliest memories were of her parents' home on Fishgut Alley, on the island called Crab, which faced out directly over Ocean. Her mother had kept house upstairs while her father ran his chandler business downstairs— although by the time her fuzzy childhood images cleared, he was already expanding into adjacent quarters and larger interests. That building had long since been replaced by warehouses.

Year by year Horth Wigson had extended his reach, doubling and redoubling his worth and workforce. Everything he turned his hand to turned to gold. He owned all of Crab now, except for one jetty on the northeastern corner. He owned most of Blueflower, which adjoined Crab on the west so that the two of them enclosed the basin of Weather Haven, a natural harbor secure enough to give him an advantage over all his competitors. Year after year he tore down more hovels, built more warehouses, extended his mansion. Any footprint-size patch of ground in Skjar was precious, yet Horth's windows overlooked a private park. He imported full-grown trees and was planning his own zoological collection. His residence outshone the palace of Satrap Eide.

As the onagers hauled the chariot across the bridge from Blueflower to Crab, Frena broke a long silence. "You will drop me at the door, Verk, and then go straight back to Uls. He will rest better if you are there."

Verk shot her a startled look and almost knocked over a woman carrying a water jug on her head. She screamed abuse after him.

"Tomorrow," Frena said, in what she hoped was the same calm and confident voice, "you will bring Uls to the Healers on Chatter Place. I will tell Master Trinvar to send someone with gold to wait for you there. And tonight I will tell Father what happened and insist that it was all my fault. I promise," she told his skeptical expression. "I think he has a lot more on his mind now than a lost sword and a scrape on my arm."

"My lady is kind," Verk said. He did not argue, so she must have found the best solution to their problem.

BENARD CELEBRE

was wakened by daggers of light stabbing through his eyelids. For a moment he thought it must be Cutrath coming to kill him, and his heart leaped in terror. But it was only Thod, his depressingly cheerful apprentice, all dewy-faced and doe-eyed.

"Twelve blessings this fine morning, master!"

"And on you," Benard growled. "Water?"

"At once, master!" Darkness returned as Thod dropped the tarpaulin and ran over to the well.

Benard sat up, wincing at the resulting thunderclaps inside his head. He could hear priests warbling morning hymns, accompanied by screaming roosters in the surrounding houses. He could hear voices as people went by on their way to prayers. His shed stood in a corner of the abandoned builders' yard behind the new Pantheon, almost the only empty space in Kosord. As a home it was sadly cramped, just three walls of mud brick and the fourth only a curtain of oiled cloth hung from a beam, but he could work in there in rainy weather. The interior was a catastrophe of clay models, faience figurines, tubs of raw clay, tottering heaps of chisels and mallets, balks of timber, jars of paint, bags of coloring for glazes, boxes, baskets, polychrome tiles, boards for sketching, and gods knew what else. One thing old Master Artist Odok had signally failed to teach his best pupil was tidiness.

Hiddi . . . His body still hankered after Hiddi. Had she really been the vision she had seemed, or had her beauty been only in the bedazzled eye of her beholder? He must not judge the child for choosing to serve the god of madness. What seemed to him like utter degradation might be better than the life of a peasant's wife, endlessly producing short-lived babies.

Benard dragged himself upright and began picking his way through the disorder. He felt as if he had not slept at all, and apparently he would not be eating today either. His pelf string had held at least a dozen twists of copper last night when he went off with Nils to celebrate, but now it was bare. Even the epochal torment in his head could not have cost that much, so he must have bought matching headaches for half of Kosord. Granted that the priests were better at commissioning work than paying for it, but when they did pay him, the sudden riches never lasted long. So he survived on his fee from Thod's family, a bag of meal every sixday, and the next was not due until tomorrow.

If he lived that long.

Werist Cutrath was an infuriating, unnecessary, unwanted complication in the life of a man who wanted nothing more than to spend the entire day chipping stone. Benard's needs were few: his art, his art, and his art. Once in a while he enjoyed a riotous celebration like last night's. He appreciated women, women appreciated him; although most of his friends were humble folk, he had worshiped holy Eriander in some of the best bedrooms in Kosord. There was one woman he loved to desperation but could not have. The last thing he needed was a fight to the death with Cutrath Horoldson, especially when there could be no doubt as to whose death.

He grimaced as Thod opened the drape again, hurling sunlight everywhere. Benard accepted a jug of Kosord's fetid, lukewarm well water and drank greedily. Thod hopefully located a chisel and maul.

"No hammering yet," Benard said. "I need a board."

"At once, master." Thod put a brave face on his disappointment. He liked nothing better than to spend the entire day chipping marble as Benard directed, convinced that this would build muscles to impress the light of his life, Thilia, daughter of Sugthar the potter. Thod was eagerness personified, laboring untiring from dawn to dusk, five days out of six. Whether he possessed enough of an artist's eye to please holy Anziel was another matter.

"But first, run and ask Thranth if I can borrow his good loincloth again. And his sandals!" he shouted as Thod took off like a stone from a sling. Thranth was his brother, a harness maker, and relatively wealthy.

Benard tied up the curtain and squinted out at the day. Although Kosord had no good building stone, it did own a quarry of warm-toned marble that was perfect for sculpting golden Vigaelian bodies. Three great blocks stood around in various stages of completion. Mayn, goddess of knowledge, was the easiest of the Bright Ones to portray, because only Her hands were visible, holding Her traditional distaff and spindle, but he was pleased with the way the stone revealed the woman inside—trailing folds where fabric hung loose, smooth surfaces when it clung to flesh at shoulder or advancing knee, even hints of the face under the veil. Almost as if the marble were transparent. Praise the lady.

Next to Benard's kiln stood a roughly hacked out Sinura, goddess of healing, wrapped in Her snake, but no one except Benard knew that the raw block nearest the shed contained Weru, god of storm and battle, just waiting to be exposed.

By the time Thod came trotting back from his brother's harness shop, Benard was rummaging in his cluttered nest. "You haven't seen my razor anywhere, have you?" Vigaelians reacted badly to black beards.

They found the razor but not the polished scrap of bronze he used as a mirror. In his present state he was likely to skin himself anyway, so he let Thod shave him while he—*Ouch!*—planned his visit to the palace.

"Lot of teeth lying around the streets this morning," Thod remarked shyly.

"Teeth? . . . Um, yes." *Ouch!* As well as instructing his apprentice in his craft, a master should set a good example of proper civic behavior, but knuckles as bruised as Benard's could not be explained away. Nor could his hangover be concealed. He told the tale, stressing the mitigating circumstances of betrothal celebration and damsel-rescuing, and not mentioning divine intervention.

Thod made admiring noises when he heard about the fight. "Do you know who this rapist was, master?"

"Cutrath Horoldson."

"The satrap's son?" Fortunately Thod was stropping the bronze blade on a fragment of tile at the time, or he might have cut his master's throat. "But he's a Werist! Oh, master, master! That's suicide, to hit a Hero!"

Possibly, but it had been worth it. Since childhood Benard had been waiting for the news that he was either about to be packed off to a home he barely remembered or put to death for something done by someone else. Now he could die happy, remembering Cutrath spread out in the dirt.

"I trust in the lady to help me out of this."

"Praise the Beautiful One!" Thod agreed, looking puzzled.

Benard did not explain, because he wasn't sure exactly what he was going to do. Certainly he was in mortal danger. No Werist, especially one as new to his collar as Cutrath Horoldson, could ignore such an insult. Any other man would flee the city, but Benard was a hostage on parole. The day he failed to report to the palace guard, he would be an outlaw, an escaped prisoner, fair game for anyone. The only people who could possibly restrain Cutrath were his parents. Lady Ingeld would certainly intervene if Benard asked her to, but even a peaceable artist drew the line at hiding behind a woman's skirts, and Cutrath probably wouldn't listen to her anyway.

He would obey his father, but the satrap was no friend of Benard's. Horold might side with his loutish son and specifically order him to avenge the family honor, or he might choose to regard the incident as a criminal offense and sentence the culprit to be flogged, branded, or hanged as the fancy took him. Since no other solution found its way through Benard's thundering hangover, those risks would have to be taken. He was a firm believer that where there was life there was hope.

✦

Hurrying off to the palace, clad in Thranth's smart linen cloth with the sun hot on his back, Benard felt reasonably respectable. He had combed out his black tresses, oiled them, and tied them back with a red headband some girl had given him once, which he had rediscovered a few days ago under a jar of umber pigment. He carried a plank of balmwood that Thod had sanded clean for him.

Mud brick would last forever if it was kept dry, but every heavy rain would undermine a wall or two somewhere. As often as not the whole side of the house would then be flattened and rebuilt, raising the level of the street and converting the next flood into a neighbor's problem. Thus, through uncounted generations, Kosord had lifted itself high above the plain. The highest point of all was the temple of holy Veslih, surmounted by the bronze canopy above Her sacred fire. Around that, in splendid confusion of roofs and levels, sprawled the palace and everything else, descending higgledy-piggledy to the outlying shanties of the poor.

The palace was approached up wide steps of bricks glazed white and green and red. More polychrome bricks adorned its walls; sunlight flamed on the bronze pillars flanking its high doorway. Just inside that was the guard room, to which Benard must report each day. In the ten years since he was apprenticed to Master Artist Odok, he had forgotten this duty only once; the unpleasant results had improved his memory dramatically.

At full strength Horold's host numbered more than twenty sixty, although he normally kept only two hunts in Kosord itself, billeting the other three in other cities. His satrapy, covering about a third of the Face, contained many other hosts whose leaders were nominally subordinate to him, but any Werist put in charge of an army soon developed revolutionary ambitions. The Heroes found peace an elusive concept. Even summer training exercises were regarded as failures if they did not get out of hand.

Compared with the rest of the host, the palace guard was a joke, a handful of men too old or maimed to fight plus a number of boys in training, all under the command of Flankleader Guthlag, who should always be seen as early in the day as possible. Benard found Guthlag on his usual bench, rolling knucklebones and quaffing beer with three young Werists sporting the white sashes and leather collars of cadets. By noon they would owe him a fortune; before sunset they would win it all back. It seemed as if he had made a good start on his drinking already, for his pall had sagged into a clumsy rumple, while the youngsters' looked sculpted, not a fold out of place.

He scowled at his visitor with bleary pink eyes. "Early for you, isn't it? Did you wet the bed or did she just kick you out?"

To any man except a warrior, Benard would have retorted along the lines of "We thought we heard you coming back," but one could never trust a Werist's sense of humor, not even Guthlag's.

He bowed, which made his head throb harder. "Lord, the miserable low-life Florengian beetle reports that he is present as required."

"You were a slug yesterday. How did you get promoted?"

"Lord, that was before she kicked me out."

Elderly Werists were rare. Guthlag Guthlagson—that patronymic meant that his father was either unknown or had refused to acknowledge him—had run with the Kosord host back in the days of State Consort Nars Narson, before the coming of Stralg. Werists were not supposed to outlive their leaders, and Nars's hordeleader had certainly died with him in the massacre. Old Guthlag's survival was never explained.

He was a withered stick now—pate all leathery and chest hair white, skin draped loose on his arms and swollen purple cords disfiguring his legs. His fingers were twisted and his hips stiff, yet he showed none of the dehumanization that Werists called battle hardening. Age had marred him, but only as it marred other men, which suggested that he had done little fighting. Nevertheless, the old warrior did keep the vicious youngsters of the guard in line, and in the past he had been known to cuff ears when the Cutrath rat pack nibbled too hard at the Celebrian hostage. If he knew of the satrap's son being on a blood hunt today, he would certainly drop a warning, but he just rolled his eyes as he saw Benard help himself to a stick of sausage some guard had left on the table unguarded.

"What's that?" He pointed to the plank.

"Just a sketch. May I ask a question, lord? I don't intend to pry into the mysteries of Weru, but—"

"I wouldn't recommend it."

"Of course not, lord. I got into an argument last night—"

"From the look of you I'm not surprised."

"Er, yes, lord. Someone said that Werists could assume their battleform at will, and someone else insisted that they could do so only on the command of their leader. Is that secret information?" What he wanted to find out was how the newly initiated Cutrath was likely to come after him, but he wasn't going to tell that story unless he had to.

The room had chilled perceptibly. Menace stared through pale eyes.

"I suggest," growled Flankleader Guthlag, "that you mind your own business, artist. Have you ever seen a warbeast?"

"No, lord."

"Pray you never do. It is usually a fatal experience for extrinsics." An audience always made the old rogue surly. On his own he was sometimes good company.

Benard bowed. "Yes, lord."

"Show us your picture. These ignorant brutes need some culture."

The cadets scowled at his humor but wisely said nothing. Benard cleared a corner of the table and laid down the slab, which was blank. "I haven't drawn it yet."

"Glad to hear that. Thought I was going blind." The flankleader tried a suck on his straw and pulled a face. He handed the beaker to a cadet, who took it over to the corner to ladle more beer from the krater. "And a new straw!" Even Guthlag could never drink beer straight from the jar, with all its husks, gritty dregs, and yeasty scum.

Benard went to the hearth and fumbled among the cold ashes until he found a few pieces of charcoal. He came back and studied the wood, while silently reciting the invocation.

"You watch this, now," Guthlag mumbled toothlessly. "If you want t'see the blessing of a god at work."

"Goddess!" corrected the largest cadet. "What sort of man would swear to a female god?"

Benard did not hear more. He was reaching back to the day he first came to Kosord—he had been only eight, but visual memory was part of his lady's blessing. He had been very ill, too, not yet recovered from the hardship of the Edgelands, where he and Orlando had almost died, despite the best efforts of poor Dantio being both father and mother to them. They had descended onto bleak and bitter moors near Tryfors. Orlando had been detained there, screaming piteously. Benard had been brought to the court of Satrap Horold, Dantio taken farther downstream to a fate untold.

But it was not his lost family Benard wanted. Nor yet Ingeld, who had mothered him back to life. He struggled to define the other image, and gradually it took shape as if emerging from a white mist of years. He sent his rogation to holy Anziel and felt Her blessing quicken his fingers—fast strokes to define the hard edge of nose and ear and teeth, softer for the rounded edges of cheekbones and neck. Fingertips to smear the shading . . . fainter swirls for the flowing blond curls. Darkest of all the brass collar, and then it was done, a three-quarter profile of a man of about thirty, arrogantly aware of his looks. Unlike most Werists, he was clean-shaven and wore his hair long. The sketch even caught the glint of eyes that in life had been a fierce and most brilliant blue. His nose had been curved, then—not the pruning hook of his brother the bloodlord, but a strong, masculine nose. His teeth had been perfect, which was rare.

"Blood!" Guthlag muttered. "Blood and torment! I'd forgot."

"What's a pretty-boy namby doing wearing a Werist collar?" demanded one of the cadets.

"Is that supposed to be a joke?" snarled another.

"*Blood!*" Guthlag roared. "Stupid slugs!"

All three jerked to attention and parroted "My lord is kind!" in unison.

"Don't you know him?"

One by one they recognized the likeness and muttered oaths. The man Benard had recalled was not the creature who had been whirling around his satrapy in a chariot last sixday, celebrating his youngest son's initiation. Perhaps these three apprentice monsters had not fully appreciated what battle hardening could do—and would eventually do to them if they fought enough. This was the first summer Benard could remember when Horold had not been away campaigning. Werists could survive incredible wounds, but every healing left them less and less human. This was their corban.

"He really look like that?"

"That he did," Guthlag snarled. "What'ch goin' do with that, boy?"

"Show it to him," Benard said. "It's an excuse to ask a favor, is all."

"You're out of your mind!"

"Why?"

The flankleader shook his head in disbelief. "You think he wants to be reminded?"

Benard thought about it. "Why not?"

The old Werist growled low in his throat, like a true watchdog. "Better you than me, lad. And in court?"

"Court? Today?" If the satrap would be holding assize and giving audience, Benard must catch him first, or there would be no chance of a private chat before Cutrath found him.

In the distance, horns blew.

"*Oh, gods!*" Benard grabbed up his sketch and raced out the door.

♦

The great court of the palace was pentagonal, with a covered balcony all around and a center open to the heavens. The walls were formed of panels of brightly glazed tiles depicting people and gods in red, black, white, and green, separated by massive steles inscribed with the laws of holy Demern. Benard had once been friendly with a member of the scribes' guild who had tried to explain to him all the complications of writing: signs that stood for names, signs that meant grammatical elements, signs that meant sounds, and signs indicating how to interpret other signs. It had given him terrible headaches. Add to that, the oldest tongue was so obscure that the meaning of the written law could be deciphered only by Speakers of Demern, who knew it all by divine inspiration anyway.

Until the coming of Stralg, Kosord had been ruled by the consort of the hereditary dynast, who was always a pyromancer—a Daughter of Veslih. The state consort had always been chosen from among the Speakers of Demern, but Horold had banished the cult from his satrapy because a Speaker would automatically denounce him as a usurper. Consequently, although only Speakers were supposed to make legal rulings, Horold acted as his own judge, holding an assize every first-day he was in the city. After distributing justice, he would receive petitions—merchants seeking contracts, landowners wanting to register titles, citizens with disputes to be arbitrated, officeholders aspiring to promotion, and a swarm of miscellanies—until his patience ran out. Humble folk might return every sixday for half a year before he found time to hear their pleas.

Benard reached the door as the second horn call was sounded, meaning the satrap was on his way. With the courtyard so crowded, his chances of receiving a hearing today were remote, and his quarrel with Cutrath could not be presented in public anyway. However, this was the last place Cutrath would think of looking for him, and not even he would dare to commit murder here.

Benard stepped boldly up to the scribes at their high desk to give his name and rank and show his seal. He knew most of the people around the palace, but the chief scribe was new since his day. He was portly, sumptuously robed, piggy head shaved hairless. He waited expectantly, mawkish professional smile slowly fading toward contempt.

"Er . . ." Benard said. No one would ever be allowed to see the satrap without offering a bribe or two, and he had nothing to offer. "Um. A sketch of your beautiful children? Or your lovely wife?"

A couple of the lesser flunkies were seized by coughing fits. The fat man scowled and colored. "I hardly think so," he said in a shrill soprano. "Wait upstairs."

Benard scurried off, shuddering at his own clumsiness. How could he have been so inept as not to see that? Obviously the gods would die of old age before his name was called now. Tonight he would ask Ingeld to arrange a private audience. Up in the balcony, he located an unoccupied pillar, leaned plank and self against it, and prepared to endure the rest of the day. His hangover deserved to be set in glazed bricks, immortalized in the chronicles of Vigaelia.

As the final blare of horns died in echoes, priests in garishly tinted robes trooped in, chanting psalms. Benard could participate in public rituals like this, which were very different from the carnal sacrifice Hiddi had expected in the temple of Eriander. Even now the slightest thought of Hiddi was enough to send quivers through his groin. He wondered hopefully if he might have been too strict in his interpretation of the rules and made a note to ask Odok, who was head of his lodge and the light of Anziel on Kosord.

Dusky male Florengians, prisoners of war with the cropped ears of slaves, were carrying in baskets of tablets, placing them behind the throne. The pyromancer who brought in the sacred flame was another Florengian, a hostage named Sansya, a few years younger than Benard. He recalled her as a terrified child, arriving at court very shortly before he went off to Odok; now she was a striking young woman, drawing every man's eyes. In Benard's opinion, the flame-colored robes suited her nut-brown skin better than it did the Vigaelians' pink. The jet hair he remembered had turned a rich auburn, but that was a result of her initiation into the Daughters of Veslih. If Ingeld had chosen to stay away and delegate today's augury to a deputy, then no important business was scheduled.

The priests fell silent. Sansya had stopped at the hearth, where logs of fragrant honeywood were stacked ready. She spoke the invocation to Veslih, then knelt to tip the coals from her firepan onto the pyre. Flame and oily smoke spouted up so suddenly that she recoiled and almost overbalanced. A universal wail of surprise dwindled into a worried buzz.

The outburst was fortunately timed, for it muffled Benard's yelp of pain as the point of a dirk jabbed into his left buttock. He spun around to face Cutrath. He should have realized that the first thing the satrap's cub would do would be to ask Guthlag if the hostage had reported in yet today. A major war could not have produced as much blood as there was in young Horoldson's eye, but then, his hangover was working around a badly swollen jaw and no doubt a pounding lump on the back of his skull. Although no one else seemed to notice the confrontation, the space around them expanded as spectators wandered away to greet more distant friends.

"I am going to kill you before the day is out, turd."

"My lord is kind." That wonderful phrase could mean anything, or nothing. "The noble lord understands that his slave was wretchedly drunk."

Useless. Apology was a display of weakness and no apology could excuse an offense as enormous as Benard's.

"I will break every joint in your body, ending with your neck."

He probably could. Benard was beefier, but he lacked the training and the bloodlust. Even if he won at roughhousing, the kid would just battle-form or call for help. "My lord is kind."

"No." Cutrath shook his head and winced at the result. "As unkind as possible. Enjoy your last morning, vermin. I'll be waiting outside to begin." He kicked Benard's ankle and stalked away.

Benard sagged back against the pillar again. He had survived the first encounter. The worst danger had always been that Cutrath would come after him in battleform; one warbeast could massacre a whole platoon of extrinsic swordsmen, let alone a solitary sculptor.

The satrap was standing in front of his throne, almost directly below Benard. From that angle Horold did not appear too grotesque, only very large and hairy. An ominous hush had fallen over the court, for Sansya was still kneeling at the fire. It seemed to Benard's untutored eye to be blazing normally now. Someone had primed it with too much oil—that was all, surely?

Horold lost patience. His voice was hoarse and violent, like a bull roar. "I ask you again, Veslihan! Does our holy guardian bless this meeting?"

Reluctantly she rose, still staring uncertainly into the flames. "I don't . . . I think . . ." Then she gabbled out the required oracle: "My lord holy Veslih blesses this house and welcomes all who draw near in Her name praise the goddess amen." She spun on her heel and fled the hall with red-gold robes rippling, auburn hair streaming. Without question she was on her way to inform Ingeld of whatever she had seen. Nevertheless, she had pronounced the blessing and there was no need for wholesale sacrifice or public penance. Matters could proceed.

"Amen!" shouted the congregation. The satrap took his seat. The scribes settled cross-legged in back of him; the two nearest the throne poised ready with stylus in hand and freshly rolled layers of clay ready on their boards.

"Begin!" roared the bull.

The herald called out the name of the noble Huntleader Darag Kwirarlson—the satrap's men would always be given precedence, even ahead of criminal matters. Darag petitioned his dread lord for a monopoly on pepper imported into Kosord and its purlieus for the next twelve years, free of all taxation or royalty. He gave no reason why he should profit in this way, and Horold did not ask for discussion.

"We gladly grant this petition of the valiant son of Kwirarl."

The scribes' styli jabbed rapidly at the clay. The keeper of seals came forward to mutter over their chicken tracks and approve them. The tablets were then removed to be baked and more were brought.

After Darag came two other Werists, appealing for amendments to the records of certain lands they had somehow acquired. Horold did ask for objections this time, but no one was foolish enough to raise any. The effect of the change seemed to be that the free peasants currently dwelling on those lands were henceforth bound to remain there as serfs, they and their descendants forever. The tablets were approved.

Horold's seal was much like Benard's, a stone cylinder about the size of a finger joint with a hole bored through the length of it for a thong and a picture carved on the outside. Rolled over wet clay, seals recorded their distinctive images. Benard's was made of agate and showed a hawk in flight, a symbol of his goddess; the satrap's would be of more valuable stone—onyx or chalcedony—with images of a wild boar. Horold's carried a lot more power.

Next came a footpad, a youth who had bludgeoned a traveler to death for the sake of his purse. He denied the charge; the Witness testified that he was guilty. Horold did not even call for the appropriate law to be read, because everyone knew the penalty was impalement. When the deadly little cylinder had sealed his fate, the boy was led away weeping.

So it went. The satrap never demanded to hear the relevant decrees of holy Demern, probably in case the scribes would not be able to read the appropriate panel, or even find it. More often he asked for precedents, and then they would consult the tablets in their baskets and mutter among themselves before advising him what penalty his predecessors had imposed in similar cases. Benard, when not struggling to stay awake, was impressed. The bloody-handed tyrant was doing a fair job of maintaining law without divine guidance. Ominously, evidence that a brawl had been begun by a gang of Werists was ruled irrelevant, but any man would favor his cult brothers over extrinsics. Apart from that bias, the satrap accepted the seer's evidence, listened to the accused's excuses or explanations, then decreed no more than the legal penalty, sometimes less: once when he sentenced a debtor to slavery, he let the man's wife and children return to her family instead of being sold, too.

At times he even displayed the cruel humor Benard so well remembered. A young cobbler was convicted of rape, for which the standard penalty was castration. His wife and parents entered a plea for clemency on the grounds that he was an only child and still lacked an heir to carry on the family. The victim had suffered no permanent harm or pregnancy and her husband had accepted her back to his bed. Horold inquired about precedents. Tablets were clattered and a scribe reported that State Consort Nars had never reduced or postponed sentence in rape cases.

"But were any of them cobblers?" the satrap inquired. "Cobblers work sitting down. Cut off his feet instead. He won't catch any more victims then. May holy Eriander bless his marriage. Next."

✦

Flankleader Guthlag said "Come!" and peeled Benard off his pillar. "I had a word with the chancellor. You're next!" He pushed Benard's shoulder with a gnarled hand.

"But . . ." But he didn't want . . . But, but, but . . . Clutching his sketch, Benard went downstairs with Guthlag.

Satrap Horold cut off the current defendant in midwhine. "Forty lashes. Next?"

"A petition, lord," the herald said uneasily. "The hostage Benard Celebre."

"Hostage?" the satrap repeated in disbelief. He scowled with bestial little eyes at the supplicant creeping forward on hands and knees. "Little Bena! You may rise." That meant Benard could sit back on his heels instead of keeping his face on the floor.

"My lord is kind."

"You have grown."

So had he. He had always been big, but now he was as gross as an ox, spread out in all directions, although what he had added seemed to be more bone and brawn than fat. His purple pall concealed most of his torso, but all visible parts of him bristled with coarse yellow hair, like ripe barley, and this shrubbery almost covered his Werist brass collar and the numerous bands of gold wrapped around his bulging limbs. Even his eyebrows had spread up his forehead. His boots obviously did not contain human feet; the proudly curved nose Benard had sketched had vanished into a snout, the lower half of his face protruding between two jutting tusks.

The monster sighed. "The years pass! Master artist? Sworn to Anziel? This was well done."

"My lord is kind." Amazingly so.

"All Florengians are artists, not fighters. That was what we were told. You suppose my brother still believes that?" The piggy eyes glinted dangerously.

"My lord, I am ignorant of such matters." The Florengian war was far away and what Bloodlord Stralg believed was of no interest to Benard.

"A hostage should keep himself better informed. Well, what do you want?"

That was what a sixty of much worthier petitioners were wondering.

"My lord is aware," Benard said, this being the formula for *I'm sure you don't know,* "that his lowly servant has been contracted to supply statues of the Bright Ones for the new Pantheon."

"I know the priests talked me out of a wagonload of gold for some useless project." The satrap clicked claws impatiently on the arm of his throne. "What of it?"

"Holy Weru, lord. As my lord is the light of Weru on Kosord, I had hoped he would give his slave direction on how the majestic Weru should be portrayed. I presumed to bring a sketch . . . lord . . ."

He gestured to the herald who had taken his board from him. The man approached and knelt to show it to the beast on the throne. Satrap Horold, with his snout and tusks and evil little piggy eyes, looked down at the godlike face he had possessed fifteen years ago.

He grunted. Then he beckoned Benard to rise and approach the throne. This was a signal honor, but it involved no small danger. As Guthlag had hinted, Horold might decide he was being mocked and disembowel Benard with one slash of his paw.

"When did you do this?" he asked, in a low, slurred growl. He had trouble speaking below a bellow.

"This morning, lord."

The ancient throne of Kosord was not an especially high seat, yet Benard had to look up to see the giant's tusks, and it was an effort not to pull faces at his rank animal stench.

"From memory?"

"Yes, lord."

"Incredible."

"My lord is kind."

"Describe this new Pantheon."

"My lord, the gods will stand above their respective shrines . . ." Life-size freestanding statuary was a new art form, an idea imported from Florengia. Before the war, Vigaelian artists had rarely ventured beyond bas-relief or faience figurines. Since man-size statues could not be packed over the Edge, artists like Odok and now Benard were working from sketches and making up the rest as they went along. They could follow old traditions or flaunt them almost at will.

"How big are these figures?"

"The priests wanted human—I mean—*life* size, my lord." *Sweat, fool!*

"And wearing what?"

"Whatever tradition and the priests require, lord." Benard must be careful not to get carried away in describing this wonder he was to create. A man must keep all his wits about him when dealing with a despot. "With appropriate attributes. Some clothed . . . some not."

"What will Weru be wearing?"

"Whatever my lord directs."

"Then show Weru unclothed."

"My lord is kind."

While Benard considered how to ask for an edict of protection while he worked without mentioning Cutrath, the satrap forestalled him.

"Give him a sword—but no collar for a god, of course." The monster's jowls distorted in what might have been a smile. A long black tongue came out and washed his tusks. He snuffled. "You have given me grave offense in the past, little Bena. What misdeeds have you been up to now that you suddenly seek my favor?"

There was no possibility of lying in the presence of a Witness. Benard found enough saliva to whisper, "Uh. My lord's most miserable slave, while drunk, used . . . er . . . insulting language to my lord's glorious son, the magnificent warrior Cutrath Horoldson, and now fears for his life . . . my lord."

The monster chuckled and scratched a hairy ear with a curved talon. "I should hope so. That's all?"

"May it please my lord."

"Seer?"

The white-shrouded Witness glided closer without interrupting her spinning. "Lord?"

"What really happened?"

"My lord!" Benard wailed. *Not here!*

"Silence!" snarled the satrap.

"The artist challenged your son to a fight over a woman and knocked him out cold, lord."

Seers did not whisper. All the court heard.

It held its collective breath.

Horold snuffled. He opened and closed a fist a few times; the long black claws seemed to extrude farther. "My son?" he croaked. "This *trash* did? *When?*"

"Just before dawn."

"Who saw this?"

"The woman, and two warriors of Cutrath's flank."

Benard waited to die. The satrap's own questions had exposed both himself and the heir he had so recently honored to utter ridicule. A Werist's normal reaction to such insult would be lightning homicide, and Horold was visibly trembling with the effort needed to maintain control. But such public violence would make matters even worse, showing how deeply he had wounded himself. His piggy eyes scanned the appalled court, seeking any hint of a smirk or a snigger. He released a long breath . . .

"Well, that is most interesting! Where is my son now?"

"Up in the gallery near the west stair, my lord." The seer stopped her spinning long enough to wind the thread up on the spindle.

"Herald, call for Cutrath Horoldson."

Benard wondered why his jangling emotions had not knocked the seer flat on her back by now. Was Horold going to let Cutrath perform the execution? With his teeth . . .

"Artist!"

"My lord?"

"Weru is patron god of Kosord. You will make the Terrible One twice as tall as any of the others. More than twice."

But my contract with the priests . . . "My lord is kind. Alas, the marble . . ."

"What of the marble?" The satrap's roar echoed. The congregation shimmered back a pace, but Benard could do nothing but sweat faster.

"The blocks are already cut or on order, my lord. And the difficulties of transporting so large a block, and of finding a large enough slab which is not marked by unsightly veins of mineralization—"

"Scribe, record that the hostage Benard is to be supplied with transportation to our marble quarry and all the help he needs to cut the block he selects and transport it back to Kosord, all at our expense. Advise the guard that his parole is extended to permit this. Give him coppers to . . ." The black lips curled again. "No, not our little Bena! I'll send someone more responsible along to take care of the expenses."

"My lord is kind!" This was better than anything Benard could have dreamed of! A journey to the quarry could probably be spun out indefinitely. Cutrath would have to wait.

"Your escort can also make sure you find your way home safely. Herald, return that sketch to him when he leaves." Evil porcine eyes studied Benard for a moment. "Take it to our wife. Let her have it as a keepsake. Ah, my misbegotten excuse for a warrior son approaches."

Not having been summoned as "Warrior Horoldson," Cutrath was creeping forward like a civilian.

"You may rise," his father said.

"My lord is kind." Cutrath sat back on his heels and stared agonizing death at Benard.

"Always," the satrap growled. "You pride yourself on your manly physique, do you not?"

"My lord is—"

"Answer!"

Cutrath choked, as if he were about to vomit from sheer rage. "I believe I am not unworthy of my noble ancestry, my lord."

"Girls tell you how handsome and strong you are?"

"Some do, my lord."

"How many, exactly?"

"Um . . . Two?" Cutrath whispered, eyeing the seer uneasily.

"Have any ever called you a useless runt?" Horold roared.

His son shuddered and seemed to shrink. "None, my lord."

"They should be more perceptive. Our artist hostage here needs a model for his portrayal of holy Weru. You will pose for Benard. As often and as long as he requires. *Nude!* Scribe, record this edict. Record, also, that the artist remains under my mercy. This forbiddance applies to all members of our host. There will be no inexplicable accidents, Cutrath! No beatings in dark alleys."

"My lord is kind." He was white to the lips.

"You think so? You have disgraced all the Heroes of Kosord. Report to Huntleader Kwirarlson for punishment and beg him not to demean you further with any show of clemency. Scribe, we are indebted to the hostage Benard Celebre for exposing the worthlessness of our son." Horold tugged off one of his gold armbands. "Record also that we give him this ring as a token of our favor. Next case."

The entire court exploded in roars of approval as the smarmy courtiers cheered the satrap's leniency and wonderful generosity. They quite drowned out Benard's astonished thanks. He bowed and backed away from the throne, wondering what in the world he was supposed to do with a slab of gold.

ſeuen

FRENA WIGSON

knew there was something wrong the moment she swept into the mansion. Servants bowed to her or knelt, depending on rank; they smiled, or looked shocked if they saw the cut on her shoulder. But there was something wrong. Master Trinvar, the steward, was hastily summoned to proclaim a formal welcome.

She thanked him. "Inform the master that I have returned. Tell Inga I want a hot bath right away. Has Plumna had her baby yet? Have my jewel cases brought from the vaults. I trust my rooms have been cleaned and aired? Swordsman Uls has broken his arm. Verk will bring him to the Chatter Place Sinurists for healing tomorrow, so pray dispatch a generous gift to them. I shall want music this evening. Verk still has my chariot, but inform the stable master that the left wheel is slightly off-true. Are the extensions to the servant quarters finished yet?"

Her queries answered, she hurried up to her rooms. Horth had broken with the Skjaran tradition of building in wood. The Wigson mansion was of stone, faced with tile, marble, and mosaic, shimmering inside and out. He never stopped enlarging, decorating, and furnishing with art. New things of beauty were displayed in prominent places, but after a few thirties they would be ousted by even newer prizes and moved to less public sites. When they were in danger of sinking to the servants' quarters, he would resell them. He boasted that he never lost on such trading, although it was the merest hobby.

Several life-size carvings in ebony had been added to the main staircase since Frena left, and she made a note to admire them in detail when she had a moment. She was not surprised to discover that the priceless Ashurbian funeral urns they had replaced now adorned her current rooms. No, the surprise was that her wardrobe had not been moved to somewhere even larger and grander while she was gone. The urns were an improvement on some now-absent malachite fish.

Her mother had always insisted on a bedroom overlooking gardens, but Frena preferred the waterfront. She loved the bustle and excitement, ships coming and going, brawny sailors and longshoremen toiling away. Ocean was bizarrely different from land. It seemed just as flat, and yet it ended in a sharp horizon not half a menzil offshore. Ships went *over* that edge, so that their hulls disappeared before their sails, or appeared after them. She found this fascinating and incomprehensible. Her longtime secret dream was of a handsome sailor sweeping her away in his ship in a trading voyage all around Ocean, lasting for years, visiting dozens of exotic cities and romantic islands. Father could supply the ship; the problem would be finding a suitably hunky sailor with refined manners.

Soon Inga led in a parade of damsels with jars on their heads, and in no time Frena was floating dreamily in her porphyry bathtub. Plumna sponged away her coat of road dust while Lilin busily laid out clothes, scents, and other necessities. Inga frowned at the cut on her shoulder and suggested summoning a Sinurist.

"It's nothing. A rock flew up and hit me. Now tell me all the news."

Good ladies' maids never gossiped, of course, so they had to make a mild pretense of resistance before serving up all the meaty dishes they had been saving. They began by repeating what Verk had already told her—Horth had been abducted before dawn the previous day by the satrap's Werists, and returned later in an unusually agitated condition. He had even called for wine, although he normally drank only ibex milk, and had gulped it while dictating the summons to his daughter. Verk and Uls had left before noon.

"There's talk of a big party, mistress!" Ni confided. "Stuff being brought in from the country."

Since her mother died, Frena had been Horth's hostess. She had organized some of the biggest parties Skjar had ever seen. She could not imagine *why* he should want to entertain when everyone with any wits had fled the city, but that would certainly explain why he had sent for her.

Later Lilin, who was married to one of the tallymen, let slip that Horth had been closing negotiations and calling in loans, as he did when he needed large amounts of bullion on hand. No feast could require gold on that scale.

By the time Frena swept down the stairs, past the ebony sculptures, she had learned everything the household staff knew, which was normally fifty-nine-sixtieths of what mattered. Ominously, she had only just missed meeting High Priestess Bjaria, who had come calling on her father with a sneer of lower priestesses in train. They had all been treated like royalty and laden with gifts when they left. What the two principals had discussed had not been audible to anyone else, but the servants clearly thought they could hear wedding trumpets in the near future. So could Frena. She was girded for war.

◆

Horth's normal workplace was opulent and designed to impress. His gilded chair was inset with ivory, jade, and mother-of-pearl, and also raised so he could look down on visitors and petitioners—servants, scribes, guild masters, ship captains, rival traders. In the hall's vastness he could negotiate without being overheard, yet a gesture would bring scribes and tallymen running from the far end. For more honored guests he descended from his glory and sat with them at equal level, on stools near the windows. The truly revered—the satrap or his wife, consular agents of other cities, the four or five heads of mercantile houses he chose to regard as his equals—were usually received outdoors, in the greater privacy of the water garden.

It was to this shaded glade that Frena was directed, being given the customary warning not to brush against foliage on the way in. A narrow curving path brought her to the little pentagonal court concealed within the fleshy jungle. Trilling fountains muffled whatever was said there, and any spy approaching to eavesdrop would learn nothing except the deadly properties of Navarian choke cherries.

Horth was slumped despondently on a chair, gazing at the paving, half turned from her. She wondered if she had been taking her summons too personally. His troubles might have nothing to do with her at all, other than a need for support. They had no family except each other.

"Father?"

He looked up sharply. "Frena, my love!" He rose to embrace her. She knew by his awkwardness that his back was hurting him again, and responded carefully. He was wearing thick-soled shoes, which normally meant company was coming, but there were only two chairs present.

Horth Wigson was singularly unimpressive at first glance and on closer inspection even more so—short of stature, spare and narrow, hollow-chested. His head was hairless, too large, and egglike, with prominent ears and a face tapering downward to a wispy beard. He lived on barley cakes and ibex milk, so the only excessive flesh on him anywhere was under his eyes, two crescents like pale segments of grapefruit. Those wan eyes blinked a lot, peering at the world in a permanent state of sad incomprehension. He was hard to overestimate. Yet even Frena, who must know him better than anyone, rarely knew what he was really thinking.

"Did you have a good journey? Please, please be seated. Have you eaten? We can go indoors if you wish . . . hoped it might be cooler out here. So hot . . . It will be better when the rains come." He was massively overdressed as usual, enveloped in brocade robes of gold and peacock blue.

The best method of defense, in Frena's experience, was not attack—for that could lead to pitched battle against overwhelming odds—but a vigorous flanking movement with enough implied threat to disturb established positions. As she sat down, she sent her skirmishers onto the field.

"Father, I heard a horrible story recently. I was told that rich people steal farmers' lands away from them by foreclosing on loans the poor men had to take out when their crops failed. Is that really true?"

The pale eyes blinked. "You mean is that really stealing? Or do you mean do starving peasants borrow from rich people? Or do rich people foreclose their loans? Or do you mean do I do such things?" He had a soft, disarming voice.

"Do you?"

He spread jeweled hands. "My agents are authorized to make loans to hungry peasants, yes. Usually sacks of grain, repayable when the harvest is in. They do require security, of course. If they didn't, do you think the debts would ever be repaid? Should my servants just give my grain away? Is that what you mean?"

"Well, no . . . But—"

Horth rarely came nearer a smile than a look of tolerant amusement, which is what he displayed now. Frena remembered that he must know her a lot better than she knew him.

"Let me ask you this, my dear. A peasant dies and his six sons divide the land between them. Each of them raises six sons and so on. Eventually the plots must become too small to support their owners, do you see? A young peasant may get by at first, but he will want a wife, and year by year his brood will grow in size and number. Drought, blight, and flood are the peasant's lot, and children his curse. Sooner or later he will fail and need help. Once he falls into debt, the chances that he will ever climb out again are very, very slim. Should he borrow from me at all? Should I help him when he asks?"

"Er . . . I don't know."

"I'm not sure I do either, my dear," he said sadly. "But were I in that peasant's fix, I would exchange my scrap of land for something more rewarding—a mill, say. Or a kiln, or a fishing boat." He sighed. "But then, I am not a peasant."

No, he was a very shrewd negotiator. Frena had been routed. He usually let her spin out the maneuvering longer than this.

When she did not speak, he placed his hands together in a familiar gesture, fingertip to fingertip. "As I'm sure you have already heard from the servants, my dear, I was called to the palace yesterday. A matter of business, mostly, but your name was mentioned."

"By whom? The satrap or that awful wife of his?" *Saltaja, without a doubt!*

Her father winced. "I know we cannot be overheard here, but remember that the satrap has Maynists to advise him. They can probably see us and hear us even here. A careless word could cause a lot of trouble, Frena."

Not the satrap! Frena could not imagine dumb old Eide bothering to spy on anyone, but she wouldn't put it past the Queen of Shadows.

"Of course, Father. Just in case a seer's watching, I'll tell you that I quite like the satrap. Even if he does have horns, he's a lot less grotesque than some of the other monster Werists I see wandering around the city." She laughed at his frown. "Don't worry! I'm old enough to guard my tongue where it matters."

"I hope so. It was your age that was mentioned. You're sixteen now."

"Yes, I know."

He tapped fingertips together. "Satrap Eide and his lady wife are . . . The problem is the Pantheon. It's falling apart, in great need of repair. The satrap wants to rebuild it. But the cost will be—"

"He wants *you* to rebuild it, you mean? Well, that's hardly fair. You're not a polytheist. You never go near the Pantheon."

"He wants me to make a contribution," her father said reprovingly, "which I said I would do gladly. And if my god does not object, then I fail to see what business it is of yours."

Startled by the rebuke, Frena nodded. "I'm sorry, Father."

"Your name came up because High Priestess Bjaria is wondering when you—"

"When I was going to have my dedication, I suppose? What business is that of hers?"

"Don't be tiresome, Frena. Of course it's her business. Most girls make their vows at fourteen or younger. It is very irregular to wait past fifteen."

"Only for the poor. The rich often wait longer." The dedication ceremony was official recognition that a girl had become a woman, so it was also the signal that her parents were open to offers. Unless they were wealthy enough to be choosy, a wedding would usually follow within a season. Nubile maidens were always in demand to replace wives who died in childbirth. "You promised me faithfully—"

"I *know* what I promised you, child!"

She jumped. He never raised his voice to her!

"I spend my life making and keeping promises, and I know exactly what I promised you—that I will accept no marriage offer you do not approve. Gods know I do not need a bride price. Nothing in the world could reward me for losing you, my dear, and I have missed you terribly while you have been away. But I never promised you could put off puberty until you reached menopause. You're my hostess, you wear a seal, you give orders to servants— it's unseemly that you have never made your vows. Scandalous, almost. It's being remarked on."

Stern did not suit him.

"By *whom?* Since when have you ever cared for gossip? You never go near the Pantheon. Mother never went near the horrible—"

"And see what happened!"

"What do you mean?" Frena cried, leaping to her feet.

Horth looked very small, sometimes. "The reason I do not offer sacrifice in the Pantheon is that I am a henotheist, as you well know. As everyone knows. Your mother did not have that excuse. Florengians worship much the same gods, but she found our rites strange. She was undoubtedly lax in her religious observances, and I blame myself bitterly for not foreseeing the danger. Most people did not understand her reasons. They jumped to fearfully wrong conclusions."

Frena shuddered. "I am sorry, Father." She began pacing, to the nearest fountain and back. They never discussed this, normally.

"It is too late for recrimination, but I should have seen that you are running the same risk. You must make your vows right away. High Priestess Bjaria has agreed to officiate in person, and I want you to organize a very lavish celebration. Spare no expense! Let the whole city know that you have done homage to the Bright Ones."

He had begun by mentioning his visit to the palace. Then he had implied that the dedication ceremony had been suggested by High-Mucky Bjaria, although she had come calling on him this morning, after he had sent for Frena. Had she also been present at the palace yesterday, or was he molding the truth to a more convenient shape?

"Who is hiding a needy bridegroom behind this, Father? Am I to be fighting off some snotty, spotty priestess's grandson, or a brutal, brainless relative of Satrap Eide's?"

"Frena!"

"Sorry," she muttered, although she wasn't. Bridegrooms and marriage and babies could wait. She wanted to travel and see more of Vigaelia. She had plans to set up an art factory, to encourage artists and craftsmen. Horth's wealth ought to defend her from unwanted suitors, but it would not keep the satrap away. "When do you want to do this?"

"The high priestess and I agreed on six days from now."

"*What?* You're crazy! Half a year!"

Horth rose. In his present footwear he was taller than she. "I am tolerant, Frena, but I am entitled to more respect than that."

"Sorry, Father. I spoke wrongly."

"Apology accepted." He smiled tolerantly. "You had better go and start planning."

Truly! Reports on Kyrn could wait, but Uls . . . She wished she had mentioned him sooner. "Uls broke his arm, Father. He was in a lot of pain, so we left him at By-the-Canyon and Verk drove me in. He will bring him to the Healers tomorrow. I told Master Trinvar to send a gift."

As well try to smuggle a mouflon lamb through a wolf pack as slide a half-truth past a Ucrist. Horth's eyes narrowed. "And how did Uls break his arm?"

Frena drew a deep breath. "Your hamlet of Bitterfeld—they were having some sort of ceremony and we drove too close. They didn't like us snooping, or something. Anyway, they threw things—"

"What sort of ceremony?"

Frena recoiled from his sudden shout, and then shouted right back. *"They were going to bury a man alive!"*

"No!" Her father collapsed on his chair, his face white. "And they thought you were coming to rescue him? Oh, Frena! How could you be so— What was Verk thinking— *What did you do to Verk?*"

"Do to him? Nothing at all. Whatever do you mean, *do* to him? I had no idea what was going on. I just wanted to see. Verk behaved perfectly, and we drove away as fast as we could." She stared at Horth. His eyes were oozing horror. "Father, what's wrong? Are you faint?"

He licked his lips. "You must take your vows, do you hear? Must! We'll make it three days from now, not six. Oh, why did I not see that this might happen? Tell Trinvar. I'll send word to the Pantheon."

Stupefied, she could only repeat "Three days?" like an idiot. "Oh, that's absolutely—"

"Three days!" Horth said, glaring, and she knew him well enough to know that he would not be moved.

eight

BENARD CELEBRE

knew that Cutrath would gain his revenge eventually, and now there was no doubt that it would be fatal, but the kitten had been declawed for the time being. Cheerfully reflecting that everyone must die eventually, Benard strode off through the warren of the palace. He was rich! Never in his life had he owned a speck of gold, or even expected to. The strip that had barely closed around the satrap's gross arm fitted nicely on Benard's thigh, hidden by Thranth's loincloth.

His way led him past walls of gleaming polychrome bricks, across courts and halls, and also up ramps and stairs, heading toward the temple of Veslih and the women's quarters beyond. All the way he was exchanging smiles with familiar faces, pausing frequently to discuss Nils's engagement and the evils of hangovers. He even ran into Nils's mother, who said he looked malnourished and promised him a man-size meal if he came to see her that evening. He promised he would—she was a widow and often lonely.

The lady Ingeld, while being hereditary dynast of Kosord, light of Veslih on Kosord, wife of the satrap, and mother of Cutrath, had also served as foster mother to a long series of young Florengian hostages. This part of the palace had been Benard's home from his arrival in Kosord until he turned thirteen. Although Kosord had never confined royal ladies behind bars or set eunuchs to guard them as some cities did, adult male visitors needed good reason to enter, and must obey the rules. The sketch under his arm provided a perfect excuse. What her reaction to it would be, the gods alone knew—perhaps a near-fatal attack of nostalgia, for she claimed to have loved the monster once. Even dogs might be loved.

As he neared the temple, he heard the ominous echoing beat of kettle-drums, the signal that she was conducting a formal pyromancy. This was not a holy day. The logical assumption must be that Ingeld put more stock in whatever omens Sansya had glimpsed in the court than Sansya had.

Moments later Benard emerged at the base of the pyramid. The sacred fire under the bronze tholos on the apex was currently hidden by the crowd of priestesses and acolytes standing among the pillars; a small congregation of worshipers had gathered around and below them, like snow on a mountain. This place had a better claim to being the beating heart of city than did the Pantheon or the satrap's court. Women's ceremonies were held here—marriages, child namings, purifications—and here Ingeld took augury.

He had last visited the temple during the baleful time following the Festival of Demern. Some years the fasting, abstinence, and lamentation would last several days, sometimes only one, or even none at all, depending on the weather. When Ingeld saw the holy star, Nartiash, at dawn, she relit the sacred fire to proclaim the first day of a new year and read the omens in the flames.

Benard had been present in the throng, sleepless and hoarse from a night of wailing, and had heard her prophecies, which had been guarded without being alarming. Horold had ordered extra sacrifices but had allowed the usual celebrations to proceed. Had some error roused the gods' ire since then, or had Sansya been imagining things today? Of course, whatever she had seen might apply only to today's audience, whereas Ingeld had been viewing the whole town's prospects for the year. From Horold's point of view the morning's proceedings had certainly not turned out well. Cutrath's opinion could only be imagined, and not with a straight face.

There, standing higher than the palace roofs and the triangular red sails of the riverboats, Benard could mark the Wrogg winding off across the plain until even that mightiest of rivers vanished into the blur they called the wall of the world. In the spring Kosord was an island, for even at low water the Wrogg flowed higher than the level of the plain, so a normal flood would overtop the levees. In years when it did not, famine usually followed. This year's flood had been fair, not spectacular, but the canals crisscrossing the plain were still full and green crops were just appearing in the fields, so the harvest seemed secured.

Kosord itself was almost invisible from above. The little courtyards of the houses were speckles of greenery, but the reed-thatched roofs were much the same mud color as the streets or walls—or the river and plain beyond, for that matter. The people going about their business were so well hidden under branches or overhanging eaves that the Bright Ones Themselves, peering down from Their blue heavens, might well assume that only the bustling riverbank was inhabited, for it served as dock, market, and main street.

The sun glare's was molten bronze on tender, bloodshot eyes. Shading them with his hand, Benard peered around and marveled anew that the world was so overwhelmingly huge. To east and north the sky was deep indigo; southwestward it paled to buttermilk. The great bulge of Ocean lay in that direction, but so far off that it was lost in the sky's blue.

As he hesitated, debating whether to wait for Ingeld or head home and catch up on lost sleep, a clawed finger poked his ribs. He looked down and laughed.

"Twelve blessings, old mother." He gave her a careful hug.

Molith was Ingeld's most trusted servant, and incredibly ancient. Her gnarled face split in a smile, toothless and welcoming, but not wide enough to imply that all was well.

"We heard that you had died of a wasting sickness."

"It has not been that long!"

"Too long." The smile had gone. "The lady said to go by the roseberry trees and wait for her."

That was a surprise. "Thanks, old mother."

She caught his wrist in a frail grip. Filmed eyes peered up anxiously at him. "Oh, be careful, lad!"

"Of course. I'm always careful." He wandered away, trying to be inconspicuous without actually slinking.

Ingeld must have given those instructions before she began the pyromancy, which was before anyone could have told her of the events at the audience. So how had she known he was coming?

Stupid question.

Scary answer.

✦

Having been hunted through the palace so often by Cutrath and his pack of stone-throwing curs in bygone years, Benard Celebre knew it as well as any mortal could. He made his way to a rooftop littered with servants' sleeping mats. From there it was an easy slither over a wall and a short drop into a wooded park where men were not supposed to venture, although it was known to the young bloods of the palace as the Baby-Making Place. There he was supposedly visible to rooftop guards, but they were merely armed men, not Werists, and would be paying scant attention in the heat of the day.

A massive roseberry tree grew in one corner. Clutching his sketch in one hand, he jumped, caught a branch with the other, and pulled himself up into the foliage. The boughs interlocked with those of an adjacent roseberry, providing safe passage over a wall whose coping bristled with bronze spikes. He dropped nimbly to the grass in an even more private courtyard and made his way to an unobtrusive but extremely solid gate in the corner.

It was bolted, of course, but he knew that bolt very well. Laying a hand on the timber, he closed his eyes and sent a silent prayer to holy Anziel, calling up visions of the private garden beyond. When he was satisfied that there was nobody there, he reminded Her of the beauty he sought and asked Her to open the way for him. That was a little harder, but soon he sensed the bronze slide aside; he remembered to open and close the gate gently, knowing how its pivots squeaked. A stroll across a flower-decked lawn, between two shaded ponds where gold and silver fish floated in reflective silence, brought him to the lady's room.

Ingeld was both a state and religious personage and her private life was rarely private, so her chamber was very large, as befitted a hall of state, and pentagonal because it was sacred. Attendants bathed her in that huge bath of black granite, she stood on that dais to give audience, and even the children she had conceived and borne on the oversized sleeping platform had been matters of state. Five slim columns around the pentagonal hearth merged at head height to form a chimney reaching to the high corbeled roof. Although the day was warm, coals in a small brazier glowed to honor holy Veslih.

For sheer beauty as well as the memories it held for him, this was Benard's favorite room on all Dodec. Although the style was utterly different, something of its taste and beauty stirred dim memories of his father's palace in Celebre. A balmwood stool, a table holding alabaster pots of unguents, inlaid chests—the room held many lovely things and flattered them with opulent use of space. Cool in summer, with one side open to the garden's dappled flowers and silky pools; snug in winter behind massive doors of bronze-clad timber, when bright rugs deadened the chill of floor tiles and a vast log fire roared and crackled on the hearth, defying the storms . . . this was a fittingly perfect place for Ingeld. Soft mats of ibex hair adorned the sleeping platform. A faint familiar scent of her haunted the room. He saw that the bath was still beaded with water, as was the tiled gutter that drained it; she would have bathed before going to consult her goddess.

Brilliant polychrome glazes adorned the bricks of the walls, two of which bore bright friezes above shoulder height. The one depicting the Twelve, the Bright Ones, had been Benard's masterpiece, which had won him acceptance into both the artists' guild and the mystery of the Hands of Anziel; later it had gained him the Pantheon commission.

He looked instead at the other, Ingeld's personal wall of memory, executed by Master Odok. The central figures depicted what she claimed were good likenesses of her long-dead parents, who had died together on the day Stralg seized the city. Nars Narson, the last state consort, stood there eternally in his black robes, silver-maned and exactly as bony-jawed and stubborn as his legend required. The lady Tiu wore the robes of a pyromancer. Ingeld said her mother's hair had been the same rich bronze as her own, but glazing technique had limited Odok to using a gold luster, a three-firing technique formula normally used only by potters.

Off to the side stood the twins, Finar and Fitel, a little older than Cutrath was now, smiling proudly as newly initiated Heroes in brass collars.

They had been six years older than Cutrath, and sixty-sixty times as worthy to be immortalized, although one picture would have served for both. Odok's glazes had barely cooled from the kiln before the twins had gone off to the war and died without ever reaching it.

Now another portrait had been inserted in Ingeld's wall of memories. There really was no accounting for a mother's delusions. Although Cutrath smirking in his new brass collar should not be regarded as an improvement to any room, even a latrine, Benard grudgingly conceded that the old master had excelled himself, for this was obviously more of Odok's work. The background tones matched the original perfectly; every fold of the pall crossed every tile boundary in perfect alignment. And when he stepped back to admire the whole, Benard reluctantly conceded that the young brute really did have an impressive body. Pad out the muscles to full adult mass, correct the brawler's battered features, catch that ghastly arrogance half as well as Odok had done . . . and Cutrath would do very well as a model for unholy Weru.

Disgusted, Benard leaned his sketch board against the wall below Cutrath's feet to show how much more handsome Horold had been, then wandered across to the sleeping platform. He kicked off Thranth's sandals and lay down. Ingeld's scent enveloped him in a mist of nostalgia, but he detected none of Horold's sour animal reek. That one deserved a stall with dry straw, nothing more. Benard assumed she was not required to function as the monster's wife these days, although that was not something one could ask. It was not something a man could even think about.

He was facing his own work, the frieze of the Twelve Bright Ones. He found it unsatisfying. Nowadays he always used models. Back then he had been content to rely on invention, and now the results seemed bland and unconvincing. Holy Veslih stood out from all the rest because She bore a strong resemblance to Ingeld herself—gorgeous, slender, vibrant, like a living flame. He had improved on Odok by combining copper luster with gold to achieve a closer match to robes and hair, and so far the results seemed to be stable. Holy Weru had a look of Bloodlord Stralg as he had been on that frightful morning outside Celebre, fifteen years ago. A few other faces were vaguely recognizable.

His gaze settled on holy Eriander. The temple displayed the god-goddess as an obscene combination of the sexes, a repulsive collage of organs. Benard had depicted a hermaphrodite youth, draped, taller than the women and shorter than the men. No one had objected to this innovation, even High Priest Nrakfin, and the statue in the Pantheon would be done the same way. The face . . . Knowing no hermaphrodites, Benard must have invented those ambiguous features, and yet they were annoyingly familiar. He was still trying to remember who might have inspired them when his eyelids became too heavy to stay open any longer.

nine

INGELD NARSDOR

preferred to practice pyromancy at night, with sparks and voices twining upward to the stars above the hypnotic thunder of drums. Then the Daughters became swirling pillars of flame in their dance around the hearth, while glowing coals flickered myriad images. The ritual lacked the same drama in daylight, yet today's images had been unusually clear. Any fool could see pictures in a fire; the god-given skill of the pyromancer was to know which pictures mattered, to tease out divine resolve from the infinity of the possible.

The seers claimed that all prophecy was vain because the gods could not be bound. There was some truth in that, and at times Ingeld thought she could watch sixty-sixty futures dancing, as if the Bright Ones debated their plans in a vast divine committee. But the Maynists were not entirely correct, for Veslihans never claimed to see beyond their own realms. The peasant wife muttering prayers to her cooking fire differed only in degree from Ingeld, initiate of the highest level and first among the Daughters, seeking guidance on the future of Kosord in the sacred flames at the summit of the temple. One ruled a hovel and the other a palace, but both of those were households sacred to holy Veslih. If the goddess chose to make Her intentions known, the other gods would not interfere.

Last night, as was her custom, Ingeld had led the acolytes in prayer in the adytum. Inexplicably, she had seen Benard Celebre in the dark between the embers, indicating danger. That he was in peril was no surprise and she was overdue to warn him of the latest troubles, but the omens seemed to imply that the danger was to the city, which made no sense. She had been sufficiently concerned to send a herald around to his shack. He had not been home and she needed no divine guidance to guess that he was sleeping elsewhere, for he still had an astonishing ability to inspire women to mother him. At dawn she had visited the adytum again; again she had seen him, and this time heading for the palace. Images in a brazier could not compare with those in the sacred hearth itself, so she had decided on a full pyromancy, sending Sansya to the assize in her stead and warning Molith to admit Benard when he arrived.

That he was bound for Horold's audience had never occurred to her, but in the very first true images, she spied him already in the balcony of the court. The portents for Kosord were clearer than any she had seen in years— a baby shining, a letter shadowed, a boat that was sometimes good, some-times bad. Those would be the sparks to ignite the blaze, but beyond them she spied only tumult and confusion and shadow. Time and again as images formed, the coals collapsed, obscuring them as if the gods had determined to set great events in motion without agreeing upon their outcome. But why everywhere Benard? Wherever she'd looked, there was Benard in the back-ground. Baby, letter, boat, death, death, death . . . and always Benard. Why was he suddenly so important?

✦

Pyromancy was an ordeal that left her simultaneously exalted and ex-hausted. When it was over, two acolytes supported her while she addressed the anxious crowd that had gathered.

"I foresee no great evil," she told them. "Unsettled times approach, but the gods are merciful. Be mindful of them and the troubles will pass." They knelt to her as she descended the steps; she entered thankfully through the bronze doors, out of painful sunlight into the women's quarters, shadowed and cool.

Fortunately, she had other—mortal—sources to inform her what had been happening in Horold's audience, and old Molith nodded when queried with an eyebrow. So Ingeld was forewarned not to go charging into her bed-chamber with a retinue.

Pleading a need to rest, she entered the room alone and even managed to close the door without slamming it in fury. Just as she had feared, Bena was stretched out on her sleeping platform, dead to the world. No doubt he had spent most of the night rollicking with some slut. *Oh, that young idiot!* Could even Benard Celebre be so blind to danger? Horold would see this as delib-erate provocation, and his seers would tell him of it.

She swept across the room like a pillar of fire, fully intending to haul him off the platform by his ear. But the closer she came, the more her resolution faltered, until she came to a stop, staring down at him in aching wonder. Oh, Bena, Bena! He was no beauty by day, being dark and hairy even by Florengian standards, with quarryman chest and shoulders that belied his noble birth. His face was as solid as battlements, all jaw and forehead and cheekbones. And yet, boy and man, he had always been beautiful in sleep, with those incredible lashes spread on his cheeks; awake, he could melt any woman with one glance of an artist's eyes—gentle, limpid, all-seeing.

She turned to look at the twins' smiling faces in the tiles. Had they lived, they would be this age now—mature but still young, in the prime of their strength and yet untamed by the withering of dreams. And back to Benard . . . Strong but never aggressive, easygoing in most things and infinitely stubborn in the rest, combining wrestlers' brawn with the delicate touch of butterflies.

Especially she remembered Benard in that terrible summer six years ago, when Finar and Fitel had set off to join their uncle in Florengia. Horold had been away suppressing some minor revolt or other, but word of the avalanche had gone first to him. Ingeld had learned of it from his letter ordering Cutrath into Werist training, breaking the promise he had given her when she agreed to bear him another son. One blow had deprived her of all her children and all pretense of a marriage.

In her agony and rage, she had sought comfort from a boy half her age, a boy even younger than the twins she mourned. Benard had given it unstintingly, knowing his compassion might cost him his life. At first she had asked only the solace of holy Nula, but as he held her in his arms through a long night of tears, holy Eriander had come to offer support also. If either mortal had invoked that god, it had been she, not Benard, although even then he had been no innocent. He could easily have refused her, telling her to remember her age, and his, to reflect that she was the light of Veslih on Kosord, who performed countless marriages every year and lectured every bride on the importance of fidelity.

For a season they had been lovers. With Benard she had found the happiness her marriages had lacked. Many in her household must have guessed, but there had been no open scandal and holy Veslih had not burned Kosord to the ground in retribution.

Horold had found out, of course. All he needed do was ask his resident seer what his wife had been up to—those *busybodies*. The brutish-looking man who had left in spring to go campaigning had returned in fall as a thing that walked on its hind legs. Their ensuing battle had been as memorable as any he could ever have fought, with him calling her a whore and her demanding to know what sort of shoats he expected her to farrow. In the end they had stopped fighting without ever making peace. He had known that any harm to her would cause the people to rise in a rebellion that he could suppress only by crippling the city for years to come.

Fortunately Benard had been the one man in the satrapy beyond his reach, a state hostage whose death would rouse the fury of his brother Stralg or, worse, their sister. Horold was terrified of Saltaja. So the unspoken terms had been that there would be no open break, that Benard would not die, and that Ingeld would sleep alone in future. Horold had not set paw in her bedroom since. Ironically, she knew that she was married to the best of the four sons of Hrag, that none of the others would have been so forgiving.

It had been a very long time since a man lay where Bena lay now.

"Benard Celebre!" she snapped. "You are a fool!" She whirled away, marching across the room in sudden rage. When she turned, he was upright already, feet on the floor, swaying as he peered at her with sleep-sodden eyes.

"Uh? You told me to come here."

"That was before I knew that Horold was going to send you!" She swirled over to the arches, around by the bathtub, back to the door again, robes dancing.

He sat down heavily and mumbled at his toes, "You are not making a huge quantity of sense, my lady."

"Fool! Can't you see the danger?" she shouted, still pacing wildly. "He insulted Cutrath and forbade him to hurt you. He heaped gold on you so the court cheered in wonder. He even sent you to me. Simpleton! Half-wit! Jarhead! You must go. Now!"

Then she saw how he was looking at her and cursed again. He knew the signs—she was overwrought and flushed from the fire. Pyromancy always left her aroused and vulnerable; her mother had confessed the same. Horold had known, back when he was still human, that a visit right after an augury would not go unrewarded. A long time ago, that! But she was not too old to feel the need, and Benard could read her as easily as he could shape clay. He rose to his feet again and tried to intercept her. "Ingeld—"

"*Don't touch me!* Can't you see it's a trap, fool? You're a dead man, Benard Celebre, a dead fool. Hurry. Leave before it's too late."

"No, I don't see." His vision was always selective.

"I mean he's shown you favor so he won't be the second most obvious suspect when bits of you turn up in the midden. But that's what he intends to do—disassemble you, claw you to bare bones. Benard, Benard! How could you possibly do anything so unspeakably stupid as to *challenge* Cutrath and then *win?* In front of his *friends?*"

"It was win or have all my guts kicked out." He smirked, pleased with himself. Great, lumbering bear!

"Silence! And why were you such a pea-brain as to come to court and brag about it? Why did you let that stupid Witness hag vomit it all out for everyone to hear? Why did she *know* what had happened? Answer me!"

Eyes of oiled ebony gleamed. "Make up your mind. I thought I was supposed to remain silent. Stand still, woman, you're making me giddy. Oh, gods, I want to kiss you!"

She flinched back. "*No!* He'll ask that Witness trollop what you did in here. They're *bitches!* Horold can ask anything about anyone and they'll tell him. She witnessed? There was no hedging or double-talk?"

He frowned. "No. I mean yes. She witnessed."

"How?" Ingeld howled. "Why are you so important that she sees what you do?" The Maynist's interest was inexplicable, but it confirmed the pyromancy. This seemingly insignificant artist was not insignificant at all.

"I expect it was Cutrath she was—"

"No! No! Last sixday he disappeared on a drunken binge. Horold asked where he was and the seers knew only that he was out of range, not in the palace. Last night they must have been seeing *you!*"

"Perhaps she could hear my thoughts this morning."

"Mayn's blessings do not include reading thoughts, only emotions. You must go now, Benard! Oh, look at you! Those fingernails! Are you eating properly? What's that all over your kilt?"

"Charcoal . . . blood? Twelve curses!" He was more upset by that tiny bloodstain than he had been by her prophecies of sudden death. "It's not my kilt. I'll have to buy Thranth another."

"I'll give you some copper . . ." She hurried over to her treasure chest.

He laughed. "I don't need copper. Horold gave me gold."

"Don't be absurd. You can't buy clothes with gold. Here, don't argue." She found a pelf string heavily laden with twists of copper, some large, some small, and looped it over his head. "Bury the gold somewhere safe and don't forget where. Now, please, will you go?"

He reached for her and she evaded him.

"Not yet." He was broad and stark, as stubborn as a team of onagers. "Ingeld, heart of my heart, Horold is not going to storm out of his assize to rush over here and decapitate me. You know him. If murder is his aim, then he'll take a long time to plan it and savor it beforehand. He loves a good hate."

She drew breath to argue, but he was quite right. The dreamer could be perceptive when he bothered.

"He knows what happened six years ago," Benard said. "His tame seers will tell him we've been nothing but friends since. If he does decide to kill me, he will; no doubt about that. If I worried about it, I'd have gone crazy years ago."

"He would have *done* it years ago if you weren't the bloodlord's hostage. But he'll get his chance eventually. Listen. Werists come here with dispatches from Stralg. Usually I don't meet them, but Horold wasn't around and I had a chance to be hostess and hear their gossip. The war's going badly, Benard. One man let slip that Stralg lost more ground in the winter. He's being driven back toward Celebre."

The sculptor shrugged his big shoulders.

She resisted an urge to try shaking him, which would not have worked. "Listen to me! You know the slaves and hostages and gold stopped coming years ago. Now it's just more and more Werists going out, about twenty sixty a year. And still he's losing!" She feared that Cutrath would be next—Horold would not commit himself on what Stralg had written, but the bloodlord had drawn all the other young males of his family into the abattoir, so why should the last one be favored?

"You know I care nothing for the war."

"You'd better start caring. Your father's been true to his word all these years, ruling the city as Stralg's puppet, but if the Florengian partisans are at his gates, then everything may change."

Benard's polite indifference did not change, so she switched to more drastic means. "Remember Tomoso?"

"Of course. Great kid." His smile curdled into suspicion. "Why?"

"His father was a Stralg puppet, like yours, ruler of Miona. Cavotti's rebels surrounded the town while Stralg was there and burned it down on his head. He lost . . ." she shrugged ". . . many, many men. Stralg's orders to Horold were to roast Tomoso over a very slow fire."

Benard winced. "No! *No!* Even Horold . . . He didn't!"

"No," Ingeld agreed. "He didn't. He cropped Tomo's ears and sold him to slavers."

Benard swung around to stare out at the garden. He could hide his face, but the muscles in his back were taut as ships' cables. She longed to put her arms around him. Why must the gods be so cruel to someone so gentle?

"Why?" he said hoarsely. "What harm had he done? What good did that do?"

"Just spite. You'll never understand how a Werist thinks, Benard, so don't try. Saltaja's worse. Horold was being as merciful as he dared. It's the truth." Horold was the best of the whole horrible Hrag brood.

Benard said, "He won't be merciful with me. If it happens, it happens. There's nothing I can do about it."

"I hear he's sending you to Whiterim quarry."

"Me and a Werist or two to make sure I don't run. Thanks for the news. I had better go now."

"There's more."

He glanced around, trying to look exasperated instead of showing whatever he was really feeling. Just old bitterness, probably. He never seemed to fear the future, but he detested any mention of his past. "More murdered hostages?"

"I think so, but I'm not sure. None in Kosord. No, I mean that I asked the couriers about Celebre. They said your father was in poor health."

"Ingeld!" He sounded exasperated. "I care nothing for the war and less for my parents. They gave me away, remember? The only person I care about in all Dodec is you. You I love more than life itself. You were a mother for me; mother and lover and the only woman I want, but I can't have you. I should go." He headed for the garden.

"The others?" she said.

He stopped in the arch, without turning, a dark shape against the light. "What about them?"

She could not recall him ever showing even this much interest before, so deep was his hurt. "I've heard nothing recently, I admit. The young one, who stayed in Tryfors with Therek?"

"Orlando."

"He was still alive a year or so ago, when Therek came by here. He said something like 'The duckling that follows the dog thinks it's a puppy.'"

"Doesn't sound promising. Dantio's dead?"

"So Saltaja told me. She wouldn't bother to lie. If she'd cut his throat herself, she'd admit it."

"And Fabia? She's a smelly little bundle that cries all the time."

"I expect she's past that by now. She went to Jat-Nogul, to Karvak. Saltaja told me that she disappeared in the sack, when the rebels killed Karvak. She was assumed to be dead. I think you're the last, Benard, you and possibly Orlando." She longed to hold him.

"I wouldn't know him if I saw him and I'm sure he's forgotten me." He began to move, paused. "My mother?"

"She is acting as regent for your father, they said. Oh, Benard, listen to me! They will send one of you back to succeed your father, and it looks like it must be you or Orlando. The moment Horold hears you aren't needed as a hostage anymore, you're dead. Somehow we must get you out of Kosord. I know it will be difficult—"

He swung around and came to her in two long steps. Black eyes blazed down at her with a fury she had never seen in them before. She cringed back, amazed to realize that even Benard might be dangerous.

"No it won't; it'll be impossible. Horold's warbeasts will run me down and kill me. But I'll risk it on one condition."

She shook her head: *No!*

"Yes!" he said. "You come with me. Just us two. You're married to nothing human, your son is grown up. We can slip away together. If I have to work as a peasant or chop wood all my days, I won't care."

She smiled despite herself. Being Benard, he might even believe what he said. "That would be nice, wouldn't it? Except for Horold's seers telling him where we are and the fact that I am a Daughter, bound to Kosord's hearth. Good idea! And if by some miracle it were possible, strangers would congratulate me on my handsome son and ask why he wasn't married."

"Wouldn't bother me."

"Yes it would. Go and visit the Nymphs, and then you'll see things more clearly for a day or so."

Strangely, he flushed. "No I won't."

She shook her head. "It's a wonderful dream, but it's futile and dangerous even to discuss."

"I'll bring the chariot to the steps at dawn."

"I'll send a girl of about your age. Be careful, Benard!"

He shook his head and was gone.

Ingeld went after him to bolt the gate. On the way back, she stopped to watch the fish, which often helped her find calm.

She needed to scream.

That stupid *ox* of a boy! How could anyone so observant be so blind? He paved streets with broken hearts and did not realize. His work made every other artist in the city weep tears of envy, but he gave it away without a thought. He walked through walls while dreaming of clouds. He flatly refused to admit the frightful danger hanging over him. Why, suddenly, was he so important to Kosord? A baby, a ship, a letter, and Benard. Why Benard?

Her husband and her son were undoubtedly planning to kill the man she loved. Cutrath had always known that she loved Benard more than him. Poor Cutrath! He had never been able to match the twins in his father's eyes or the hostage in his mother's.

The golden fish did nothing to help, and when she stepped back over the threshold, she saw a plank leaning against the wall. That was the drawing that had caused all the trouble, the face of the man she had married. *Why* had Horold ordered that sent to her? Her temper flashed out in a curse. The wood exploded in a blaze of sparks and billowing smoke, leaving only drifting flakes of white ash and a black smoke stain on Cutrath's image in the mural above.

ten

THEREK HRAGSON,

brother of the bloodlord and satrap of Tryfors, was the light of Weru on Nardalborg—when he was there, which was not often enough. The rest of the time Huntleader Heth did what was required and did it very well, but Therek still took every excuse he could find to come up to the moors and spend a day or two there, where life was simpler. The swearing in of a new class of cadets was ample reason.

This was supposedly spring, yet a blizzard howled around the walls. Summer on these desolate fells could be missed with a sneeze, and fall was a myth when there were no trees to drop leaves. The snow would soon melt, of course, adding more mud to the tracks, but up in the high country, edgeward, some of it might hang on. That was bad, because this year's crop of Werists was on its way. The first of them had been trickling into Tryfors when he left.

Heth had not long ago sent last year's leftovers on in the first caravan of the year; he would need at least four more runs to move the new crop over the Edge before winter, and anything that slowed down the first three would make the last one dangerously late. Worse, Therek had a strong hunch that his darling Baby Brother Stralg was shortly going to demand a sixth. Call it warrior's intuition; he would bet half his battle honors on it. Every caravan depended on caches of food and fuel stocked by at least three pack trains. Late departures tempted the gods; Heth might lose a train up there, and he could not spare the mammoths, let alone the men. And Stralg was scream-ing for every additional Hero he could get.

The great hall was battened tight against the storm, lit by sputtering, stinking torches. Flames danced, shutters rattled, and Florengian slaves rushed back and forth with jars of beer. The assembly had just finished eat-ing, not yet finished drinking, and was about ready to start fighting. Therek looked out over tables flanked by big men in striped palls, a wild, all-male scene, noisy and fiery, implying danger lurking. Most assemblies of Werists ended in ructions, but that was just man play—unauthorized battleforming was savagely punished and hence rare.

Good to see so many. He kept the Nardalborg Hunt at full strength, around four sixty, but the rest of his host had been bled dry to keep Stralg supplied. Tryfors Hunt was back up to about three sixty, but the Fist's Own was down to two. Cullavi Hunt and the Fiends existed only on baked clay. He kept shifting packs from town to town, changing their stripes so that no one would realize how few men he really had. All the governors in his satrapy claimed to be in even worse shape, but they would naturally say that.

Only here could Therek imagine he was back in his campaigning days, those long summers in the field with Stralg and his other brothers and a few old trusties like Gzurg Hrothgatson, who was sitting beside him now. They'd begun two dozen years ago, disciplining heretic Werists who would not submit to the new bloodlord, and that had been a raw job; it had turned to sport later, when they were establishing Stralg's hold over the cities and mainly fighting extrinsics. Most of those old comrades were gone to the Dark One now, and those that were left were showing their years. Like Gzurg and his crocodile teeth.

Or Therek himself. Even an extrinsic was old at fifty-three, and very few Werists lasted so long, so he was lucky to have so few infirmities. The faces near him were all blurs, but he could count the cavities in the teeth of tonight's candidates because they were sitting at the far end of the hall. He scanned those fourteen eager young faces, wondering how many Gzurg had passed, and which. Old or not, the Toothed One still had his training skills, and he had driven those boys through fire and ice for the last few days. It was amazing that only two had dropped out. Both were expected to recover.

How many and which? All warriors enjoyed gambling, especially with subordinates who dared not argue the odds very hard. The rules were traditional—you tried to pick either men you thought would make the cut, or the one who would come in first. That paid the best odds, of course, and Therek had always had a good eye for winners. This year the favorite was a promising young brute named Snerfrik, huge and vicious. Therek had even wondered if Snerfrik might be one of his, but the seers said not, and seers were never wrong. But Snerfrik was so obviously destined to be runtleader that no one would give decent odds against him, so this time the hostleader had changed his strategy, betting on those who would make the team. He did not think much of the three probationers he'd brought up with him from Tryfors—they'd have done better to wait a season for the next testing there.

Thirteen faces were well tanned and windburned, but one was even browner. The darkie hostage must be good, for Therek had found lots of eager Nardalborg metal wanting to ride on the odd man out. He'd gotten some astonishing odds from those who couldn't see that he had rigged the game before it even began.

He chuckled to himself and drank a private toast to the destruction of all Florengian vermin. Ten years or so ago it had seemed a good idea to move his collection of hostages up here to Nardalborg, where they could have no chance of running away. The Celebre kid had been by far the youngest, and there had been no children of his age to play with except sons of Werists. Having been assured that they beat the shit out of him on a daily basis, which was good for all concerned, Therek had not worried.

Until the day he'd seen a dung-faced Florengian youth stalking around in a probationer's rope collar! His immediate interview with Heth had been fiery, to say the least, but the damage had been done by then, and he could not overrule the huntleader without damaging his authority. All he'd been able to do was refuse to allow any such trash to be tested anywhere in his entire satrapy. The more Heth had insisted that the whelp was a born fighter, the more Therek had explained that *you could not trust a Florengian!* They were traitors, perjurers, turncoats.

Those oath-breakers had killed his other sons.

And they were cowards. Stralg had raped the entire Florengian Face as easy as reaping corn. A torrent of loot and slaves and hostages had spouted over the Edge to Nardalborg and on down the great river, enriching all Vigaelia just as the life-giving silt of the annual flood fertilized the plain. When there was no opposition left, the bloodlord had begun to withdraw, planning to replace his garrisons with locals he had trained. That had been his mistake. Every single man Stralg had initiated into the cult defected. Then they started training and initiating others like themselves. The war had flared up again, but this time with Vigaelian Werists facing Florengian Werists. Three sons of Therek Hragson had died fighting those faithless brutes. He would *never* trust a Florengian, *never!*

Nor would Gzurg Hrothgatson, for certain. Earlier in the year Gzurg had reached the end of his fighting days. It had been a close call, as he admitted, for on his last changing he had nearly failed to come back, and a man trapped in battleform would be dead in a day.

The trouble was healing. Fights, even between well-matched Werist forces, rarely lasted more than a few minutes. Good chases might take half a day, but the body could forgive even those if they were not too frequent. Sooner or later, though, a man's luck ran out and he was wounded. A Werist healed much faster in battleform—he could also recover from damage that would kill him instantly in normal shape—but the effort could be so great that the body forgot the way back. Gzurg's next change would be his last.

So Stralg had sent the old Hero home to Vigaelia to see what he could do to speed up recruiting. Having invited him to test the Nardalborg candidates, Therek had finally allowed Brownie Boy to try his luck. The dupes in the Nardalborg Hunt who had been willing to bet on him had failed to see that Gzurg, after all the years of fighting, all the bloodshed and betrayal, was far more likely to take up embroidery than ever to let one more detested Florengian Werist into the cult. Therek was going to rake in a fortune tonight. The Orlad vermin hadn't realized it, obviously, sitting there with naked treason burning in those freakish black eyes. Oh, was Baby Turncoat ever in for a disappointment! He didn't know his hostleader had seen through his duplicity and was watching him even now.

"Have y'ever counted up, broth'r," Gzurg growled, leaning closer in a blast of sour beer fumes, "how many men you shent to the Dark One in y'r time? *Pershon'ly* I mean?"

"No. Have you?"

"Till I ran out of fingers." The hostleader brayed a drunken laugh at his absurd understatement.

"'ve you ever counted up the girls you bedded?"

"No; 've you?"

"Yes."

Gzurg's great teeth clashed shut as he hiccuped. "Shay, wash tryin' 'member—what wash the name of that duke up near White Lake tried to argue us because he thought his shordsh-men had us shoe-rounded? You 'member?"

"Don't recall." Therek just hoped the old lush would be able to remember the names of the candidates he had passed.

"Think't was before we shack'd Jat-Nogul."

No, it had been the year after. "Still don't recall."

"Never forget it. Dozen men with swords out all aroun' him and you changed and went through 'em ina blur and cut his throat and were back out again 'fore he hit the groun'!" The drunken brute guffawed and took a long suck on his straw.

"You ready to give your speech?"

"Sure. Then we can get down to some *sere-yes* drinking, mm?"

Therek stood up. And up. Werists tended to start big and grow bigger. He had always been skinny and tall, and now he towered half again over any extrinsic—if he straightened up, which he preferred not to try. He spread his talons on the table, leaning forward to scan the hall. The lads called him "the Vulture" behind his back, so his seers told him. He liked that, although "Eagle" would have been more respectful.

Elbows rammed into ribs and silence fell quickly.

"Fifteen years ago," Therek squealed—he had no teeth left, so his voice tended to whistle, but that was his listeners' problem. He could chew with his gums. "Nardalborg was a traders' staging post, a collection of tents and sod huts. It was here that our dread bloodlord, my brother—"

Pause for obligatory cheering. It was here he'd said farewell to

Stralg—with a silent *Good riddance!*—and settled down to enjoy the life of a satrap: wealth, women, and power. The hills were stiff with good game and every summer would bring forth a rash of small rebellions that he could enjoy stamping out, often in concert with his brothers and Saltaja's husband, Eide. Surprisingly for Heroes, the four of them had worked well together. Having the Witnesses of Mayn on their side had given them an insuperable advantage, and the only thing better than a good fight was a good fight you couldn't lose. The land was quieter now, alas. Since the Florengian war had sucked away all the manpower, it would be hard to organize two decent opposing hordes.

In the good old days, Therek had regarded Nardalborg as the cesspit of the world, much preferring Tryfors, with its zesty nightlife. Nowadays not a female in the city would look at him twice in her worst nightmares, not even the Nymphs. He'd come to prefer the masculine world of Nardalborg, where he wasn't tantalized so often.

He smiled and the cheering choked into silence. "It was here that Stralg assembled the great horde that he led off to his conquest." Which still had not ended. He turned to his neighbor. "And one of the men who went with him that day . . ."

During the renewed hubbub, he noted that the fourteen candidates were on their feet cheering Gzurg as hard as any. For days the Crocodile had battered and exhausted and maltreated them, so now they cheered him? Men were strange. Perhaps they were just showing how tough they were. Therek sat down and sucked beer and waited for his bets to pay off.

When Gzurg shouted, his voice came through clear and hard, and he seemed to have sobered himself up, at least temporarily. He ran through a few quick platitudes and went to the part everyone was waiting for. Copper, silver, even women, would be changing hands in a moment. He paused and peered into the gloom. "Are the candidates present?"

"There." Therek pointed.

"Ah, good. First, my congratulations to Satrap Therek and Huntleader Heth. I have rarely passed more than half a class of candidates. In this case, out of the sixteen who presented themselves, I am proud to approve ten."

He grinned that terrible display of teeth again as he waited for the cheering to subside. "First—and I will add that he is an *easy* first, a man who displays courage, toughness, dedication, and honest bloodthirsty ferocity such as I have rarely been honored to witness . . ."

Therek watched Snerfrik preening under the praise.

"—coming in well ahead of his nearest competitor, is . . . Candidate Orlad."

The hall stilled. Even the wind dropped for a moment, and the slave waiters froze, wondering what was wrong. In the distance mammoths trumpeted. As the Florengian hostage walked forward, dark eyes shining with triumph, five hundred pale eyes watched in total silence. He had been odds-on favorite to pass, but *First?* Gzurg must be crazy. He'd drunk his brains away. Or been hit on the head too often. Put a filthy Florengian belly-worm ahead of fifteen honest Vigaelian lads?

And now Therek would have to hold the bastard's hands and listen to the freak parroting an oath he had absolutely no intention of keeping . . . would have to put the winner's chain collar on him . . . And, oh horrors! would have to embrace him.

No, this was intolerable. This was an insult to holy Weru and Therek himself and the memory of those three sons who had died. *The only good Florengian's a dead one.* Something fatal must be arranged. Soon.

eleven

FRENA WIGSON

was fighting for her life with a black blanket of darkness wrapped around her head. Rushing water tugged at her ankles, trying to throw her down, while wind flailed rain back and forth. She was barely able to think in the tumult, certain only that if she fell she would be washed away and lost. And she must hurry. Danger pursued her. Its form was vague, a growling, fanged noise lurking in the storm, hiding its approach under the roar of the storm, but creeping ever closer as she fought her way step by step up the slope.

She was in Skjar. The air reeked of Skjar. The alley was typically Skjaran, with rough timber walls tight about her, with unexpected outcrops of rock and sudden changes of level and grade. The walls were coarse where her hands pawed at them. Her breath came in painful gasps, a stitch stabbed in her side. Rain streamed over her face and soaked her clothes—tore at her clothes, as if the storm sought to strip her naked.

Meaningless rags and planks went swirling by her. She must be adjusting to the darkness, for she could make out a slight widening of the way, not worthy to be called a square, but a place where two alleys crossed, one steeper than the other. Windows were barred, doors firmly bolted. Water frothed and leapt over the stones, washing away the gravel of the road. Wind wailed in rooftops. She saw no one else around, but sensed the monstrous danger slithering closer to her heels.

A small door in one corner, a curiously misshapen shape between a wall and a rocky knob, held the answer. There was the salvation she sought. As she clawed her way along the wall toward it, fighting the rising water and the spiteful wind, she saw the crooked door begin to open. What lay beyond was blacker than the night, blacker than eternal space or bottomless caverns. Even the torrent in the streets did not dare enter there. Wider and wider, and a figure emerging, a less-dark darkness taking shape in that uttermost darkness . . . a woman . . . smiling, beckoning . . .

"Mother!" Frena screamed. She scrambled wildly toward the door, but the smiling figure retreated within, fading into the stygian black, still smiling, beckoning. Frena tried to follow and met resistance. She wanted to enter and someone or something held her back. "Mother! Mother!"

✦

She sat up, trembling and choking. It was the same dream again, but knowing it was a dream made it no less terrifying. Her sheet was soaked as if she had bathed in it, and her head throbbed. Sweat was normal for Skjar, terror was not. The glimmering night lamp showed nothing wrong: sleeping platform, carved chests, delicately shaped chairs, mosaic and hangings, Ashurbian funeral urns . . . all as it should be. But every time she drifted off to sleep she had this nightmare of her mother. By rights she should ring for Master Frathson, her father's oneiromancer, so he could explain the portents and look up the offerings required to avert the gods' wrath; but her mother had always mocked the old man and his skill. Dreams were phantasms sent by the Mother of Lies, she'd said, and best just ignored.

Frena touched the sore place on her shoulder, and her fingers came away black in the dim light. *Blood and dark* . . . No, that wasn't right. *Blood and* . . . something. No matter. In her dream struggles she had opened the cut the rock had made at Bitterfeld.

She *could* have rescued that man, had she realized in time what was happening. A bold effort could have done it: two chariots, two swordsman, and she screaming curses to frighten the mob. It had been when they turned away that the pack had gone for them.

Dawn could not be far off—she had been up until long after dark with scribes and tallymen and stewards, making plans. Time had frothed by in a deluge of meetings, decisions, edicts, and even a few temper tantrums to break down resistance. At dawn the invitations would go out, still warm from the oven, and by morning a sizable fraction of the population of Skjar would be working on her dedication.

The underlying ritual could not be simpler. A girl of poor family went with her mother to any altar of Veslih and offered the goddess a flower or a barley cake, making her vows without a single priestess in sight. It was the rich who showed off with banquets and parades, with the girl's mother driving her to the Pantheon, where all her family and friends and her parents' friends waited to witness. Then the new woman would make a vow and a sacrifice at each of the twelve shrines, before driving her mother home, leading the parade of chariots to the banquet.

Frena's problem was that the people she wanted to invite had almost all fled to the hills. Nobody would willingly miss a grand feast in the Wigson mansion, but how many could return before Father's absurd deadline? Three days? They would all assume she was being rushed into wedlock before the baby arrived. Even collecting food in time would be almost impossible. Guests must be given expensive gifts. And entertainment? She must have dancers and musicians, tumblers and mimers, even performing animals, but the professionals had followed their patrons to the hills. Arrgh!

She sat on the edge of her sleeping platform with her head in her hands. It throbbed.

On such a night . . .

On just such a night, three years ago, heat and worry had kept her from sleeping. She had donned a robe and gone downstairs to see how her mother was faring. For three days Paola had lain abed, bandaged and splinted, coughing up blood and suffering terribly. Healers would not normally accept a patient so grievously injured, so close to death, but Horth's wealth had persuaded one—braver or greedier than the rest—to offer an attempt at a cure. Paola had refused him. She had refused all aid from holy Sinura, and even holy Nula. She had persisted in her refusal despite her daughter's tears and her husband's entreaties. Although Horth had fetched the best extrinsic apothecaries and surgeons available, internal injuries were beyond their skills. Paola's life had been visibly ebbing away.

Yet that night Frena had walked in and found the sleeping platform empty, her mother gone, and Quera—that sad excuse for a night nurse—snoring in a chair. Somehow the immobilized invalid had vanished. Curiously, young Frena had not run screaming for her father. She had not wakened Quera, nor yet raised the alarm among the servants. She had run back to the inner court to search among the trees and flowers, knowing that the garden she tended personally was her mother's favorite place, the view she always wanted from her room. A trail of discarded clothes and bandages had led Frena to Paola's corpse, facedown under some bushes.

The cold earth . . . *Blood and the cold earth?* No, that wasn't right.

Paola had been laid to rest where she died—in a respectable grave, it was worth remembering, in a marble sarcophagus and faceup. Half the population had come to the service. She had been a loving, most utterly perfect mother, not an evil monster. Her almsgiving had been the wonder of the city. Everyone who knew her had loved her well.

But . . .

But she had not merely been lax in offering sacrifice in the Pantheon. In the long dark of the night, Frena could not recall *any* instance of her mother going there to offer sacrifice. As the wife of one of the wealthiest men on the Face, she must have seen fewer of life's troubles than most women, but had there been no sicknesses or worries to prompt her to importune the Bright Ones? No friends or favored servants in trouble? In her final illness, why had she rejected all physical help from holy Sinura and comfort from holy Nula? And the manner of her death—had some ghastly aspect of Xaran dragged the dying woman from her bed, stripping her near-naked, before sucking out the last of her life under some bushes? Or had Paola Apicella returned voluntarily to a dark mistress and the cold earth?

Had the watchdog Quera been incompetent or victim of some evil art?

If Frena for the first time in her life did not trust what her mother had been, she must also admit that, for the first time in her life, she did not trust what her father said. His excuse for rushing her into a dedication ceremony in such disreputable haste did not ring true. What did he know or suspect that he would not discuss?

twelve

ORLAD ORLADSON

threw off his covers and was on his feet before the last note of reveille faded. Shivering. He heard groans and grumbles from adjoining stalls.

The sun was not yet up, and he could barely see the bunk he had just left. In contrast to its prolonged and bloody sunsets, Nardalborg's dawns were dramatic. The sun's coronal glory rose into a night sky full of stars that refused to fade until the ineffable disk itself came burning up over the Ice. For a few moments the world was monochrome white—glittering white castle set in stark white moorland; there was never a night without frost or snow at Nardalborg. Only when the sun itself showed above the horizon did the sky reluctantly begin to turn blue.

This was the day he must march out and face the world; face down the other nine, he and his little flank of runts. He was alone in his stall. A stall it was, with a drape across the front, a shelf, a few hooks, just a blanket and sleeping rug on the floor. This was how cadets and probationers were billeted. Last night there had been celebrations and women's voices in his neighbors' stalls. Normally there would be no lack of willing female companionship for a new runtleader, perhaps even for a *Florengian* runtleader, if such a thing could be imagined, but Orlad kept clear of women. They offered too many opportunities for hurt. When he had won his brass collar and shown the men what he could do, then he would show their women also.

Donning a Werist pall without help was no small matter. Start by tossing one end back over the left shoulder, long enough to reach the kidneys. Drape the rest across the chest, wrap it around to cover the back, then the left hip, privates, right hip, buttocks; bring it up across the back, under the left arm, and over the right shoulder. If it had been judged correctly, the end should come to the kidneys, level with the other. All correct so far. Then—moving gingerly because this was when it might collapse—take up the sash and tie it around the waist in a half-knot. That should hold everything in place. Theoretically. There remained the problem of moving at all under what felt like an ox's weight of wool. When the quartermaster had dropped the baled cloth across his eagerly outstretched arms last night, Orlad had staggered under the sheer weight of it. He had spent half the night practicing by starlight, and now the time had come for him to go forth garbed as a Werist, instead of a scabby civilian in tunic and leggings with a rope around his neck. The years of chafing were over.

To have come in first was the stuff of dreams. Gzurg would never give praise without cause, and he had praised the Nardalborg training highly. To be approved by a Hero such as the legendary Gzurg, to be trained by Heth, and to swear one's oath to the great Therek, the Vulture himself—all these were lifelong honors, humbling starts to a career. But to be first was best of all. Ten new cadets. Nine runts and one runtleader. Nine leather collars and one chain.

Gzurg had warned Orlad what was coming, but no one else had known. Everyone had been struck dumb. Later, of course, they had cheered Snerfrik! They hadn't seen that the more they rattled the rafters for the man who had come second, the more they had really been honoring First. There had been no other surprises until the end, when Waels had sneaked in under the bar as number ten. His name had been greeted mostly with puzzled silence, until someone had explained, "Pusmouth." *Oh, yes, Pusmouth . . .*

Orlad inspected himself with his hands and decided the folds across his chest were rumpled. Determined not to make his first appearance as runtleader in a poorly wrapped pall, he stripped, spread the absurd garment on the floor and began folding it again for another attempt. Feet and voices went by in the corridor.

"How much authority does a runtleader really have?" he had asked Gzurg.

"As much as he can take; no more than he can hold." The old rogue's laugh had displayed all sixty-four teeth. "You, son, had better draw some lines in the sand very quickly and defend them to the death. Preferably someone else's death."

Only on his fourth attempt was Orlad satisfied—and almost out of time. A Werist! A pall-draped, chain-collared Werist! Cadet Orlad, in stripes of orange (for the Vulture's host), green (for the Nardalborg Hunt), and white for cadet. After so many years of yearning and trying, he was at last dressed as he had longed to be. The white would go soon enough. He had sworn the oath; now he belonged to the god.

A pall was a very drafty garment. He felt certain it would all drop to the floor at any minute and leave him naked, but that was its purpose—Werists assuming battleform had no time to waste struggling with clothes. He felt ridiculous, but that, too, must pass in time. He was stiff and bruised from the tests, which had been even more grueling than he had expected, and badly short of sleep, but all these were part of the process. The cut on his arm where he had drawn blood for his oath was healing well. He felt great.

Runtleader Orlad stepped into his sandals, pushed aside the curtain, and strode forth. Half the curtains were still closed, and he could even hear snores from some of the stalls he passed, but most of the men billeted in this dorm were nothing to do with him. If any of his flank were late for roll call, then he would take action. He was almost at the door when a curtain slid aside and out came Pusmouth. Good timing!

Orlad stopped. "Death to your foes, Runt Waels."

Pusmouth nodded hastily. "My lord is kind."

"Not lord." Orlad practiced a Werist frown and was pleased to see the kid flinch.

"My *leader* is kind." Waels waited cautiously to hear what was wanted. No one knew much about him. He was one of a trio of probationers sent up from Tryfors to participate in the tests. He had seemed so young and unassertive that the oddsmakers had given him little chance, but last night when the other two Tryfors boys slunk out with the jeers of the entire Nardalborg Hunt howling about their ears, he had remained. His nickname came from a wine-colored birthmark covering the lower half of his face. His gossamer beard could not hide it yet and probably never would.

"Stand by that window," Orlad said. "Turn around. Good job. Looks perfect. Now me. Is my ass hanging out?"

Today the runts would formally pair up and from then on each man would be responsible for his buddy in a dozen ways, including inspecting the hang of his pall.

"My leader is kind. If I may . . ." Pusmouth made a minute adjustment to the hang of Orlad's pall. "I believe that is better, leader."

"Thanks." They fell into step along the corridor. Orlad was not one for small talk, but a leader should know his men and he had no experience of Pusmouth. "Congratulations. Feels good, doesn't it?"

". . . Very . . . leader. And congratulations to you, Runtleader Orlad. If I may say, from what I saw in the tests, you amply—"

"You may *not* say. No sandal-licking! I don't need to be told I'm good, whether I am nor not."

"My leader is kind."

They left the dormitory building and walked into ankle-deep slush and a wicked wind that wanted to test their skill at tying palls. They sped up, leaning into the blast. A group from gold pack passed them, nodding and smiling to acknowledge the new runts. The first shock must be wearing off.

"So why did you hesitate when I congratulated you?"

"I do not recall hesitating, Runtleader."

"Yes you did. You're thinking you were tacked on as a *spare,* weren't you? Odd man out? Tryfors trash?"

Pusmouth stared straight ahead into the wind, eyes watering, cheeks flaming almost as red as his birthmark, lips turning bluish. After a moment's thought he said, "The idea of *spare* did occur to me, Runtleader. It is only a legend, I am sure."

They were almost at the mess door.

"How often does it happen at Tryfors?"

"There have been a few cases."

"Here," Orlad said, "it has happened eight times in the last ten years." Eight out of twenty cadet classes had suffered a mortality in training. Some of those might have been genuine accidents, but there was a whispered tradition that the last name on the list tended to be unlucky. "I suspect that we may be due for a ninth, but you are in much less danger than I am."

"You were *first!*" Pusmouth looked startled as he held the door for his superior to enter.

"A Florengian runtleader? You know that no Florengian has ever survived Werist training at Nardalborg?"

Waels grinned. "Because no Florengian has dared try?"

Orlad went by without answering. He sensed no threat in this boy, perhaps even some compatibility—hideous birthmark meets skin too brown.

The mess hall was big and high, but today's wind was disposing of the smoke. Today the overlarge windows offered expansive views of the moor and a temperature close to freezing, but most of the year windows were kept shuttered in Nardalborg. Men from red pack departing the mess made some jocularly insulting remarks about the low class of vermin that were being let in these days. Orlad did not bother to smile.

Inside, most men sat on stools at long tables, eating and arguing. There must be a runts' table somewhere. There was also a cutting table, where men just stood and tore at raw flesh. That was not yet his idea of breakfast, although he knew it soon would be. He headed for a counter laden with bread, cheese, fruit, and vegetables.

Pusmouth automatically followed his leader Orlad. That was a strange concept for a lifelong outcast, that nine men were now expected to obey his orders. *Expected,* but not *required.* A warrior who spoke back to his flank-leader risked death or close to it, but a cadet could appeal to higher authority. Gzurg had warned him. *As much as he can take; no more than he can hold.*

Even Gzurg had admitted that runtleader was a tough assignment. When a Hero was promoted, he was set over strangers. A new flankleader was moved to a new flank, packleader to new pack, huntleader to new hunt, and sometimes even a hostleader to a new host. But a runtleader was merely first in his class. It would be hard to promote the first-among-equals idea if the class could not see a Florengian as an equal. He had his chain collar and about a year on most of them, two years on some. That was all. The real authority belonged to Huntleader Heth, a hard, humorless man who played no favorites. Would the huntleader back him up or cut the ground out from under his sandals?

By the time Orlad had filled a basket, he had located the runts' table by locating Snerfrik. In a hall full of huge men, Snerfrik stood out. Or sat out, to be exact. He was half a head taller than almost anyone, and he lacked nothing in breadth—give him ten years as a Werist and he would be a true giant, like Satrap Therek. That was why he had been favorite to win the leader's chain. He had certainly been the favorite in the wrestling test, but Orlad had thrown him, and that joy was a close second to coming in first.

He headed for the table, saw his approach being noticed. Would they rise for him or snub him? His dander began to bristle as he planned possible responses. No, it was too early for line-drawing. Deliberate insubordination before he had even opened his mouth would be rank mutiny.

Stools scraped back. Every man was standing at attention by the time he reached his place. But five men along each side meant twelve in all, a full flank, and Orlad realized that he had forgotten to include Vargin and Ranthr. They had been runts in the last class and for some reason had not been initiated with their peers—just how or why they had failed were secrets of the god's mysteries. They were allowed one more chance, which put them in Orlad's flank.

Years ago, these two had been his peers, but he had been held back and they had gone on. Now, suddenly, they were thrown under his authority.

They would be the first to test it, he decided. They knew the ropes, so even Snerfrik would probably defer to them. Vargin was a superb fighter—as Orlad had rediscovered many times to his cost—but that was largely because he was too stupid to know when he was beaten. Recruiting officers never worried about *wits*. Ranthr was smarter, in a sly way, so he was the one to watch. The pressure would come from him.

Yet interlopers might not be a bad thing. Even without a word spoken, Orlad sensed the tension. The cadets had seated themselves in the order of their standings, with the end stools left for the runtleader and the possibly doomed spare. But Vargin and Ranthr had taken the places on either side of Orlad's, claiming seniority. Everyone was waiting to see what he would do.

He laid down his bowl. "At ease. Death to all your foes, runts."

They spoke in almost perfect unison: "My leader is kind."

He sat and they all did. He looked around the table without a smile.

"Last night we swore an oath. Now we belong to the god, so together we must strive to become worthy of His blessing. We owe it to holy Weru to help one another in this quest. We are brothers in this flank, even if we are not yet numbered among His Heroes. I think we risk offending our god if we come to Him in the company of a man named *Pusmouth*."

All eyes turned. At the far end of the table, Waels blanched, making his birthmark flame even redder. Puzzled glances swung back to Orlad.

"A more fitting name for a Werist would be Bloodmouth. So my first decree as runtleader is that Waels will henceforth be referred to as Waels, or Bloodmouth, but nevermore as Pusmouth. Penalty is two strokes of the rod."

Waels was grinning as if he had just survived a bad fright. "My leader is kind," he murmured.

"Who does the honors?" Ranthr asked.

Orlad contemplated the battlefield and saw no pitfalls yet. "I do. You will learn that I have a strong right arm. Anyone who catches me at fault gets to return the favor." He bit into an apple.

More grins. So far so good. The first order was acceptable and would probably stick, unless Waels made a complete idiot of himself in the next few days. Once the ox starts moving in the right direction, the next step comes easier.

Big Snerfrik was obviously unhappy about the way Ranthr and Vargin had effectively demoted him from second to fourth. He fidgeted for a few minutes while everyone ate assiduously and the rest of the hall buzzed on uncaring. Then he barked out in his gravel voice, "What happens today, leader?"

Orlad had no idea. He chewed, swallowed, and drew his first line in the sand. "First thing that happens is I assign pairings. I may as well do that now."

"But—"

"Yes?"

"Nothing . . . my leader is kind." Snerfrik and Vargin exchanged glances. Perhaps Snerfrik considered himself second-best choice and expected Orlad to take him as partner. Or he might have misgivings about being honored that way. Likewise, Vargin and Ranthr had been down the road before, so either would be a good catch. Waels would be last choice, obviously, after Hrothgat, who had come in ninth.

"I warn you all now," Orlad said, "that I intend to have no failures. All members of this flank will pass or die in the attempt. The strong must help the weak, so I take Bloodmouth as my buddy. Snerfrik will take Hrothgat, Caedaw take Charnarth . . ." He ran through the list, dealing from top and bottom alternately until he put the middle two together. Then— "Vargin and Ranthr, you'll partner each other."

The runts' table had become a tiny oasis of silence in the hum of the hall. He abandoned the thought of another bite of apple as he realized that his challenge was going to be accepted. His whole mouth seemed to pucker, dry as salt.

"I don't want Ranthr," Vargin said. "Other runtleaders let their men choose buddies."

Vargin was always too stupid to know when he was beaten, meaning in this case demoted. He had dug his own grave.

And perfectly timed, for Huntleader Heth was striding in their direction, so the new runtleader could stand or fall right now.

"I'll give you one heartbeat to withdraw that remark, runt."

"I agreed to be Snerfrik's buddy."

The apple in Orlad's hand crumbled to paste without his willing it to. "Runt Vargin! Run and ask the harbor master how many children he has now."

"Run yourself, shit-eyes."

Perfect timing. Orlad could now pretend to notice Huntleader Heth looming behind Waels. He sprang up. "Flank, attention!"

Several stools toppled as the eleven followed his lead. Then Orlad bowed in proper Werist fashion—feet together, back horizontal, eyes staring straight down, which in this case meant with his nose almost on the table, for a count of three. This put him at a disadvantage if his leader wanted to stun him.

"At ease," Heth said. The huntleader was a respected warrior, with no known weaknesses except a humorless dislike of drunken orgies; there were also vicious rumors that he was faithful to his wife. Despite his many campaigns, the only battle hardening he displayed was a general increase in size and an abnormal thickening of his neck and shoulders, which gave him a bull-like appearance. His head was oddly cubical, but Orlad could remember noticing that as a child.

The cadets sat, all except Orlad. The huntleader eyed them thoughtfully, as if sensing something amiss.

"This morning, Runtleader, drill your men in stripping, and then rest them till evening. None of you will be getting much sleep for the next few days. Make sure they feed well now, then make them fast. Report to the shrine at sundown bell for instruction and meditation. We'll proceed toward the lifting of the first veil."

Yes! to that, whatever it was. "My lord is kind. We are eager to begin."

"Good. Carry on . . ." From the slowness with which he turned, Heth probably knew he would not get far.

"My lord!"

"Runtleader?"

"My lord, I regret to report a disciplinary problem."

The Werist scowled. His square face darkened; his massive shoulders seemed to grow even larger. "Already?"

"Yes, my lord."

"That is probably something of a record, not one to brag of."

"My lord is kind."

"What sort of problem?"

"A punishment I assigned has been refused."

"The offense?"

"Refusal to obey an order."

"What order?"

"The man refuses to accept the cadet I assigned as his buddy."

"And the punishment?"

"Harbor master, my lord."

The harbor master—whoever that notoriously fruitful man was, for Orlad had never had cause to meet him—was stationed down in Tryfors, which was supposedly three menzils away, but a menzil was a very loose measure. In good weather, a strong and superbly fit cadet like Vargin should just manage the trip between dawn and dusk, one way. Having to run there and back again was rated worse than a second-level beating, and last night's snow would certainly delay him.

"And what additional punishment have you assigned for refusing the first one?"

"I had not gotten so far, lord. Five strokes for each day or part of a day he is absent?"

Heth pursed his lips. "You will have to learn to be stricter than that, Runtleader, or they'll be taking advantage of you right and left."

Triumph! Orlad struggled to conceal giddy relief behind a stern, warrior mien. "With respect, my lord, I do not want to cripple the man on a first offense."

"As you will." Heth shrugged. "If he persists, report him to me and we'll run him for the hunt."

An inexcusable surge of nausea almost made Orlad gag, but he managed to gulp the obligatory "My lord is kind" at Heth's departing back. Reproaching himself for unbecoming weakness, he looked down at Vargin and saw utter terror.

"You heard the first and second punishments, runt. Will you take them or go for the third?"

The delinquent lurched to his feet. "My leader is kind," he croaked. "Permission to go now?"

"Granted." But there was no point in killing the idiot. "Vargin?"

The great loon turned. "Leader?"

"Wear whatever you like. Take food and a canteen."

"My leader is kind!" Vargin sounded as if he meant that, for once. He headed for the counters to gather rations.

Orlad sat down and regarded ten appalled faces. Ranthr and Snerfrik were almost green, wondering which of them would be next. There would be no further trouble.

"Runt Ranthr, will you run through the stripping drill for us?"

"My leader is kind," Ranthr mumbled, and then parroted, "*On the command 'Strip!' the warrior will drop his pall.* My leader is kind. And of course:

On the command 'Dress!' the warrior will don his pall, helping his buddy to do the same."

"We'd better find a warm place to try that." Orlad tore off a crust and stuffed it into his mouth while he considered the problem. A pall could be removed with a yank at the sash's half-knot and then one hard tug. The heavy cloth would drop like a landslide. "How long does a good squad take?"

"No time at all," Ranthr said. "Instantaneous upon the command."

"So we'll do it faster!" Orlad ripped off more bread. One or two of the others had began to eat again also. Most were still too stunned by the onset of full warrior discipline. *Run him for the hunt?*

"We all belong to holy Weru now," Orlad said. "We are all going to be initiated into His mysteries. And we are going to do it in record time. Does anyone doubt that?"

There was a long pause before Waels ventured to inquire, "How much time did you have in mind, leader?"

"Before the last day of the Festival of Weru."

No one dared look at anyone.

"With utmost respect, leader, that is only half a year." As the leader's buddy, Waels was assuming the dangerous office of spokesman. "I don't think any class has ever gone from probation to initiation that fast."

"But we will. In the last ten years the last caravan has always left about a sixday after the end of the Festival. We will be ready so we can cross the Edge before winter closes the pass." Orlad glanced around the table. "Or are you cowards who want to sit around until next year before you join the blood-lord's horde and start killing Florengian oath-breakers?"

They shouted denials like good little Werists.

Orlad smiled approval. "I can't wait."

thirteen

FRENA WIGSON

gazed out her window at the lifeless docks. Not even slaves could work on a day like this, when the sun was a blur of brightness in a pallid sky and Ocean a lead sheet behind masts and rigging. She wore an appropriately virginal robe of white linen with a sprinkling of pearls. Her tar-black hair was demurely coiled but adorned with a ruby comb, which was somewhat daring for the Pantheon, a subtle display of insurrection.

Accepting noon for her appointment with High Priestess Bjaria had been a misjudgment. By the time she crossed to the bedroom door, she was damp with perspiration. Her chariot was waiting for her at the front door, with Dark and Night in the traces, but she was surprised to find Verk driving. Servants set down mounting steps for her, and he offered a strong hand to help her aboard.

"Uls is well?"

"The lady is kind to ask. He is fully recovered."

She took the reins and he raised the brake. Why Verk to escort her, instead of her usual driver or one of the other house guards? Had Father arranged this, or was Verk contriving to speak with her in private? She did not inquire, because she had developed a stabbing headache, and it was growing steadily worse. As the chariot rocked and bounced across the bridge to Temple, thunder and lightning inside her skull felt fit to burst it.

Having no female relatives, she had informed Father that he would be Mother to drive her there. Although he had not driven a chariot in years, he had laughed and said he would be honored. She would drive home, though. She was determined to follow tradition and lead the chariot parade back from her dedication. So this trip was rehearsal as well as the obligatory preliminary call upon the garrulous high priestess.

"Are you all right, mistress?"

She wondered how green her face must be for him to have noticed. "I am fine. I just wish I had thought to bring wool to plug my ears." High Priestess Bjaria was the worst blabbermouth on Dodec.

Temple was one of the larger islands, the most rugged and irregular of all, and clearly had been formed when a section of the canyon wall collapsed and the river cut new channels through the resulting dam. Houses had spread over most of it so that it looked like a lumpy reptile scaled with roofs, but in places its bones were exposed as piles of gigantic rocks. The Pantheon stood on a green-furred hump, one of the few wooded areas in the city, and was reached only by climbing a long flight of stairs. Score twelve extra points for the weather, twelve more for headache.

From the bridge to a busy street, then another, which headed straight to a cliff, snaked through a notch in it, and emerged in a steep-sided bowl whose floor was an uneven graveled yard. Scores of other chariots were waiting there, some being tended by their owners' servants, others by green-clad Nastrarians employed by the Pantheon. The onagers' braying echoed back and forth, and the stupid brutes kept answering themselves. Worshipers bustled in and out through several entrances, but they must all ascend the rocky hillside by the same wooden staircase. Verk drove as close to the base as he could. There she must leave him, because weapons were not allowed and to take attendants when calling on gods was regarded as poor taste.

She handed the reins to Verk and prepared to climb down.

"The master sent for me," he said, not looking at her.

She paused. "But did not impale you."

"No, mistress. He was very concerned to know why you insisted on approaching the mob."

So was she. What had led her to be stupid? That was not like her. "I hope you explained that I was merely being nosy?"

"Not in those words, mistress." His tone was oddly flat.

She could have rescued that man!

Verk handed her down. Slinging her leather satchel on her shoulder, she braced herself for the climb. The headache pounded harder than ever, not helped by the wailing of beggars trying to extract alms from stolid citizens going by. The stolid citizens ignored them, as did the clergy in their many-colored Pantheon robes. When the cadgers noticed Frena's purse, they redoubled their howls, scrambling after her on their knees with hands outstretched, but she hurried past them and began the ascent, following a couple of priests. The stair zigzagged, changing slope and direction frequently. It was wide enough for two people going up to pass two coming down, but the treads were in alarmingly poor condition, the handrails splintered and not entirely secure. Renovations were clearly overdue.

"Fabia Celebre?"

Something touched her arm. She ignored it, plodding painfully upward.

"Frena Wigson, then."

Frena was startled to discover that she was being addressed by a seer—a woman, judging by her voice, tall, slender, and completely swathed in white cloth. Her lower body was covered in a white skirt or robe, a cape fell below her waist, hiding even her hands, and another cloth draped her head. She must be melting inside all that.

"I am Frena Wigson." She had never spoken with a Witness before.

The speaker moved alongside. "Keep climbing and do not act surprised. I have an important warning for you."

"How do I know you are what you pretend to be?" And why were they speaking Florengian?

"You have an unhealed cut on your right shoulder and your shift is embroidered with blue daisies." She sounded young. "Am I a seer?"

"Er, yes. What warning, Witness?"

"You do believe that I speak only truth?"

"You addressed me by another name."

"I wanted to see if you knew it. You were not always Frena Wigson."

"I wasn't?" Frena croaked. Her heart was pounding much harder than it should be. Her mouth was dry, her headache excruciating, and the two old priests ahead were climbing faster than she was. She did not need crazy seers babbling riddles at her.

"No. You have been lied to all your life, but only to keep you out of danger. Now your ignorance may put you in worse danger."

If anyone other than a seer mouthed such nonsense . . .

"Then who am I?"

"Your real name is Fabia. You are the fourth child of Piero, doge of the Florengian city of Celebre, and his wife, the lady Oliva. You were taken hostage when Celebre fell to Bloodlord Stralg, fifteen years ago. Your heartbeat is alarmingly fast, my dear. Take a moment's rest."

Frena leaned against a mossy rock and the seer stood beside her, one step up. A family group climbed past. A group of women descended. The headache was flashing streaks of green light brighter than sunshine.

"Fabia?"

"Fabia Celebre."

"What's a doge?"

"A sort of elected king."

"What is the danger?" Besides dying of headache.

"Premature death. Very briefly: You and your three brothers, all older than you, were brought to Vigaelia as hostages. For the last fifteen years, your father has ruled his city as the bloodlord's puppet, thereby keeping war and grief away from it. Our sight cannot extend to another Face and my most recent information is about a season old. He was said to be very ill then. Celebre is becoming strategically important again, as it has not been for many years. One of his children will be returned to Florengia to take over after his death. The others will not be left alive as potential challengers. Now do you appreciate your danger?"

"Brothers? Where? Who?"

"We have no time for irrelevant detail. The Queen of Shadows is Stralg's regent on this Face. She will decide which one of you will live. At the moment she leans toward marrying you off to a man she can trust and sending you back with him to legitimize his rule, but she may change her mind."

"She organized this dedication?"

"Certainly. She terrified your father by threatening to denounce you as a Chosen of Xaran."

Frena hung to the rotted handrail and tried fiercely to focus on the seer through the flickering green lights. Pain was wringing out her brain like a wet cloth. "Why are you telling me this? I thought Maynists were Stralg supporters and counselors. Why are you pretending to thwart his sister?"

"Never pretending!" The seer's voice displayed some welcome human emotion at last—anger. "Fabia, Fabia! We serve the monster unwillingly, believe me, and only to fulfill an ancient compact, which most of us believe must now be discarded. Although only a minority in our cult think as our leader does, only her views count, and by accosting you I am sorely bending my vows of obedience. Do you feel well enough to proceed? Some officious priest will certainly start prying if you remain here very long."

Frena forced herself to resume the climb, although her feet felt like boat anchors. People coming down were glancing curiously at the seer, not at her.

"I don't think I can believe all this."

"Try, because your life is at stake. *I am a Witness of Mayn!* We speak only truth."

"Yes, Witness. I am sorry. Does my father know of this?"

"Of course."

"And as soon as I have made my vows, he will receive an offer for my hand?"

"An offer he will not dare refuse."

"Who is the lucky bridegroom?"

"Saltaja's present choice is a son of her brother Horold, satrap of Kosord. The youth's name is Cutrath and he has just been, or is about to be, initiated as a Hero."

A *Werist?* Ugh! Frena could not imagine a worse choice of husband. "My father . . . Horth . . . has always promised that I will not be forced to marry against my will."

"You will be now. No one who opposes Saltaja Hragsdor ever prospers."

"Why are you bothering to tell me if I have no choice?"

"Suicide is always an option," the seer said cheerfully. "But rarely an attractive one. Partly because I serve the goddess of truth and you should know the truth. Partly to try and frustrate the Queen of Shadows, for she is evil. Partly—and I am not supposed to tell you this—because you are what we term a *seasoner.* It is a subtle concept, almost impossible to explain to an extrinsic. *Seasoning* is a potential for greatness, and very rare. High Priestess Bjaria is an important woman in this city but has no 'flavor' at all. Your foster father is completely insipid, despite his unbounded wealth. Stralg is a seasoner, and so is Saltaja."

"Then why should I want it? What's it good for?"

"It is found in those who make history. It does not guarantee that they *will* do so, for many seasoners are buried by the wayside, their destiny unfulfilled. But when the gods wish to change the flavor of the world, they use a seasoner to do so. We rarely encounter seasoning before it is manifest, which is one reason we are interested in you, Fabia Celebre. Your time has not yet come."

"You are being metaphorical, I trust? You view the world as the cook pot of the gods?"

"Why not? If your flavor is the taste the gods want, then yours will be the seasoning they apply. Or you may stay forever on the kitchen shelf. This is the closest a seer will ever go to foretelling the future."

This was madness!

The seer sighed. "You cannot believe. No matter. But consider the only family you know. Horth Wigson is a basically a good man, for a Ucrist, and you will put him in extreme peril if you resist the inevitable."

Right foot, left foot, right . . . Cold rivulets raced down Frena's ribs and the air was too thick to breathe.

"I understood—" Frena corrected herself. "What he always told me was that he went over the Edge as a young man and met my . . . met Paola in Florengia, married—"

"I have no evidence that he has left Skjar since the day he arrived. How well does he speak Florengian?"

"Just a few words. Paola taught me and . . ." Frena stopped as the import of her words registered. *Why* didn't Horth speak more Florengian than that?

"It is known that Paola Apicella was hired, or coerced, as a wet nurse at a place near Celebre, to bring the hostage baby, namely you, to this Face, where you were assigned to the custody of Satrap Karvak, another Hragson. He died when rebels sacked Jat-Nogul. Apicella escaped and brought you to Skjar, where she married a promising Ucrist. The Witnesses tracked you down, of course. Saltaja was content to leave you where you were, anonymous, until she had need of you."

"As you also—" A blaze of pain made Frena drop her voice. "As you also have need of me? Suddenly everyone is trying to use me. Stralg wants me; you want to balk Stralg. What are you offering? Will you rescue me from this situation?"

The slender woman shrugged. "Witnesses observe, record, and never meddle. Besides, to expose our petty resistance efforts to Saltaja at this time would be most unwise."

Frena thought, *Ha!* "Well, you say I am not Horth Wigson's natural daughter, but I have not lived with him all my life without learning to shun an exchange that only works one way. If you want my cooperation, you must offer something in return. No matter how strategic this city you mention, being queen of it would hardly compensate me for being married to an animal. These Florengian aristocrats you cite apparently gave me away as a baby, whereas Horth and Paola were everything a child could ask for in loving, caring parents. I do know that the lady Saltaja has a dubious reputation, but I always find her to be a cultivated, knowledgeable lady." So *there!*

"You fear her without knowing why. Can I bribe you with hopes of revenge? Saltaja had Paola Apicella murdered."

"What!" Frena stumbled to a halt, grabbed the rail with both hands, and peered blearily at the Witness. "Did you say—"

"I did. I would testify in court before a Speaker that Saltaja Hragsdor sent a flank of Werists after your foster mother with orders to beat her to death and leave the body on Wigson's doorstep. She is not a very subtle person."

"No!" Deliberate murder seemed even worse than the random violence of a gang of drunks. "Why would she do such a thing?"

"Regarding motives, I can only speculate. She certainly suspected your foster mother of causing the death of her brother, Karvak. She may have worried that Paola would initiate you into the ranks of the Chosen. Saltaja was convinced that Paola was a chthonian."

They were standing very close to the top of the stair now, but whatever lay ahead was hidden behind a fence; the path made a right-angle turn through a gate. A jabber of young boys came yelling and screaming out and plunged down the steps in a human avalanche. The yard was far below, all the waiting chariots small as children's toys.

Shivering despite the heat, Frena asked the obvious question. "And was she?"

The seer seemed to word her answer carefully. "Fabia, our goddess does not let us pry into other divinities' mysteries. Satrap Eide is obviously a Werist, because he wears the collar and also has vestigial horns, but Weru has other cults you've never heard of. If a woman wears a live fireasp as a necklace, she is undoubtedly a Nastrarian. Did you know that Ucr, your father's god, also supports a cult of thieves?"

"No! Truly?"

"Membership in the Chosen cannot be detected, no matter what the witch-hunters say."

"Mother never came here, to the Pantheon," Frena admitted.

"Apicella may have just disliked hypocrisy. She could have come, I am sure. Gods tend to be jealous of their votaries, but if the Dark One kept Her Chosen from visiting other temples, they would soon all be unmasked and destroyed. There is *no* perfect test!" The Witness turned, as if looking at something, although the heavy cloth over her head and face must be completely opaque, as it showed nothing of her features, only sweat stains.

"She was not an evil person!"

"I never said she was. I know no unassailable definition of evil. The Old One is greatly feared as keeper of the dead, but we all go to Her in the end. That some of Her minions may be evil I do not deny; that some may not be is a tenable hypothesis. And Saltaja did have evidence—the strange circumstances of her brother's death, Paola's success at escaping and remaining undetected for years, her coup in marrying a man of wealth who could protect her. Even, although this came after the fact, the remarkable toll she took of her assassins and the long time she took to die. One aging, unarmed woman beset by a gang of young louts and she kills even two of them? Is this probable?"

"You are manipulating again!" Although she wanted to shout, Frena managed only a croak. "You tell me that the Chosen are not evil and they have powers to overcome even Werists? Are you suggesting I swear allegiance to the Mother of Lies instead of the Bright Ones?" That was the real question, wasn't it?

"I am suggesting no such thing. The decision is entirely yours. I detect that you are suffering extreme physical distress, possibly a headache. This may be no more than a result of eating bad meat, although I regard that hypothesis as improbable. The most likely alternative, although there may be other explanations that I have not thought of, is that you are already promised to a specific god. This puts you in conflict with your purpose in coming to the house of the Twelve, and the conflict will have to be resolved. A dedication is a form of choosing."

"You're suggesting that I belong to the Dark One," Frena whispered, visualizing open graves.

"She is certainly the most likely candidate."

"But I never pledged allegiance to Her!" Frena wiped away the perspiration running into her eyes.

"Infants can be pledged by others, especially their parents or those in charge of them. For instance, foster mothers." The seer sounded very much as if she were fishing for information. She would be disappointed. "The allegiance must be ratified in adulthood. This is why the dedication ritual requires you to renounce all other gods in general and the Old One by name."

"Then I will be free of Her?"

"So the priests assure us. If you wish to try doing so here and now, just saying the words may reduce your stress to more tolerable levels. Alternatively, if you intend to pledge full loyalty to Her, then a declaration of that intent would probably be equally beneficial to your present comfort. I suspect that it is your undecided status that is causing the problem. As I have said several times, there is no way of detecting the Chosen—a chthonian could speak the words of the renunciation without flickering an eyelash." The seer looked away as if hearing something Fabia couldn't. "We have been together too long. Twelve times twelve blessings on you—"

"Wait! Just suppose I did decide to . . . to investigate the alternative. How would I proceed?"

The seer stood in silence for a long moment, a cloud of draperies. "I suggest you question your foster father's employee, Master Pukar. Based on his habits, if he is not a chthonian himself, he must know some who are . . . But exercise extreme caution!"

"Wait!" Frena caught the seer's cape. "You would aid a Chosen?"

She jerked loose. "I said I knew no definition of evil, Fabia Celebre, but 'the Children of Hrag' comes very close. I will aid anyone who opposes them, anyone at all, and I am not alone. But beware! There are nine Witnesses in Skjar just now, and not all agree with me. Trust no one who does not come in the name of Mist."

"Mist?"

"Our leader in this. Twelve blessings, Fabia Celebre." White robes swirling, she strode nimbly up the rest of the stairs and vanished through the gate.

◆

High Priestess Bjaria was of mature years, majestic in stature, stentorian of voice, and the biggest bore on all Dodec. She could sit through an entire banquet without ever seeming to draw breath, while eating more than anyone else and chattering on whatever subject currently held her personal fancy. Frena was careful never to invite her unless Saltaja was certain to be present, because the satrap's wife was the only person who ever dared interrupt her.

Yet she was inept, not ill-intentioned. She received Frena in a large and crowded robing room—dim, breathless, smelling of rot—and enveloped her in an odor of godswood and a giant sweaty hug. After a mere three or four sentences she pushed her visitor back to arm's length to peer at her with well-bagged eyes.

"Are you feeling well, child? You look poorly. Nerves, I assume; perfectly normal for any girl just before her—"

"Headache . . . weather—"

"Ah, the humidity, I know exactly how you feel, we have a priestess of holy Nastrar who is absolutely *devastated* in the wet season, throwing up all day long . . . Why don't we go straight over to the shrine of holy Sinura and you can say a quick prayer, perhaps leave a small offering, and I am sure the goddess will send you some relief."

"No, I'm quite all right," Frena said hastily, any other form of speech being impossible near the reverend Bjaria. "When we get there—"

"As you will. Then let me begin by introducing . . ."

The high priestess presented a dozen minions and two dozen deputy minions, some male, some female, all unnecessary, but all expecting a gratuity from Frena's purse. None of them managed to slip in more than two words of greeting before Bjaria swept the entire procession off on a tour of the Pantheon.

Very soon Frena discovered that her headache had dropped to a bearable level. She had made a decision of sorts, she realized, by refusing to appeal to holy Sinura—she had decided to put off a decision until she had a chance to reflect on the Witness's astonishing revelations. Daughter of a *doge,* whatever that was. *Fabia* was an intriguing name, exotic. Aristocratic. She must practice thinking of herself as *the lady Fabia.* Three brothers? Ruler of a strategically important city?

Murder?

Like a mother goose, Bjaria led her entourage along a tended path through irregular parkland, up and down, winding between rocks and ancient trees from one shrine to another, all around the top of the hill. Other worshipers and clerics scuttled out of her way, wide-eyed. Today the monologue was on the history of Temple Island and Skjar itself, the need to preserve and restore. Although she did not mention Horth's gold, that was obviously what had provoked this interest.

She kept saying *very old.* "Holy ground from ancient times, even older than the Arcana in parts, evidence of *very old* primitive worship . . ." All the shrines were made of wood, some in styles of great antiquity, *very old.* The timbers themselves were quite recent, of course, but for centuries every building had been replaced at intervals of about twenty years, the copy reproducing the original as exactly as possible. This work was now overdue and being planned. Bjaria's only endearing quality was that conversation with her required no effort whatsoever, not even speech.

"This shrine of holy Weru is *very old,* perhaps the oldest of the preserved designs, because the gorge is called after Him and there is no doubt that in the so-called Expansionist Period the city regarded Weru as its patron god, but of course in those days Skjar was not much more than a pirates' strong-hold, although we mustn't say such things, must we, even if we know they're true, and anyway it was their expertise at building more seaworthy ships than anyone else that let the expansionists extend their sway over half the shores of Ocean, and all the lake so that was why holy Hrada was regarded as His consort and They were worshiped as joint patrons—"

Frena managed to squeeze in a word. "I have always understood that holy Hrada is a *virgin* goddess?"

"Well nowadays of course," the high priestess said airily, "but this was a long time ago." She barged ahead in blithe unawareness of what she had just said. "A donation of an embroidered scarf is traditional but we can supply a jeweled container for a reasonable fee . . ."

It was most curious that the seer had seemed so tolerant of the Dark One. It was also very comforting. Perhaps Frena's . . . Perhaps Paola Apicella had been both a Chosen and also the loving person whose memory Frena . . . Fabia . . . cherished. To believe that would resolve a whole mountain of misery and incomprehension.

"Holy Demern's shrine obviously dates from *very old* dynastic times when He and holy Veslih were guardians of Skjar, as you can see from the roofline and upturned gables and there is an inscription which seems to note the number of rebuildings . . ."

Did Frena really have any decision to make? The outcome was inevitable. Two days hence Horth would drive her here, to the Pantheon, with an escort of armed guards. Many sixty friends, employees, associates, and hangers-on would witness her dedication, including her renunciation of Xaran and all other gods outside the Twelve—of which she could remember none offhand. If she balked she would be dragged away and buried alive, which would absolutely ruin the afternoon—

"Did you say something?"

"Oh, no, Holiness." *Just a nervous snigger.* "My headache is much better. Do please continue."

"Then as I was saying, the so-called Democratic Interregnum does not seem to have left any lasting marks on the Pantheon, but of course it was very brief and there are conflicting reports on the religious developments of the period, and while the idea that holy Cienu was the divine sponsor of the revolution may explain why its effects were so transitory although naturally I do not mean to imply any disrespect toward . . ." And so on.

And so on.

Fabia had three brothers, three older brothers! Three! She had not had a chance to ask the Witness where they were, who they were, what they were. Would she like them or they like her? Would they have the same likes and dislikes she did? Had they been raised in palaces or kitchens? Had they been apprenticed to trades, trained to be doges, or perhaps even degraded to peasants? The moment she was *officially* informed of her true status, then she must inquire about her brothers. And warn them of their danger!

". . . course the oligarchy brought Skjar its greatest prosperity, because it concentrated on trade and thus claimed holy Ucr as its patron with Anziel as His consort because what good is wealth if it does not enrich our lives artistically and all of these reconstructions you see here date from that period just before Bloodlord Stralg overthrew the council which was over twenty years ago now—I can remember it but I'm sure you . . ."

Did the woman *never* stop talking?

Fourteen

FRENA WIGSON

arrived home only to be sucked into another whirlwind of meetings, arguments, and objections, which she suppressed with a dozen or so proclamations. She then demanded a cool tub, a fresh robe, and some refreshments served on her favorite balcony overlooking the harbor. The cut on her shoulder was still seeping blood. Inga tried again to fasten a bandage there, but even Frena was now wondering if she should send for a Sinurist.

She soon forgot it, though. Relaxing on a couch and nibbling candied sweetmeats while Plumna and Lilin played and Ni sang for her, gazing out at the blue Ocean framed in the canyon mouth, Frena shed almost all of her headache. The seer, had she been present, might have seen that as a sign that Frena had made her decision. She had not, of course; she was still weighing her options. She eventually felt strong enough to send for the archivist of the inferior inventories.

That meaningless title belonged to Master Pukar, one of Father's scribes. He came and went a lot, and even his official duties were mysterious. His unofficial duties—according to servants' gossip that Frena had collected over the years, and which the seer's remark this morning tended to confirm—included some very unsavory tasks around the house. That was one reason she disliked him. He was plump, and while some plumpness could suggest cuddliness—the quilted Bjaria's, for instance—his did not. He also seemed to be completely hairless; his mouth was loose and slobbery; he bore a perpetual odor of fish. He made her skin crawl in all directions.

She did not hear him approach over the strumming of Plumna's dulcimer and almost jumped off the coach when she realized he was standing there. A white linen wrap draped him from armpits to ankles. Wet lips smiled, fat hands clutched together on his potbelly, and his eyes did not meet hers.

"How may I serve my lady?"

Frena waved a hand to dismiss the girls, their departure giving her a moment to collect her wits. There was another couch available, but she did not invite him to sit down. He would not expect her to. She reached for a candied grape and a whiff of fish odor dissuaded her.

"I was informed today that you are a Chosen."

Master Pukar was standing just a fraction too close, smiling down at her body. He continued to do so.

"You do not wish to comment?" Frena demanded, rattled.

"Chosen for what, mistress?"

"A Chosen of—" She caught herself before she said the forbidden name. "A chthonian."

"Ah."

"That is a serious charge."

He sighed, scanning her thighs. "It is indeed. Naturally I deny it. I do have some dubious acquaintances, though. Does my mistress require some chthonic ritual performed? How many days since you bled?"

"*How dare you!* Insolence! I should have you flogged for that!" Her face burned painfully hot.

"I am so sorry," Pukar said, lisping slightly. "A natural misapprehension. Perhaps my lady will inform me how else—"

"I am well aware that you procure miscarriages for misguided servants. Most of them blame their troubles on love potions you sell to unscrupulous male servants. I do not normally discuss such matters with my father, but—"

"That fish will not bite, mistress." Pukar's smile had now settled on her left breast. "Your father refuses to know things he does not wish to know, and he values domestic harmony. I perform many little tasks that he desires but never specifically orders. If you are hoping to blackmail me with kitchen tattle, then you will be disappointed. You would endanger him also."

Frena took a few deep breaths to rein in her temper. He was cleverer than she had expected. "I am also aware of the fees you charge in such instances. Three nights from the pretty ones, briefer but more humiliating services from the older and plainer ones. You can likewise forget about blackmailing me into anything like that."

His bow was little more than a nod at her navel. "Then let us speak plainly, as . . ."—he smirked—". . . partners. Your mother was a Chosen. True, there is no evidence, but your father hired me soon after she was . . . 'returned to the womb,' as they say. One may speculate that I replaced her as provider of some lore or service. Now you are being forced into a dedication to the Twelve, so you must choose between them and the Dark One to whom your mother bound you. You wish to discuss a complete initiation."

"All of that is evil slander!"

The great white slug studied her left breast. "My humblest apologies. I was misled by the wound on my lady's shoulder into assuming that she had tried a sacrifice on her own."

"Wound?" Of course the maids would have chattered.

"Made by a sharp stone, I suspect? A metal blade is anathema. Ah, I see from your flush that I am correct. You even knew enough to use your left hand, obviously. The blood sacrifice is the essential core, but very dangerous without proper procedure and peripheral ritual. Guidance is essential. Shall we discuss terms?"

"Gold."

"What a sweet voice you have." His stare wandered down to the vicinity of her hips. "How much gold?"

"What exactly am I buying?"

"Guidance. Instruction. Merely spilling a few drops of blood on the earth will not suffice. You must offer sacrifice in a place sacred to the Mother of All and swear the correct oaths. There are rituals, as I said, but it is a brief service, light compared to the years of toil and humiliation some cults require. I should be happy to provide a knowledgeable mentor to lead you to the place and guide you through your vows to the Ancient One."

No question that the promised mentor would be fat, hairless, and slippery-eyed. *Blood and dark*? No, that wasn't right. *Cold earth* was part of it, though.

"What powers does She grant and what corban must I swear?"

Pukar beamed at Frena's thighs, so enthusiastically that she wondered if he could see through the cloth. "She rewards according to your offering. You swear only to endure. She is also Death, but when She gathers in the night, She knows and spares Her own. If I told you my true age, you would not believe me."

"Yesterday I saw a mob burying a Chosen alive."

"How do you know he was a Chosen, mistress? How did they?"

"You mean, if he dies, he is innocent; if not, he is guilty?"

"I never said She granted immortality. We all die in time."

Frena shivered. "I will have to think about it."

"But not too long, mistress. Your appointment with the Twelve is only two days away and it will bind you with knots you will find hard to dismiss as mere insincerity if you later wish to acknowledge Mother Xaran. My! I spoke Her holy name and am not struck down. The mentor I mentioned will naturally require payment in advance. Five measures of gold."

"Never. Two might just be possible."

"Five. May the ground below your feet be bountiful, mistress." Master Pukar bowed to her crotch and departed as silently as he had come.

◆

Every day must end eventually.

Frena sat up, trembling. *Darkness? . . . noise . . .*

Rain at last! It spattered on the floor under the windows—not a full monsoon, but a heavy downpour even so. The air seemed just as hot, but would cool soon. She rose from her rumpled sheet and stumbled over to close the shutters by the trivial gleam of her night lamp. Then she flopped back down on the edge of the platform, head in hands, and thought it over yet again.

Pukar was impossible. Supposing she could meet his price, which she couldn't, she could never trust him to deliver what he promised. Even the seer had not been certain that he was what he would not deny being.

Common sense said she should take her problem to Father . . . to Horth—she could *not* think "*foster* mother" or "*foster* father"!—but he had lied to her all her life and she still did not know how much he knew. Had he been aware that his wife was a Chosen, or was that one of the things he refused to know, as Pukar put it? She could not ask Horth for help.

Perhaps there was a clue there. If the Chosen were the cult of Xaran, then it was a cult like no other—no great temples, no priests or teachers, just solitary devotees, hunted and hated. Saltaja needed a puppet to run that Celebre place, and a Chosen would never be a puppet. A Chosen might even have the power to avenge Paola's murder!

Frena-Fabia had to solve this alone. Her shoulder was bleeding again. Offer blood in a sacred place, odious Pukar had said. There might be one such place close at hand.

◆

Not daring to bring the lamp, she fumbled along the corridor. This wing of the mansion mostly held public rooms. Only Father and she slept in it; the dozen guest rooms were never used. The swordsmen patrolling the grounds were not supposed to come in, but might if they saw a light moving around. Her toes found the top step. She began to descend, being very careful because she remembered the black carvings and did not want to send any thundering down ahead of her. Her sandals made tiny hushing sounds on the marble.

That awful night of three years ago haunted her still. Then, as now, the house had been dark and seemingly deserted. Then, as now, she had seen a light under the door of her father's counting room, for he rarely stopped work to eat or sleep. Then, as now, she had gone in the opposite direction and on down the stairs. Since then the staircase had been made wider and more imposing; her mother's old quarters had been ripped out to extend the inner court, which was now surrounded by a covered walk. She floated along this cloister until she stood at the archway nearest the place where Paola had gone to die. If anywhere nearby was sacred to the Old One it must be there. It was certainly sacred to Frena.

The rain had grown heavier, although still nothing compared with what would come when the wet season arrived in earnest. No wind penetrated the confines of the building, but rain fell down into the court with its persistent hiss and the staccato plop of drips from eaves and branches. It magnified the heavy leafy and earthy scents of the garden. It was life, the life-giving gift of the gods. Shivering, but not from cold, Frena stood in the cloister and remembered that persistent dream. The door. Her mother. Beckoning. She could not recall any dream so vivid. *Blood and cold earth* . . . No, not that. *Blood and birth* . . . And something else. A saying? A proverb? A poem?

Words she associated with her mother—Paola Apicella, not some mythical aristocrat far away on another Face.

She was going to be drenched. Water would do her no harm and a wet towel or two in her room would raise no unspoken questions in the morning, but a sopping-wet robe must provoke speculation. She slid the fine linen off her shoulders and let it fall. Yes, that felt right. Mother-naked, she stepped through the arch, out onto wet paving. The rain was warm and heavy enough that in moments she was as wet as she could be, wet as the moment of her birth. She hurried along the path, splashing in puddles, feeling her hair settle into clammy ropes on her back, feeling the caress of leaves as somehow friendly, as if plants were happy in the deluge.

Across the grass. Here. Here was where she had found her mother. This far Paola had crawled, shedding bandages and splints. She had not managed to remove them all, but when she reached this point she had been almost as naked as her daughter was now. And here she had died, on the bare earth. Bare earth? No, *cold* earth!

Frena crouched down and peered into the shrubbery. The bushes were grown larger, like small trees, and now the site was marked by the five stones that traditionally outlined a grave. Leaves dancing in the rain tapped her shoulders as she wriggled in under the branches.

Yes! That was it: *Blood and birth; death and the cold earth.*

She rubbed fingers on the cut-made-by-stone, then laid her blood-smeared hand on the black loam. It felt soft, strangely comforting. Comfort swelled into joy. There was love there, and warmth, and a presence. She sensed a murmur of welcome that was not heard, an embrace that was not felt, a familiar scent not smelled.

"Mother?" she whispered.

The answer was still just love. *Endure!* it whispered.

She grew cold. Eventually she tired of waiting and retreated to the cloister. She was playing a dangerous game, now. Solitary rituals in the dead of night were enough to condemn anyone. Even wet footmarks in the cloisters might be deadly evidence. She made a grotesquely long step through the arch to put herself on her discarded robe, then dried her feet and legs before replacing her sandals. She hurried through the darkness to her room.

There she stretched out on the platform and said a final prayer. The Ancient One was the Lady of Dreams. *Send me a dream,* Frena prayed. *Not that one about the flood and the door. I got that. Something new! Show me something helpful!*

✦

The Woman was taking her turn in the front rank around the fire, eight anonymous people huddled up tight for warmth, cowering down in vain effort to stay inside the windbreak of the next row out. The wind was sharp bronze, cutting through all her wrappings of wool and fur, and the cold of the ground seeped upward into her flesh. Her neighbor coughed; other coughs replied. There was not enough air, and what there was burned throats and lungs, cracked lips and nostrils. The men's beards were caked with ice.

Camp had been pitched in a hollow that offered no shelter from the killer wind, and even the hulking Werists lacked energy to pitch tents. That sputtering fire would die out long before dawn. The caravan had not passed even a twiggy shrub in days, but tonight they had found a mummy, some ancient traveler who had died there and just dried up, lying by the wayside. The Heroes had broken the husk in pieces and tipped the last of the oil on it. Thanks to the wind, it burned.

Against the black velvet of the heavens, the stars were beyond belief, webs and gauze of diamond dust. Very far to the west, a conical peak showed over the horizon, gleaming like a ghost. That was Varakats, the ice devils said, the sign that they had crossed over the Edge. But the long descent still lay ahead; everyone understood now that some of them were not going to make it. Perhaps none would, and future travelers would use them as tinder.

The wind was a razor up close; farther away it was a carnivore whining amid the rocks. The worst burden of all was lack of sleep. To lie down was to suffocate in the thin air. From now on, without fuel to melt snow, there would be no drinking water, making thirst a greater torment than hunger or fatigue.

Massive hands grabbed her and dragged her bodily over the people behind her, who ducked and raised arms to defend themselves. She was dumped outside the outer circle, sprawling backward, trying to defend the precious burden inside her parka. The Werist who had done this stepped over the sitters to take her place next the fire.

"You are supposed to protect us, pig!" she cried hoarsely.

He ignored her, either not understanding her tongue or just knowing she lacked strength to cause trouble. The ice devils made no aggressive display of *brawny bare limbs up here as they did on the plains; they wore cocoons of wool and fur like everyone else and then wrapped their palls around on the outside, but they still saw violence as the solution to all problems.*

The tiny bundle inside her furs was torpid and cold. She had known since the hostleader called for camp to be pitched that the time had come, but lethargy had stayed her hand. If she did not do the thing now, it would be too late. She crept away from the camp unseen, or if she was seen, no one now cared enough to call her back. No one cared if she lived or died, or if her charge lived or died. Soon they would stop caring if they died themselves, and that would be the end. Then they would all die together from lack of will.

Beyond the first high boulders she located a patch of rock blown clear of dust. What she was to do must be done very quickly. There was no light other than starlight, but darkness was her friend. She could see quite well enough for her purposes, the Mother's purposes.

She threw down her mitts. Her fingers were icy inside them already and would swiftly freeze without them. The cold earth here had been frozen solid for untold ages. She laid a hand on a polished rocky surface and opened her mind to the deep tide of the world, the comforting presence of the Mother. It came instantly, an exigent upwelling of power that startled her, dazzled her, and almost made her pull away. She realized that she had never communicated through raw bedrock before. Always she had known the power as a nourishing force filtered through gentle, living loam. Here the underlying elemental strength was undiluted, undisguised, and all its darker facets shone with terrifying brilliance, as if in this immemorial frozen waste the life force had been frustrated and sought release through her flesh.

Was what she planned even possible? What would such intensity do to the babe? The child might easily be consumed and die, but it could certainly not last another pot-boiling without a blessing, so the risk must be taken.

She selected an angular flake of rock, dragged up a sleeve, and made a cut on the back of her wrist. She let blood dribble on the rock, laid her hand on the stain. Then came recognition, acknowledgment of sacrifice. And love, of course. But ruthless love, love in its most adamantine aspect, the sort of love that will count no costs. Again she hesitated, fearing . . . But it must be done, for better or worse.

"Mother," she whispered, "hear me, help me. Grant me strength, Mother, to succor this little one I bring You. Grant her the strength to live, so that she does not die in this horrid place."

Now she must move fast. She tugged with laces and buttons, clumsy in her haste. There could be little in her teats to suck, and the babe at her breast had not cried for ages. She pulled it out, foul in its soiled wrapping because there had been no usable moss around for days. It whimpered faintly as the cold bit. She wondered if she had waited too long. The suppliant should be stripped for first contact, but there was no time; a body so minute would not survive more than a few heartbeats in this temperature.

She turned the babe over, and made a cut on the underside of the tiny thigh. For a moment she thought there was not enough blood in it to bleed, but then a drop or two fell on the rock.

"Mother, I pray You choose this child to be one of Your own. Take her living body, or take her spirit, as You please. But I beseech You to give her life that she may serve You in future days."

She pressed the tiny hand to the tinier bloodstains, already frozen. The child uttered a sudden lusty cry, as of outrage at such treatment. Then another, even stronger.

With a shout of joy the woman snatched it up and plunged it back into the warmth of her bosom. It was like embracing a fish, but the tiny lips found her nipple at once and began to suck. She sighed with rapture as she felt the milk surge. A tide of warmth flowed out from her teat, through the babe and through her also. Even the love of a man, even the ecstasies Stavan had been able to inspire in her, could hardly compare with the sucking of a babe.

She closed her garments over her charge, warm already.

"There, there!" she muttered. "Now you are Hers, as I am. But you will live. It is better so."

◆

When her heart stopped hammering so crazily, Fiena rose and found her bronze hand mirror. She examined the back of her thigh by the jerky light of a lamp almost out of oil. She found no scar there, but that was hardly surprising after so long and so much growth. She sprawled back down on the platform, knowing she would sleep no more that night. How could she possibly find five measures of gold, trust Master Pukar if she did, get away with him unobserved to wherever the sacred place was, or even trust him not to deal foul with her then? She had only one more night left.

No headache now—she had made her decision. She knew what she wanted to do. For Paola's sake. But she would need help from the Old One.

Fifteen

THEREK HRAGSON

paced his chambers in twilight gloom. *Click . . . click . . . click . . .* Where was that accursed seer? What could be keeping the woman?

He paused at the window to stare down the trail to Tryfors. The sky was a wild effulgence of red, orange, and salmon, with the sun a distorted bloody blur. Sunsets lasted forever in Nardalborg.

He spun around and headed back. *Click . . . click . . . click . . .* Indoors, in this light, he could not see his bench and table, or even his sleeping platform. He timed his pacing by the scratch of his claws on the boards.

From the east window he could look up the trail, toward the Ice, and there the sky was already velvet black, sprayed with stars. This morning he had studied the incoming caravan descending the pass for an age before the watch noticed it and sounded the alarm. He'd been depressed to see how small it was. In the old days there would have been an endless train of slaves bent under their masters' booty; but now there were just a handful of traders, a dozen or so repatriated wounded, and a couple of apparently healthy Werists whose satchels doubtless contained dispatches from Stralg.

Why was that Witness taking so long? It would be dark soon.

Back again to the west. He'd intended to return to Tryfors right after the oath taking, days ago. Gods knew he had enough work waiting down there with green troops pouring into the city on their way to die for Stralg in Florengia, and Heth did a fine job of running Nardalborg without his hostleader breathing all over his collar. Therek had stayed because of that accursed Orlad hostage. The look in the kid's eyes! Not when Therek hung the chain on him and gave him that disgusting ceremonial embrace—he'd been only a hard, warm blur then. But earlier, a few minutes before, when that drunken ruin Gzurg Hrothgatson had been announcing his distorted judgment, the brownie had been lurking at the back of the hall. He had known what was coming, obviously, without realizing that anyone was watching him. Ha! Therek had seen the treason burning in those freakish black eyes.

So instead of heading back to Tryfors the next morning, Therek had sent for a seer to join him, and she'd arrived by yak wagon this morning. All he needed was her confirmation of what his own judgment told him—just in case Saltaja ever asked—and he was going to put that young brute to death. Chain collar? Hang him in it!

Knuckles rapped on timber.

He said "Enter!" and pretended to study the scenery.

"Lord!"

It was a man's voice—probably Heth, but one word was not enough to identify him. Therek could not make out the color of his sash. "At ease. What do you want?"

"My lord is kind." Heth straightened. "A caravan has come."

"I saw."

"It brought these for you." Came the distinctive sound of clay tablets being clattered down on wood. "And others, of course, which I will order sent on?" He meant, *Do you want to peek at them first?* It was years since Therek had been at Nardalborg when an inbound caravan arrived, so Heth was not sure of his procedures. He was smart enough to guess that there might be such procedures, though.

"Send them on by all means. I assume the largest collection is addressed to my sister. Did you think I would pry into her mail?"

"Of course not, my lord."

He would if he dared. He'd risked it once, just once, many years ago— one night when he was monumentally drunk he had started to brood on the unfairness of Stralg sending all the latest news to Saltaja and almost none to him, so he'd told a scribe to pick out the latest of several tablets from the date on the covers, then crack it open and read out the contents. Covers were broken in transit easily enough, but apparently seers could tell the difference. He hadn't known that; his sister had, and her summons had arrived about a season later. He'd tried to ignore it, mentally telling her to go to the Old One, but he'd been too afraid that she might do just that, but not in the way he wanted, and in the end he'd obeyed. For some reason she had been at Jat-Nogul that year, at the far side of the Face, and it had taken him all winter to get there. When he finally did, she had merely slapped his face, told him she would kill him if he ever did it again, and sent him straight home. At least, that was how he remembered it, but his aides had insisted he'd been gone for three days. He had never dared tamper with Saltaja's correspondence since.

Uncertainly Heth added, "Shall I send in a scribe . . . my lord?"

"No. What's the gossip?" That might be more credible than Stralg's fictions. "What news from Florengia? Any great battles won?"

"Indeed, yes, my lord. The Heroes are jubilant over a great victory at a place called Miona. The rebels attempted to besiege your honored brother there, my lord. Although he was seriously outnumbered, he cleverly lured them into the town and then withdrew, burning it down on top of them. Their losses were enormous."

It was impossible to tell from the huntleader's flat military tone whether he believed that fable. Therek did not. He would give half his talons to be able to see Heth's expression, but at close quarters faces were only a blur to him now.

"Were they there in person, these Heroes?"

"I don't believe so, my lord."

"Where is this Miona? Near the pass, or far away?"

"I . . . I didn't think to ask, my lord." Heth's voice sounded more wary.

Therek laughed and turned back to the windows. "Come here."

Heth moved to his side. "My lord?"

"You don't understand what's happening, lad," the satrap said quietly. "Shouldn't call you that, though, should I? You're what . . . twenty-eight?"

"Thirty."

"Ah. Well, at thirty and a huntleader you ought to see the game in the shrubbery." He forced a little chuckle and laid an arm around Heth's magnificent shoulders. "Remember back when you were initiated? You wanted to charge off to Florengia right away. You'd have set off alone that very night if I'd let you. I insisted you wait until you'd made at least flankleader."

"I remember." The tone was flat, admitting nothing. "And then you told me it was too late, that I'd missed the war."

"I believed it, lad. I did. But then he made his terrible mistake."

"You mean in initiating natives, lord?"

"Of course I do. What else could I mean? Those mud-faced, black-eyed, slithery cheats! Traitors, all of them!"

"They will suffer for their treachery."

"Will they? You think so? The Florengian horde probably outnumbers Stralg's now. Their warriors are as lethal. Why do you think he keeps screaming for more men? He is *losing!*"

"A temporary setback."

"I don't think so." *Click . . . click . . . click . . .* Therek realized he was pacing again. "There is less ice on their side of the Edge!"

"My lord is kind." Undoubtedly Heth knew what Therek meant, but a good Werist must never say such things.

Therek could. "Even for couriers it is easier to cross in this direction, son, with the harder going on the downhill side. To bring a horde in this direction would be *much* easier. That's the scorpion in the blanket! That's why the war must continue at all costs. If Stralg cannot hold the north—Celebre and the road home—then he is going to come scrabbling back over the Edge with a Florengian horde breathing on his collar. You think Nardalborg can hold them? Those brown horrors will pour into Vigaelia in their sixty-sixties, burning our cities, raping our women! And all this because Stralg trusted Florengians!" He was ashamed to hear his voice break. "They killed your brothers!"

"Yes, lord."

In his time, Therek Hragson had fathered four sons and some daughters on a variety of women. He'd given the women good settlements, letting them keep the girls while he hung on to the sons. Now he wished he'd thought of keeping the girls for grandsons, but he hadn't. Three sons he'd admitted to, and every one had sworn to Weru and taken the brass collar. He had said farewell to each of them here in Nardalborg and watched them march off to fight for their uncle. Hrag Therekson, Stralg Therekson, Nars Therekson—mighty warriors all, and Florengian oath-breakers had killed them.

"That's why I keep you secret, son. That's why you must bear the shameful name of Hethson. Stralg took three of my sons. The Florengians killed them. And Karvak's two. And three of Saltaja's. Two of Horold's died on the way there." If either Stralg or Saltaja ever learned about Heth, they'd take him as well.

"Yes, lord."

"Florengian swine! I hate them, hate them! And that stinking brown whelp of a Florengian here in Nardalborg—*you* talked me into letting him take the tests, Huntleader! I won't forget that. Then that bonehead Gzurg actually *passed* him, so I had to give him his collar. I had to watch him spill his filthy blood at my feet. You made me accept an oath from a stinking brown Florengian traitor, knowing every word he uttered was lie. I even had to embrace the scum!" He shivered with revulsion. He still wondered how he'd managed not to strangle the maggot there and then. All he needed was a word from the seer and he would do it. Personally. Why was she taking so long?

"Well, what do you want?"

"Just bringing you the dispatch and the news, my lord."

"That's a lie. You're no page. Out with it." He might not be able to see his son's face at this range, but he knew how to glare at it, and he heard the worry in the reply.

"My lord is kind. I came to say, my lord . . . to inform you . . . I have given permission for the cadets to touch the Presence. Tonight. My lord."

"No! No, no, no! That's ridiculous." Accidentally jostling a bench, Therek roared in fury and slapped it across the room; he heard it shatter against the wall. "They're not ready. They can't be. You're making a—"

"Father, will you hear me?"

Therek could not recall ever hearing Heth give him that title. It winded him. The Florengian mutineers had butchered three of his sons, he must not lose the fourth. He nodded dumbly, staring out at the eastward stars.

"Father, I have never seen a runtleader like Orlad. Every morning I tell him what I want done next and he's already done it! He's run those boys through six days' training in half that. I know it sounds impossible, but he's done it. All twelve of them! They're reeling. It's inhuman, but he's done it. They're out on their feet, but he keeps on pushing and they respond. They follow him like goslings. He treats himself harder than any and they follow. They know all the responses, word-perfect. I tested, my lord—of course I did! And I swear they are as ready to touch the Presence as any cadets I have ever seen. Don't waste this, lord! I beg you! If they don't go tonight they'll collapse and it will be a thirty before they can be brought up to readiness again—if they ever can be. Twelve cadets, Father, *all twelve ready!* Gods know we need them."

Therek growled deep in his throat. Readying a man to touch the Presence for the first time was the trickiest part of initiation. The postulant must be strung to breaking point, on the very edge of snapping, or the ritual would fail, and a first failure often meant no later success. It might even kill him. Exhaustion, hunger, and lack of sleep were all vital, but too much and the boys just crumpled. Heth was rarely wrong on this.

"Take eleven and break that other one's neck."

"That won't work, lord! They're following him. Without Orlad they'd just collapse in confusion. They're beyond thinking."

"No! I've told you, you can never trust a Florengian!"

That should have been the end of it. Werists did not argue. Incredibly, Heth persisted.

"Father, if what you say about the war—"

"No! He's a hostage! And a hostage for Celebre, which even Stralg admits is likely to prove critical. Saltaja asked me about him in her last letter, if he was still alive and available. Suppose the old king, or whatever he is, dies and Stralg calls for Orlad to replace him—and we send him a *Werist?* What sort of puppet ruler would a Werist make?"

"I can't see Orlad as anyone's puppet even now, lord."

Again knuckles rapped on the door. With relief, Therek barked "Enter!" This time it was the seer—he could make out the white blur of her robes. He barely waited for her to close the door.

"Well? What kept you? What's he thinking? He's plotting treason, yes?"

"We are not alone, lord." She was a fussy slip of a thing, this one, and young, from the sound of her voice. Women! It had been so long!

"I am well aware of that."

"As you will. The reason I took so long is that you forbade me to let anyone know what I was doing. Since I couldn't ask him direct questions, or have others do so, I had to rely on chance conversations, and he is currently so exhausted that he is barely capable of speech. The arrival of the caravan provided a fortunate opportunity for—"

"And what *is* he plotting? Is he subverting his entire flank against me?"

"Far from it, lord. What he says is exactly what he means, with absolutely no reservations. He is fanatically loyal to you and Huntleader Heth. He admires you so much he will not even let the cadets refer to you by the nicknames others use. He is determined to see the entire class initiated in record time, and his motive for doing so is so that he can join your brother and fight against the Florengian Werists."

"Wrong! You're *wrong!* You have *got* to be wrong!"

The woman screamed before he reached her.

Heth jumped between them and grabbed his father in a mighty hug. "Satrap! Wait!"

Therek struggled free. "She is lying! That cannot be right. He's a Florengian himself."

"Please let the seer finish, my lord. Carry on, Witness."

The Witness was curled up in a ball on the floor. "Carry on?" Her voice was shrill and shaky. "Had you not moved so fast, Huntleader, that crazy monstrosity—"

"Get up!"

She unwound. "He was going to *rip* me! You explain to him what would have happened then, because I have tried and failed. The agreement between the Heroes and the Witnesses would have—"

"Oh, shut up, you prattling sow," Heth said. "And get up. He didn't touch you. Tell him why Orlad hates his fellow Florengians."

"As long as the satrap behaves," she whined, dusting herself off. "The boy doesn't hate all Florengians, at least not much. He despises the Florengian Werists, regards them all as oath-breakers, because the first initiates had sworn loyalty to Bloodlord Stralg."

"You see, Father? All his life, here in Nardalborg, he has been derided for—"

"Blood!" Therek strode back to the window to let the cold wind cool his rage. "Stupid floozy. So you tell me there is one Florengian I can trust, just one who will not turn on me the first chance he gets?"

"I do not prophesy. I say only that you can trust him now."

"Ha! So I *can't* trust him?"

"I repeat what I just said."

"I think what the seer means, lord," Heth said, "is that fanatical loyalty can be fragile. There is no room for compromise in such allegiance. If a man who supports a cause fanatically decides that the cause is unworthy, he will change sides and support the opposition with the same absolute zeal. Am I correct, Witness?"

"I report facts, Huntleader. I do not make hypotheses."

"Blood!" Therek said again. "A dead Florengian wouldn't even make good manure. Read me that report."

"I am not a scribe, my lord."

"I know that, half-wit! But you can tell me what it says."

He always had a Witness read his correspondence to him, because he did not trust scribes. When he dictated anything important, he had the seer read it back to him later. He tapped claws on the floor impatiently while she shuffled the little bricks.

"All of these are from Bloodlord Stralg to you. This is the first—"

"Begin with the latest, dung-head!"

There was a pause as she cracked the clay envelope on the table edge and extracted the tablet itself.

" 'In the sacred name of the most mighty—' "

"Never mind all that offal! I can guess he begins with a demand for more Werists, right?" He always did.

"Er . . . yes, my lord. He, er . . . he says that he must follow up his recent success at Miona, that the enemy are summer people and will not fight in winter, but to Vigaelians their weather is nothing, so he has a natural advantage in—"

"Toad piss! Florengia has no seasons; winter and summer all alike. How many this time?"

"Er . . . he expects Tryfors to supply one complete pack, at least two flanks being experienced men. You are also to send your best huntleader . . . my lord."

Impossible! Therek could not possibly spare forty-nine men and he was certainly not sending Heth. Heth was being discreetly silent. In the last few years he had watched men head out in sixties and sixty-sixties and only a dribble of cripples return.

"How many more caravans does he expect me to squeeze in before winter?"

"He did not say."

"Then how many men in total, mm?"

"He did not say, my lord . . . here."

Therek missed it, but Heth didn't. "Where *does* he say it?"

"With respect, my lord, I am authorized to advise only the hostleader."

"Answer him!" Therek bellowed, and then answered for himself. "You read the other dispatches! *You can read them without opening them?*" Why had he never thought of that? The bag-head cows had never told him they could do that. They never volunteered anything! He wondered if Saltaja knew they had that ability.

"I cannot read a sealed dispatch, lord."

"But you can tell the meaning?" Heth asked.

"If I am close enough to it," the seer admitted glumly, "and the content is important."

Therek chortled. "And were you close enough to the other dispatches that arrived today? Of course you were. You wouldn't have missed that chance to snoop. What did my dear brother write to our sister, mm? Tell me that!"

"All of it, lord?"

"Start with the most interesting news and I'll tell you when to stop."

She sighed. "Yes, lord. He wrote that he suffered a major defeat at Reggoni Bridge. Rebel Hordeleader Cavotti had sabotaged—"

"The Mutineer!" Therek screamed.

"The Mutineer, then. He had sabotaged the bridge and it collapsed when your brother's hunt was crossing, dropping the men into a gorge. The vanguard was isolated. It was attacked by the freedom fighters—"

"Rebels! Oath-breakers!"

"—and destroyed. The bloodlord lost more than sixteen sixty men, almost an entire host. He wants as many replacements . . . His exact words in this case, my lord, were that your honored sister is to send 'as many men as the lunatic Therek can be forced to move over the Edge.' My lord."

Therek contemplated wringing her neck and reluctantly decided not to. "Heth, can you get five more caravans out before winter?" They had never managed six in a season before.

"I can but try, my lord. The weather will decide."

"Can you make the caravans bigger?"

"No!" Heth said firmly. "Not without more slaves and more mammoths. And if we did find some way to stock the food caches for more than four sixty men, most of the shelters will barely hold even that many. They were built for smaller caravans. Four sixty is the absolute limit . . . my lord."

Then Therek had an idea, a beautiful idea, a shining constellation of an idea. "Don't bother reserving a space for Warrior Orlad."

"My lord is kind," Heth muttered uncertainly.

"All those recruits . . . eager but inexperienced," the satrap mumbled. He chuckled gleefully. But he couldn't do it here, not at Nardalborg. Not one of themselves. Very bad for morale, that would be. "Tonight you may proceed as requested. I am sure Runtleader Orlad will do very well. Give all the cadets my best wishes. Dismissed."

"My lord is kind."

"Oh, and one other thing . . . When, in due course, Runtleader Orlad is initiated, as I am sure he will be . . . send him to me, in Tryfors."

He heard Heth shut the door. The white blur of the Witness remained, cowering as far away from him as she could get. All those splendid young new warriors! Before sending them off to battle, it would be only fair to give them some practice in running down Florengian Werists.

ſixteen

FRENA WIGSON

spent another day in a blur of preparations for her dedication banquet. Replies to the invitations came flooding in—not that baked clay tablets could flood, but many of the responses were brought by runners, leggy youngsters capable of reciting astonishingly long messages verbatim. They did not exactly flood either, but they did trickle sweat onto floor tiles, for the rain had stopped and the heat was more insufferable than ever.

Food was arriving on groaning oxcarts. The beer was brewing, filling the entire residence with heady odors of yeast. Still more decisions had to be squeezed in between dress fittings and the uncountable little crises that ran everywhere like arpeggios on a dulcimer. Horth was nowhere to be seen. Although his days were always devoted to business, when Frena was at home he usually managed to share a meal with her—nibbling barley cakes and sipping ibex milk while she, like as not, gorged on goose in ginger or trout stuffed with oysters. That day she dined alone, while Vignor the storyteller chanted some of his ancient tales to keep her from brooding. She saw Master Pukar just once, in passing. He smiled and bowed. She nodded and swept on by. She would sooner trust a fireasp.

Still, every day ends. The time came when she could bolt the door on Inga and Lilin and the rest, on her father and his staff, on Pukar and the world. Exhausted, she rolled herself out like dough on her sleeping platform and closed her eyes. At that point the Problem leaped at her like a starving catbear.

The mother she had loved had belonged to the Old One and she herself had been promised to that goddess. Even without the previous night's vision, it should have been obvious that only divine aid could have brought a tiny baby through the Edgelands alive. For Paola's sake, Frena should honor that promise and make her dedication to Xaran, not the Twelve. But how could she manage it, and with so little time? Obviously her prayer had been heard. She had been shown the past. Tonight she must ask for guidance for the immediate future. Exhausted though she was, she had no trouble staying awake until the household slept.

Muffled in a dark robe, she felt safely invisible as she crept along the corridor on her pilgrimage. Her father was still at work, a sliver of light showing under his door. When she reached the archway out to the grass, she stopped to listen. Very far away she could hear the inevitable mating cats, yapping dogs, and drunken revelry from the sailors' hostels in Fishgut Alley. The house itself was a tomb. *Bad thought!* The stars that shone just now above Kyrn—the Wagon, Graben's Sword, Ishrop and Ishniar—were almost never visible in muggy, canyon-bound Skjar. But nothing stirred nearby, and she had no excuse not to proceed.

She hurried through the gardens to the grave. She was of two minds about stripping, but in the end it seemed wisest not to dirty her robe, so she removed it and hung it on a branch. The cut on her shoulder had scabbed over, but she found a sharp flake—probably builders' marble—and scratched out a few drops of blood.

"Mother?" Feeling absurd whispering to earthworms; it was hard to remember how serious this was. There was none of the *presence* she had felt before. Last night had been mystery and sanctity. Tonight was pure farce. "Mother . . . Xaran . . ." She had never spoken that name aloud before. It sent such a thrill of fear through her that, stubbornly, she repeated it.

"Most Holy Xaran, I will swear fealty to You at Your holy place if You will guide me. I will swear by *blood and birth; death and the cold earth,* if only You will show me how."

Somehow an appeal to Paola Apicella had become a prayer to the Mother of Lies, but there was no perceptible answer. Eventually Frena rose and returned to her room, feeling rather sheepish and reminding herself that the Old One spoke to her children in dreams. There might yet be an answer.

✦

Paola Apicella wore the chill of the night like a cloak of ice, but that was mostly because she was still so weak. She could not lift a full spadeful of dirt, only spoonfuls, and she could not have dug at all had the soil not been so loose. She shivered in the wind. The spade made tiny shuff . . . shuff . . . *noises. She had come all alone, because the others would not have let her come at all, and they would not have known the right place to dig. She had let the Mother guide her, so she was sure.*

Shuff . . . shuff . . . the air smelled of decay and death.

She had gone into labor just as the ice devils started driving off the herds and the men ran out to stop them. By the time her water broke, the men were all dead. By the time the long labor was over, the women and boys had finished burying them . . . here, in a mass grave.

Shuff . . . shuff . . . They had told her the babe would not live, she should not name him. But she had named him after his father. She wanted him so much, and she had tried so hard. He had struggled, been a fighter, but it had done no good. The Mother had taken him back. Praise the Mother.

Shuff . . . The spade struck something soft, not a rock. Stavan's arm, perhaps. The hole was not very deep, but it would have to do. She paused to catch her breath, wipe her forehead. She was cold and yet sweating. She must finish this quickly.

She took up the little bundle, little Stav, unwrapped him enough for a last kiss, and then she knelt and laid him in his father's arms. She spoke a prayer to the Old One that She might care for them both. Then Paola filled in the hole and went back across the field to the village.

◆

The cottage was cold. She was hungry, for the outlanders had stripped the village of everything edible, even the dogs. She curled up on the mat in the blanket that still bore Stavan's familiar scent. Her breasts ached with milk. No food in the village, no men, but that was not her concern. She was beyond caring.

She must have slept then, because she was awakened by deep male voices shouting in some unknown tongue. So the ice devils must have returned. They could not be looking for food this time.

Screaming, then more shouting, then the door of the hut being kicked open, flaming torches streaming fire in the dark . . . She cowered back in the far corner of her bedding, not afraid, just too hungry to care, too bereft. They yelled at her in their guttural tongue, then a smaller man spoke at her in Florengian with a twisted accent, talking about babies, about food.

◆

It had been a rich man's house, for it had stone walls, tiled floors, and solid furniture, but now it reeked of the ice devils, that repellent stink, half animal, half unwashed man. They put Paola in a room to wait, but there was a fire for light and warmth—hunger had made her so cold!—and one of them came back and thrust a bowl of gruel at her. She scooped it up with fingers and gulped it down, almost choking; it was lifesaving.

Then a woman screamed, angry male voices rumbled, more torches with oily flames poured into the room. Behind them came a man half naked, carrying a small package. He thrust it at Paola, almost threw it at her. Its shrill wails brought back the pain in her breasts. She pulled up her smock at once and put the babe to suck. The crying stopped and ripples of joy flowed through her. Not little Stav, but someone to love, to live for, to take her milk. Boy or girl? She had not thought to look.

She looked up and saw the woman in the doorway, staring. She was a Florengian, with milk-swollen breasts visible through a badly ripped dress. One side of her face was red and puffed; eye swelling, lips bruised, hair torn. The man barked something impatiently. He had bloody scratches near his eyes. She started forward, he caught her arm. Was she the mother or just another wet nurse now wanted for other duties?

The girl lifted her smock to let the woman see the babe sucking, and smiled to say that she would love and cherish it, be it boy or girl. For a moment they stared at each other, and then the woman's spirit seemed to crumble. She nodded resignedly. The man snarled and thrust her out the door ahead of him, impatient to do what he wanted; she went in silence, resisting no more. All that mattered was that the ice devils had given Paola a child to feed, so they would have to feed her also.

Praise the Old One, who had answered her prayer!

ſeventeen

BENARD CELEBRE

was already hammering marble when the priests began their morning psalms. That was the last possible moment he could leave if he was to reach the palace at sunrise; keeping a Werist waiting was a sure road to unhappiness. Reluctantly he tossed maul and chisel into the shed, exchanged his smock for the new secondhand loincloth he had purchased with the copper Ingeld had given him, absentmindedly wiped his hands on it, weighted down the drape with the chunks of rock he used for that purpose, and set off at a trot.

In Benard's absence, Thod was supposed to help Sugthar the potter, which meant he would mostly ogle his adored Thilia.

Satrap Horold's orders that Benard visit the Whiterim quarry had seemed like deliverance from certain death at the time, but there had been no signs of Cutrath since then, so the matter no longer felt urgent. In fact, the trip was unnecessary. He could tell the priests what he needed and they would send word to the quarry master to cut the block and deliver it on the next spring flood.

Furthermore, Benard had started work on the third block of marble. If it could not be holy Weru, it must serve for another god. No sooner thought than realized—he had hardly begun to consider the matter when holy Anziel flooded him with inspiration. Never had he felt Her divine fire so strongly, as if the stone had become transparent and he saw the goddess Herself standing inside it, looking just as he had seen Hiddi that night at the temple. Without models or sketches or even guidelines on the block, he started cutting away everything that was not Hiddi to expose his statue of Anziel. Already he had the rough shape outlined. To leave it like that was agony; he was going to be thoroughly miserable every minute he was away from his work.

✦

Having gone around the long way rather than cut through the palace, he arrived breathless at the stable yard. Even there he kept a wary eye open for Werists, for they would not consider mere toe-tramping or sucker-punching covered by Horold's edict against violence.

A car and team stood ready, with the onagers being comforted by a young Nastrarian; their eyes were closed and the long ears drooped in bliss. The standard, workaday chariot was merely a battered wicker box on two wheels, lacking the fancy trimmings and webbed floor of vehicles driven by people like Ingeld. Benard had been taken on four chariot trips in his life and been sick to his stomach on all of them. The inside was already crowded with somebody's personal bindle and two plump wineskins. Wine could only mean that his driver and custodian was to be Flankleader Guthlagson, who seemed an odd choice, but would be more pleasant company than any other Werist. Being no admirer of the satrap's son, he had practically congratulated Benard on humiliating the lout so epochally.

Benard climbed in and sat on the bindle to think about Hiddi—Hiddi the statue, not the flesh-and-blood one, whom he had not seen since their first meeting. He had decided to show her with her chin a little higher than she had held it when she posed for him at the temple. This would produce minor changes in her neck, and . . .

Old Guthlag came hobbling across the yard, his pall already rumpled. Beside him trudged a hulking Werist cadet carrying a leather bag. Benard stood up. The hunk said "Here!" and swung the bag up to him, but the artist's eye had noted how far the titan had been tilted as he walked and how much effort was needed to lob that load. Benard caught it with both hands and against his thighs instead of where it had been aimed, so he did not drop it and it did not disable him. The chariot rocked, provoking snorts of protests from both onagers and Nastrarian. The Werist had the grace to look impressed as well as disappointed.

Benard lowered the bag to the floor. It chinked. What in the world did they need so much gold for?

Guthlag said, "Ready?"

"Ready, lord."

"No baggage?"

Benard just shook his head. He gave the old man a surreptitious hand up, gripping his wrist and not his arthritic fingers. He was surprised to find himself on the left side.

"You expect *me* to drive? Lady Ingeld used to say it would be easier to teach onagers to paint. The only time she ever let me try by myself, I nearly tipped the car over. *Wow! You're going to let me drive?*"

"Boy, it's time you grew up!" The growl came in a gale of beer fumes. Beer was the old man's usual tipple, but beer could not be transported in chariots. Neither the beer itself nor the crocks would stand the bouncing. It was a surprise that Guthlag thought he could.

"Yes, lord. Right away." Benard unwound the reins, remembered to check that the brake was up *(handle down, remember!)*, took a firm grip on the rail, and yelled "Ready!" at the Nastrarian. Reluctantly the youth returned to the world of people and stepped aside, withdrawing both himself and his god's blessing. The long ears shot up. With angry brays, the brutes lurched forward against the neck straps. The chariot hurtled along the yard, heading straight for the far wall, where each brainless ass would inevitably try to turn outward and create complete disaster. A pull on the right-hand onager's reins—a *stronger* pull—brought the car around in a death-defying U-turn. As it settled back on both wheels, Benard aimed the team at the gate and resisted an urge to close his eyes.

Out in the alley, he could do little more than hang on as they careered down the long, winding slope to the river, through crowds, carts, wagons, and carrying chairs. Guthlag blew long warning yodels on the bull's horn. Pedestrians and livestock leaped aside, howling curses and choking in the roiling clouds of red dust.

"Which way?" Benard yelled.

Guthlag stopped bugling long enough to snap, "Left!"

Left it was. They veered madly around an oxcart, and after that life became a little simpler. True, it was there, where land and water met, that the main business of the city was conducted. Being both quay and road, the levee teemed with people buying and selling, loading and unloading, coming and going. Porters toiled like ants under seemingly impossible burdens; wagons rumbled between high piles of wares and gaudy market stalls. The wealthy rode by in carrying chairs or chariots, whose drivers screamed and cracked whips at the mob, yet went no faster because of it. But at least there was space enough to dodge and no wall for an incompetent driver to butter bystanders against.

"There!" Guthlag said as they swept out of town. "That wasn't hard, was it?"

"I'd rather chisel marble," Benard muttered under his breath, but he did feel pleased with himself. Heading upstream with the wind in his hair and the sun in his eyes, he even began to enjoy life. The traffic was light, just the occasional wagon or chariot, and his onagers had lost their first furious speed. On the rutted track the car bounced. And bounced. And bounced. It also swayed, pitched, and rocked. The trick was to keep one's knees slightly bent, so they said.

Hard as it was on him, it was much harder on Guthlag. The rheumatic old warrior clutched the rail with hands all knobbly and twisted. His brass collar bounced up and down his scraggly neck, his face repeatedly twisted with pain.

Benard eased back on the reins, and the winded onagers condescended to slow to a trot. "How far to Whiterim?"

"'Bout a menzil."

A chariot should get there before noon. "Do we go through any interesting places?"

The Werist opened his eyes, the better to scowl with. "Only place on the plain that's interesting is Kosord—an' even that's half a finger from boredom."

"How about Umthord? Isn't that where holy Sinura's sanctuary is?"

"What if it is?" the old man snarled. "Heroes have no truck with Healers, nor them with us. Stop. Need a drink."

Discard first theory—despite his grotesquely swollen joints, Guthlag had not been sent along on this expedition so he could seek a healing in the famous sanctuary. So why so much gold?

The onagers did stop on Benard's signal, much to his surprise. Giving the old man the reins to hold, he knelt to untie a wineskin. Guthlag took a very long drink.

The sun was brutal already, the long baking of summer that ripened crops. The clouds impressed Benard—innumerable little puffy clouds scattered like grain on a slate and extending forever. Landscape was soon obstructed by hedges or houses or *something,* but that heavenly ceiling stretched on in all directions until it was lost in the haze of the wall of the world. To his right flowed the river, which was another and far greater highway, coils of ochre-colored oil peppered with three-cornered sails in red-browns. In the other direction lay endless green spreads of growing grain mottled with silver ponds.

"What'ch waitin' for, boy? Drive on, an' stop daydreaming."

"Yes, lord. Giddyup!" Benard slapped the onagers with the reins.

"You got the brake down."

Ah, yes . . .

✦

After a long period of bouncing, Benard said, "Any word of Cutrath?"

Guthlag cackled. "Pimple's still in the sweatbox. You miss him?"

"No. Who does?"

"No one I know of."

"So you don't think I'm in any danger?"

"Arr! Didn't say that. You're in plenty danger."

"Even after what the satrap said?"

"Hope so," the old man said grumpily. "Honor of the host's at stake. Course, it'll take some planning. Anything happens to you, then Horold'll have to ask a seer who dun't, right? Means the pimple wouldn't dare do anything himself, 'cause he knows his daddy'll beat him bloody for disobeying. No local Hero will, for same reason. But a twist of copper in a beer house can buy all the thugs you want, and there's Heroes coming through town all

4559757

the time, heading for the Edge. Uphold the honor of the cult, see? By morning the culprits are long gone and you're feeding the eels."

"My lord is kind," Benard said, but he said it to himself. If it happened it happened.

He still did not know why Guthlag had brought a fortune in gold along on a simple two-day outing, but he knew better than to ask. Besides, there were more interesting things to think about. The Anziel statue was like a sore tooth, impossible to ignore for long. The angle of Her gaze would be critical—

✦

After the second wine break, Guthlag's painkiller began making him talkative. "That drawing of your'n really took me back," he mumbled. "Handsome man, then, Satrap was."

"Even when I knew him. Must have been a vision in his youth."

"He wash at that, lad. Spec I wound be here if he hand bin."

"My lord is kind," Benard said blankly.

Guthlag cackled and elbowed his arm. "Stuff that! You ever heard tell of the fall of Kosord?"

"Just scraps and rumors." Much more than he had ever wanted to hear, in fact, but he was obviously about to hear more. Perhaps he would learn how Guthlag had survived when the rest of the defenders did not.

"Aye. Well the pyromancer foresaw it, o' course, lady Tiu. She saw Stralg's horde on its way. He'd seized Skjar an' Yormoth an' a few other cities already, and Kosord would give him control of the plains, so no surprise. Hordeleader Kruthruk had been predicting he'd try for Kosord next. Fine man, Kruthruk." Guthlag spat nostalgically. "Course Stralg was running 'bout a host an' a half by then, 'bout twenty sixty. Kruthruk couldn't field even a couple of hunts, so the odds would ha' been at least five to one."

"*Would* have been?"

"Aye. Well, the lady read it in the fire and announced the news, and State Consort Nars was the light of Demern on Kosord. A Speaker has to give true judgment, no matter what his own interests—his blessing and his corban are the same. Nars judged his city would fare better if it didn't resist. He ordered Kruthruk to take his men and go over to Stralg. Kruthruk refused."

Benard had heard that tale before and decided then that he would never understand Heroes. He still thought so. "Better death than dishonor?"

"Some of that," Guthlag admitted. "More that his brother had been a candidate for bloodlord, so Kruthruk wanted Stralg's guts for rat bait."

"Even if that meant all his men dying too?"

"Their duty. Said he would let Weru decide. Stralg drew up his horde on the plain and they agreed to fight it out that night. Then the state consort insisted Kruthruk give his men the choice. 'Bout half of them went over to Stralg—knowing, o' course, that he would send them into battle first to let them prove their new loyalty."

Ouch! "That doesn't sound like very good judgment to me."

"Then you're no Speaker!" the old man barked. "Stralg was bound to win, see, and he razes cities that defy him. He'd be in a better mood if his own losses were lower."

"You're right, I'm no Demernist." Benard had often wondered if his father's title of *doge* had been the Florengian equivalent of a state consort. Who else but a Speaker could give his children away to a monster? "That's too cold-blooded for me."

"Thaz what been a Speaker izzle bout." Guthlag hiccuped. "The cause was hopeless, so Nars's god told him he'd best serve his city by dying 'longside his troops."

Benard pointed to a mound in the distance. "What place is that?"

"Umthord."

"I thought we went through there? A priest told—"

"Naw. Stay on the levee."

Benard drove on, passing a line of near-naked peasants wielding hoes in the everlasting war against weeds. He waved and was ignored. The sky seemed oppressively big, out here on the plain.

"And the lady Tiu chose to die with her husband?"

"That she did. She drove the chariot and brandished a sword so that they would treat her like a combatant. Knowing what Stralg's horde did to women."

"Why? Surely even Stralg would not dare touch a Daughter of Veslih!"

"She said it'd be best for the city, because Stralg would never trust her and she couldn't trust him. Nils tried to tell her she was wrong and *he couldn't do it!* Saw him standin' there with tears running into his beard and he couldn't tell her she was wrong. So they went off together. But they had Kruthruk assign one man to guard Ingeld until the new overlord took over the city."

Ah! "How old was Ingeld?"

"Sixteen." Guthlag sighed.

So did Benard. He couldn't imagine Ingeld at sixteen, for he kept seeing her as she had been six years ago, when they were lovers.

"Kruthruk picked me," Guthlag said, "oldest man in the host. Talkin' makes me thirsty."

Benard reined in again. The night battle outside the walls had been a massacre, they said. He hadn't known about Kosord's Werists fighting on both sides and slaughtering one another, but he could believe it. After that, even, the citizenry had tried to contest Stralg's entry, leading to riots, retaliation, and the bloodshed Tiu had died to avert.

"Drive on!" Guthlag belched and wiped his mouth.

Benard remembered the brake, whapped the onagers. "How much defending did you have to do?"

"Enough." Such modesty was unheard of in a Werist.

"The rioters broke into the palace, didn't they?"

"Faugh! The rioters were just extrinsics with spears. I splattered some gobs of flesh around an' after that the rest stayed well back. But Stralg's warbeasts was more serious. I took out three of them before their packleader got there and called them off. When Stralg himself arrived, I was still blockin' the door, still in battleform, all reekin' of gore. He had Horold in tow. Told me he wanted to talk to Ingeld, an' she came out."

The lady had seen much trouble in her life, but that interview must have been one of the worst moments. She had never told Benard this. He had not even been born then. It was shocking to realize all the things that the world had gotten up to before he was there to see.

"This was the jade stair?"

"Naw, the west door."

Benard tried to conjure up the scene. He knew the passage well enough . . . narrow and straight, about fifteen steps . . . he counted them in his memory and there were fourteen . . . darkness, rushlights flaming and smoking, making shadows dance. Much blood, Stralg and his men crammed in at the bottom, perhaps a few bodies . . . Ingeld defiant at the top and the monstrous Guthlag-thing crouching beside her. Or looming over her—it would not be wise to ask the man to describe his warbeast. Bleeding . . .

Guthlag growled. "Stralg said she could marry his brother and swear to be loyal, else he'd give her to the troops, which was it to be?"

"So she accepted the handsome Horold?"

"No. Ah, you'd have been proud of her, lad! She laid out some terms of her own. One of them was that I be spared. So I was. Stralg himself said I'd earned that."

"Praise indeed!"

Guthlag sighed nostalgically for what must have been the greatest moment of his life. "Ah, the Fist's a Hero's Hero. 'Member you asked about battleform? Well, here's your answer: Yes, we can put it on anytime we want, but snot allowed. Man changes form without orders, he's headin' for a load of what your friend the Pimple's goin' through right now. And, my lad, changing's not something done lightly. It hurts! All your joints grind, your bones bend. A man needs to be mad to go through with it. Or really scared. Doesn't matter which in a real fight, because them already changed will turn on shirkers, so when the leaders form, we all form."

"What other terms did Ingeld demand for her marriage?"

"Hard to say." Guthlag scratched busily. "In battleform, anything more'n simple words gets pretty tricky. Lost a lot of blood, too. An' I was trying to watch half a dozen Werists, wondering what to do if they all came up the stairs at me at once. So I didn't get much of it. Something to do with sons . . . And her husband was to go free."

"Her *what*?" Benard squealed, causing the onagers' long ears to pivot in alarm. The old man's chuckle told him he'd reacted as required.

"So wash it to you if lady was married before, my lad?"

"Nothing." He glanced at Guthlag and saw that his denial did not convince. How many people knew or suspected that he'd once been Ingeld's lover? "What was his name?"

"Ardial Berkson. A Speaker, o' course. Nars's chosen heir."

"How long had they been married?" Had she had any say in her father's choice? Had she loved him?

"'Bout a sixday. He was standin' on other side of her, cool as bronze. Anyway, when Stralg balked at something, she said, 'Packleader, kill me.' I was packleader of the red, then, see?"

"No! Oh, no, that's too much! I've know I've swallowed a lot of whoppers in my time, but that one chokes me."

"Watch your teeth, boy," Guthlag growled. "I'm telling you Mayn's truth. We had it agreed. I was to kill her rather than see her taken alive. That wasn't the final code word, though."

Ingeld was capable of it, Benard decided, like her mother. Whether she would have been capable at sixteen was another question. "Obviously Stralg believed her."

"Stralg had a seer with him. Asked if she was bluffing. Seer said she wasn't. So he agreed. She went to his brother whose looks musta' helped some. Handsome as a god, he was. Ardial wash an ugly cuss an' fishy cold, like all Speakers. He just bowed and walked away between the Werists, stepping over corpses. I was allowed to swear fealty to Horold. First thing he did was order me never to put on battleform again."

It took Benard a moment to realize what his companion had just said. He glanced again at the twisted hands and knees, the pain-racked face. Werists had no need of Sinurists because they could heal themselves in battleform.

"He's probably long forgotten that order. Can't you ask to try?"

"Werists don't beg, boy."

Surely self-defense must be a permissible excuse? Had Guthlag brought the gold along as bait for an ambush so he could battleform in a fight with bandits? No, that was absurd. Was Benard supposed to try and run away with it and be hunted down?

"This journey isn't easy for you, lord. Why didn't you send someone else?"

The resulting pause was so long that Benard thought the old man wasn't going to answer, but eventually he growled, "Came along because Satrap told me to. Said I was the one who had to keep track of you anyway, and I was the only man in his host he could trust not to gut you soon as his back was turned."

"That was kind of him."

"Aye. He wants to do it himself, see?"

Benard knew that. "At least Horold's honest. Did he mention when?"

"Naw. He did say I gotta run you down if you try to escape."

"I have no intention of—"

Guthlag cackled unpleasantly. "Just as well, because it shard to think about anything in a chase sept the game, un'stand? Catch something an' not kill it—snot likely."

Benard stared straight ahead, but his stomach was churning. "I do *not* intend to try running away."

"That's what her ladyship told me." The old man affected a prissy falsetto. "'I'm just afraid dear Benard will never abandon all that marble,' she said. 'The darling boy thinks of nothing except his art.'"

"Ingeld did *not* call me a darling boy!"

"No. She called you a bullheaded idiot."

At last, Benard saw the plot. How could he have been so blind? She had said marble to the Werist, but marble was not the problem and they all knew it. The problem was Horold wanting to kill him. She wanted Benard to run away.

"So the real reason you came was because Ingeld asked you to and this gold came from her, yes?" Meddlesome woman!

The old man cackled drunkenly. " 'Gotta do something to save him,' she says."

A kind thought, maybe, but Benard was hurt that she had tried to buy him off, even if she had not seen it that way. He would *not* go unless she went with him. Why couldn't they see that sometimes it took more courage to do nothing? True, he rarely went to see her, because the satrap undoubtedly spied on her through his seers, but the thought of *never* seeing her again was unbearable. One day she would understand that the only way to save his life was to run away with him.

He waited until Guthlag needed another drink, which was not long.

He reined in. There were several boats in sight and more coming, all with bare masts and oars out as they let the current swing them around a great curve, close in to the bank. As the Werist raised the almost-empty wineskin to his mouth, Benard leaped from the chariot. He went down the bank in three great strides that almost smashed his ankles, and launched himself in a dive that should have cleared the fringe of reeds and landed him in the water with a spectacular belly flop.

Something intercepted him in midair. It must have beaten him to the water's edge and turned there, because it threw him sideways and landed him flat on his back in the reeds. He looked up at monstrous open jaws and fangs like chisels, eyes glaring, talons out, and a foul blast of hot wine fumes.

He was going to die. It was going to tear his face off. Guthlag had warned him what happened in a chase, warned him a warbeast was too stupid to understand language. But there were brays of terror in the background and a frenzied rattling. The onagers had panicked at the sight or smell of the warbeast.

"The chariot!" Benard screamed. "The gold! Get the gold!"

The talons touched his forehead and stopped. Benard lay petrified, staring up at the horny, hairy paw that would be the last thing he would ever see. The Guthlag-thing raised its head to look after the fleeing team and chariot.

It uttered a snarl of fury and was gone, flying up the bank and racing off after the onagers like a giant cat.

Benard went the other way, hit the water, and started swimming with all the power he had, foaming through the water toward the nearest boat. It would give him a ride back to Kosord. Guthlag would not abandon the gold to follow him. No matter what Ingeld wanted, Benard Celebre was not going to run away from a little turd like Cutrath, nor a big turd like his father either, and she would just have to learn to live with that fact.

eighteen

PAOLA APICELLA

stood by the door, not daring to go out on the balcony lest the crowd down there see her and harm her, mindless rage-beast that it was. Torches flamed and sputtered in the night, the fires of war. The battle was reaching in through windows and over walls; she could hear missiles striking shutters, strife downstairs—voices raised in fury, sounds of destruction, animal howls as Werist tangled with Werist.

Behind her, the child slept the sleep of innocence in her crib. One wavering flame above the little bronze lamp revealed a room of luxury, full of lustrous hangings, soft mats, plump quilts. Palaces were very fine, but it was time to leave. Paola crossed the room to the lamp. She held it to the hangings, and when she had sent fire licking up those in three or four places, she tipped oil and burning wick on the sleeping platform. The bedding leaped eagerly into flame and acrid clouds that stung her eyes and throat. Now the defenders had more than the attackers outside to worry about.

She scooped up the child, so heavy now! She was not soon enough, for something heavy dropped on the balcony in a scrabble of claws. A monstrous black shadow towered up against the glow outside, then shimmered and shriveled and became a very large Vigaelian, soaked in blood and sweat, naked except for a brass collar. He was panting almost too hard to speak.

"She-fiend!" he gasped. "What have you done? Give me the brat." He strode forward, one hand reaching for her throat and one for the child. "We need you no longer, chthonian."

She had done what was needed. The babe was weaned and now the woman had seriously upset the satrap by setting his palace alight, so he was going to kill her.

Hate!

He reared back. "Stop that!" He tried again, and this time he fell back far-ther. "What are you doing? Stop it!"

Hate-hate-hate! *She advanced, still clutching the child, who also had strength that the woman could draw on. The Werist backed away, screaming curses, trying to fend her off with wild swings of his fists, although she was not even close to him. He came to the doorway and his screaming took on a new note.*

"Weru! Holy Weru! Help me!" He backed right out onto the balcony, howl-ing in terror. The crowd-beast recognized him and screamed its rage. Missiles pattered like hail. A bronze-tipped shaft sprouted from the Werist's chest. Then another. He twisted around, displaying the feathered ends, staggered a few steps, took two more hits, and toppled over the balustrade. The mob cheered him all the way down.

Paola turned back into the smoke and hurried the child away to safety.

◆

A clap of thunder like the end of the world jerked Frena upright and awake. She gasped for breath, hearing the drumming of terror in her heart. Sweat trickled down her face. No reek of smoke making her eyes burn, no raging mob outside, but the vision had been as clear as life itself. Where? When? *Api-cella escaped* . . . What was the name the seer had mentioned? Jat something. *Satrap Karvak, another of Hrag's sons . . . died during the sack of Jat-Nogul . . .*

Another stunning thunderclap sent Frena dashing, naked, to the win-dow. One should be careful what one prayed for, Horth always said. She had prayed to the Old One to save her from having to visit the Pantheon.

A bad enough storm could do that, but she did not want to see half of Skjar leveled in the process. Usually the canyon sheltered the city from the worst winds, but it could channel them, too, and waves could do even more damage. Rarely a storm surge lined up with the gorge and caused massive flooding and destruction. Again the heavens roared.

The rainy season was about to begin in earnest.

◆

All morning a curtain of black rose steadily up the sky. By noon the waters had turned from bright blue enamel to lead, and an ominous swell was fondling the quays as if testing their strength for the battle to come. Everything movable had been trussed or stowed or battened, and most ships had been towed around to the safety of Weather Haven. Thunder rumbled constantly.

"We'll all die!" Ni whimpered.

"Don't be ridiculous!" Frena snapped. "You've seen storms before. This house is built of stone! It's the safest place to be."

The fan Ni was wafting at her made no difference whatsoever. Everyone was staggering and gasping in the steamy air, hurrying to ready her ladyship for her departure—Inga making final adjustments to the mother-of-pearl combs holding up her hair, Plumna applying the final touches to the silvered fingernails, Lilin kneeling to adjust the flower petals on her slippers. The rest were trying to tidy up, and outside the sun had disappeared.

"If the gods are kind my lady will make it home again before the storm," Inga said soothingly. Efficient Inga had led the team dressing Frena for the great occasion—several pot-boilings of bathing, primping, curling, scenting, powdering, and painting.

Or the gods might rain on her procession as a penance for ever having flirted with the Old One. These visions she had been having—were they anything more than evil deception from the Mother of Lies? If the Old One wanted Frena to swear to Her, then why had She not shown her how it was done? She was so giddy from stress and lack of sleep that she hardly cared which god or gods she would accept today. Since before dawn she had danced a wild gavotte of overseeing cooking, baking, table preparation, the arrivals of fresh produce, wine decanting, stabling, checking and double-checking a myriad other details. No one had ever organized so large a feast in so little time! Then had come the preparation of Frena herself, but even in her bath she had been kept abreast of the preparations by a constant stream of reports. The jugglers had arrived, the geese had been put in the ovens, some of the guest gifts were late, the wine jars were being cooled in wet rags . . .

A mere three days ago this miraculous white gown had not existed. White was the traditional color for dedications and all agreed that it set off her coloring to advantage. Overruling impertinent protests from Inga, Frena had chosen a daringly low-cut bodice. She had the figure to support it, so why not let the world admire? For three days and nights, legions of sleepless seamstresses had labored to pleat and hem and, above all, stitch on pearls. More than ten sixty pearls shone like summer dew, defining and stiffening the bodice. Another few sixty formed the choker she wore on her neck, about as many the two matching bangles, and there were even more in her tiara. She preferred not to think about recent mortality among oysters.

Inga held up the mirror so she could make a final inspection. No great beauty peered back at her. White face powder was the customary makeup for maidens going to make their vows; on her complexion it would look ridiculous, so she had spurned it. An adequate face, but no one would ever mistake her for holy Anziel come visiting mortals. A young Veslih, just maybe— motherly, competent, defender of the hearth. Not, she hoped, Mother of Lies, Womb of the World, or any of the Dark One's even less flattering titles. No one ever made images of the Old One.

"Thank you all," she said. "You have done marvelously. Let us go down so my father and everyone else may see the fruits of all your hard work."

"The master is waiting outside, mistress."

"Then bring him in at once!" Frena said crossly. When Horth appeared, she curtsied low.

He bowed. "Oh, my chick has grown up! Behold the swan."

Not a swan, a cuckoo. He had lied to her all her life, but she did not hold it against him. He had raised her, protected her, cherished her. The doge man in Florengia had given her away.

She was amused to see that Horth was not resigned to skulking in her shadow, even on this, her special day. His robes were more dazzling than hers, ablaze in embroidery and gems . . . a jeweled cap to hide his baldness, dye to make his beard less hazy, shoes even higher than normal. She embraced him carefully, not wanting to knock him over.

"Exquisite, my dear! Turn around. Your mother would be proud. You are truly gorgeous, Frena! Oh, I shall have to summon half a dozen of my best tallymen to keep track of all the marriage offers I will hear tonight."

"It's quite easy, Father. You just keep saying no! Yes?"

He chuckled. "Yes, 'no' it will be. I keep my promises." But according to the Witness, he would shortly be offered a candidate who could not be refused.

As they set off along the corridor arm-in-arm, with her skirts whispering exciting secrets to the tiles, she sensed his limp and knew his back still troubled him. She slowed down, taking this last chance for a private word with him.

"Father, listen. I don't truly believe that the satrap's wife cares one raindrop about my reputation."

"Frena—"

"Let me finish, please. Gods know her own reputation stinks high enough, and if Skjar had to vote for the most likely Chosen in—"

"Frena! I asked you not to—"

"Listen to me! If it turns out that the Queen of Shadows has a match in mind for me, you will be in trouble if you do not cooperate. I hope I'm wrong, but please don't put yourself in danger by sticking to that promise you gave me."

She glanced at him to see his reaction, but he showed no signs of taking her words seriously. Indeed, he laughed as they turned the corner and started downstairs.

"Frena, Frena! Don't worry. I hope you won't rush into matrimony, my dear. I don't want to share you with anyone. But if any woman can afford to pick and choose, you can. I shall be very lonely when you fly off to a husband, and all my wealth cannot dispel loneliness." That was an unusual concession from him, but he was keeping something from her, some plot, perhaps.

Halfway down the stairs, she paused to enjoy the applause. Most the household staff had gathered to watch her arrival, and all the shop employees were there as well. She was running late, for there must still be well-wishing and gift-giving from the employees, with exactly five of the most senior men being allowed to kiss the debutante—those selected having been advised beforehand. Master Pukar was not one of them. Then off to the Pantheon and . . .

She was still five or six treads from the bottom when shouts of protest from the doorway alerted her to trouble. Horth staggered to a halt; she steadied him, and heard him mutter something she suspected was a prayer. Brass collars were advancing through the crowd, people shuddering away in alarm from brutal stubbled faces, massive bare limbs. Their leader halted at the bottom of the stairs, fists on hips. He had eight Werists at his back.

"Huntleader Perag Hrothgatson!" Horth exclaimed, resuming the descent with Frena still on his arm. "Twelve blessings on you, Hero, and your fine warriors. You have doubtless come to inspect the security arrangements for the visit by our noble satrap and—"

Perag had a sneer to swallow an ox. "Ain't he gorgeous, lads? Which one's the prettiest, do you think?"

Horth's smile did not waver. "May I offer you and your men some refreshment, Huntleader? Too early in the year for wine, I'm afraid, but we have some fresh-made beer."

Including two soured batches that would do perfectly for these brutes.

"I came for you, boy. My lord wants you."

"There must be some misunderstanding." Horth halted two steps up, so his eyes were more or less level with the intruder's. "Satrap Eide and his lady are invited to our feast."

At close quarters the Werist smelled bad and looked worse. His height and width were incredible. Verk and Uls and the rest of the house swordsmen stood against a distant wall, livid with fury and shame, completely irrelevant.

The Werist shook his head contemptuously. "Tell him when you see him. Take him, lads!"

It had been rehearsed, obviously. Moving impossibly fast for their size, two younger thugs jumped forward and grabbed Horth's arms. Hoisting them high, like flagpoles, they wheeled around and ran him out of the hall, bearing him backward with his humiliation visible to everyone. His jeweled cap slid down over one eye and his head only barely cleared the lintel.

"This is outrageous!" Frena yelled. "The satrap himself ordered this . . . ordered . . ."

The Werist's leer stopped her.

"Not bad! Dusky beauty, they call this, lads. Tradition is, men get to kiss the maiden."

Frena bleated, "No!" She tried to back away, up the steps, but his great arms reached out and plucked her like a berry. He crushed her to him and forced her lips apart with his. It was the most disgusting experience of her life—feet clear of the floor, back bent almost to the breaking point, and that animal slobbering in her mouth. She punched and kicked and gained nothing. When he had done, he laughed and handed her to the man beside him, who repeated the process. Fingers pawed and squeezed her. Without letting her touch the floor once, the brutes passed her along the line as if they were sharing a wineskin. The last one set her down on her feet and she fell backward into somebody's arms. Now she had some idea of what a collective rape would feel like—performed in front of the whole household, including all of Horth's swordsmen.

"Wine!" she gasped. "Vinegar! Brine! Anything!"

Someone handed her a beaker of wine. She rinsed her mouth and spat into a bowl conveniently offered. "Ugh! Filthy brutes! Don't they ever bathe?" The intruders had gone.

"It makes little difference with that lot," Verk said. He was white-lipped with fury.

"My lady, your hair," Inga bleated. "Oh, your train!"

Frena drained the rest of the wine. "Mother of Death take my hair!" she roared. "And take them! Verk, follow me. Are the chariots ready?" Without waiting for an answer, she plunged into the crowd and it opened for her.

nineteen

HORTH WIGSON

was dumped roughly in a chariot and his elbows tied to the rail, so he was bent over backward facing the rear. That position would have been awkward for any man; for him it was torture, and he was certain the two Werist whelps knew that. They pulled his hat down over his eyes and left him to suffer while they waited. Normally he would just add such humiliation to the bill, and the pain in his spine was trivial compared to the agonies of molten bronze the gods churned in his belly after every meal, but such open brutality was a very bad omen. Obviously his secret plans had been discovered. He had been very careful to commit no illegal act, nor had he confided in anyone, even Frena, but a tyrant who commanded the powers of seers could condemn a man for even thinking treason.

Thunder roared. A gust of icy air whirled through the heat and disappeared again.

Then Perag Hrothgatson said, "Ready?"

"The load's on board, my lord. Did you get a good grope?"

"Indeed. That's prime stuff, lad! Don't get to play with dugs like that very often."

This was all for Horth's benefit, of course. Hrothgatson was Saltaja's favorite henchman and had very probably led the mob that killed Paola. Had Horth ever managed to buy proof of that, he would have arranged for the Werist to die, but *very probably* was not enough to justify execution. The real culprit had been Saltaja, anyway. Alas, a Chosen was vulnerable to nothing less than a maddened mob. Or perhaps another Chosen—Master Pukar had been working on the problem for years without finding any sure way to strike at her. Now time had run out.

The man who jumped aboard, making the chariot lurch, certainly smelled like Perag, but nothing more was said. He whipped up the team, and they rattled off over the cobbles. With thunder roaring almost continuously the streets must be almost empty, but more speed meant more bouncing and so was of little consolation to Horth, who was flapped up and down like a rug until he thought his back would snap.

✦

The chariot rumbled over only four bridges before it stopped, so it had not gone as far as the palace. That was another bad sign. From the reek of urine and rotting meat, Horth could guess he was on Blackstaur, which was the tanners' island, but also home to other unsavory trades, as if evil stench attracted evil deeds. Many hands hauled him from the car and ran him indoors and down steps. When a door creaked open and then slammed shut behind him, the noise echoed spookily. A push sent him sprawling on slimy flagstones, stinking of sewer.

"Up!" Something hit him in the ribs, not hard enough to break any. He rose and pulled off his hat. He was in a cellar or crypt without windows, lit dimly by a single lamp and very crowded by three Werists, one of whom was Hrothgatson. "String him up!"

The same two bruisers as before tied ropes around Horth's wrists and hung him in the center of the cell with his toes barely touching the ground. Then they armed themselves with cudgels and waited, grinning eagerly. Horth was not in the least surprised when the huntleader produced a cloth and blindfolded him. This was all standard technique to put him in a cooperative mood. He had never been subjected to quite so much of it before, but he knew of others who had. He also knew of many who might have been, but had never returned to tell.

"Now, lord?"

"No hurry. Give him time to think."

The door thundered shut.

More bluff. Horth was supposed to start worrying that his tormentors might still be in there with him, about to strike without warning. They had left him fiendishly uncomfortable, dividing his weight between strangled wrists and toes already cramped; and yet that position did ease the fire in his back.

Although Werists were known for their brutality, the satrapy was popular in Skjar. The plutocracy Stralg had overthrown had favored the rich, taxing the poor and keeping them firmly in their place. Eide Ernson kept everyone in place, but he levied no taxes at all. On clay, he owed Horth more than sixty-sixty-sixty measures of gold, probably the largest single debt in all Vigaelia. Horth knew he would never see one copper twist of it again, because any request for repayment would be answered with bronze rather than gold. This did not trouble him. When another "loan" was demanded, he would negotiate some small favor that would cost the satrap himself nothing—a ten-year monopoly on salt, for instance. Thus Eide levied no taxes; Horth waxed even richer, ready to be fleeced again in future; and the poor paid anyway.

This time the satrap or his wife wanted more than mere gold. Obviously they were after Frena—as even she had guessed—and Horth would give up everything he possessed rather than surrender his precious daughter into their talons. Saltaja was capable of understanding that, even if her blockhead husband was not. Alas, all pleasures were temporary, as a Ucrist well knew. All loved ones were hostages.

> *Tomorrow's joys and yesterday's,*
> *Are sweeter than today's.*

He had learned of the danger four days ago, when Perag had dragged him up to the palace at dawn so the Queen of Shadows could issue her absurd threats of denouncing Frena as a Chosen. Even the identity of the bridegroom she had in mind had been so obvious that Horth had seriously contemplated sending the two swordsmen to Kyrn with orders for Frena to flee. After a little consideration, that plan had seemed too risky and impetuous. Besides, a girl's dedication ought to be the finest celebration of her life, and he had not wanted to deny her that. Happiness was too rare to waste. He had decided to wait until tonight, after all the guests left, and then break the news and offer her the choice. The ship would have been ready. Knowing Frena, he was certain she would rather be a lifelong fugitive than the wife of a Werist.

He had been careful, but no one could outwit the Witnesses of Mayn. Now Saltaja would cut his throat or beat him to death, whichever pleased her, and then use his seal to transfer everything he owned to the satrap. It had been done to others before him. Frena would go to her fate as broodmare to a brute.

✦

Horth—the Wigson came later—was born in a wattle hovel on a scrubby islet in Ocean, to a mother who never quite recovered from one baby before starting another. Small, undernourished, and generally picked on, he had an utterly miserable childhood. His father was a sailor who came home at long intervals to drink up his pay, launch another baby, beat his wife, abuse his children, and brawl with his friends. His departures were cause for universal rejoicing. There was more to eat when he wasn't there.

Horth was roughly the tenth of twelve or fifteen, depending on how one counted stillbirths and miscarriages. The survivors all disappeared at puberty, heading for golden Skjar to find work, which was very easy at that age if you were not fussy about what you did or was done to you. Horth minded. He minded very much, and he was not cut out for hard labor, either.

What he wanted was wealth, and he soon decided that a steady supply of eggs beat one meal of roast goose. In a moneyless economy, that was not a trivial insight. Most rich people saw wealth as ownership of land or power and despised trade as beneath their dignity. Even merchants often thought of things bought with copper as different from those bought with silver, and likewise with gold. Converting one metal to another was just another barter, more haggling, so a universal scale of value was a difficult abstraction.

Having a knack for numbers and bargaining, young Horth talked himself into a job in a market and then an apprenticeship in the tallymen's guild. As soon as he had been inducted master tallyman, he was invited to join the Ucrist mysteries. It was typical of that cult that it had no priesthood and claimed no grandiose name for itself or its members: no "Heroes of . . ." or "Hands of . . ." Just Ucrists. Its shrine was a stuffy rented cellar and it met only when one of the brothers or sisters nominated a candidate for membership. Most initiates were far too busy to bother attending and knew that their god would approve of that attitude. Besides, there was something ridiculous about a congregation of wealthy merchants, ranchers, and mine owners standing around by lamplight singing psalms.

The rules called for a minium of five sponsors, a quorum that could be mustered only by bribery. The aspirant borrowed a measure of gold from each sponsor at a ruinous rate of one sixtieth every sixday. Even in Skjar, that interest was worth having, and since the postulant would likely need several years to repay the principal, the total return was substantial.

Horth easily convinced his employer and four of the man's friends to sponsor him. He so impressed some others that almost a dozen people turned up to witness. By the rules, after the sponsors had testified that the tokens they had loaned him were of full weight and purity, the aspirant divided the five between two pots, one of gold and one of clay. Only then did he make his vows. Whatever had gone in the gold pot was an offering to the god and disappeared—holy Ucr expected to be recompensed for the trouble of attending rituals. The contents of the clay pot remained for the new initiate, who could either repay some of his creditors on the spot or use it as grubstake for his future fortune.

But it wasn't as simple as that.

Postulants seeking initiation into a mystery were never left in doubt about the blessings its members received. The price the god extracted was sometimes less clearly expressed—"written on the back of the tablet" as they said in the bazaar. Thus holy Ucr offered prosperity, while the oath that He required contained no mention of a corban, just an innocent-seeming mention that the postulant would make prosperity his "only joy." It was understood—a gentlemen's agreement between mortal and divine—that wealth and happiness would follow in the proportion of the measures in the two pots. Few candidates dared give the god more than three of the five, reserving two for themselves. To give Ucr four was regarded as foolhardy.

Horth was a man in a hurry. He dreamed of really great wealth, not mere comfort. He wanted to go home—just briefly, admittedly—to rescue his mother from her benighted poverty. He would probably also modestly assist his brothers and sisters, were he able to find them. He especially dreamed of showing his father what a rich man looked like and what a good team of bodyguards could do to repay certain ancient grudges. This being his highest ambition, he put all five measures in the gold pot.

Judging by subsequent events, the god was impressed by this offering. The mortal witnesses certainly were, to the point that many were receptive when Horth came calling a few days later to propose, in strictest confidence, partnership in a venture he had in mind. Within a sixday of being initiated, he had paid off his inaugural debt completely by borrowing more at much lower rates. Within a year he was free of debt and two of his sponsors had become his employees.

He never found time to revisit his birthplace. When he finally got around to sending someone in his stead, the man returned to report that Master Wigson's parents had been dead for some years and no one knew where his brothers and sisters were. As usual, tomorrow's joy had failed to materialize. Today's work soon drove it from his mind.

◆

Vicious cramps were knotting his legs and pain made his eyes water under the blindfold. Tears were for trivia, not for real grief. He had not been able to weep when Paola died, and he would not if they took Frena from him now. Corpses shed no tears.

Poor Frena! He had so wanted to give her a splendid day!

> Tomorrow's joys and yesterday's,
> Are sweeter than today's.

Where *did* that come from?

◆

The two great joys of his life had come to him late one afternoon a few years after his initiation, when he received a caller—a young Florengian woman with black hair in ringlets and fierce, dark eyes. He was upstairs in his counting room and had given orders that he was not to be disturbed, yet somehow she won her way past the doormen, walking in and taking a seat without being invited. She had a girl child with her, a toddler who stood by her mother, holding on and staring at Horth in silence, with unfathomable eyes.

Horth stared back, for he trusted the instincts the god had given him and they said there was profit to be made from this woman.

"What can I do for you, mistress?"

"Much. And I can do much for you."

He waited. The dark eyes grew even fiercer.

"This child is a hostage from an important city in Florengia."

"If you expect me to help you extract ransom from the children of Hrag, then you are sadly deranged."

She shook her head contemptuously. "I was hired as wet nurse to bring her here." She had remarkably little accent if the story was true, for the war was only a year old, so she could not have arrived in Vigaelia more than a season or so ago. "Later they tried to take her away from me."

"It is customary," Horth said, "to guard hostages closely. Granted that one so young would not think of escape, her guardian might."

"Her guardian did." She smiled grimly.

"When and where? I have no wish to find a pack of Werists clawing their way in through my window." He was puzzled by his increasing certainty that she would bring him profit; it was a feeling he often experienced when looking at a cargo of copper ore or swan feathers, and it was never wrong. But he could not see the means yet.

"Jat-Nogul."

"Ah!" The fish began to bite. "Rebels? The palace was burned in the sack, I understand. Satrap Karvak died."

"Yes, he did." The woman's smile sent a tremor of dread prickling all the way up his backbone. Surely not!

That possibility changed matters considerably.

But why not? Two gods might be better than one.

He took a moment to think before saying, "I do not view the slaying of any child of Hrag to be a crime. If anything, the reverse. Public statues may be in order. Do you know any of the details?"

"Yes."

"Are you—"

"Do not ask."

They stared at each other in thoughtful silence. She was no longer smiling. He who fences with the Old One needs a long sword, as they said in the bazaar. On the other hand—and Horth could play more hands simultaneously than almost anyone—his god was still whispering "profit" in his ear. Two gods *would* be better than one.

"You want sanctuary here, or transportation home to Florengia?"

"Marry me. Adopt the child. You are rich and going to be richer. You can afford a wife. I make a good wife." She smiled mockingly. "Wet nurses are seldom virgins."

"I suppose not." Horth, to his astonishment, felt himself returning that smile. She had an undeniable attraction, in an earthy sort of way. He had been meaning to look around for a wife but had never found time. "And what else do I get out of this, apart from your very appealing company?"

"We look after our own."

"Wives are expected to. Be more specific."

"Prosperity to you and ruin to your enemies."

"I do not approve of murder, if that is what you mean." She had endangered herself by saying as much as she had, and he was now in peril too. If

he refused her and she were genuine, she might put the evil eye on him. And
if he did not report her, he might find himself an accessory to charges of rebellion. Or worse. Since holy Mayn's Witnesses would not testify in chthonic
trials, holy Demern's Speakers could not pass judgment, and justice belonged
to the mob.

"I am not in the habit of killing people," she said huffily.

"Can you offer me any evidence that you are what you are hinting you
are?" He could not bring himself to say the word.

"I found you, did I not? Your lackeys let me pass, didn't they?"

He nodded. Those were convincing arguments.

The child turned and held up her arms. The woman lifted her onto her
lap. "I have made you a fair offer. Do you accept or not?"

He took one more moment to think. He considered throwing her out—
assuming he was able—but the prospect felt very wrong. "Marry you?"

Cuddling the child, she said, "My baby here says we have been married
at least two years. You can invent a story."

He said, "Yes. All right. We're married. What's your name?"

She laughed. He laughed.

Strangely, after all these years, he remembered that unexpected shared
laughter as vividly as he remembered the shared bed that eventually followed,
although the sheer intensity of the pleasure she revealed to him that night had
been one of the greatest surprises of his life. He had been a reasonably competent husband thereafter, until failing health affected his virility.

She shrugged. "How does 'Paola' sound? Paola Apicella. Name your
daughter, master."

"Frena," he said at once, his mother's name.

It had taken his agents almost a year to pry out the rest of the story and es-
tablish the child's identity. By then it had not mattered. He never learned the
details of Paola's background, for she had been a person of no importance.

Had she truly been a Chosen? He had never again tried to ask her. She
had been loving and well loved. She could not be compared with the Queen
of Shadows, whose foes died with ghastly speed and regularity. He had
wondered, sometimes, when a business rival had sickened or met with misfortune, whether Paola's curses had assisted Ucr's blessing, but there had
never been any way to tell for certain. He did not even know if the odious
Pukar was what he claimed to be, or just a very slick imposter fleecing him.

Yesterday's joys . . . Three years ago he had lost the mother and now he

was going to lose the daughter. There was no joy in that prospect, no joy today. Alas, he had long ago learned that nothing replaceable was worth a
care. All the incomparable wealth he had gathered, and the thing he prized
most—

The door of the cellar creaked open.

✦

There were several of them. They let him hear their footsteps moving
around him, but took their time before speaking. Despite his confidence, he
was strung tight in expectation of sudden bone-shattering agony.

"Ready to talk?" growled a low voice. "Mmm?"

Even without his familiar mooing mannerism, Eide Ernson always
sounded like a hungry, rather sullen, bull. He thought like one, too.

"How may I serve my lord?" Horth was admitting nothing. Any man
dangling in a dungeon would address his captor as "lord."

"I want your daughter as wife for . . . a certain young man." Eide, simple
soul, had almost said more than he had been told to say.

"A match approved by my lord would be an enormous honor. But I fear
our ancestry is not worthy."

"Yours, no. Do you know who she is, mmm?"

Who else was present? Saltaja included her bovine husband in important
meetings only when she needed testimony from a Witness. If a seer were
present, Horth must not lie.

"I know. She does not. Her foster mother did not tell me—I made it my
business to find out." There were times in negotiation when knowledge
must be concealed. There were other times when it could be volunteered to
advantage. "I have made it my business to keep abreast of Celebrian affairs
ever since. Frena's father the doge rallied somewhat in the spring, but his
health still causes great concern. I understand that a successor must be found,
but I naturally assumed that one of Frena's brothers would be selected."

Outflanked by unexpected information, the satrap grunted.

"Is he telling the truth?" inquired the throaty voice of Saltaja Hragsdor.

Silence.

"Is he telling the truth?" Eide echoed.

"He is speaking what he believes to be the truth, lord," a woman said in
the singsong voice of a seer witnessing. "His information concerning Celebre must be hearsay, as is yours."

"Mmm? Hadn't heard about the doge man rallying before."

Eide and the seer were both in front of Horth, and Saltaja lurked somewhere behind, and very likely there would be Perag or another henchman to wield the club if the meeting turned sour.

"The prisoner's information may be more up-to-date than yours, lord. I can judge only what he believes."

Eide grunted again. "Do you consent to the match, mmm?"

Horth drew a deep breath. "Will my lord do me the honor of describing the young man I shall be so honored to welcome into my house?"

"Who do you expect?" asked the Queen of Shadows.

"It would be absurdly presumptuous of me to—"

"Answer, or I'll have Perag break your legs." Saltaja had the reputation of never bluffing.

"My lady is kind," Horth sighed. "The last I heard from Kosord, the city was preparing to celebrate the imminent initiation of the satrap's youngest son into the Heroes. He is two years older than Frena. Since all your own sons and all your nephews were sent over the Edge as soon as they were blessed, Cutrath would seem to be a very logical candidate to become puppet ruler of Celebre."

"Mmm?" Eide bellowed. "He's been spying on us! Seer, how does he know that?"

"Ask him, my lord."

"How do you know that, prisoner?"

"Speculation based on public knowledge, my lord," Horth said.

"He speaks the truth."

Saltaja's voice cut through like a silver knife. "And do you welcome this match, merchant?"

He drew a deep breath. "No. I have always promised Frena that I would let her choose her husband. Meaning no personal disrespect to your nephew, my lady, for I have never met him, I do not think my foster daughter would favor a Werist."

"So what were you planning to do about it?" The menace was clear.

"Submit, of course! What else could I do about it? You have seers, you have Werists. Could we run away? Leave all my wealth behind? You think I am crazy?"

"Then why have you been packing chests with gold?" Saltaja demanded. "Why did you have them moved aboard a ship in Weather Haven in the night? Why did you send hampers of your clothes and the girl's with them?"

Trapped!

There was no acceptable answer, and Horth remained silent, waiting for the battering to start. They would kill him and take it all, declaring Frena underage and a ward of the satrapy. They had done as much to others before him. He ran sweat and every muscle in his body cringed.

He was saved from having to answer by the voice of the Witness. "I am not normally permitted to volunteer information, but under the circumstances I should advise you that a major storm surge has struck the city. Many sixty have drowned already and this cellar is about to be flooded to the roof."

twenty

FRENA WIGSON

flew out into a yard darkened by the black tent of storm now pitched over the gorge. A deafening flash welcomed her, whirlpools of leaves danced across the stable yard, flights of black birds gyrated in panic, and a steady drumroll from the stables told of onagers kicking their stalls. Three teams had been harnessed already and old Permiak was struggling to keep them all calm, which was an impossible job in this turmoil, even for a Nastrarian. One of the chariots was hers, all bedecked with ribbons and blossoms in celebration, with Dark and Night harnessed to the yoke.

She boarded in a flying leap, holding her skirts up around her knees. She pulled the reins free and smacked the onagers with them in one wild move. The chariot seemed to spring clean off the ground. She hit them again before it came down.

"Mistress!" Verk screamed, sprinting after her.

"You follow!" Her yell was probably lost in another bellow of thunder. She took the gate on one wheel. Lavender fire streaked the clouds. Hauling the whip from its socket, she gave the onagers more hard whacks. They shrieked and went even faster.

The road was empty, of course. No sane person would be outdoors now. Thunder roared, and the first raindrops, big as grapes, splashed icily on her

skin. The bridge to Blueflower was straight ahead. It came at her like an ar-
row, but even as it grew, it faded behind a gray gauze of rain. By the time she
reached it water was falling from the sky in rivers, beating on her like sixty-
sixty hammers.

Wheels growled as they raced over the timbers. Up on to Chatter Place,
another big shipping island. Tearing down a street with not a soul in sight.
She lacked her alms bag, her veil, the two lily blossoms, and several other
things needed for the ritual. Not to mention the sad state of her dress, her
hair, her makeup. These things mattered not to Fabia, because she wasn't
going to the Pantheon. She was going to the palace to give Eide and Saltaja
a piece of her mind. Two pieces, one each. She was driving under water,
barely able to recognize the way from Chatter Place to Eelfisher. Huge swells
were running, surging up almost to the bridge deck—indeed, she could see
the bridge swaying ahead of her. That was ominous. She glanced seaward
and saw only fog.

Where were those Werist swine? She had expected to catch up to them
by now. Even if the satrap owned the finest onagers in the world, Dark and
Night should have been able to outrun them when they only had Frena as
cargo. The brutes might have gone by way of Lobsterclaw instead. She
peered around but saw no sign of Verk and Uls behind her, or anyone at all
for that matter, but she couldn't see far. Streets were brown rivers. The air
was a sea, the train of her dress a mess of filthy tatters. Shivering violently
and trying to remember the last time she had been cold, she took another
one-wheel corner and shot out onto the bridge to Temple. The deck was
empty, booming under the wheels.

Lightning turned the gloom milk-white; instant thunder struck like sixty-
sixty sledgehammers. Night and Death panicked and bolted. She dropped her
whip and almost lost the reins; when she regained them she clung like death
to the rail and screamed at the onagers to go faster. Under the roar of the rain
lay a deeper, more sinister sound. Something that should not be there loomed
up in the mist downstream, something advancing purposefully up the channel. Fabia howled and tried to rein in.

She couldn't see much, but there was a ship, certainly, and what looked
like the remains of houses, and this wall of death rode relentlessly up the
channel on a high gray wave. The bridge was doomed and so was she, unless
she could reach the far side before that mess arrived.

"*Faaaaaster!*" She flogged the onagers with the reins. The car took several long leaps, veering madly from side to side, when one nudge against the paling would spill Frena out and very likely smash the chariot to fragments. The ship was above her now, tilted so she could see weeds encrusting the hull, riding a tumbling wall of froth full of gnashing timbers. The chariot's wheels spun along the deck, faster than they had ever gone before and still slow as nightmare, for the end of the bridge seemed to come no closer and death was reaching for her in that swelling mountain of water.

Fortunately, she made it out from under the ship and other flotsam before the wave hit close behind her, crumpling and burying the bridge. The onagers saw it or felt it, and seemed to redouble their speed. As the final span lifted and broke apart under their hooves, they reached land, but certainly not dry land. The chariot sprayed up the slope with the storm surge frothing at its wheels, then raced along a street with a smaller wall of water still pursuing. Frena no longer pretended to be in control, or even aware where on this rock pile of an island she was. They had missed the turnoff to the Pantheon. The onagers took a right fork, then a left, and came to an intersection where a muddy torrent raced across their path. Then she saw a door she recognized from her dreams.

"Whoa!" She reached for the brake just as one wheel dropped into a pothole as big as a bathtub. The river was cold as death and deep enough to break her fall. It lifted her, rolled her, and seemed to be carrying her straight back into the killer storm surge. Dazed and choking, she struggled to her knees and grabbed hold of the wall. She caught a glimpse of one wheel disappearing downstream, but otherwise her chariot and onagers had vanished.

She stood up, still clinging to the wall. Water sucked at her shins; mud slid away under her toes. She stumbled, bare feet finding all the sharpest rocks, but heading uphill anyway because there might be more waves yet. Although she passed a couple of doors, she never thought of banging on them to beg for shelter. The alley jittered in and out of sight, daylight-bright lightning alternating with utter, sepulchral dark. Between the clashing, clattering madness of thunderclaps, she heard another, ominous sound, the roar of hail. In seconds the torrent turned white with floating ice, and soon hailstones were battering the buildings all around her—big hailstones, the kind that could do serious harm.

But by now she was at the door, a curiously misshapen door in a corner between a wall and a rocky knob, just as she had seen it time and again in her dreams. She stumbled over to it, never hesitating, and when she reached it her feet were clear of the water for the first time. The fastening was a simple latch, but she had to struggle against the pressure of the wind to force the flap open. She squeezed inside and let it slam shut behind her.

✦

For a long while she just stood in the dark and shivered. It might not be much of a refuge, but it was better than drifting out to sea as a corpse. There were no ghosts, no voices, only strangely leafy, earthy smells. Thunder continued to rage and for a while hail rattled persistently against the planks behind her, then stopped as quickly as it had begun. The rain roared on—a storm like this might last for days.

Careful fingers found living rock on one side, rough-dressed stonework on the other, and a low roof of flagstones. Toes, even more cautious, located a step up. Then another. The air was not cold, but the waterlogged remains of her gown were. She was almost tempted to strip it off, but discretion suggested waiting until she knew where she was—she might lose it, and then what? Ten steps brought her to a level passage. She took stock again. The tunnel was now a true cave, or rather a slanted gap between two massive rocky slabs that leaned against each other; the roof was dangerously low on one side, too high to reach on the other. Someone had packed gravel in underfoot to make a level floor.

Soon the wall on her right disappeared. So did her nerve. The danger of becoming hopelessly lost seemed all too obvious. She sat down and hugged her knees in misery for a while. But obviously that was not going to help; she must go on or go back into the storm . . . and either her eyes were playing tricks in the dark or there was a very faint glimmer ahead. The thunder's petulant rumbles were coming from that direction. She rose and began feeling her way along the left-hand wall, testing every step.

Blood and birth; death and the cold earth.

That she had been brought here could not be doubted—but surely not by the Bright Ones! The Dark One was also known as the Womb of the World; the grave was a return to the womb. Had Paola come here sometimes, instead of going to the Pantheon? This was a well-traveled path, a prepared way. The Pantheon must be somewhere overhead.

Frena came at last to a grotto. The roof was lost far overhead, but in at least two places it was open to the sky, admitting enough light for her dark-adjusted eyes to distinguish the outlines of a huge, irregular chamber. When lightning flashed, wet rock faces twinkled like silver moldings. The floor squelched below her bare feet, but she could not tell how much was moss and how much just mud. The air felt soporific with fetid, humic odors, which she did not find unpleasant; and, yes, there was sanctity here, immortal timelessness. Water dripped everywhere in staccato irregular counterpoint, but also trickled serenely. She tracked that sound to its source, to drink and lave her muddy hands.

The altar was a wide flat slab against one wall, like a slightly tilted sleeping platform, and the image inscribed in the wall behind it was the outline of a very obese woman, styled in pillow shapes—head, breast, belly, buttocks. High Priestess Bjaria had mentioned traces of *very old* worship on Temple Island. The Old One. The Womb of the World.

Frena removed her dress, confident that there was enough light for her to find it again. Most of her ornaments and jewels had gone. She debated making an offering of the rest and then discarded the thought. Naked, aghast at her own audacity, she went to kneel before the altar and was not surprised when her groping fingers found jagged fragments of rock on the floor in front of it. She cleared a space for her knees. *Blood and birth; death and the cold earth.*

"Mother?" she whispered.

No response.

Louder, boldly: "Mother, I have come as you bade me. You saved my life in the Edgelands when I was a helpless infant, so it belongs to you. Only tell me what you want of me and I will obey." She took up a sliver in her left hand and slashed her right palm. That hurt, but it was supposed to. She let the blood dribble onto the stone, then laid her hand there, bowing her head.

"By *blood and birth; death and the cold earth,* I swear to obey and endure." Pause. She sensed power seeping up through the rock like a welcome. Love and joy played a silent song, and she felt a strange warmth. It might only be her imagination, and she dared not look in case it was, but she had a strong impression that someone else was there with her . . .

"Not bad," Master Pukar said.

Frena cried out in shock and sprang to her feet, stumbling and banging her knee against the altar rock as she turned. He glimmered like an oversized white maggot in twilight.

"I wondered if you would find your own way here. The bond must be very strong already." He came closer. "But that is only the beginning, my dear. A dribble of blood from a cut hand? You expect the Mother to be satisfied with that?"

She detected his sour, fishy odor. His words were fishy too. She backed up a step and almost lost her balance. The floor was treacherous for bare feet.

"Keep away from me! What do you want?"

"It is not what I want, child," he lisped, "but what the Mother requires. You really think a *virgin* can become a Chosen? You have more precious blood to offer, the sacred blood of maidenhood." He tugged, and his wrap fell away in his hand. It made almost no difference—he was still a great pale worm in the gloom. He was also much larger and stronger than she was.

"No!"

He sighed. "But you promised to pay the price and to endure. This is the sacrifice required of a maiden who wants to be a Chosen. Here, spread that out and lie down." He threw the cloth onto the altar.

"No! I will not!"

"What are you going to do? Scream?" He laughed sweetly. "No one will hear. Even if they did, you know what they would do to you, finding you in here." He grabbed for her.

She tried to run, but she was barefooted and he still had shoes. He caught her arm before she had taken three steps. "Come, my dear. You are required to sacrifice blood, dignity, and some pain. Shall we begin with a kiss?"

"No!" She squirmed as he pulled her into an embrace and offered that soft, slobbery mouth.

Hate!

Pukar released her and stepped back. "What did you do? That hurt!" He sounded more puzzled than worried.

Hate! Hate! Liar and procurer and blackmailer. Killer of unborn babies. Detestable slug.

"Stop!" Now he screamed, trying to shield his face with his arms as if she were an intolerable brightness. He reeled back faster.

She followed, still *hating,* wondering if she could frighten him away altogether—and, if not, how long she could hold him off with this strange power she had been taught. *Hate! Hate! Hate!*

Now his scream was piercing. Stones rattled away from his feet and fell, clattering down, down. "Mercy!"

"Mercy? You don't know what that means!" *Rapist!*

Hate!

He took one more step back and began waving his arms wildly to regain his balance. She could have saved him, perhaps, but without an instant's hesitation she stepped forward and pushed hard with both hands. He vanished. She heard his scream stop as he hit, starting a rush of loose stones. He hit once or twice more. The clatter of falling pebbles died away into silence.

◆

He was certainly not conscious down there, wherever "down there" was. If he was alive there was nothing she could—or would dare—do for him.

Trembling, she went back to kneel at the altar. She did not know what to say . . . but that was just because she had not decided what she was thinking. Was she sorry? No. It had been self-defense. He had been prepared to use force on her because he thought he was the stronger. If one-twelfth of the stories about Master Pukar were true, then he deserved what had happened.

Would she do the same again under the same circumstances?

Yes.

"Holy Xaran, I, *Fabia Celebre,* give thanks for this deliverance. I offer the blasphemer Pukar as sacrifice to You. Accept his blood and death as my offering, I pray You."

After a moment she added, "Amen."

twenty-one

FABIA CELEBRE

dressed again in the remains of her sodden gown. Shivering from cold and delayed shock, she found and appropriated Master Pukar's leather cloak, into whose capacious inner pocket she stowed her pearl bracelet and the few other trinkets that had survived. His wrap she tossed into the shaft after him as a shroud. She found no lamp, but the possible significance of that absence did not occur to her until she was almost back at the outer door, navigating the unlit passage with little trouble. Of course a Chosen would be able to see in the dark! That realization shook her more than anything that had happened yet, even Pukar's death. She was one of *them* now. Had Pukar been one or an imposter? The seer had warned her that there was never any way to tell.

Inconspicuous slits and knotholes in the ancient door provided a complete view of the alley outside, so that Mother Xaran's worshipers could depart unseen. The thunder had moved on but rain still roared and the alley was a stream. Fabia had very little idea of where she was or even where she should be trying to get to—home, palace, or Pantheon? The same monster wave that had smashed the Eelfisher bridge must have taken several others, so the way home would be a long detour around by Live Ringer and Handily. The palace was no closer and she could not go there looking like something spurned by seagulls. The Pantheon was nearest and would offer help.

A few people in cloaks and hoods splashed along, bent against the downpour. Fabia halted a woman at random and traded one of her precious mother-of-pearl combs for directions and a pair of reed sandals—chuckling at the thought of what Horth would say if he knew. After that she could manage a better pace, limping through the mud and rain while her business associate stared after her openmouthed.

The rocky bowl where the chariots waited for their owners to return from the Pantheon was a knee-deep lake packed with wailing multitudes and angrily braying onagers. Rain was hammering down unhindered, but as much of the stairway as she could see was dangerously crammed. There were also far too many onagers in the crowd, like snakes in a vegetable patch, and if she reached the steps without being kicked or bitten or both it would be—

"Mistress! Mistress Frena! *Aee!*"

—a miracle.

Black hair did have its uses. Verk was standing high, obviously in a chariot, waving both arms wildly. She acknowledged the wave and headed in his direction. The ribbons and flowers on the car were almost as bedraggled as she was.

When she arrived he looked her over and said *"Aee!"* several times. "I must take you to the sanctuary of holy Sinura at once, mistress."

Suddenly she felt incredibly weary, as the stressful days and sleepless nights caught up with her. "No. Just home. The Healers will be overloaded with far worse injuries than mine. I took a tumble, is all. Nothing serious." The cut on her hand would not be noticed among all the other scrapes.

Yelling and cracking his whip, Verk began the tricky process of guiding the onagers out of the crowd, but they were almost uncontrollable, driven out of their asinine minds by the rain and tumult.

"What are all these people doing?" she demanded.

"Giving thanks for not being drowned, mistress."

The disaster had allowed her to make her vows of the Old One as she had wanted, but she did not like to think that it might have been sent for that purpose. "What about those who did drown?"

His pale eyes twinkled. "They were impious people who deserved what happened."

They laughed together. Unkind, yes. Blasphemous, certainly. But they were alive when so many were not, and it was only human to rejoice. Between cursing at idiots of two and four legs both, Verk explained how he had seen the bridge go, but only after Fabia had already vanished into the rain. He had taken a roundabout way to the Pantheon and been waiting and watching for her ever since, overhearing news of terrible destruction on the seaward islands—Crab, Blueflower, Saltgrass, and Strand—and lesser damage as far upstream as Slanted. Naturally, he had no information on what had happened to Horth since the Werists had carried him off.

She gave him a vague account of her accident, reflecting that if she told him the whole story he would faint right out of the chariot. She had not yet grasped all the consequences of her actions. From now on her life would never be free of danger. And what had she gained, in return for a lifetime of jumping at shadows? A *long* lifetime, supposedly, if she could avoid being buried alive too early. She could see in the dark better than before, which might be useful, but what of the strange power that had destroyed Pukar and Satrap Karvak? A knack for making men walk backward was certainly not a skill to be displayed in public, and of limited usefulness, since she could not count on finding rebel archers or bottomless chasms in the background very often. It might be a form of the evil eye. The seer had hinted that Paola had brought down some of her Werist assailants in her death struggles, and polytheists could not do that. Fabia needed a teacher, but she just could not imagine herself hailing down Saltaja Hragsdor with a cheerful demand for lessons in cursing.

Fabia had *killed* a man. She tried not to think too hard about that . . .

"Verk?"

"Mistress?"

"Why did you come here and wait for me? You must have known I was heading for the palace?"

The chariot lurched down the muddy street. Verk stared straight ahead, rain dribbling from his helmet to his craggy, fresh-shaven face and on down his shiny mail.

"A lucky mistake, mistress."

"Yes, but now tell me the real reason."

He squirmed. "Last night, mistress . . ."

"Well?"

"I had a dream. I was in that place and many, many people were wailing. And you were there, calling me . . . mistress." He shot a nervous sideways glance at her, eyes all white.

Dreams came from the Mother of Lies, of course. And Fabia had tried to rescue the Chosen at Bitterfeld. That was why he looked so frightened.

"Then it was a miracle. But I will see that Father rewards you well."

She was very tempted to add, "And I give you my blessing." But Verk had been very loyal, and it would not be fair to terrify him even more.

◆

The crisp smell of the sea bore sinister, sour overtones. Weed and debris on the streets were the first signs of flooding, but not the last, and soon the destruction was total—ships on top of houses and houses on what had once been ships. Skjar had not been smitten so badly in many lifetimes. Many bridges had gone, but Verk found a way back to Crab, where great stretches of island had been swept clean.

Horth's extravagant habit of building in stone had paid off, for the Wigson residence remained standing, solitary defiance in the midst of desolation, with lights showing in downstairs windows. There had been damage, of course—doors and shutters ripped away, the grounds devastated, the main floor gutted. Dazed servants were digging golden goblets out from heaps of sand, seaweed, and shattered furniture.

Fabia's appearance was greeted with cries of joy. Dozens crowded around her, gabbling out all the good news hidden behind the bad. The first warning surf had come surging over the docks just after she left, they said, while everyone had still been in the great hall, no doubt enjoying a juicy gossip about the master's abduction and his daughter's unorthodox departure. Master Trinvar had rushed everyone upstairs and there had been no casualties, as there surely would have been had the staff been scattered throughout the whole complex as usual.

So the goddess of death had spared this house? The Bright Ones expected praise and sacrifices when they behaved nicely, but even to suggest these for holy Xaran would be regarded as blasphemy.

Fabia had just established that there had been no news of the master himself when more cheering from the entrance announced his return, and Horth limped forward into the torchlight. His hat had gone, his jeweled robes were muddy and sodden, and the city's richest inhabitant resembled a bedraggled, shipwrecked bindlestiff, but he seemed to be unharmed, which was all that mattered. Fabia ran to him and they hugged, two battered waifs jabbering delight and relief, tears and laughter. She explained about her narrow escape on the bridge and the chariot upset.

He sighed. "So we will have to start over. You will have to organize a new celebration. We must ask the high priestess to set a new date for your vows."

Thereupon Fabia had what seemed like a brainwave. The idea of swearing false oaths was repugnant; Paola had passed on her dislike of hypocrisy. "Celebration, yes, but when I reached Temple and the bridge fell behind me, and the storm came, and . . . well, I realized that there could be no banquet or anything today . . . but I found that little shrine on Steep Street and made my vows there. Very simple, just the bare ritual, no celebration. But that part's done!"

Horth's expression was oddly distrustful. "Congratulations!" He embraced her again.

Had her fast fable been plausible? She *had* made her vows, and Master Pukar had witnessed them, even if the ceremonial had been not quite what he had expected. Surely a single little lie today was better than forswearing herself to all the Twelve a few days from now?

"And Verk found me on Temple! I have never been more glad to see anyone in my life. You must give him a really big gift, Father!"

"I shall indeed!" Horth glanced around and then lowered his voice, excluding the servants. "Did Perag and his men pester you after I left?"

"They forced their filthy kisses on me. I do not like Huntleader Perag Whatever-his-name-is, Father."

"He fouls the world like dog dirt!"

Fabia was startled to see naked hatred flame up in his eyes. She had never known the gentle merchant speak so or look so.

"You know him of old?" she asked cautiously.

"He is suspected of . . ." Horth's bland visor dropped back in place, as if he caught himself about to say too much. "... very serious crimes. But no one can prove such allegations."

The Witness had indicted Saltaja's involvement in Paola's death. But what had the satrap's wife to fear from the satrap's justice? With new understanding of Verk's cynicism about Skjaran courts, Fabia sought a safer topic.

"That brute is unimportant. Whatever can we do here? We are ruined! Your ships? The house! Oh, Father, you have lost everything."

He smiled and squeezed her hand. "I have not lost what matters most. I have greater resources than this. My ships are safe in Weather Haven, my competitors' are sunk. They will be ruined and I shall rise stronger than ever." He sighed and she guessed what was coming. "But I do have important news for you, my dear." He glanced around again and the few servants still clustered nearby hastily returned to work. Only old Master Trinvar was close, holding a torch, and he was hard of hearing. "This seems wrong, my dear—telling you in this midden. Let us go upstairs and send for some wine."

"No, spit it out here. The floors upstairs are clean. I was right? Silver trumpets and ribboned sweetmeats?"

He nodded ruefully. "I truly had no choice, my dear, as you foresaw. I keep thinking of you as a child, but you're truly a very resilient young woman now. Very few could shrug off such a day so easily. We must get you to a Sinurist before you leave, so you are in shape for—"

"Leave?"

"The lady Saltaja—" Horth fell silent, scowling angrily over her shoulder. Half a dozen Werists had entered the hall, with the distinctive figure of Satrap Eide himself rolling along behind. Hateful, sour-mouthed Perag was not among them, but behind the hostleader, with white robes glimmering in the gloom, came a seer, picking her way daintily through the nauseating debris and holding her skirts above her ankles.

Fabia sent a quick but silent prayer off to her goddess, the Mother of Lies. Nine Witnesses in Skjar, she had been told. This one was too short and too plump to be the one who had accosted her at the Pantheon, so whose side was she on?

Eide was peering around. "We seem to be too late, lads, hm? But it must have been quite a party!" He bellowed laughter while his men smilingly said that their lord was kind. The satrap enjoyed his own jokes, while rarely understanding others'.

"Such a party it would have been, too," Horth said sadly, to Fabia or just to himself. "I often think that the harder one pursues happiness, the faster she runs away."

"But if you would just sit down under a tree she would come and join you!" Fabia gave him a one-armed hug. "Come, let us offer our guests a friendly beaker of hemlock." She led the way forward to greet the satrap.

Eide Ernson had the largest head Fabia had ever seen on a human being, although thinking was not what he used it for, as evidenced by the horn stubs on his temples. His neck and shoulders were to scale, but from there he tapered down to quite spindly legs, and his arms were unexceptional—all his limbs being visible because he wore a Werist pall. Naturally top-heavy, he always swayed as he walked; now the weight of waterlogged cloth made him roll like a cockleshell in a high sea. She had never known him to be anything but cheerful and courteous, but she suspected his bovine stupidity was not entirely genuine—his habit of making mooing *mmm?* noises while he talked was too good to be true—and he was undoubtedly ruthless, powerful, and dangerous.

"Fire and blood, girl!" he boomed as Fabia rose from her curtsy. "Your father is strict, mmm? Who won this battle? Did he finally beat a consent out of you?"

"She took a fall from a chariot, my lord," Horth explained. "I have not even had time to pass on the good news."

"News?" Fabia said brightly. "What news, Father?"

"You are betrothed," the satrap said, staring at her with huge, sad, bovine eyes. "My nephew—wife's nephew, rather. Son of her brother Horold, up in Kosord, mmm? Name of Cutrath."

"He is just two years older than you, dear," Horth added, eyes sending anxious warnings. "And newly initiated into the Heroes."

Bliss! Teenage monster, what every girl dreamed of. Even forewarned by the seer, Fabia needed all her self-control to feign pleasure. "Oh, *Daddy!* How wonderful! What is he like? Tall? Handsome? And our roots are so humble! What have I done to be so honored?"

Horth would be grateful for the support. Eide would not care whether she meant what she said or not, and his escort probably expected her to swoon with joy at such news. She hoped the dumpy seer in the background had a strong stomach for hypocrisy.

The satrap shrugged his mountainous shoulders. "It's a long story, mmm? Wife can explain on the way. Going to go with you for the wedding, mmm? In Kosord."

So Saltaja would be her jailer? The only ray of sunshine on this pestilent landscape was that Kosord was a long way off, so there would be plenty of time to consider a plan of escape. The deepest blight was the prospect of many sixdays in the company of Saltaja Hragsdor.

Endure!

"Oh, that *will* be nice! Gods!—the trousseau I will need! And of course I must help Daddykins redecorate here." She sighed. "It will be just ages before I can meet my new lord. But, oh, I can't wait!"

She was overdoing it. The Werists exchanged smirks. Even Eide's big eyes narrowed a fraction.

"You won't have to, child. If my wife says you're leaving tomorrow, you leave tomorrow."

"And I am coming with you," Horth said.

She gaped at him, speechless. He, who rarely even left the house and never the city? Where would he find his barley cakes and ibex milk in a riverboat?

He gave her hand a warning squeeze. "We shall organize a great wedding in Kosord to make up for your spoiled dedication."

She faked a squeal of joy so she could hug him and whisper "Hostage?" in his ear.

He kissed her cheek with a soft *uh-huh* of agreement.

So any plan of escape would have to include both of them—the Florengian hostage and the hostage for the hostage. "That is so kind of you, Father! But what about your business? What about this house?" She gestured at the disaster all around them.

"I have good men to run my affairs until I return, dear." He turned. "Master Trinvar, there must be many, many homeless in Skjar now. Pray convert this house into a shelter for them until I return. The satrap and his lady have very generously offered Mistress Frena and me hospitality at the palace until we leave, for it escaped damage."

Of course a few sixty squatters in Horth's mansion might discourage the satrap himself from moving in during the owner's absence. Before Fabia could comment, a new voice spoke—a throaty, vibrant voice as musical as a silver flute.

"Your benevolence is commendable, trader," said the Queen of Shadows.

Saltaja Hragsdor was a tall woman who invariably wore the black robes of a widow, even to a black wimple and floppy black cuffs covering her hands. In the glimmer of Trinvar's torch she was only a disembodied face. It was a remarkable, not a beautiful face, very pale even for a Vigaelian, with bloodless lips and prominent nose and mouth; it was also unusually long and narrow, as if her head had been squeezed in a vise. She advanced through life with high disdain, seemingly expecting walls to open at her approach.

Fabia hastily curtsied as Horth bowed and spoke an apologetic welcome.

Behind Saltaja loomed a pair of very large young men. Where other highborn ladies went attended by maidservants, Saltaja preferred a body-guard of Werists, usually just two, but always young and handsome. Bazaar gossip naturally insisted that they followed her into her bedchamber, but her husband must assign them to her service and did not seem to mind. Nothing could have interested Saltaja herself less than bazaar gossip.

The icy arrogance turned its attention to Fabia. "Your dedication, child? Did you make your vows today as planned?"

Fabia sent another fast prayer winging to the Mother of Lies.

"Yes, she did," Horth said.

"She has a tongue of her own."

"I made my vows, lady. Very hurriedly, I admit. I was just telling Father about—"

"Witness?" The satrap's wife never took her pale eyes off Fabia. "Is she telling the truth?"

For an instant that felt longer than a sleepless night, Fabia contemplated an open grave and the shortest-ever career as a Chosen. Even if the unknown Mist and her minions preferred her cause to Stralg's, they could not be expected to tell outright lies. No Witness *ever* did that.

The satrap picked up his cue. "Answer the question. Is she telling the truth?"

"Yes, she is," said the seer.

Fabia bowed her head lest her face betray relief and glee. The Queen of Shadows had not asked the right question.

Eide mooed ruminatively. "Then that's all right?"

"Apparently," his wife said.

"Mmm? Then welcome to the family, Fabia Wigson, or whatever your name is. That nephew of my wife's is no great thinker, but if he's anything like his uncles, you'll have no complaint in bed, mmm? Strong as a horse, mmm, lads? May holy Eriander bless your union."

Holy Eriander could go and do horrible things to herself, as far as Fabia was concerned. A *Werist* husband? Would nightmares make him change into a warbeast in his sleep? Would he have hunting dreams like a dog, wiggling his paws in bed?

Would he ripple his muscles for her to admire . . .

. . . perhaps posing in front of an open window . . .

. . . several stories up . . .

?

twenty-two

ORLAD ORLADSON

felt his teeth rattle every time the great drums spoke, their sepulchral roll reverberating through the high-corbeled chapel. Man-sized flames danced in the fire pit, illuminating rough-cast walls of boulders and giant timbers, and also the figure of the god, huge and terrible in white mosaic—certainly made of bone chips, but whether or not they were truly *human* bone, as the probationers were taught, was known only to Satrap Therek. *Brmmm!* Eleven runts knelt in a horseshoe before the great central blaze, sweating rivers in their palls. The Hero witnesses stood farther away, in comfort—tonight these were the warriors of gold pack, four dozen of them. But other initiates lurked in the shadows at the back of the chapel, and Orlad was sure those included Packleader Ruthur Landarson and probably Hostleader Heth, who kept a close watch on the cadets. Tonight was First Call, said to be the most critical moment in the whole training program.

Brmmm! The echoes faded. Everyone in Nardalborg knew that the Heroes were meeting in conclave tonight and no extrinsic who valued his life would approach the shrine.

Runt Vargin was being examined, kneeling on the far side of the pit, with firelight shining on his naked back. Packleader Frath Thranson was examiner, standing directly under the god. He was farther from the fire, but his pall probably made him even hotter than Vargin. He held a two-handed bronze sword before him, resting on its point.

"What is life?"

Brmmm! roared the drums.

"My life is my corban!" Vargin shouted.

"Louder!"

"My life is my corban!" Vargin screamed.

He would not be warned again—he was lucky to have been warned once. There were twelve questions in the catechism. The first and last were fixed; the other ten could be asked more than once and in any order. Responses must be correct and instantaneous.

"What is victory?"

Brmmm! No eavesdroppers would hear the sacred responses over that thunder.

"Victory is my duty!"

"What is pain?"

Orlad wiped sweat from his eyes. He could not remember when he had last slept or sat down to eat. Life seemed to have been a single long torment of drill, practice, study, and exercise ever since Satrap Therek hung the chain collar on him, three sixdays ago, so that now he was simultaneously reeling from exhaustion and more keyed up than he had ever been in his life. He was runtleader and he should be out there leading, but the rules said that Vargin and Ranthr must go before him. Ranthr had sailed through the catechism and had made First Call successfully. He was now back kneeling with the rest, getting bloody from trying to grin while gnawing a meaty bone, which was the traditional award but obviously not something he craved.

Idiot Vargin was not doing as well. He was hesitating on every response, although Orlad had drilled him half the night on the catechism.

"What is blood?"

Brmmm!

"Blood is my . . . er . . . blood is . . ."

"Wrong!" Frath roared, raising the great sword.

At this point in the ritual, that move was merely the gesture of dismissal, but Vargin screamed in terror and hurled himself back, almost tumbling into the fire pit. By the time the sword descended on the place he had left— slowly, so as not to break the bronze—he was running full-tilt for the door, not fully upright yet, but still howling.

Orlad streaked. Two Heroes in the line of witnesses jumped aside to let him through and he caught Vargin in a flying tackle before he had pulled the heavy flap open. They crashed into the timber together, slamming it shut. *Boom!*

"Let me go!" Vargin howled, eyes rolling in terror. He tried to struggle free, but Orlad clung like lichen.

"You're not going anywhere! You have one more chance at First Call. You'll take it tonight and you'll pass!"

"No!" Still Vargin fought. He was larger than Orlad and slippery as an oiled eel. "Not tonight! Next sixday!"

Orlad hooked a foot behind the madman's ankle and flipped him hard against the door again, winding him; then pinned him there. "No! You're going up again tonight!" It was obvious that a sixday from now the man would have worried himself into complete idiocy. In the Heroes, "last chance" meant *last* chance.

"Leader?" said Waels. He, Snerfrik, and Charnarth had come to help. The runts were not supposed to go running around making a scene in the middle on this most solemn occasion.

"Hang on to him," Orlad said. "Stay here unless they order you back to the fire, and drill him, drill him, drill him! Make him give you the answer to every question the light asks—quietly, of course. He knows it, really. He's going up again tonight and he's *going to pass!*" He grabbed both of Vargin's ears and pulled the bigger man's head down so he could glare right in his eyes, nose-to-nose. "Shame me and I will rip your throat out! Understand?"

Vargin did not reply, but he *looked* as if he believed.

Orlad trotted back to kneel in his place. Frath had gone and two Heroes were adding logs to the fire and poking it with bronze rods to make it burn hotter. Ranthr had curled up on the floor and gone to sleep, a permissible reaction to the release of stress.

Brmmm!

Now came Orlad's turn at last. He was unafraid. He could recite the responses backward or sideways. All that really mattered, as Hostleader Heth had told them several times, was that a man must believe in the ways of Weru. The Heroes were the best of men, the manliest to rule all others.

Then a new examiner came marching forward, bearing the great sword. He stopped before the image and turned to call out Orlad's name—Heth himself! That was an unexpected honor, and a brief mutter of surprise from the witnesses suggested it was an unusual one. Orlad tried to keep his face solemn as he rose, bowed, dropped his pall, and walked around the fire to kneel on the far side, facing Heth and the god. Werists always stripped before changing.

He waited. The fire was going to take the skin off his back. Rivers of sweat ran from his armpits, his hair, everywhere, while the stone flags under his knees were cold and hard. Smoke nipped at his eyes.

"Who are you?" Heth asked. He gave no warning, but the drummers' warrior reflexes brought the thunder instantly: *Brmmm!*

"The footprint of the god!" Orlad screamed. Echoes rolled.

"What is terror?" *Brmmm!*

"Terror is my weapon!"

"What is blood?" *Brmmm!*

"Blood is life!" Louder yet.

"What is rage?" *Brmmm!*

"Rage is my friend!"

"What is life?" And so on. It was easy enough when a man really believed. Why had Vargin found it so hard? In what seemed no time at all he heard the last question:

"What is fear?" *Brmmm!*

"I do not know!"

Orlad was annoyed to hear a small cheer greet his success. The catechism was only the beginning.

"Rise."

Only the savagely crackling fire disturbed the silence. The drums spoke no more. Orlad stood, staring confidently, even happily, into Heth's eyes. How long he had longed for this moment!

"Who comes?"

Orlad reached for Heth's brass collar with his left hand. The metal was cool and damp. He waited, mind searching, for he must not give the next response until he was sure. *Yes!* Yes, there *was* something new in the hall—a power, a presence between him and the mosaic on the wall . . . or perhaps behind him. Location did not matter, there *was* something. Huge. Dangerous. Dark? This Bright One was bright with the brightness of blood. Amazingly in that furnace, he shivered.

But he could speak in truth: "It is my god."

Heth nodded approvingly, a smile flitting over his lips. He raised his right hand. "Do this." His face reddened. Sweat beaded on it, trickled down into his stubble beard. Changing was easy enough in battle, when a man's life was at stake and all his friends were changing also. To convert one limb in cold blood was a vastly different prospect, requiring deliberate acceptance of pain. There were tales of guides losing control and changing completely, then turning on the novices who had caused their distress.

Even the stoic hostleader could not suppress a whimper as his hand began to swell. Fascinated, Orlad watched it grow to twice its normal size, and change—black pads on the underside, white fur on the back, and five great deadly talons on the edge. The bear's paw was the simplest of all transformations.

At the same time, Orlad felt the blessing of the god flowing through the man's collar. It was like no sensation he had ever encountered before, but it was there and somehow he grabbed it. And held on. Somehow. Power like a rope of lighting danced inside him.

"Concentrate on one finger," the instructors had told them. "All you have to do is make one fingernail grow and you have made a start. Many thirties of learning lie ahead of you yet. Just one nail will do to begin."

Whatever Ranthr had achieved had satisfied Frath but had not been visible to the watchers. Orlad was a better man than Ranthr and would die to prove it if he must. One miserable nail would not satisfy him.

But it would be a start. Orlad willed one nail to grow and all that grew was pain. Angry, he tried harder and soon felt as if he had plunged his finger into molten bronze. The nail stayed just as it was. Fury came to his aid: *Rage is my friend.* He pushed through the pain. *Pain is an honor.* Better-man-better-man . . . Hungrily he sucked power from Heth's collar and thrust it at his finger. *Change!*

Grind. Burn. Orlad staggered as the ordeal surged stronger. More rage: he concentrated on the enemy, the Florengian traitors, false Heroes who had taken the god's blessing and then betrayed their lord. They were the foe, the subhumans, the snakes who had given all Florengians a reputation for treachery. Fury filled him. A red tide swam before his eyes.

It happened! His finger sprouted a walnut dagger. Exultant, he forced the other four into that imaginary furnace, and four more daggers rose from their tips. *Yes!* Done it. Now he could wield the power. Faster it came, smoother, easier. He was beyond pain. He commanded his whole hand and every bone screamed.

Heth was muttering "Easy, easy!" but Orlad ignored that. This was the challenge he had wanted. The Florengian hostage would show them! Little Mudface would show them. Pain was an honor. There had been so much pain for so long that grinding a hand to paste was nothing.

"Easy, easy! That's enough for First Call."

The hand grew larger. Blood thundered in his ears; his other arm trembled as blessing spurted through it from the collar.

"That's enough!" Heth barked. "Stop! Turn back."

I will die first . . . More power, more pain. And there it was! A bear's paw as huge and deadly as Heth's—talons as long or longer, furred in sable black instead of white.

He yelled in triumph and brandished it overhead as if threatening the god. A huge cheer filled the chapel.

Now for the arm . . .

"Stop!" Heth roared, striking Orlad's other hand aside to break the path to his collar. Both bear paws vanished, although not without a jolt of agony that made Orlad reel. His lungs froze. There was no air. The whole world swam. As his knees buckled, many hands caught him; two men held him upright so that Heth could swing and land a killer punch on his chest. They all staggered. Then another. Firelight was sinking away into darkness. On the third punch something snapped—probably a rib—but Orlad sucked in a huge breath of air. His heart shivered and resumed its usual beat.

Then everyone was thumping his back and pumping his hand. Someone wrapped his pall loosely around him and someone else held out a slab of bloody meat. *Yes!* He grabbed it like a beast and began tearing lumps out of it while the laughter and congratulations clamored. Never had anything tasted sweeter.

"All right?" growled the huntleader.

Rubbing the throbbing bruises on his chest, Orlad grinned sheepishly. "My lord is kind."

"Next time do as you're told." Heth turned away.

Orlad should feel triumphant, but fatigue was rolling over him in black waves. And he couldn't stop, couldn't just curl up and snore like Ranthr. Snerfrik was next, so Orlad must go and take his place coaching Vargin; and he must make sure that Vargin tried again tonight. Watching eleven successes should give him the faith he lacked. Maybe then Orlad would be able to sleep. For a sixday.

Long and hard was the road to finding and perfecting his true battle-form. But Orlad Orladson had begun.

Part II

◆

Summer

◆

twenty-three

BENARD CELEBRE

was at home, working on the statue of holy Anziel. It was noon in summer and there were almost no spectators around to bother him. *Clang! Clang!*

Rumble . . .

Angrily Benard changed hands, placed the chisel where he wanted it, and swung again, spattering chips like hail. *Clang! Clang!*

Rumble . . .

The thunder came not from the cloudless heavens but from his belly. He had rushed out before sunrise to start work and hadn't stopped to eat.

Out of range of the flying rubble, Thod was making *grrk . . . grrk . . .* sounds as he smoothed holy Sinura's left ankle with a sandstone rasp. He was also chattering like a starling, reporting everything his mother had overheard in the bazaar the previous day.

"You shouldn't repeat that," Benard muttered absently for the sixtieth time, estimating if he dared hold the chisel *there* and strike like *this*. He visualized the heart of the stone and where it would cleave. *Clang!* . . . Good. He had cut very close to Hiddi's shin, but not too close. He stepped back to admire the play of symmetry and asymmetry, the long curve from slightly tipped shoulder to the weight-bearing foot, the symbolic hawk perched on Her wrist, bird looking up, She smiling down. He did not consciously insert such trivia; the goddess did, and he carved as She directed. Her likeness stood knee-deep in uncut marble. He was not quite certain about her feet.

"I'm done, master," Thod said. "You mark some more for me?" Then he looked beyond Benard and said, *"Eek! Master! Run!"*

Cutrath Horoldson was stalking across the yard toward them. Benard dropped maul and chisel, wiped his hands on his smock and waited to see if this was the end. Murder would not worry a Werist much—in Cutrath's case it would help to restore his reputation—but public disobedience of an express command would be punished severely.

He came to a halt a few feet back and glared. Thod was trying to hide behind Sinura.

"I have to pose for you, slug."

Benard shook his head. "It isn't needed, lord. I know what you look like. The statue will be you exactly, twice life size, as your honored father decreed. You will dominate the Pantheon. The extra marble is being cut, but it can't arrive before spring." He saw some of the stress melt from Cutrath's tendons and sinews.

"I'll be gone from here two days from now."

"I know what you look like. I'll remember."

"You don't know what *all* of me looks like," the Werist said with menace.

Benard resisted the temptation to say he would call in Hiddi as a consultant. "My lord is a true servant of his god. I am faithful to holy Anziel. I will carve your image as perfectly as I know how. Like this." He gestured at Her statue.

Cutrath looked surprised. "That's Hiddi!"

"I saw her that night we . . . we . . . that night."

"That's very good," Cutrath admitted.

Benard was glad he had dropped his maul earlier, for that remark might have caused him to drop it on his toes now. "Thank you!"

"But you haven't seen all of *me*."

"I'll be generous."

Cutrath thought that over, too. "Very well," he said, and turned and walked away.

Benard stooped to retrieve his tools.

Thod's worshipful grin had appeared from around Sinura's half-shaped hips. "*Really* generous?"

"In perfect proportion," Benard said sternly. "Anything else would not be art."

Rumble . . . said his belly.

He cursed and wiped an arm over his streaming face. The sun was murderous. "Fetch me some . . . No, wait. I'll get it myself. Come and round off this corner for me." He scratched an outline. "That much. And that." He handed over chisel and maul, feeling his hands quivering from the work—time for a rest. As he headed across to the well, a beaming Thod prepared to build muscles.

Four priests in variegated robes emerged from the Pantheon, causing

Benard to mutter under his breath again, but they turned and went off toward the river instead of coming to badger him as he had feared. Priests were pests, always wanting to inspect and criticize and bring guests to admire. So was hunger. And sleep. *Anything* that came between a man and his art was a pest.

He pulled up the rope, drank about half the bucket's contents, and tipped the rest over his head. As he started back to the future Anziel, a carrying chair emerged from the nearest alley. This time he swore aloud, something anatomical about pigs.

The chair was enclosed by a canopy and gauzy curtains so he could not see the occupant, but only a woman's conveyance would be so brightly gilded and enameled. The armed guard trotting ahead of it was a Florengian, as were its bearers, two brawny, deep-chested men. The guard was younger than they, slender and nimble-looking, wearing a sword on his back. All three were well turned out, with kilts of good quality, hair and beards neatly trimmed, although at the moment they were as breathless as if they had run all the way from the Edge, dusty and streaked with sweat from their exertions. The bearers set down the chair close to the statue of Mayn.

However annoying the interruption, Benard must be gracious. Women whose husbands could afford such a retinue were sources of future commissions. He wished he had not left the front of his shed undraped, showing all its intestinal clutter.

"Your mistress works you hard," he said in his rusty Florengian.

"I do not speak that language."

Only now Benard noticed the seal thong around the swordsman's wrist. His ears were not cropped, as the bearers' were. By the Twelve, artists were supposed to *see!*

"I beg your pardon, master swordsman. I assumed you were a prisoner of war."

The man smiled graciously. "A natural mistake, master. I am a freeborn citizen of Podarvik, two menzils from here. My parents still live there."

"There is cool water in the well. I am Master Artist Celebre, if you would be so kind as to present me."

"That's not needed," said a woman's voice. A hand glittering with seven or eight jeweled rings emerged from the drape.

Benard bent to kiss it. Then he recognized the perfection of its line and texture, the scent of her skin. He jumped back, startled. "Hiddi!"

"Who else?" She threw back the drape. "Go water the team, Nerio. I'm quite safe with this fellow."

The swordsman bowed and trotted off, gesturing for the slaves to accompany him. Hiddi favored Benard with a smile to slay armies.

"Master Benard! We meet again." She was enthroned in her chair, draped in a sort of pink spiderweb that did not reach her knees. Ropes of garnets, coral, and amber encircled her slender neck, her wrists bore a dozen bangles of gold, silver, and jade; jewels sparkled in her hair, in her ears; a tiara of pearls adorned the flaxen pillow of her hair. She was enjoying Benard's amazement.

Part of that was despair, though. How could he ever hope to match such perfection? What marble could equal the translucency of her skin?

She favored holy Anziel with a glance of twin sapphires. "You made that? How clever! Is that an owl?"

"It does not do justice to the original," Benard said warily. Having recalled that he had a gold arm ring buried under his sleeping mat, he had worked out why the Nymph had come calling. It was surprising that she had not caught wind of his windfall long ago, since Horold's donation had been so public. Benard was no longer a penniless artist, but that situation could be rectified.

"I am 'stremely impressed." Hiddi managed to look bashful. "It was terrible of me not to at once recognize your name that night you . . . *Thod!* Go and play by yourself for a while. We grown-ups are talking!"

Thod had been listening with ears like winnowing fans and eyes not much smaller. He knew her! Whatever would little Thilia say if she heard that? At Hiddi's snarl, he turned an impossible shade of scarlet and shot a horrified glance at his master.

"Off with you!" Benard said, and Thod vanished in a spray of marble chips. "You know my apprentice?"

"I know them all. But as I was saying," Hiddi continued, obviously trying to make her voice sound less like a refugee's from a pig farm and more like a high priestess's, "I shouldn't have overlooked the name of the greatest artist in Kosord. As a collector of beautiful things myself, I am very honored to know you, Master Artist Benard." She flaunted her kohl-darkened lashes.

She was a child dressed up, robbing her mother's jewel box to play at being a queen or great lady. She was also unnecessary. Whether Nymphs were purely benevolent as they claimed or vicious gold diggers as their reputation labeled them, Benard needed no such distraction interrupting his work just now . . . except maybe a quick glance at her feet. On the night they met, he had not taken adequate notice of her feet. Understandably. He could invent feet, but they would look wrong, at least to his overcritical eye.

"The lady is gracious to praise my art."

"That, too." She smiled coquettishly. Her face, her body, were delectable, incredible, but her flirting was clumsy and lame.

Puzzled, Benard said, "What can I do for you, mistress?"

The Nymph's sigh strained the muslin over those flawless breasts. "I still have to show you how thankful I am to you for rescuing me from those Werists." Earnest.

He bowed. "Say no more. It was my pleasure."

"I would be willing to show my gratefulness." Sickly coyness.

"I really am very busy today, Hiddi. I would appreciate a quick glance at your ankles, though."

"Just ankles?" Flirtatious.

"And feet."

"You should be more ambitious. Come back to my house with me and I'll show you all the pretty arty things I have, mm?" Imploring.

The prettiest of all were in plain view through her wrap. The lashes could not possibly be real—they were probably made of feathers and glue—but the rest of her was all genuine, every delicious morsel. Other appetites stirred. He could feel his resolution melting like snow in high summer. *Rumble!*

Hiddi smirked. "I'll feed you! I have a wonderful cook."

"No images of holy Eriander?"

"Not one, I promise!" Amazingly young, very desirable, she was somehow contriving to appear innocent while implying that her intentions were anything but. Her scent alone was intoxicating. Hard hammering had made Benard's hands tremble; her smile could make all of him flap like a flag, and his body was already saluting the view through that web. She sat at ease in the shade; he was being broiled.

"I have no gifts to offer you," he protested.

"Am I so stupid? If I wanted gifts, I wouldn't show you this." She rattled bracelets in a clash of metal. "And I wouldn't come begging from a man who lives in a kennel."

He *did* want to work on the statue while there was daylight. Nymphs *did* have a bad reputation for enslaving men and bleeding them of everything they possessed. On the other hand . . .

The other hand held several good arguments on its sweaty palm, not least of which was that he must eat sometime. He could not hope to hold on to his gold, because wealth was his corban. And he was curious to see her collection of loot.

"I'm not dressed to go visiting."

"I'll undress you when we get there." Teasing.

"No gifts, no god, no talk of love?" he said sadly. "Just rank animal copulation? Like a cat—one yowl and it's over?"

"As rank as you want, master."

"I do not enjoy being treated like an animal."

"You *are* an animal," she said sweetly, sure of her success now. "All men are."

"I suppose we seem so."

Slaves and swordsman came trotting back, dripping and apparently ready to begin another journey. Thod followed them cautiously.

If gauze could be slammed, Hiddi slammed the drape. "Then follow. Home, Nerio. Benard—*heel!*"

✦

He took a moment to outline some work for Thod, then sprinted after the chair as it vanished into the alley. He caught up with it just before the first fork. In these narrow ways, he made no effort to join the swordsman out in front. He had not expected to have trouble keeping up with older men so burdened, but Hiddi's slaves were trained to their work and kept up a fiendish pace, charging through crowds and narrow gaps like runaway onagers. The journey was much longer than he expected, uphill to the palace complex and then around to the fashionable side of the city. They stopped eventually at a gate set in an adobe wall. Nerio rang a bell. In a moment the gate was opened.

Winded, Benard staggered in after the slaves, down into a shaded courtyard. Someone handed him a soft towel and a golden goblet of cool water flavored with some astringent fruit.

He drank, wiped, and drank again before he felt able to judge his surroundings. The garden was spacious, running from a dwelling of three or even four rooms at one end to obvious servant quarters at the other, the sides being blank walls clad in vines. The overall effect was exquisite. He had been

raised in two palaces and had visited rich folk's homes many times to discuss
or carry out commissions, yet he had seen nowhere with more harmony and
appeal than this miniature forest. He had stepped down into it from alley level,
which meant that it was old, and obviously those massive trees were ancient.
Their spacing around the obligatory fishpond blended with flower-spangled
shrubs and glazed-tile paving in a perfect union of balance and peace. This
haven had been designed and executed by someone with admirable taste.

First impressions curdled as he appraised the painted terra-cotta animals
and plaster figurines. Whoever had added those did not know what taste
was. Gaudy cushions and low gilt tables were being set out for dining. Half
a dozen slaves—all male, all Florengian, a couple of them little more than
boys—were laying out meats and fruits and well-shaped loaves. His mouth
ached. *Rumble* . . .

Swordsman Nerio was likewise engaged in wiping off sweat and red
dust, but he was also issuing orders to servants, who ran to carry them out.
He noticed Benard's attention on him and wandered in his direction, still
breathing hard but clearly amused.

"You are surprised?"

"Who owns this place?"

"Why, the lady Hiddi." Nerio had learned his wide-eyed innocence
from her.

"She is married? Or had a rich father?"

The wide-eyed innocence was very close to wide-eyed mockery. "I cannot
discuss the lady's affairs, master artist. I am sure you may ask her yourself."
He spoke a more citified brand of Vigaelian than Hiddi did, and his smile
was almost a smirk, brazenly hinting that he enjoyed his employer's favors.

Hiddi now approached, having descended from her chair still cool and
ravishing, and now openly amused by her guest's breathless, sweat-soaked
condition. He had never seen woven mist like her dress. There was very little
of it to see.

"You approve of my residence?" she inquired, spider to fly.

"It's magnificent, my lady." It had been until she started making it over.

"Only my very *special* friends get invited here, Benard."

"I am honored."

"It will be a treat for you. My cook is an expert. I *always* eat off gold
plate, of course."

In Benard's experience, gold plate was absurdly impractical stuff, chilling hot food instantly. "I am really impressed."

"I think, though, that you should be rubbed down before being fed your hot mash. Follow me." Hiddi floated toward the house.

He followed, fascinated by the movement of her hips and keeping his hands off her only by great effort. "Your goddess rewards you well."

"Of course He does." She swept into a shadowy chamber where one of the younger slaves was tipping water from a steaming jar into a bath. "That will do, Cosimo. We shan't need more."

The bath was set below floor level, impractically wide and shallow. The room was luxurious, with glazed tiles on the walls and floor depicting flowers and shrubs full of birds that made the room's dimness burn with brilliant colors. Unfortunately, Hiddi's taste predominated. The effect was hideous enough to hurt Benard's eyes. He could guess the hack artist who had done it; wealthy people heaped gifts on him for creating such monstrosities. Suspecting a trap, he scanned the room carefully for inconspicuous images of holy Eriander, but found none.

The boy padded out on bare feet, sneaking a monumentally inscrutable glance at Benard as he passed.

"You favor Florengians, I see."

"Animals, like all men," Hiddi said, testing the water with a foot no goddess would spurn and no peasant could even imagine. "All slaves, since I can enslave any man I fancy anyway. Of course, I march them through my bedroom all night."

He squirmed at her sarcasm. No woman had ever disconcerted him so much, not even Ingeld. But there was no drawing back now.

"Of course. Six at a time, I presume?"

"Are you going to bathe like that, or undress?"

"I don't need help to wash myself."

"Wash? You never had a woman in a bathtub, Florengian?"

None of her business. "I shall need instruction."

"I'll call for Nerio." The pink gossamer floated down around her feet. Without removing a single jewel, Hiddi stepped into the water and turned to face him. "You only need a moment, don't you? One quick yowl, you said?"

"What I need," Benard said, pulling off his smock, "may be a lot less than what I take."

As it turned out, there were several yowls and a terrible lot of splashing at the end.

✦

Much later, and in another room, Hiddi said, "Sun's setting. I must go and serve my god."

They were sitting on the edge of the sleeping platform. She was running a tortoiseshell comb through her silken hair, and Benard had been mentally rearranging furniture. He still had an arm around her. He wondered where his clothes were.

The platform bore soft mats of red and purple, which clashed with the wall hangings, which fought with the rugs. The room held far too much ill-sorted *stuff*—chairs, chests, tables, even a grotesque image of Eriander, which he had covered with a drape before joining Hiddi on the sleeping mat to repeat their earlier lovemaking in the bathtub. The entire house was an artistic junk heap, an obscene misuse of wealth. Her cooks and gardeners were skilled, her house servants well trained and respectful, but the only real beauty in the place was Hiddi herself. Sometime during the afternoon Benard had removed all her assorted jewels, having persuaded her that she was both lovelier and more cuddlesome without them.

He should not be so petty. All his bodily needs had been satisfied without stint. Life bore a rosy glow.

"When can I see you again?" he asked.

Her smile was a purr. "You enjoyed romping with your little Nymph, mm?"

"A day to be remembered always. I trust I gave satisfaction?"

"Indeed you did." He waited for her to bring up the subject of his gold.

But what she said was "You are a true artist! Come and see me any time you like, Benard. I serve the god at night. I'm here all day." She rested her head on his shoulder. "I don't have many friends. I have to sleep sometimes, but I won't mind you waking me. I'll tell Nerio to let you in whenever you want."

twenty-four

FABIA CELEBRE

came awake with a start. She had been sleeping soundly, with one hand, as had become her habit, stretched out beyond the edge of her mat to rest on the cold earth. She had been dreaming of darkness and how to make it. She opened her eyes and saw nothing.

The Wrogg was certainly the greatest highway of the Face, writhing in vast loops of reeds and sluggish water across the flat lands, navigable from Lake Skjar almost to its source in the Ice. Prevailing winds blew sunwise in summer and the Wrogg flowed the other way, so the swarming riverboats, which in sum housed more people than any city of Vigaelia, could ride the breezes upstream and rely on the current to bring them back. The riverfolk were almost a race apart, worshiping simple nature gods and speaking their own tonal dialect known as "Wroggian." They shunned villages and towns, preferring to pitch tents on the levees at sunset. Many of them boasted that they had never slept under a roof. At dawn they raised red triangular sails and moved on.

Fabia was in her personal leather tent, so tiny that she could not sit up in it. She could not have been asleep long, for the riverfolk were still singing, celebrating a chance reunion with friends they had not seen in years and might not meet again for many more. She was used to that by now. What had awakened her?

Came a whisper, "Fabia Celebre!"

Ah! She nodded.

"I am Mist." The voice came from outside and at her level, as if the speaker were lying on the grass to evade the guards' notice.

Wide awake now, Fabia rolled over on her side. "It is about time! Why have I heard nothing from you until now? It's ages since we—"

"Not so loud. When did you expect to hear from us? The nights you spent in the palace next door to its mistress? During the voyage across the lake, when you were hung over the rail like bright green laundry? Or perhaps at Yormoth, where you *shared a room* with the Queen of Shadows? Or since then, while you've been guarded by a dozen Werists and never a stone's throw away from her? Are you not worried that she may keep watch on you in her own dark ways? You think it is easy for us to come at you unobserved?"

"Sorry." Tolerating mockery was a skill Fabia had only recently acquired, although this soft-spoken teasing was easier to take than the Werists' vulgarities. "Is tonight different?"

"Slightly less lethal. Saltaja has withdrawn downstream to bathe, and the Werists are still distracted. But we must be quick."

The Werists had been distracted for several nights now, because a boatload of Nymphs had been tracking the flotilla, camping nearby and offering participation in their strange worship. Eager though his men were to oblige them, Huntleader Perag saw to it that the captives were never left unguarded.

"Can you smuggle Horth and me away?"

"Why? Where to?"

"But we'll be in Kosord any day now and I cannot sleep for nightmares of being married to one of those brutes."

"Your snores were louder than a hungry onager," the seer said dryly. "So you spurn the honor that the children of Hrag offer you, marriage to one of their own? Are you still of the same mind you were in the Pantheon?"

"I am opposed to Saltaja and her brood, but what can I accomplish against the Queen of Shadows?"

"More than you may think, child." Surely that soft, wry voice was familiar? "You are a seasoner."

"Born to greatness?"

"Only if you admit both good and evil greatness—Stralg and Saltaja both have seasoning in abundance. And it cannot shield you against ill chance. You may still die young and unfulfilled. Again I ask: Are you still on our side?"

"I think so. I am on my side, and my brothers', and Horth's, and my true parents' . . ."

The seer chuckled. "Spoken like a Chosen. No, do not protest. I speculate, merely. Chthonians do look after their own. So, Fabia, my ally, I tell you that Light-of-your-heart Cutrath has left Kosord, heading for Tryfors and the Edge. No wedding trumpets will sound for you in Kosord."

Fabia breathed a very long sigh of contentment. "Thank you!"

"Be very careful with this wisdom. Saltaja does not know yet. She is without news. Several boats bearing dispatches to her have passed you on the river. For that we must thank the disaster in Skjar, because the satrap could not leave with his city half ruined, and without him she cannot command the Witnesses."

"How can you possibly know—"

"I must go," the seer said. "She is coming back. You will find Satrap Horold's wife a fine lady who understands what forced marriage to a Werist means. Keep cultivating Flankleader Cnurg. I also have news for Horth Wigson. Tell him that he may find old friends in Kosord at the Jade Bowl. But again—be careful!"

"Wait! What happens when we find my beloved is flown? And tell me about my brothers."

"What has Saltaja told you of them?"

"Nothing that seems helpful. The youngest is a Werist in Tryfors, the middle one an artist in Kosord, and the oldest dead."

"Close. Orlando is still a cadet, but near the end of his training. He is said to be formidable, so he could aid your cause considerably if he chose; but he is unfailingly loyal and thus much more likely to betray you to his lord. Benard is a Hand. You have met some of those?"

"Many. Practical as a wax ax?"

The seer chuckled. "But a *beautiful* wax ax! Twelve blessings—"

"Wait! Who killed Paola Apicella—Perag Hrothgatson?"

There was a pause. "Where did you learn that?"

In a nightmare. Soon after Yormoth, Fabia had started praying for enlightenment about the murder. At first her petition had been refused, but she had persisted, and a few nights later had been shown the start of the attack—her mother walking home with her swordsman escort, shapes leaping from the shadows. Fabia's own screams had awakened her before she saw any more, and had roused the entire camp as well. Ever since then, the young Werists had been generous with advice about what would help her sleep better and offers to provide it. But in those few ghastly moments she had heard Perag Hrothgatson's voice directing the assault.

"Horth suspects," she said, knowing the seer would detect the equivocation. "So it is true?"

"Perag was in charge. Now I must—"

"No, wait! I know your voice. It was you who accosted me in the Pantheon."

"Well done," the seer said, without sounding pleased.

"But not the Witness who testified to Saltaja that I had made my vows."

"Did she speak untruth?"

Fabia cursed herself for stupidity, trying to match wits with a seer. Should she answer yes or no?

"I was in Skjar that day," the voice went on, "and I saw you take your vows, Fabia Celebre. It is true that the disastrous storm was overloading us, but the eyes of Mayn do not see as your eyes do. We see truth and my sisters and I saw you take your vows. What you said, where, and with whose help were not revealed to us. You may have been in the house of the Bright Ones or below it in the realm of the Mother. Few of my sisters would agree with me, I admit, but I personally do not care if you gave a lily to Veslih or spilled blood to the Old One, just as long as you oppose the vile Saltaja. If you are now a Chosen and she discovers this, she may destroy you or try to enlist you. I do not pretend to read anyone's thoughts, let alone hers. May whatever gods you serve guide you through perils to come, Fabia Celebre."

"Wait! What happens when I reach Kosord?"

There was no reply.

◆

At first light Fabia dressed hastily, hoping for a private word with Horth, but Flankleader Cnurg was asleep across her tent door as usual, and came instantly alert, like a watchdog. She nodded sourly and walked around him. The levee swarmed with Werists in various stages of nudity as they turned their palls from bedclothes into day wear.

Horth was already kneeling in the crowd around the fire, participating in the group's usual hasty breakfast. Strangely, the endless boredom of the river seemed to agree with him; he had gained an appetite and lost his painful leanness. He was being idle for the first time in his life.

The party numbered fifty-three. Fabia and Horth had brought no servants and Saltaja only a single handmaid, the moronic Guitha, but the Queen of Shadows had not skimped on guards—Huntleader Hrothgatson led a pack of young Werists on their way to join Stralg's horde in Florengia. They were more jailors than protectors, of course. Cnurg, flankleader of the center, was Fabia's shadow, and Ern, his counterpart of the rear, kept equally close watch on Horth. The rest were never far away.

They traveled in a convoy of five boats: *Blue Ibis, Mora, Redwing, Beloved of Hrada,* and *Nurtgata.* The sixty or so men, women, and children who crewed these vessels lived in complicated, ever-changing relationships never explained to passengers. New faces might appear overnight and others vanish. People changed vessels from day to day, just for variety in company, and Fabia was certain they exchanged sleeping partners as readily—argument and bad feeling would build toward explosion and then suddenly vanish, leaving new smiling pairings and new scowls of jealousy.

With so many people striking camp, attending to toilet, and snacking on leftovers from the evening meal, the dawn departure was predictable confusion. She found herself a safe haven between a smoldering fire and a heap of bales and there, where she would not likely be stepped on, hunkered down to chew a crust and shiver herself properly awake. She laid her free hand on the cold earth of the levee and registered the power of the Old One.

Perag was strutting around, being objectionable. The huntleader was a foulmouthed bully, detested even by his own men. No doubt Fabia's nightmare of him murdering Paola had been sent by the Dark One, but the Mother of Lies had not lied in that instance, because a Witness had now confirmed his guilt. It was time to bring the murderer to justice, lest he vanish out of Fabia's reach when they reached Kosord. Ever since Yormoth she had been requesting and receiving instruction from the Dark One and now she had dreamed everything she needed.

Saltaja had not yet emerged from her pavilion. There was time, but it must be done before they left land and Fabia lost contact with the Mother.

First Fabia must create a darkness to shield herself from notice. *Dearest mistress, You must sometimes cloak Your children and obscure the sight of others. Do so now, I pray You, and protect Your servant.* Thinking *veil,* she wove strands of obscurity around herself. This was her newest skill, but she felt confident that she was using it correctly. The sparkle of light on the river dimmed, and even the chattering voices seemed to fade as if muffled by fog.

Now the hex. She had never seen snow in her life that she could remember, but she had heard tell of it, and in her dreams she had been standing in a field of malice like black snow. Gathering up a handful, she began small: *One for spitefulness and maltreating the men you command.* Then she squeezed a second handful into the first to make a black snowball: *Two for disrupting my dedication party. Three for forcing your foul kisses on me that day.* And so on. *For twice abducting and humiliating Horth Wigson.* Finally much larger handfuls for the despicable assault on Paola Apicella. By then Fabia had amassed a seething mass of hatred. It felt adequate, but if nothing happened in a few days, she could try a stronger hex. *By blood and birth; death and the cold earth,* she mentally threw the malice at Perag. There were no visible results at all, which was as it should be. She dissolved her veils of darkness.

Saltaja had emerged with Guitha and her tent was already being dismantled. It was time to embark. All that Fabia had left to do to complete her hex was the lie: *Instruct them, my lady, that if I were truly one of Your Chosen, I would not dare strike at him so blatantly in front of another chthonian who is my foe and has vastly greater experience and knowledge of Your ways. Convince them all that Perag's misfortunes must be pure chance, a sending from holy Cienu, and nothing to do with me. Amen.*

✦

The passengers followed the riverfolk custom of shifting from boat to boat, and that morning Fabia scrambled down the bank to embark in *Ibis,* closely followed by Cnurg and another eight Werists, mostly from right flank. Generally the riverfolk kept to the stern, leaving the area between the two masts for baggage and cargo, reserving the bow and its seating for passengers. She took her favorite place at the end of the starboard shelf, where she could lean back against the side and watch what the sailors were up to. Cnurg sat close to her, inevitably. Most of the Werists shunned the benches and perched on various barrels and crates they had collected. Two remained standing as punishment for some minor offense, their haggard expressions suggesting that they had been on their feet most of the night.

The last to board were Perag and Saltaja, who took the bench opposite. Fabia smiled a welcome, mentally consigning the day to a dunghill.

"Twelve blessings on you, my lady. And on you, Packleader."

Saltaja inclined her head in imperious acknowledgment. However evil, she was at least courteous. The Werist just scowled at the mockery. Although he now commanded only a pack of four flanks, he still wore a huntleader's green sash; everyone but Fabia still granted him his former rank.

The moment the lines were cast off, the riverfolk began squabbling. Fabia watched with amusement, unable to understand their curious twanging speech, but reading their gestures and emotions easily enough. Evidently some of the male sailors had been helping Nymphs worship Eriander in the night, so the women were threatening to start offering favors to Werists. The brighter Werists caught on and called out promises of cooperation until Perag barked at them to stay out of it. The argument spread wider when *Hrada* came near enough for shouted exchanges.

The Wrogg was not as huge here as it had been at Yormoth, and boats swarmed on it like midges, tacking back and forth in complex dance. The vessels were long, lean, and open, offering no shade from a sun much fiercer than Skjar ever knew.

Fabia's childhood ambition to explore all Vigaelia now lay in ruins. So far she had found travel hideously boring. Although many towns and villages lay along the great river, all she ever saw from the boats were the levees, for they were high enough to cut off her view of anything else. The coastal ranges had dwindled until they were lost behind the wall of the world. Some days she managed to organize sing-alongs or, rarely, conversations that did not consist entirely of Werists bragging about their toughness, but neither was ever possible when sourpuss Perag was present.

So she watched the flights of birds, waved to passing boats, and puzzled over her visitor in the night. The seer had not told her what would happen in Kosord. Nothing, probably. She would just be dragged on upriver until she overtook the unwanted Cutrath Horoldson. If the Witnesses had any plan at all, it probably required the *flavorful* Fabia to return to Celebre, with marriage an unfortunate but necessary formality to get her there.

"Did you pay your respects to the god in the night?" she asked Cnurg. That gangling, freckled redhead was a year or two older than most of the others and showed signs of growing out of the brutalization so obvious in the other Werists. Some of them were easy to look at, if not to listen to, and she could feel sorry for all of them at times. They had been ensnared as children by promises of glory and manhood, and now found themselves being rushed into an insatiable war that took no prisoners. Their youth was an advantage, they assured her—young Werists were the most deadly. She did not ask how many of them were likely to survive their first year in Florengia.

Cnurg smiled toothily. "Not *god,* my lady! Goddess! Yes, I gave Her an outstanding offering."

"Outstanding?" exclaimed Brarag, who had his back to Perag. "Did you not hear the Nymphs laughing when they saw it?"

"On your feet, warriors!" Perag barked. "Both of you!"

Cnurg and Brarag snapped upright and chorused, "My lord is kind!"

He left them standing there. He was crazy.

Fabia fumed for a moment and then let rip. "Pray inform me, Pack-leader, just how your men offended?"

"Mind your own business, slut."

"Are you afraid a foolish joke will rot their fighting mettle, or do you think my smile will seduce them from their duty? Is your pettiness so deep that you cannot bear to think of men not being in mortal terror of you every second? Or are you just peevish because you did not sleep well last night?"

Perag glared at her, flushing. She could sense all the other Werists holding their breath. The huntleader clenched his fist and began to rise. Saltaja laid a black-draped hand on his arm.

"Leave her to her future husband to discipline!" she commanded resonantly. "And you, Fabia? You slept well last night?" Assuming she did not know about the seer, the woman's instincts were incredible.

"Indeed I did, my lady." Fabia spoke with a sweetness she was far from feeling. "And yourself?"

"I sleep very little."

That closed the conversation. Perag stayed on his keg, scowling at the prisoner. If he were forbidden to beat her, he would just take out his spite on his men.

Almost nothing was known about the children of Hrag prior to Stralg's baleful rise, but Saltaja was reputed to be the eldest. It needed no master tallyman to calculate that she must be almost sixty, yet there was barely a line to be seen on that elongated, bloodless face; perhaps her agelessness had started the rumors that she was a Chosen. Her only concession to travel was a broad-brimmed black hat and apparently infinite patience. She seemed to have bewitched Perag. His men were convinced that he yearned to be invited into her tent, and they attributed his persistent bad temper to a lack of success. No one wept for him.

◆

Thinking again about her visitor in the night, Fabia realized that the seer had spoken as if she had personal experience of the voyage so far. Indeed, she was almost certainly one of the riverfolk in the convoy, because she had been present in Skjar not long before Fabia left, and no one could have journeyed any faster upriver than Saltaja had. The Witness must be disguised as a sailor!

But which? Fabia ran through the boat crews in her mind without success. There were more than a dozen adult women in the flotilla, but the singsong dialect disguised voices, and they spent most of their days just sitting and talking, sheltered from the sun and wind inside voluminous burnooses. Although they might strip down to very little when there was work to be done, they owned a half-dozen slaves—all Florengian prisoners of war, who scowled at Fabia from shame or resentment and avoided her—who attended to most of the hard labor. Yet even the slaves seemed healthy and well nourished. Better by far the placid river life than the grinding drudgery of a peasant.

◆

The day dragged on. One could count boats, or clouds. At the stern one could trail lines to catch supper. One could wait for the hex to start producing results.

◆

Around noon, the riverfolk would rummage through the cargo and hand out snacks of fruit, cheese, pickled fish, or whatever they had traded recently. In his usual boorish fashion, Perag went first, pushing aside hungry children. Moments later he screamed.

Wild shouts of "Jumper!" roused everyone and for a few minutes *Blue Ibis* was a scene of chaos. Fabia had never heard of jumpers, which were apparently tiny but greatly feared spiders native to the flat lands. One must have come aboard with one of the tents, or perhaps the basket of roots . . . When the jumper had been hunted down and hammered into a small black stain, everyone could relax again. Except Perag.

He was thrashing on the deck boards, moaning in agony. Already his left arm was twice the size of the other and turning purple. His face was distorted—eyes bulging, lips everted, grossly swollen tongue protruding. Several of the Werists were shouting "Change!" at him, but he either could not hear or just could not change. He clawed a few times at his brass collar as if it were choking him. He did seem to be conscious, though.

"This is horrible!" Fabia said. She had gone to sit by Saltaja. "I can't pretend to like the man, but no one deserves to suffer so. Surely there must be a sanctuary we could take him to?"

The Queen of Shadows was watching her henchman's convulsions with the disapproval due a display of bad manners. "Sinurists will never treat Werists," she intoned. "If he could change form, he might be able to shake off the poison, but it would seem that he is unable to call on his god to help him."

"Perhaps we should pray for him."

"Perhaps we should," Saltaja agreed.

Fabia prayed: *Mother of Death, do not release him yet. Make him suffer enough!*

Eventually Cnurg took charge and ordered Perag trussed to restrain his convulsions; it took six men just to do that. The riverfolk shrugged and recommended keeping him doused to cool the fever. When his screams became too oppressive, Cnurg gagged him.

Flankleader Ern in *Redwing,* on being informed of the calamity, assumed command and suspended all punishments.

No one spared Fabia a single suspicious glance.

♦

Late that day, for the third time on the journey, the convoy saw a sun wife, a bloated patch of brilliance some distance below the sun and equally impossible to look upon. Horth had explained to Fabia that sun wives were merely sunlight reflecting on the dome of Ocean, which was so far away now that it was lost in the blue of the sky. A sun wife needed only the right angle and unusually clear weather to form, he said.

But the riverfolk regarded sun wives as blessings from their gods, so they chanted a hymn of thanksgiving; the Werists countered with a paean to Weru, and one song led to another. *Blue Ibis* finished the day's journey with a rousing general singsong.

twenty-five

INGELD NARSDOR

stepped into the adytum, the holy of holies in the temple of Veslih, leaving Sansya to close the heavy door behind them. It was a cramped five-sided chamber with room for only a dozen or so worshipers around the bronze brazier in the center. The fire that lit it and kept it oppressively hot was even more sacred than the one in the tholos on the summit, for it was never extinguished and had been lit eons ago by holy Veslih Herself in the legendary city of Gal. Many layers of rich rugs padded the floor. The walls were very high and glazed in random patterns of cool green and blue tiles, with small openings under the roof for ventilation.

Only Tene, the most junior Daughter, was present, kneeling in vigil before the flames and bare to the waist. Ingeld moved across to join her, although not so near that they would have exactly the same viewing. She knelt, dropped the top of her gown, loosed her hair to fall in red-gold veils over her breasts, and bent her head in silent dedication and appeal for guidance. She sensed Sansya joining them on her other side. The only sound was a faint crackling of the logs.

Sansya had fetched her, claiming that she had seen the babe, a portent that up until now had been revealed only to Ingeld herself. She had first seen it back in the spring, and that was a long time for a vision to be so restricted. Even Tene had not discerned it, and her sight was brilliant—clearer and wider-ranging than Ingeld's had ever been.

When the ripples on her soul had calmed, she raised her eyes to contemplate the coals. A boat, of course, going away. That was Cutrath. She kept trying for a closer vision of him, but all she ever saw was the boat, and often only its sail. Almost instantly an ember shifted and the boat was gone, although he could not be aware of her sight or even of his own desire to block it. She did not try to overrule him. Cutrath had never been willing to share anything, even himself; the more he needed love, the more he rejected it. She was happy just to know that he was alive—and also surprised that he was still relevant to Kosord, for his brothers had disappeared from view long before they died.

Boats approaching, five of them. They could not be far away now. And for days now this little fleet had been linked to an ax; yes, there it was, a double-bladed ceremonial ax of silver with a long handle and shiny crescent edges. Ingeld knew who that was. She pointed.

"What do you see there?"

Tene had been close to trance—it was so easy for her—and she jumped. "My lady! . . . Where? Oh! A bird, my lady."

"What sort of bird?"

She gave a nervous little laugh. Tene was very beautiful, slender and fair and glowing with youth. Even in daylight she was gorgeous, and one glimpse of those high, rose-tipped breasts caressed by firelight would drive a man clean out of his mind. There was better to come, for in the three sixdays since she had made her final vows to Veslih, her flaxen hair had begun turning bronze and her eyes to gold. "A nighthawk, my lady. It is a white bird we have in the hills. It hunts by night, like an owl."

Ingeld smiled, mostly to herself. "Good omen or bad omen?"

Tene was obviously shocked to hear the light of Veslih speak of omens. "The peasants fear it, my lady."

"I don't blame them. I cannot see your bird, but what I do see is my own warning. How many days until she arrives?"

"Who? Er . . ." Tene looked back into the coals for a moment. "Four days, my lady. The feast of Ucr."

Ingeld exchanged glances with Sansya. "Incredible, isn't she?"

"I am wrong?" Tene asked, worried.

"No, dear. I mean that we two can't guess within a sixday. But I think you will find that the nighthawk is your own portent of my dear sister-in-law, Saltaja Hragsdor." Ingeld contemplated the boats. Not all evil, though. Whatever news or orders or companions Saltaja was bringing had mixed implications for Kosord. Horold had reacted with predictable horror when warned that his sister was coming.

And there was Benard, striding along an alley with a sour expression on his face. He was in even worse trouble than usual. Ever since spring, when he began showing up in the embers, Ingeld had regarded Benard as a civic matter and had kept him under surveillance, so she knew exactly where he was heading. One of Eriander's hags had her claws in him.

"There?" she asked, pointing.

"The artist," Tene said, just as Sansya said, "Celebre."

Ingeld had never met a Florengian Daughter until she inducted Sansya, and she was fascinated by the way the Veslihan change expressed itself on Florengian coloring. The heavy tresses hung like ropes of reddish metal, but it was the fiery shine of Sansya's skin that most impressed; her aureoles and nipples might have been carved from enormous red garnets, glowing like lanterns in the firelight.

Now for the babe . . . "Where do you—" No need to ask. Ingeld could see baby, baby, more baby . . . It had been born, and that was why it had gone from private portent to civic. "Big healthy lad," she muttered. She could not see the mother, or even any hint as to *where* this brat had been dropped, but a sturdy boy it was, and the flames rejoiced around it. "There?"

"I see it," Sansya muttered. "It is a blessing for the city, my lady."

"But so much blood!" Tene cried. "Surely the mother died!"

Yes! Even in the overpowering heat of the adytum, cold shivers raced over Ingeld's skin and her throat tightened. She rose and backed away, pulling her gown closed. "So it seems. How sad! Watch over it, please. Some of the acolytes ought to be able to see it now. Let me know if Our Lady reveals more."

✦

Puzzled and deeply troubled, Ingeld went back to her room to think on these things. She sent word to Horold to expect Saltaja next fifth-day, and left orders that she was not to be disturbed by anyone except Tene or Sansya. It was almost dark already. Many of her evenings were spent counseling brides-to-be, but at this season the young were too busy bringing in the harvest to have time for romance.

Thoughts of reaping reminded her of a verse in the Arcana . . . She put her head out again and told them to let Benard in if he appeared. She was not certain he was coming to visit her, but she needed a serious talk with that unserious young man, for he had been entangled with the rogue Nymph quite long enough and should be rescued before he suffered permanent damage.

Nymphs undoubtedly performed a valuable service—without them, single men would be a public nuisance, constantly bugling like wapiti. Most Nymphs were true to holy Eriander's ideal of love freely exchanged, but some became greedy or even sadistic as they aged, and this one had offended Ingeld before. A few days before he left town, Cutrath had been caught smuggling gold plate out of the palace. In that case Horold had sent a stern warning, and the snake had released her victim, but she did not deserve another chance. It was time to draw her fangs.

The big room was still hot, although mornings were cool now. Soon it would be time to have the winter doors brought back and hung. Ingeld wondered if she should order a fire laid. Short of another public pyromancy, the only way she might gain insight into the portents was by trance, and she had not risked that for several years. Patience! If the baby had been born in Kosord, then she would certainly recognize it when it was brought to the temple next sixth-day for Veslih's blessing.

And if Benard did show up tonight, then a serious talk with him might reveal more than the state of his loins. She wondered with a flash of amusement if it were possible to wander into auguries by accident. If anyone could, it would be Bena!

As she tipped water from the ewer to the basin, intending to sponge away the heat of the day, something fell on the grass outside with a muffled thump. Then another. Benard? He would not come that way without leave, and if he did, it would be through the gate, quiet as starlight. She strode over to the arches in time to see a dark shape come down, but this one fell in silence and flopped shapelessly on the ground.

For a moment she was rooted to the spot by sheer disbelief, refusing to admit that the first two had been boots and the third a pall. Then their owner came over the wall also, landing on all fours, a huge white-furred beast in the twilight. She turned and fled. He was not in battleform, but he did not need to be. She was not even close to the door when arms like tree boughs closed around her.

"I don't want to hurt you any more than I have to," he growled in her ear. "Don't bother struggling."

She gagged at the porcine stench of him, although it was mixed with scent, so he had at least tried. He had been drinking, too. She gasped several deep breaths in and out before she could speak.

"So it was yours!"

He grunted. "Been spying on me?"

"You spy on me with your seers!" She tried to pry herself loose and merely confirmed her helplessness. Her head barely reached the middle of his chest. She tried her nails on a hairy thigh, but his hide was tough as pigskin.

"They tell me you still bleed," he said. "You're still fertile. And, as of today, I know I am, too." Still clutching her tightly, he ripped the front of her gown open to the waist and began fondling her breasts. His paw was rough as earthenware. "It has teeth, but it's quite human."

She shuddered. "You are not serious!" Of course he was serious. "The mother died!"

"It was big for a newborn." He had been drinking *a lot*. "Women die in childbirth all the time."

"I am going to scream!"

"Go ahead. I won't mind an audience." He had both might and right on his side; she was as powerless in his grasp as that newborn baby. "Veslih will help, because this is Her business. You swore to the goddess. And you swore to me, too." He slid his hand lower.

It was true that a dynast owed her city a daughter to succeed her. On the night Stralg took over Kosord, Ingeld had negotiated the terms of her rape, standing between Ardial, her lawful husband, and the Guthlag beast, who had been quietly bleeding to death. She had agreed to bear two sons for that astonishingly handsome Werist at Stralg's side. But her promise to the goddess had come first, and he knew that as well as she did.

"One daughter and two sons, you promised," Horold said, methodically stripping away her clothes without even seeming to notice her struggles. When he had her as naked as he was, he carried her over to the platform. "Cutrath you agreed to later. Doesn't change the daughter. *My* daughter, to be dynast after you."

He turned her to face him. "So we have unfinished business. You're fertile, I'm fertile, and we're going to settle the matter now. I'm ready; you'll never be. Will you submit or do I force you?"

She gagged at his stench. "Get it over with, then." She lay down and closed her eyes.

◆

It probably did not last as long as it seemed, but it was terrible while it did. When he rolled off her, she lay and sobbed. The humiliation was worse than the pain and the pain had been bad. The worst part was knowing that he was right. She was old for bearing, but not impossibly so, and the goddess would hold her to her oath.

Horold stopped panting. He heaved himself along the platform until they were face-to-face again—face-to-snout. Fortunately it was too dark to see any details, but she could imagine his sneer of triumph.

"I know you have ways, wife. You don't need to hunt out some sleazy old chthonian behind the bazaar or poke around with sticks, but you will only delay the inevitable. You are going to bear me another child. The seers will tell me whose it is, and if it's any other man's, I'll kill it and start over."

She turned her head away. The timbers creaked as he left the platform. She saw his outline against the brighter garden when he went to find his pall and boots. She was still shaking, still close to throwing up, but she must make her prayer soon if she wanted to shed his seed.

Sudden terror drove away the pain: Benard *wouldn't* come through the garden, would he? But he might be dallying out in the public part of the women's quarters. If Horold ran into him now, in his present drunken state, there would be murder done.

He came back in, dressed. "You're bleeding." He could see in the dark better than any cat.

"What did you expect? When you go out, tell them to send for a surgeon. I need stitches."

"Rubbish. You'll get used to it. The girl did." He stalked across the room to the door. "Tomorrow at the same time." He slid the bolt, then turned again. "And every night until it's done, understand? That's what you tell the brides, isn't it? They owe this to their husbands?"

If their husbands were human. "I tell the men they owe their wives respect."

"If I find this door locked, I'll rip it down." He went out and the anteroom erupted in startled screams. Soon the whole palace would know that the satrap was bedding his wife again.

twenty-six

BENARD CELEBRE

carefully set down the weighty sack he had been carrying on his shoulder. He uttered a moan of relief, hauled on the bell rope, then stood and massaged his cramped hands while he waited, nodding and smiling to passersby. When the little shutter flipped open, the eyes that peered out were as dark as his own, but much less friendly.

He said, "It's me."

"The lady is resting. Go away."

Benard sighed. "You have orders to admit me at any time."

"Not now." Swordsman Nerio shut the cover.

Benard sighed at the unreasonableness of mortals and appealed to his goddess. He had, he pointed out, a work of art at his side that was much too heavy to lug all the way back to his shed and much too beautiful to abandon to the mercies of feral alley brats in this garbage-strewn lane. He heard the bolts click back, one by one. *The beauty is in the details.* He thanked Her and opened the gate.

Nerio swung around with a curse, drawing his sword. Benard had barely had time to forget Cutrath, and here he had made a swordsman enemy. It must be a character flaw. He put his hands on his hips and tried to look unconcerned. He was, mostly.

"I will kill you!" Nerio said, displaying very fine white teeth.

"No, you won't."

"But I am going to throw you out!"

Several of Hiddi's Florengian slaves were tending the plants. They looked up in alarm, and the one called Cosimo shouted, "No, master! You know what she'll do to you!"

Not caring to ask how Hiddi disciplined her majordomo, Benard wrestled his package in and again set it down carefully. By the time he closed the gate again, Nerio had sheathed his sword, but was within punching range.

"Now go away! She needs to rest!"

Benard peered past him, nothing two Vigaelian bearers patiently sitting on a bench beside an unfamiliar carrying chair. Hiddi had company. Apart from them, the yard was greatly improved since he had first seen it. The crude figurines had gone, and the furniture was more tasteful.

"I didn't come to bed her," Benard said, which was true as far as it went. He could always be persuaded. "I brought her a gift."

"I'll see she gets it. Cosimo! Now go."

Benard shook his head as the slave came running. "Cosimo couldn't lift it, and it's fragile. Twelve blessings on you, Cosimo."

"The freeman is kind." The youth winked at him from the safety of his place at Nerio's back. The swordsman was not popular with the rest of the staff now, although he had been once.

"Why carry it yourself?" Nerio snapped. "Why not hire porters?"

"I have no money to hire porters," Benard said patiently.

"Hiddi would pay them for you. They'd be happy to settle for a chance to worship the goddess with her."

"The first time we met, you told me you couldn't speak Florengian." That was what they were speaking.

The swordsman scowled. "I meant not on that occasion. Hiddi was present. She would have suspected I was telling secrets about her."

Poor Nerio! He was tall and dark and trim, handsome in his sparkling-white kilt, with his bronze sword on his back, strong arms folded, golden headband restraining his curls. Hiddi had a superb eye for beauty when it came to men; it was art she failed at. It needed no artist's eye to see the signs of strain in the wild eyes and drawn features. Benard wondered what Hiddi *had* done to him. She could be as spiteful as a weasel. In theory Nerio was a freeman, but she had him enslaved by other means, chained on a rack of jealousy and, probably, unrequited lust.

Cosimo went back to work. Benard tried to step around Nerio, who moved to block him. This was ridiculous!

"Have the new tiles been delivered yet? Have the boys stripped off the part I wanted?" Benard was remaking Hiddi's house for her, and his current project was the ugly mosaic in the bathroom.

Just then Hiddi's visitor emerged from the house and headed for his carrying chair. He was a portly man of mature years, robed very finely and seeming content with life. His servants jumped up, and he did not notice yet one more Florengian.

Nerio unbolted the gate to let the chair out and bowed to the occupant. "May the gods bless the ground beneath your feet, lord." Then, as the man handed him a copper ring, "Oh, my lord is most generous! Sixty-sixty blessings on your noble house."

As he bolted the gate behind the visitors, he pouted at his tip and then at Benard. "They don't come any cheaper than that one. Go sit down and I will announce you."

Benard manhandled his package across to the nearest bench, set it on the table, and accepted a cool silver beaker from Cosimo. Another handsome but crop-eared Florengian youth laid a basin of water before him and knelt to wash his feet. Guilio began combing the road dust from his hair.

"What is this gift, master?"

"Unwrap it and see. Just don't knock it over." Benard sat back and relaxed while the boys wiped his limbs with cool damp cloths and soft towels. Others refilled his beaker and laid out plates of sweetmeats. Luxury would pall, he thought, but it was enjoyable at times. This was as close to it as any Hand of Anziel would ever come. The shady park fussed with birdsong and insect noises. Nerio seemed to be taking a long time.

"Darling!" Hiddi came running. He jumped up to embrace her as she threw herself into his arms. She was wearing nothing below her earrings except bathwater, but that was not at all unusual for her. Her welcomes were always passionate and prolonged. By the time she released him, Guilio and Cosimo had removed the sacking from the gift, a painted pottery figurine, about half life-size. Even Nerio had joined the crowd gathered around to admire it.

Hiddi said, "Nerio said you brought me a . . . Ooh! Oh, it's lovely!"

Yes, it was. Benard considered it one of his best creations yet, a model for the full-size Eriander he planned for the Pantheon, an ambiguous, androgynous youngster with a cryptic smile. She was naked, but clutching a cloth to her chest, and the fall of drapery concealed enough to leave her sex in doubt. The pose was oddly shy, but the sleepy invitation in the eyes was not at all ambiguous.

"He's gorgeous!" Hiddi stooped to peer closely at the image and caress it, which is what a true art lover would instinctively do. She was no connoisseur but she recognized sensuality. She touched the cuneiform on the base. "What does this sign say?"

" 'Eriander.' I copied it off the shrine in the Pantheon."

"Clothed? I never seen Him with clothes on before."

Benard chuckled, happy to see his work approved. "She's not wearing any more than you are."

He had based this Eriander on the image in Ingeld's chamber. The features had turned out with the same tantalizing familiarity, although he had tried to model them on those of Thod's youngest sister. It must be an illusion caused by the ambiguous shifting back and forth between genders. Hiddi began jumping up and down with excitement, demanding that the new idol be brought to her bedchamber at once, so Benard heaved it up for the last time and carried it across to the house. He had made some progress in remaking the room, but it still contained far too much clutter. Hiddi was a slow pupil when it came to understanding the difference between quality and sheer quantity.

He set his creation in place on the sleeping platform while Hiddi removed the grotesque hermaphrodite he disliked so much.

"What does one do with an unwanted god?" she said, puzzled. "I can't throw Him out or break Him!"

"Give Her to the temple," Benard suggested. He took the offending plaque and laid it behind a chest, out of sight, where it couldn't watch him.

"This one's *much* prettier!" Hiddi hugged him again as they admired the figurine. "You are good to me, Bena darling!" She kissed him fondly. "Won't you help me make an offering to Him, just this once?" She kissed him again, even more so.

Knowing where this was leading, he broke free long enough to pull off his loincloth and throw it over the image of the god as a cover. "No. But I want you to do me a favor."

"Anything." She pulled him down on the mats. "Anything you want."

"I want you to make the first offering to the new god with Nerio."

"Nerio!?" Suddenly she was pushing him away indignantly. Hiddi could change direction faster than a bat. "Nerio is insolent! I hate him. He doesn't know his place!"

The place Nerio regarded as properly his was now occupied by Benard. "Dismiss him, then. Send him away and hire another swordsman. If you don't want me, I'll get started on the tiles." He reached for his loincloth.

"No!" She grabbed his arm. "How can you *possibly* want me to make love to Nerio? Don't you care for me at all?" Now she was a hurt child. Her moods never seemed faked. She really felt them all.

Benard folded her into his arms again and they stretched out on the mat. "I care for you very much and I want you to be happy. You're making Nerio miserable and he's upsetting the slaves. Your household isn't running as well as it used to. Now promise me—the next man you make love to here will be Nerio."

Hiddi pouted. "Oh, very well. Just for you."

"And you will be very, very nice to him? Like you used to be?"

She was purring as he stroked her thigh. "All right. I'll pretend he's you."

Benard muttered approval into the space between her breasts and nothing more was said.

twenty-seven

INGELD NARSDOR

had never baked a loaf or plucked a goose in her life and had a staff of many sixties to run the palace for her. No matter; preparations for a major festival like the Harvest Feast of Ucr still ran her as ragged as any peasant wife organizing a daughter's wedding. Paradoxically, the knowledge that Saltaja would be arriving tomorrow had turned out to be a blessing, in that Horold had flown into a panic and fled town. Confident that she would not be molested tonight, Ingeld retired early to her chamber and knelt in prayer before the hearth. The evening was chill, and she must soon order the shutters installed in the arches, but she hated to admit that winter was on its way.

Even the scent of burning godswood did not quite mask the reek of Horold that now hung in her chamber. He would return. Like Benard, the satrap was slow to change course, but nothing would deflect him when his mind was made up. Three nights now he had forced himself on her. Fortunately he did not know the proper rites for what he wanted, but the goddess could always waive ritual. Each time Ingeld had cursed his seed so it could not quicken her womb, but each rejection had proved more difficult than the last. She was using the goddess's blessing to defeat the goddess's purpose, and obviously that course would not prosper long. Veslih was showing Her displeasure by refusing to answer Her Daughter's pleas for guidance. Flames leapt in endless play, bouncing shadows off the darkness but showing nothing. Nothing except Benard, that is, which was a reminder that Ingeld must find time to rescue him from the bloodsucking Nymph.

Benard, Benard . . . Benard behind a bush? She *knew* that bush.

She jumped up and swept out through the arches into the garden, shivering as the cold air struck her heated skin. He was sitting with his knees up and ankles crossed, huddled in a dark blanket, almost invisible under the leaves.

"Just what do you think you are doing?"

"Waiting."

"Get up!"

He rose, big and sheepish. The blanket cape did not quite conceal the shape at his side. Ingeld peeked and confirmed that he was armed with a dagger. A dagger with a jeweled hilt, no less.

"Where did you get that?"

He pulled the cloth from her fingers. "Borrowed it. How long until he gets here?"

It was so pathetic she wanted to wrap him in her arms and comfort him like a child. Benard as killer? "Who told you?" she said.

"Guthlag. The whole palace knows."

"The whole palace knows my husband goes to his wife's bed? Is that so extraordinary in Kosord? Come inside before you catch cold."

Benard said, "No!"

"Sit here, then. You'll have a long wait. Horold has gone hunting. He won't be back before morning." She stepped over to a bench by the pool.

He sat beside her, wrapping a meaty arm around her, so the blanket enclosed them both. "I am serious, Ingeld. I know you aren't accepting him voluntarily."

"And you really think you would have a chance against him? Oh, Bena, Bena! Even if you could creep up on him when he's—busy, let's say—which you couldn't, and even if you stuck that knife in his back, it would not kill him. He'd battleform, heal the wound, tear you to pieces, and go back to what he was doing." She felt him shudder.

But it was wonderful to have that arm around her, someone who really cared. Cutrath was long gone. The man she had married had been transformed into an animal. Bena was all she had left.

"Surely your goddess doesn't expect you to endure that monster!" he said. "Can't you curse him—burn him or something?"

She leaned her head on his shoulder. "My holy mistress would not approve of husband immolation as proper wifely behavior. Horold is within his rights and Veslih is on his side. No, listen!" she said as he tried to protest. "I'm getting old, Benard, but I still owe my city and my goddess a daughter to rule after me. Horold remembered that, or someone reminded him, and he wants to be her father. The seers will tell him whose child I bear."

"Will they tell you what it's going to look like? Will it have hooves? Claws?"

"If you're going to shout you'd better come inside." Ingeld rose and headed back to the hearth. She knelt on the rug, and a moment later Benard's big shape settled beside her. The firelight made him seem haggard, as if he had not slept for days.

"If you won't kill him or let me do it," he said gruffly, "I know how he can be distracted so he won't bother you."

"How?"

"I have a friend who's a Nymph. She says she can handle any Werist, no matter what it looks like."

Now Ingeld was on safer ground. "Yes, I know all about your cuddly pet. Fortunately she cannot get into the palace. If the guard didn't stop her, holy Veslih would. I've been meaning to have a talk with you about her, Benard."

"You needn't lecture me," he said grumpily. "It isn't what you think."

"Yes it is. She's one of the nastiest gold diggers I've seen in all my years as dynast. She bleeds men dry. Believe me, Mistress Hiddi is going to be heading downriver very shortly."

He sighed. "I know she's greedy. So let her loose on Horold! Let her loot the palace. At least your bedroom won't smell like a pigpen."

"Stop that! You have no right to speak to me like that!"

"Yes I do. I love you."

"Benard!" Not daring to stay close to him, Ingeld scrambled to her feet and began to pace. If Horold asked the Witnesses what men had been in his wife's bedroom, what they had done, what they had said—they would tell him. "You love Hiddi, remember? And Horold would kill her!"

"She swears he wouldn't. She says she's tamed much worse."

"She's a Nymph, Benard. She's enthralled you."

He snorted, a sound of exasperation. "She's done nothing of the kind! Hiddi is in love with me."

"Grow up, Benard! Don't you know her corban is to forsake love? Unlimited lust, but no love; that's the bargain she made with her god."

"Ingeld!" He spoke softly, but he was wearing his stubborn expression, watching intently as she circled the hearth. "I've never known you to be wrong like this before. Hiddi's corban is that she can never *be* loved, but *she* can love. She knows I can never love her. I'm sorry for her. We're good friends. I'm probably the only friend she has. Yes, we do what lovers do, but she knows it doesn't mean to me what it does to her."

"Indeed? And do you still have that gold Horold gave you?"

"Don't be absurd! I couldn't keep that. Wealth is my corban. I gave it to the goddess."

"Which goddess?" Ingeld demanded triumphantly.

"Mine, of course! I cast a hawk."

"You did what?" Her confidence wavered.

"I made a rough clay likeness of a hawk, her symbol," Benard explained happily, "and coated it with wax. I carved the wax to show the details, covered it with more clay and baked it in my kiln, so the wax ran out. Then I poured the gold in and cast the hawk. I gave it to Anziel at her shrine. It was very good."

A masterpiece, no doubt, hidden in some secret chapel, never to be seen by extrinsics. "I suppose you visit Hiddi just so the two of you can be sorry for her together?"

Benard shrugged. "I've been redecorating her house, replacing a mosaic, organizing—"

"At night?"

"I can't *paint* by candlelight, but mosaic's easy because I remember what color the tiles are in daylight. I get a lot more done when Hiddi isn't there." He smiled apologetically. "I'm an initiate, Ingeld. I bed her, but I don't worship her goddess with her. I couldn't even make love to you in this room anymore—because of that." He pointed to Eriander in the frieze of the Bright Ones.

It was almost unknown for a man to resist a Nymph, but perhaps Benard's unshakable innocence could impress even the likes of Hiddi. His haggard look came from working day and night.

Ingeld had wandered too close. Benard caught her wrist and pulled her down into an embrace. She was much too aware of his strength, his maleness. He kissed her and she did not resist. It was not a sisterly kiss.

"Run away with me, Ingeld. Go tonight. By the time he gets back tomorrow, we could be long out of the seers' seeing range."

Merciful Mother! Had she been misreading the auguries? All her training, all her experience, taught her that the city's welfare must come first. Kosord was everything; her own comfort or preferences counted for nothing. Was the goddess offering to make an exception now?

He felt her shock. "What's wrong?"

"I tried to send you away once and you couldn't bear to leave your precious statues."

He scoffed. "Statues? *Statues?* You think I care about the statues? We'll stop by the yard on the way and I'll smash them to gravel for you. It was you I wouldn't leave, and if you won't leave with me now, or can't leave, then I am going to kill Horold."

"You mean this, Benard? You really, truly still want an old woman like me? You haven't grown out of it?"

His response was to kiss her again, even more thoroughly. He needed a shave, but he kissed very expertly. She could not have broken free of his embrace had she wanted to. She didn't want to. His strength was gentle, nothing like Horold's brutality. It was years since she had been kissed like that. She had forgotten how sweet it was, but her heart had not forgotten how to respond.

"Oh, this is crazy!" she muttered when it was over. She did not want it to be over. "Horold will send Werists upstream and downstream. Anyone who looked at me would know I'm a Daughter. We'd never get away, love." She would be dragged back and Benard would die.

"Tomorrow night!" Benard said firmly. "I'll hire a fast boat. No, I'll get Guthlag to do it—I'm hopeless at haggling. We'll slip away during the feast. No one will know I've gone, because Guthlag won't be there to tell them, and we'll get Hiddi to distract Horold. It'll be a sixday before anyone dares tell him."

This was starting to make terrible sense! Her heart was racing. "Saltaja's coming. We foresee her arriving tomorrow."

"Even better. The old hag'll keep him even more occupied. Ingeld!" This decisive Benard was strangely unlike his usual impractical self. "*Can* you leave Kosord with me? You've always said one menzil was the farthest—"

"There may be a way," she admitted. It was madness, total Eriander madness, but it seemed to be what the fires were telling her, and there was a way to test it. "How did you get in here?"

"Through the gate, of course."

Benard was greatly favored by his goddess. Anziel would grant requests from him that other artists would never dream of asking. She would reveal shapes inside solid rock to him, open locked doors for him. He lived in a shed and gave Her golden hawks.

"Do you know the treasury of sacred vessels?"

He shrugged. "Yes. Haven't been inside it since I was a tad."

"Can you get in there without anyone knowing?"

"Why do I want to?"

"I'll explain later. It's very important. We'll be opening it before the feast tomorrow, but at the moment it's still sealed. You have to be able to close it up when you leave so that no one will know it's been opened."

He sat in silence and stillness for a dozen heartbeats, then muttered, "It's been so long . . . There's a cord on the inside of the door going up through the roof." He was *seeing* that in his memory. "It must lead to one of the bells outside the guard room. I'd have to ask Her to unhook that, or I'll find myself neck-deep in Werists. And the ropes across the door are sealed?"

"Yes. Three seals." Three wads of dried clay on the knots, each marked with seven or eight people's wrist seals. He would have to moisten the back of each seal, remove it without cracking it, and then stick it back afterward. No mortal could do that without divine aid. But Benard's deft fingers could turn lumps of clay into flowers or butterflies or likenesses of friends.

"She may do that for me, if I ask properly."

"Go, then!" she said. "Hide that stupid dagger somewhere. If you find you can't get in, come back here. Otherwise I'll see you in the treasury when . . ." She jumped up, led him over to the arches, and pointed to the stars. "When Ishniar is overhead. Will that be time enough?"

"Plenty." He kissed her again and again she melted like a dewy maiden at her betrothal. Oh, it had been so long!

"Don't get yourself killed, love!" she said, but he had gone.

◆

Never had the sky turned slower. Ingeld fidgeted and fretted, paced, tried to pray. She could see nothing in the embers, which was hardly surprising in her jittery state. There was no real danger, she told herself over and over—no real danger as long as Benard had remembered to dispose of the dagger. If the guards heard the bell and went to investigate, they would merely arrest him and shut him up in a dungeon overnight—as long as he didn't try anything stupid, like trying to knife a Werist. It was her palace, so when the prisoner was brought before her, she would just pardon him.

The stars had frozen in place. She went to kneel before the embers. She was tempted to make a vow that she would not move from there until Veslih showed her it was time to go, but threatening goddesses was never wise. And then, as if her goddess had taken pity on her, she saw him. He was kneeling by a door, patiently working on the lowermost seal on the crisscrossed ropes. He had a jar, a lamp, and a cloth—and the dagger! He was gently loosening the clay on the back of the seal. The other two seemed to have gone already. She watched in terror. The guards were supposed to patrol the palace all night long, but she knew they rarely bothered to visit the cellars, and with Horold out of town they would be even less vigilant than usual.

Benard lifted away the third seal and set it down a safe distance from the door. He began untying the ropes. All he had to do now was pull the bolt and haul the door open. He must be confident that the bell cord on the other side had come untied. Or perhaps mice had already chewed through it, because holy Veslih must be cooperating in this, two goddesses combining to foil the god of war.

Ingeld jumped to her feet, snatched up a dark gown, and ran out into the anteroom. The palace was dark and silent. Steering mostly by memory and fingers trailing on the wall, she hastened to the Daughters' chapel. Tene and an acolyte were on duty there. Their alarm and guilt as they sprang up suggested that they had been very close to asleep, but that was good news, for it meant that there had been no alarming sightings.

"I shall keep the vigil for a time," Ingeld said, and swept on into the adytum. No one argued, especially the mousy little acolyte keeping watch over the sacred fire. Ingeld chased her out also. Let them wonder! A city dynast need not explain her decisions to anyone.

She closed the heavy, bronze-scrolled door, locking it with bolts hidden within the tracery. She dropped her cloak around her and knelt to offer a wordless prayer. No calm needed now. Calm would be out of place, and the flames were full of joy—showing Benard also, of course, but mostly joy and celebration. So she had read the auguries correctly and divined why Benard Celebre was so important to Kosord. What would happen after tonight she could not see. No boats. No dead bodies, either, but no promises that her lover would live even until dawn. He was about to fulfill his destiny. He might hold no interest for the gods after that.

The Holy Keeper had made Her will known, and Her light must obey.

Ingeld rose and crossed to the secret panel. The little hatch was heavier than she remembered it on the day her mother had shown it to her. She pressed on one side, pushing hard, sinking her bare feet into the rugs. When it had turned on its central pivot far enough to show a crack along either edge, Benard's thick fingers appeared beside hers, and hauled.

The floor of the treasury was lower, so he was looking up at her. His eyes went wide with astonishment, black crystal with the sacred flames dancing in them. He stared at the central hearth and the five dark-tiled walls rising into mystery.

"Where?"

"It is the adytum of Veslih, Her holy of holies."

He bit his lip. "I may not enter such a place. It is forbidden me."

"That is possible," she admitted. "But did not your goddess open the treasury door for you?"

"So She did!" He smiled the huge grin she always associated with young Bena, softening his blocky face back to boyishness.

When he started to move, she put out a hand to stop him.

"Wait! Benard, only once in a generation may a man enter this room, and for only one purpose. You must enter unclothed and here give your seed to Veslih, renouncing all claim on the child you will sire. Do you accept those terms?"

He stared at her in disbelief, working it out, then nodded. Then his eyes narrowed. "You will use me to block Horold. I don't mind that, but you promised we would go away."

"So we shall. This must come first."

His smile twisted with young man's lechery, so that he was again the adolescent lover she remembered. He fumbled at his waist. "Can I try for twins?"

How typical! Despite the solemnity of the moment, she laughed. "You have all night. Go for triplets if you're man enough."

She shed her robe and returned to the brazier. By then he had stripped and clambered up; he closed the panel with no obvious effort. He knelt beside her, unashamedly aroused.

"You're sure I'm not too old to interest you?" she said.

"Do I look as if I had doubts? Oh, Ingeld! This time forever?"

"Forever," she promised. "As long as the gods allow."

Arms embraced, lips met, she closed her eyes.

There was a little more lovers' babble: "You make me feel like a girl again." "You taught me how to be a man." "All these years? All those women?—and don't deny them—and yet you want me again?" "I never stopped wanting you. They were all you. And none of them was." Then no more words.

✦

Horold's savagery had left her sore, but even as a youth, Benard had always been a careful lover. And a playful one. No doubt all previous impregnations performed in this chamber had been cold-blooded ritual, dour state consorts doing their duty, but Benard as lover could never be anything but joyful. He teased and tickled and tongued her until he had her helplessly aroused, gasping and pleading for release. And perhaps the goddess added Her approval, for when the ecstasy came, it was inexpressibly prolonged and sweet, as if all the years of denial were being rewarded in one single, overpowering passion.

✦

Later, while he was leaning on an elbow, studying her body by firelight and tracing out its contours with fingertips, he said, "Holy Veslih must have kept you young for this. You haven't changed at all! If you had gained one wrinkle I would notice."

"I enjoy flattery more than I used to. You've changed, though. You're bigger and cuddlier and a lot hairier."

"And I have more stamina."

"I doubt that," she said. "But I'm willing to be persuaded."

"In a moment. Explain why this was necessary."

"I think you know. What was your mother's name?"

"Oliva. Why?"

"Part of the ritual. And now I can leave Kosord, because Horold will kill Oliva if he finds out she's yours, and obviously she cannot flee without taking me with her."

He touched tongue to nipple. "What absurd logic! But I'm not complaining." He nibbled, sucked, inspected his handiwork. "I think we can start work on the second triplet now."

twenty-eight

FABIA CELEBRE

said softly, "In Kosord, Father, you must visit the Jade Bowl."

For days she had been seeking a chance to pass on the Witness's advice. Now the two of them were leaning on the gunwale, in the bows where the wind would carry her whisper away, and no one was watching them except a snoopy white bird on the fore post. All other eyes were on the landing ahead as *Beloved of Hrada* eased in toward the bustling waterfront of Kosord.

"What is the Jade Bowl?"

"I have no idea. A friend told me." She considered telling him that there would be no wedding yet, and decided that the risk was not worth it. He would learn that in a few minutes.

Horth was still a man of infinite surprises. His pale eyes appraised her narrowly. "Did this friend also mention Huntleader Hrothgatson?"

Perag had died after three days of agony, which was what he had inflicted on Paola.

"The subject may have been raised."

Horth sighed and went back to studying the front. She realized that he would not comment further, neither now nor ever. Lately she had seen the truth in Master Pukar's warning that Horth Wigson refused to know things he did not wish to know. Marriage to a Chosen must require some such denial.

"It seems we were expected," he said.

"I expect the Bright Ones are watching over us."

Horth just frowned.

Fabia was unimpressed by her first view of Kosord. The high palace was imposing and the unfamiliar vegetation added an exotic touch, but the city itself was only a shaggy, overgrown thatched village, unworthy of its ancient fame. The waterfront was an elongated madhouse bazaar, although part of the confusion was being caused by an honor guard of Werists, which was seriously disrupting traffic. Brazen notes of trumpets had already greeted Saltaja's disembarkation from *Blue Ibis*. Some god had forewarned the satrap of their arrival. He was greeting his sister; the woman beside him was no doubt his wife, Fabia's mother-in-law-elect.

She walked up the plank behind Horth and Ern, with Cnurg breathing on the back of her head as usual, to meet a monster that could only be Horold Hragson—a boar pretending to be a man; or a man and several boars mashed into one. Saltaja was a tall woman, but she seemed like a child beside him as she waved Horth aside when he would have made obeisance. Fabia genuflected to the satrap. Streets were never exactly fragrant, but there was a particularly horrible local stench somewhere nearby.

"Rise!" He leered around his tusks at her. "You are welcome to our realm, young mistress." His voice grated like a corn mill. "And to our family, also."

"Eventually," Saltaja said. She was dangerously displeased. "Your bridegroom has gone on upriver, child."

"Left for the Edgelands about a thirty ago," the satrap rasped. "Hot blood, you know. Eager to get to the war."

"Alas!" Needing to look relieved-pretending-to-be-disappointed, Fabia sent a quick appeal for aid to the Mother of Lies.

"We shall follow and hope to catch up before he leaves Tryfors," Saltaja proclaimed. "Acting Packleader Ern, inform the boat masters that their continued service is required. They will be paid when we reach Tryfors, with an extra measure of silver apiece. Post guards to make sure they do not slip away in the night. We shall embark at dawn tomorrow." Her orders sounded like military bugle calls.

"Ah . . . feast of Ucr begins tonight," Horold protested.

"You expect me to cook for it? Carry on, Packleader."

"As my lady commands. Um . . ." Ern gulped nervously. "The masters will need funds for rations."

"Horold, have the boats provisioned."

Fabia was amused to watch the ogre flinch. He was just as afraid of his sister as the youth was.

"Don't I get to meet my future daughter-in-law?" The woman who spoke was a human flame in red-gold robes almost the same shade as her hair, younger than Fabia had expected; her smile lit up the plains. She was obviously a Daughter of Veslih, and in this case dynast of Kosord, but she embraced Fabia before she could drop into a curtsy.

"This is wonderful news! You are very lovely, my dear. My son is indeed fortunate! We all are, for Benard has always been one of the family to us, and now he really will be, as your brother." The lady's eyes twinkled like golden gems as she added, "And I know how heartbroken you must be to hear that you have missed Cutrath."

Such teasing could be a trap, but even without Witness Mist's testimonial, Fabia would have trusted this woman. "Marriage is a daunting prospect, my lady."

"Benard calls me Ingeld. So must you. Horold, Fabia can ride with me. You two will have much to discuss—Sister?"

Saltaja merely shrugged.

Ingeld glanced around at the mass of Werists, both homegrown and newly disembarked. She tossed her red-gold tresses in disgust. "Call them off, Horold. Nobody's going to be running away. Come, Fabia."

Horth had apparently been forgotten and had already made good use of the situation by disappearing. With sudden dismay, Fabia wondered if he might just vanish out of her life, so that he could never again be used as a hostage against her.

She had no time to worry, for in moments she found herself standing in a splendid chariot of gilded bentwood, drawn by two sprightly piebald onagers. The lady drove fast and skillfully along the winding, crowded alleys, but already it was evident that Ingeld would do everything skillfully. People cheered as she went by, some fell on their knees, and youngsters ran ahead to clear the way for her. No one ever cheered Saltaja! There was not a guard in sight.

Travel began to seem more appealing. The clothes were unfamiliar—the women wore neck-high robes, brighter and more elaborate than simple Skjaran wraps, the men mostly just pleated kilts. Hair was longer, smells were spicier, laughter louder, and even the alley dogs seemed to bark in an unfamiliar accent.

"I will be honest," Ingeld said, expertly driving, acknowledging the plaudits of the crowd, and making conversation, all at the same time. "My son is far from ready for marriage. A mother should not say such things, but five years would not be too long. Weru's training cultivates crass and overmuscled juvenile horrors. I was forced into marriage with one. Horold was a stunningly handsome man and certainly the pick of the litter, but life with him has not been easy." She bit her lip. "You know all about the children of Hrag, of course?"

"I understand that the sister rules the brothers, except maybe Stralg."

Golden eyes shot a sideways glance at Fabia. "Have you heard any rumors that the Queen of Shadows is not their *sister*?"

"No, my lady, I mean Ingeld . . . What else could she be?"

Ingeld smiled softly at the alley ahead. "There are dark whispers that she is their mother, Hrag's widow. She has also borne four sons to Eide Ernson. Her remarkable preservation is taken as evidence that she is a Chosen."

"No one doubts that in Skjar."

"Chosen look after their own. She raised Horold. She can still terrify him. I am taking you to meet your brother. That is agreeable?"

"Oh, yes! I always hated being an only child, and now I learn of three brothers!"

"You did not know your history?"

Fabia told of her upbringing by the wealthy merchant and his Florengian wife, and what she officially knew of her past. She heard in turn about Benard's arrival as a stricken child and his blossoming into the finest artist in the city, perhaps in all Vigaelia.

"He is not the most practical of men, but we all love him," Ingeld concluded.

"I hope my return to Celebre will not put him in danger," Fabia said warily.

Another stab of the brilliant eyes: "I hope so too. We must persuade him to accompany you to Tryfors for the wedding."

"Would he not be safer here?"

"No! Absolutely not. There he is. As you see, there is quite a lot of him."

The chariot had emerged onto empty ground, a sun-burned weed patch beside a high, circular building. At the far corner three white statues stood incongruously in front of some sort of storage shed. Two men were working on them—a leggy Vigaelian boy and a Florengian. Fabia's heart was racing. Fable was about to become reality and produce a genuine, living, breathing brother.

The man had been crouching beside one of the figures, polishing its leg with a cloth and abrasive. He looked up, scowling angrily at the interruption. Then he rose, and she saw that he was not unusually tall, just very wide and thick . . . his black hairiness was barely concealed by a leather overall that seemed to be his only garment . . . dusty, sweaty, unshaven, unkempt. Unprepossessing. A quarry worker—with a wrist seal.

He saw Ingeld and a smile like summer sunrise turned him into a huge, overgrown boy, black stubble and all. As the lady skillfully brought the chariot to a halt without ever reaching for the brake, Benard's dark eyes switched to Fabia and stretched wide.

The apprentice came running forward, all awkward arms and legs and gaping smile. "My lady! Great honor . . ."

"Veslih bless you, Thod!" Ingeld said. "Will you water them for me? And walk them a little?" She accepted the boy's hand to descend and gave him the reins.

Fabia left the car without noticing she had done so. Benard was still staring at her as if she were a sending from the Dark One. She could do no better than stare back at him. Twenty-three was not really old at all. He had incredible arms . . . wavy black hair down to his shoulders . . . eyes black, lustrous.

She stopped just before she walked into him.

"Fabia?" he said in a sort of squeak.

"Brother!"

"Mother's eyes." He touched her face with a hairy knuckle. "Cheekbones from Father, but the rest is all Mother . . . They told me you were dead!"

"No one ever told me about you at all."

Whereupon Master Artist Celebre uttered a scream that raised pigeons from half Kosord. He grabbed his sister, swung her up like a child, spun around several times. Setting her down again, he kissed her and yelled, "Fabia, Fabia, Fabia, Fabia!" He was stronger than the Wrogg in flood and gentler than thistledown. Where had he been all her life? "Oh, Fabia!" He kissed her again.

Fabia's eyelids prickled painfully. She hugged him in return, and kissed him, all stubbly.

"You two know each other, I see," Ingeld remarked.

He roared, *"Why didn't you tell me she was coming?"* Which was no way to address the dynast.

"Because I didn't know. Are you going to crush her to death?"

He laughed and apologized and kissed Fabia yet again, all at once, and finally he let her go. For a moment it seemed as if he would grab Ingeld and kiss her also, but he remembered his manners and bowed low.

"Benard, you'd better know this right away. I told you your father is very sick. He may have returned to the womb already. Fabia is on her way home to Celebre."

His face went wooden. "Female succession? What of Dantio? Is he not the heir?"

"He's dead. You know that." She spoke to him like a mother or a teacher. "And it wouldn't necessarily be him, even if he weren't."

"You are not plotting to make *me* a doge, I hope?"

"Only the gods do miracles. Benard, Fabia is to marry Cutrath."

He turned almost as pale as a Vigaelian. He yelled, *"No!"*

"Benard—"

"No! No!"

Across the yard the echoes agreed, *"No! No!"*

"Benard—"

"No! I am her eldest surviving male relative and I absolutely forbid—"

"Don't be such a puddle-brained, idiotic—"

"Over my dead body and any other bodies I—"

Fabia concluded that they were not going to sit down in some comfortable, shady place for a family chat. Back in Skjar artists ranked just above laborers, well below merchants and artisans, while Ingeld sprang from a long line of royal foremothers—twelve generations in Kosord alone—yet here these two were screaming at each other like bazaar hucksters in a slow spell. Thod, walking the team slowly by, stared with owl eyes at the unseemly squabble.

One might conclude that Benard did not approve of Cutrath Horoldson and that Ingeld thought he was being unrealistic, but the quarrel had sprung up much too fast to be only that. Fabia had seen the same pattern in her friends, in her father's employees, and even in the riverfolk. She was almost certain that Benard and Ingeld were yelling about this because they dared not yell about some other, more important thing. Curious!

"You want my opinion?" she asked.

Benard wheeled on her. "No, I do not . . ."

Ingeld said, "You keep out of . . . Yes, of course we do."

"Tell us, Sister," he said hastily.

"With no disrespect to your fine son, Ingeld, I will not marry a Werist.

Any Werist. Benard, if Stralg wants to use me to control Celebre, then he will leave no rival claimants alive. Saltaja will see you dead before she leaves here, and yelling at each other won't help the situation."

The disputants eyed each other warily and declared a truce.

Benard folded his massive arms. "How do you plan to escape the Cutrath disaster?"

"I shall need your help. As my nearest male relative, you have a duty to escort me to Tryfors."

He pouted. "Satrap Horold would rather I remain here in Kosord, in an unmarked grave."

"We'll discuss it tonight," Ingeld said firmly. "Um, everything all right for tonight?"

He grinned with what seemed like sheer boyish glee. "She's willing!" He did not deign to explain to his sister who was willing to do what.

"Get your hair cut," Ingeld said, sounding more like a mother than dynast of the city. "I'll send a chariot for you. The brother of the bride must be present at the feast. Did your robe arrive? I'll send one for Thod, too!"

Benard's huge grin flashed back, wiping ten years from him. "He'll eat himself sick and his mother will die of pride!"

"That's what feasts are for." Ingeld waved to the boy to bring the chariot.

Fabia had just taken her first proper look at the three silent bystanders, the marble goddesses. Horth would give gold by the bucket for such art. "Benard, *you* carved these? But they're . . . beyond words! Oh, I am so proud to have a brother who can do this. This is holy Mayn, of course? And this one? . . ."

twenty-nine

INGELD NARSDOR

whipped up the team and sent the chariot rattling across the yard. That had gone very well. She had not blushed like a child on seeing her lover and Benard had behaved himself as well as could be expected. Fabia could have no reason to guess their secret.

"Does he remember?" the girl asked.

"Remember what?"

"His parents giving him away—our parents."

"Yes he does. It scarred him terribly. The first time I met him, he was curled up in a ball. It was a sixday before he would uncurl long enough to feed himself." For a thirty or so, she had been the only person who could get him to straighten out. A year later—when he had finally stopped following her around the palace *all* the time, when he would sometimes talk with other people, even play with other children—any mention of his family, his home, the war, any of those, and he would promptly just curl up again. On some level, he was still doing it.

Fabia said, "Is he bitter?"

"Very."

"I don't. Remember, I mean. I was a baby."

"Of course not. Curse my sister-in-law! She is going to drag you away before we can even begin to get to know each other." But Fabia's arrival could have been a serious impediment to the lovers' planned flight, for she would certainly notice their disappearance, even if everyone else was too busy partying. So *bless* Saltaja for whipping her away again so promptly! "And you'll miss most of the feast. You don't *have* to eat until you're sick, but you are entirely free to do so."

The girl laughed, neither too much nor too little. She was strong and deep-breasted, not sylphlike like Benard's goddesses, but she sparkled with youth and health, and her royal breeding showed in poise and diffidence, wit and intelligence. Broad shoulders must run in the family. She would be wasted on Cutrath, who had not yet discovered that women had uses outside bedrooms.

Fabia might also be a spoiled brat, accustomed to getting her own way, overindulged by a wealthy father. Her demand that Benard drop everything to escort her, while not absurd, could have been more tactfully phrased. Her flat assertion that she would never marry a Werist was as unrealistic as some of his crazier logic. It was a rare bride who had any say in the selection of her husband, and girls with dynastic claims never did, as Ingeld well knew. Fabia would be taken to Tryfors under guard, and there her choice would be wedding ring with or without thumbscrews.

"Benard is stubborn, isn't he?" Fabia asked.

"*Bena?* Why, he flows as smoothly as the Wrogg."

"And only one way?" She was quick.

"Exactly one." Ingeld waved to acknowledge cheers. "He refuses to see trouble until he steps in it. Who was the man who came with you?"

"My foster father, Horth Wigson. Saltaja brought him along as hostage for the hostage. I suspect Eide is currently looting his home and business."

"Very likely. I saw him dissolve into the crowd. It was smoothly done." His absence might tempt Fabia to try an escape, Ingeld thought, and wondered if the girl knew how dangerous Saltaja Hragsdor was. "Will he be all right?"

"He will own half of Kosord within the year."

It was Ingeld's turn to laugh. "We have Ucrists here, too."

Fabia's grin was impish. "Pity them."

✦

Ingeld swept into the palace like a spring flood. She summoned the flank-leader of the palace guard; sent for a pair of golden rods; committed Fabia to the tender care of Sansya, who rushed her away, both of them chattering happily in Florengian; established that Saltaja had been given a room but was now closeted with Horold and thus safely out of the way; ascertained that preparations for the feast were in full roar, with edible meats due almost at once; added Thod to the list of honored guests to receive festive wreaths and robes; and settled a dozen other problems.

By then she had reached her chamber. She tossed a handful of godswood on the smoldering coals in the brazier and paced a few lengths while she went over her escape plan. She could not hope to deceive the Witnesses, but they never volunteered information. By the time Horold got around to asking questions, she should be far, far away.

Two youngsters knelt in the doorway, each clutching a gilded baton.

"Come in." She smiled to put them at ease. Neither was known to her and they were both so sweaty and dusty that they had obviously been working hard already, but she had expected as much today, which was one reason why she had summoned two. The other reason was that two rods made a message an affair of state.

"Both of you to High Priest Nrakfin," she said. "Make sure there are other priests in attendance, understand?"

They both nodded and the taller boy smiled slightly, so she need not labor the point. Nrakfin's aides would see that her commands were obeyed.

"Say to him: 'The Nymph of holy Eriander known as Hiddi, who dwells in the Lesser Street of Silversmiths, has given grave affront to holy Veslih. The woman must be brought in penitent garb to the Shrine of Repentance and our gravest ban shall fall on any who delay her.' Repeat."

They parroted it back, watching each other's lips for timing.

"Good. Go."

They did not merely go; they fled. It must be ten years since Ingeld had threatened anyone with exile, and old Nrakfin would gibber if he understood. His aides would pass the thunderbolt on to the light of Eriander, and it would be up to her to deliver the package.

Flankleader Guthlag was next, beaming toothlessly and bowing in proper Werist fashion—a move he had been quite unable to make before Ingeld's last attempt to ship Benard out of town.

"You sent for me, lady?"

"Indeed I did, Packleader," she said, giving him the rank he had borne in the days before Horold. "I want to ask a favor."

"Anything at all, of course."

"Not unlike the last one I asked of you. When the hostages check in today, can you arrange to see them alone?"

Only one hostage was required to register at the guard room these days, and the old man caught her meaning at once, leering his pleasure. She had never doubted that he would aid her flight. Quite apart from his lifelong loyalty to her, he had always had a soft spot for Benard and now additionally credited Bena with finding an excuse for him to battleform and so cure his rheumatism. That was not how Benard told it, but Guthlag looked ten years younger than he had before their escapade in the summer. He was even staying sober.

"No difficulty, my lady. I was thinking of taking a stroll down to the temple." Meaning he could talk privately with Benard there.

They exchanged a few meaningless remarks and the Werist departed. Guthlag would do his part, but last night Ingeld had given Benard a bag of silver for expenses. She hoped he would not mislay it before Guthlag got there.

Now back to the feast—the anteroom was again full of people with problems.

✦

Ingeld's everyday dress as a Daughter was ostentatious enough, but her festival robes were a state treasure, copiously decorated with amber, coral, topaz, rubies, carnelians, jasper, and garnets. She could not sit down in them, but she could fill a small room, and her headdress was an eruption of red and gold feathers that posed problems in all but the highest doorways. She had long ago learned to tolerate the weight and discomfort in exchange for the awe she could provoke in almost anyone. By the time she was made ready for the feast, the garden outside was shadowed and the sky burned sunset-red.

She was advised that the two Celebre hostages were awaiting her pleasure in the anteroom. She was also informed that a woman in penitent garb had been delivered to the Shrine of Repentance. She sent for Tene and Sansya.

"There is a vicious old baggage Nymph in the Shrine. Tene, summon a Witness and scribes for a trial. We'll make it quick and run her out of town. Sansya, take three or four acolytes, and don't let her within arm's length of a man, whatever you do. Show her the shackles, whips, and branding irons, and explain how they are used. Then bring her here . . . Go around by the Great Corridor and Crystal Court . . ."

She outlined an itinerary that would show Hiddi the wealth and grandeur of the palace. She would walk high-vaulted halls and wide corridors, see polychrome murals, mosaics of semiprecious stones, paneling of fruit woods and alabaster, furniture of gilt and ivory, tin and amber, rare fabrics and soft furs. She would pass early feasters starting in on meats and fruits piled high on gold and silver platters; heaps of fish and beans, dates, peaches, innumerable cheeses, cucumbers and poultry; rivers of beer fortified with mead; wine cooled in the palace cellars, all being served by many sixty servants. She would see the dancers and tumblers, hear the musicians and the laughter of jeweled nobles reclining on their couches. If that didn't do it, Ingeld thought, she was sadly misjudging her victim. Sansya looked puzzled, but went off to obey.

Ingeld called for the Celebres and threw more godswood twigs on the brazier.

Fabia entered first and Ingeld saw she had been too hasty to judge someone who had spent many sixdays on the river without a single attendant. Not sylphlike, no, but the girl did have beauty beyond the mere glow of youth. Surprisingly, her dresser had robed her in dark colors, a gown of deep blue and costly purple that gave her a strange air of mystery, and whose simple lines made her seem taller and slighter than before. It was a curiosity of Kosordian costume that the men covered their chests for festive occasions and the women bared theirs. Fabia's décolletage would have shocked Skjaran society to the marrow, but she had the figure to justify it and apparently the confidence also. The high black coil of her hair sparkled with amethysts.

Benard, in blue-green festive cloak and garland of roses, was a maiden's dream, an astonishing contrast to his habitual scruffiness. Ingeld wondered briefly which god he could model after himself, and decided with amusement that it would have to be holy Demern. Only the Lawgiver should portray that rocky stubbornness.

He could hardly take his eyes off his newfound sister, but when he saw Ingeld in full regalia, he sobered and dropped on one knee. Fabia was already down.

"Up, up!" Ingeld said. "This is a family conference, not a temple ceremony. Fabia, you look breathtaking! The feast has its queen. Are you not proud of your sister, Benard? What goddess will you style after her?"

He frowned and stared at Fabia. And she stared right back—cryptic, inscrutable, waiting.

"I . . . I don't know," he muttered. "Hrada, perhaps?"

Fabia was amused. "Me? With a loom or a needle? Or are you thinking stonemason's mallet and chisel?"

He shook his head and did not reply, still frowning.

"Come over here, dear," Ingeld said, "this is Cutrath."

"It's a good likeness," Benard growled from behind them, "except that in reality his ears are bloated like cabbages, his nose is all bent over, his teeth—"

"That will do, Benard!"

Fabia made some tactful remarks about brawn, but clearly would still not admit that Cutrath had relevance for her.

Ingeld explained the rest of the images—her parents and the twins. Then she pointed up at the frieze of the Bright Ones—Cienu with his wine jug, Nula comforting a child, and so on. "That is Benard's work. You have a very talented . . . What's wrong?"

The girl had lost color. "Nothing . . . nothing at all . . . Is that not Bloodlord Stralg, my lady?"

"It's not a great likeness," Benard said. "I barely remember him."

"It's close enough to give me nightmares," Ingeld countered.

"But you were only a pudding, so you can't possibly remember," he told his sister. "So how—"

"I do believe Saltaja showed me his picture once," Fabia said hastily, seeming flustered. "In Skjar. And of course he is your brother-in-law, my lady! I suppose he is an appropriate model for holy Weru . . . And that is you—as holy Veslih, of course! Oh, it's wonderful! Who are the rest, Benard?"

He was grinning again. "Most are composites of several people. Can you recognize any more?"

"No. How could I?"

"Holy Nula is based on Mama. Now you see how I recognized you this morning? Demern, over there, is Papa. They're not true likenesses, just childhood memories, and of course the coloring is Vigaelian, not Florengian."

"You are most wonderfully clever! I am honored to have such a brother. Will you draw Dantio and Orlando for me?"

Benard winced. "I never think about Dantio. Orlando was so young that my memories would mean nothing. He must be a grown man by now."

Fabia had made a very good recovery, but Ingeld was certain it had not been Stralg that had startled her. She had been looking toward Nula, and while Master Artist Benard might see a resemblance between the picture and the girl, Ingeld had not until he pointed it out. Fabia had not exclaimed, "That's me!" If she had been taken from her mother as a babe, how could she have retained any memory of her face? And why lie about it if she had? Curious! Nor could Ingeld recall seeing any likenesses of Bloodlord Stralg in Skjar the time she had visited her sister-in-law there.

Now it was past time Ingeld took her place at the feast, and she still had Hiddi to settle. "Benard, I do think you should ask Saltaja to let you accompany your sister to Tryfors for her wedding."

He frowned. He was hopeless at lying, and almost never did, but he must see the need to keep their plans secret even from Fabia.

"You heard the bride's views on the wedding," he said. "It will not happen. Why should I want to go to Tryfors? I remember it as an absolutely horrible place." Never had Ingeld seen him look more like a mud-brick wall. "I have a commission to finish here. I have obligations to my apprentice. You can have Celebre, so far as I am concerned, Sister. Congratulations. Give Mama my regards."

Ingeld caught Fabia's eye and they pulled faces in unison. Men!

"How about Papa, if he still lives?"

Benard shrugged. "Him too, if you want. Ingeld worries that Horold will kill me if I stay here, but she knows that her son would certainly kill me if I turned up in Tryfors."

Amusingly, the girl now looked equally stubborn. Accustomed to getting her own way, she was close to losing her temper. "It seems a shame after all these years to find my brother and so soon have to mourn him."

To keep up the pretense, Ingeld had to say, "She's right, Benard."

His scowl became even more mulish. "I don't think so. You're proposing I evade murder by committing suicide. Horold won't kill me until I've finished immortalizing Cutrath for him. You know that. Come, Fabia, I want to show you off. By your leave, my lady? If this is to be my last feast, I mustn't miss any of it."

Ingeld nodded permission and he left with his sister on his arm.

✦

Like a huge brown caterpillar, the Nymph shuffled on bare feet into Ingeld's chamber. Penitent garb was the ultimate in indignity, a narrow, sleeveless sack that left only the upper half of her face visible. She could neither sit nor kneel, and to move at all she must struggle to hold up the trailing hem and take tiny steps. Hiddi had been prodded along on her tour of the palace by two husky Daughter acolytes armed with long toasting forks.

Ingeld posed in state on the platform, a white-shrouded Witness stood near the arches, and two cross-legged scribes held styli ready. Tene and Sansya had chosen to attend, wanting to learn how to conduct such a trial. If this one went as planned, it should not seem difficult.

"Witness of holy Mayn," Ingeld proclaimed, "I am dynast of this city and I have summoned the Nymph Hiddi here before the holy Bright Ones to answer my charge that she has abused the powers granted her by holy Eriander. Do you recognize this court?"

"I do," the Maynist said.

"Are the holy ones present?"

"Their images testify that They are."

"Is the prisoner the accused I named?"

"She is."

Ingeld turned her attention to Hiddi. What could be seen of her face was scarlet with fury, and her eyes glittered like bronze knives. Ingeld could only hope that Benard had explained why this charade was necessary.

"Nymph Hiddi," Ingeld continued, "you worship Eriander in your own home instead of in the temple and enrich yourself with gifts that should have been made to your god or not made at all. I abhor you and your like. You pervert your god's purpose. Instead of dispensing His joy, you torture men with unslaked desire. The powers He gives for your defense you use to enslave. I have lost count of the wives who have come to me in tears because their husbands have given away everything to holy harlots like you, so that they and their children will be sold into slavery to pay their debts. In the last year, at least three have told me that you were the leech responsible. Do you deny these charges?"

"They are lies!" Hiddi screamed.

"Witness?"

"She is guilty."

"Then I can pronounce sentence. Nymph, will you plead for mercy?"

"Bitch!" Hiddi screamed. The onlookers gasped in horror. If that was fake anger, it was well done.

"I am the light of Veslih and greater than you, slut. I sentence you to confiscation of all your property plus eight sixty lashes with an oxhide whip, followed by eviction from our city, living or dead."

Hiddi muttered something inaudible but unrepentant.

Ingeld waited for the scribes to catch up. "We shall remit part of that sentence if you will confess your victims by name, beseeching your god to release them evermore from your toils."

"How much will you remit?"

"That will depend on how repentant I judge you." Ingeld nodded to the scribes. "We shall not have the names of innocent men recorded. You may leave. And you, Tene. Sansya, please stay."

The moment the door closed, Ingeld smiled and stepped down from the platform. "I hope I did not frighten you, Hiddi? You do understand that this was the only way I could get you in here?"

"But you were enjoying it!"

"And you earned it. Sansya, will you help Mistress Hiddi out of that appalling garment, please? There is a robe for her on that chest and I have some sweet wine here."

Sansya gaped at her. Possibly the Witness did, too, under her shroud, because Ingeld and Benard had done most of their plotting in the adytum, where Mayn was not permitted to pry. Hiddi was extricated from her penitent's sack and provided with a gown of finest silk. She was much younger than Ingeld had expected and quite obviously the model for one of Benard's goddesses.

She perched on an ivory chair and accepted wine in a carved crystal goblet, suspicion crawling over her pretty face like maggots. "Now what?"

"First you release your victims and the Witness testifies that you are sincere in your petition to the god. This room is consecrated. Eriander is up there."

Hiddi looked up and regarded the frieze. "That's Benard's work!"

"Yes it is, and if it satisfied High Priest Nrakfin, it will do for you. After that I shall remit all the rest of the sentence—I'll let you keep your loot, because I suppose some of it you earned. You may sleep here tonight. I will see that my husband comes to join you. You know what to do then, and I wish you every success."

Hiddi smiled, catlike. Sansya was aghast.

"I'm only doing this for Benard!" Hiddi said.

"You mean you won't accept presents from the satrap?"

Hiddi shrugged. "Maybe one or two."

"He's dangerous, Hiddi. *Be very careful,* because he can see in the dark like a bat. Remember, too, that he has violent followers who may try to rescue him."

"Men!" Hiddi said contemptuously. "Animals. This is very high class wine, Ingeld."

thirty

HOROLD HRAGSON

had known some bad experiences in his life, the worst being a rebel ambush outside Jazkra, when he was jumped by four warbeasts at once. It had happened soon after the twins' death, when he was less alert than usual, and by the time his host rallied to him, he had killed one of his assailants and the other three had killed him—or so his men thought. He had needed most of a day in battleform to heal and had failed to retroform properly. He had never looked in a mirror since.

His second worst experience, and also the third, fourth, and continuing on as high as he could count, had involved his sister Saltaja. He had no memory of his parents, or any ruling force in his life besides Saltaja. Terrible as Weru, she never made a threat she would not carry out. Nor had age softened her. Nay, it had not even dared touch her, for she was unchanged from his earliest memories. He had heard the rumors that she was his mother, not his sister, and did not believe them. Therek, the eldest, was not so sure, but you could never believe much of what Therek said. That she was a Chosen seemed very believable, but in sixty lifetimes Horold would never dare ask her.

Mother or not, she had always been able to cow him when she wanted to, and she was in a cowing mood that day. A daylight nightmare in her black robes, she led the way into his private courtyard, sat on the marble wall enclosing the fishpond, and began questioning him relentlessly on recruitment of reinforcements for Stralg. Forewarned of her arrival by Ingeld, Horold had ordered his tallymen to have answers ready for the sort of questions Saltaja usually asked, and had even made some effort to memorize a few responses, though numbers had never been his strong point. This time she ignored crops, taxes, and plagues, concentrating instead on how many recruits had passed through Kosord on their way upriver. How was he supposed to know *that*? They rarely even came to the palace. They'd storm the temple of Eriander and be on their way by dawn.

He summoned the tallymen and their baskets of tablets—and Saltaja tangled all of them in knots. Later, when the minions had been sent away and there were just the two of them again, she delivered the Truth as she saw it.

"At least six sixty have deserted in the last year. That's the least it can be. The real loss must be much worse."

"There's always some wastage in training," he protested. "We run them down and make examples of them."

She gave him a look he recalled from his childhood. "I am talking of initiates, not boys! Have they found some way to shed their collars and live? If not, then where are they going?"

"Probably mostly nowhere. Any governor likes to collect a larger host than he'll admit to."

"You were smarter when you still had your milk teeth. Listen and we'll try again. *Either* eleven-twelfths of the governors are suddenly holding back far more men than usual—which means there is a Face-wide rebellion brewing—*or else* about twenty-five out of every sixty recruits heading for Tryfors disappear on the way there. Or both," she added, frowning. "The leak seems to be upstream from here."

"They're recruiting trash, that's the trouble."

"They always did. But the loss in senior men is greater than it is in the youngsters. Why do you think I arrived with a escort of wet-eared boys?"

"You were frightened the older ones might gang up on you and mutiny on the way here!"

"Was that a flash of lightning I just saw? Yes. But I want a really senior man to escort me to Tryfors and back—one with a family here, so he won't be tempted to desert. Call your seer."

The satrap obediently rose and went like a page to pass the word. He was intrigued by the thought of a boatload of Werists trying to throw Saltaja overboard—which side would he bet on? If he was Cutrath, sailing off to join the Florengian slaughter, he would certainly be tempted to desert, but the lad ought to be fairly safe playing tyrant in Celebre, married to that curvy little piece, Whatshername.

A Witness came waddling into the courtyard like an ambulatory bolster. He knew this fat one. She had been around for a couple of years, and Horold normally hated to see her answer his summons, because getting information out of her was like getting eggs from a gander. He wondered if the Queen of Shadows would fare any better with her. Saltaja began snarling questions; his part was just to tell the woman to answer each time.

Even with Saltaja asking the questions, the fat seer got away with giving very few firm answers. If recruits were absconding, it was happening nowhere near Kosord.

"Where is Horth Wigson?" Saltaja demanded at last.

"Who? Er, answer the question."

"Horth Wigson is Fabia Celebre's foster father. He is not presently visible to my sight."

"And Fabia Celebre?"

"Answer."

"She is in the Hall of Hawks in the company of her brother."

"Go!" Saltaja snapped and the seer obeyed in silence.

"Almost sunset!" Horold tried not to sound relieved. "Have to go host the feast."

"Wait. The brother?" Saltaja said. "Could he rule a city?"

Horold's bellow of laughter probably startled the fish. "Benard? He'd start by tearing it down so he could remake it better. He's a *Hand!*"

"Would he take orders?"

"He never has before. If he hears them at all he just forgets them. Er, you don't need him as a hostage anymore now, do you?"

Saltaja gave him a long, steady stare. "Why do you dislike him so much?"

"Personal reasons." If she snooped around the palace, she would hear about Cutrath, not the bedroom problem.

"I see. Come here."

A stab of inexplicable terror raised his all-over fur. "Why?" he demanded, rising. Why was he so frightened? She was only a bossy old woman; he could break her neck with one hand if he wanted. Why did she arouse such panic in him that his knees shook? Just vague memories of childhood? Or that day in Jat-Nogul? Was that all? Why was he obeying her, edging closer, dragging his feet, shivering like a terrified child? Why didn't he just tell her to go to the Dark One and stay there?

✦

Gods! Horold started upright on his chair. He must have dropped off. The sun had set already. Where had the day gone?

Saltaja was already at the door. "Do what you like with the artist then, but wait until the girl and I have left."

At last! Horold smiled contentedly, cherishing visions of Benard in a soundproof dungeon, just the two of them. "You sure you won't attend the feast?" he asked unhopefully.

His sister just shook her head. Her taste ran to intimate Skjaran dinner parties with endless, pointless, incomprehensible conversations, not jolly Kosordian-style feasts that faded off into orgies on the edges. As soon as she had gone, he bellowed for a jug of mead.

Having drained that, he felt even better. Get the feast out of the way and then dismember Benard Celebre! Something to look forward to very much. He donned a fresh, well-scented pall and strode off to see if the procession from the temple had arrived yet.

✦

The feast began in the lowermost courts, with more praise for holy Ucr and appeals to holy Cienu to bless the festivities. Street level was where most people remained, with standing room only and hasty grabbing at whatever went by. Citizens of substance, who had been sent festive wreaths, were allowed up to middle-rank halls featuring benches at long tables. There the food was still cold, but the beer was drinkable. The real elite, those given both wreaths and robes, could progress on up to royal levels, and there recline on couches, nibble delicacies, and quaff wine while dancers writhed and musicians twanged and chirped. Because the harvest feast of Ucr lasted four days, the upper halls also featured dimly lit side rooms where senior guests could seek holy Nula's gift of sleep to restore their strength. Holy Eriander was worshiped there also.

Horold began at the top, where he ran into the Celebre girl, a sight to warm the cockles of any man's loins. Lucky Cutrath! Surely even that sorry excuse for a warrior should manage to breed some bulls on this buxom heifer?

"You are enjoying yourself, daughter?"

"Indeed I am, my lord. This is not like feasts in Skjar."

"I hope not. Keep her in the well-lit rooms!" he told her escort. "Mustn't have any gossip."

Her escort was, of course, the cesspool artist, Benard. Horold gave him a *big* smile. "You see you enjoy yourself too, boy." *Then it will be my turn.*

✦

Eventually his progress through the halls and courts brought him to the lowest levels, where he discovered his wife, wearing what he always thought of as her bonfire costume. She was surrounded by doting throngs, of course. As always. Kosord would have been a much harder place for him to rule without the support of its hereditary dynast, and twenty-five years ago it had looked close to impossible. Stralg had been planning a major massacre to bring it to heel —he had estimated a quarter of the population—but once Ingeld consented, the people had followed her lead. She had been a beauty then and was still lustable enough, although no one could know it when she was packaged in that absurd outfit. Horold wandered in her direction, and his presence swiftly thinned out the crowd of admirers.

"Come, wife. You have wasted enough time here. There are more important people to greet."

She agreed with little enthusiasm. "I must go, friends. I shall return later. Please do enjoy yourselves . . . Lead on, my lord."

As they headed up the corridor together, she said, "You didn't used to be such a boor. The rich you can control easily enough, you know. If the poor ever rise, though, *then* you will fall."

"Over their dead bodies."

She looked up at him for a moment. Once her head had been level with his shoulder; now it was closer to his elbow. "It's hard to tell now, but . . . You drink a lot, don't you?"

"There's a lot of me to satisfy."

"Not tonight!" she said sharply. "We have guests, at least sixty-sixty guests."

He chuckled. "Every night I said, and every night I meant. I have last night to make up for, too."

"You spurned me for years. Why the sudden rush?"

"Because I have a lot of catching up to do." He had believed all the stories of battle-hardened Werists killing their women by fathering monsters on them, but there was nothing wrong with the slave girl's whelp. She'd carried it a few thirties too long, was all. That error could be avoided next time.

"I can't oblige you in this dress."

"You won't wear that until dawn. You never do."

She sighed, and her fingers moved on his arm. "Very well. When I go to my room to change, I'll send word."

Aha! This was starting to sound more like the old days. "Getting back in practice, mm?" He'd known she'd soon start enjoying it again.

thirty-one

BENARD CELEBRE

was not known for staying sober at feasts, but that night he was going to need a clear head. Besides, he had to be nice to his long-lost sister.

"This is called the Bull Concourse," he said, pausing at the mouth of the great passage. The inside was shadowed and apparently deserted. He had escorted plenty of other men's sisters in there in his time, usually persuading them to go all the way to the end. "There's a lot of old statuary stored in there, so it's a popular place for, um, private cuddling. Your reputation will be absolutely ruined if you're seen going anywhere near . . ." He laughed clumsily. "I'm behaving like a jealous husband, am I not?" He must have told her a dozen times to stay in well-lit places. He found himself glowering at every man who came close, especially Werists. "I have no experience at brothering."

Fabia chuckled. "I've had none at being brothered. It's very flattering."

He enjoyed her smile. It did not appear very often, but it was worth watching for. Flighty she was not. Fabia was an extremely down-to-earth young lady and knew her own mind. He'd loved the determined way she had told Ingeld she would never marry a Werist.

They continued their tour. Fabia was puzzled by Kosordian informality, especially when Benard introduced her simultaneously to honored guests and the flunkies waiting on them, all of them his friends, from High Priest Nrakfin to Nils the carpenter. "I'm an unusual case," he admitted. "Not many palace brats join artists' guilds."

"More than a guild, though? Only a cultist could create such wonders."

"I don't create them. Anziel does. I'm just Her Hand."

They had so much to discuss! He asked about her childhood, of course, but it was no longer relevant to either of them. She asked why he disliked Cutrath Horoldson so much.

He explained, "Briefly, Cutrath's only redeeming feature is that he is not hypocritical enough to have any redeeming features. He's a lying, thieving, sadistic, tale-telling, lecherous, blasphemous, bullying, foulmouthed brag-gart. He also picks his nose."

Her eyes widened like forest pools brimming over. "No! Both nostrils? Isn't it your duty to defend me from this unsavory marriage?"

"Don't nag! If your Ucrist foster daddy can't help you, what can a starv-ing sculptor do?"

They went up on the roof near the sacred flame in the tholos and ad-mired the infinity of stars, trading Skjaran and Kosordian names for the constellations. He was to meet Ingeld when Hrada's veil was overhead. It had a long way to go yet.

"Brother," Fabia said softly, "I'm eager . . . I'll understand if this is too painful to talk about, but I would very much like to know what happened at Celebre all those years ago. Why did Stralg kidnap all four of us?"

She was picking scabs off his nightmares.

"Because," he said, "he's a Werist and rules by terror. He wiped out any town that defied him, spared any that surrendered. Celebre is a big, rich city and Papa had no way to defend it. He was ordered to come out and bring his family. Stralg made him swear allegiance and said he would take all of us as hostages for his loyalty. Papa quoted divine law about children not yet ten. Stralg said Weru was his god, not Demern. Papa protested that a child at suck could not be separated from its mother. So Stralg took Mama as well. That's not lawful, either."

He paused to let Fabia comment, but she just waited for more, her face a pale mask in the firelight.

"So you and Mama came with us, but that evening we were separated, leaving Dantio to look after Orlando and me. I never set eyes on Mama again—until I saw you this morning." He laughed. "This has been wonderful, Fabia, meeting you after all these years!"

She said, "Was it me Stralg wanted, or Mother?"

"Her, I suppose. She was a beautiful woman."

"But she had already borne four children."

Benard shrugged. "Maybe he just needed to rape the loser's wife to show he was the winner. Werists get sex and violence mixed up." Like Cutrath and Hiddi. *Like Ingeld being raped every night by that Horold monster.* "I never heard whether Mama was brought here to Vigaelia, just you. We three boys almost died on the trip over the Edge. Orlando was left at Tryfors; me, here; and Dantio went on to Skjar and *did* die there, soon after."

"How? How did he die?"

"I have no idea. Didn't you ask Saltaja?"

Fabia said, "She said he met with an accident."

Benard shivered like a dog shaking off water. "This is a feast! Let's not talk about it."

They went back down and he showed her more of the palace.

◆

She stopped to peer at another dark entrance. "What's down there?"

"Rats and spiders." He laughed uneasily. "Don't ask! It's called the Old Ramp, but there's nothing at the bottom except a cellar. It has a grim reputation."

"Like the Bull Concourse?"

"Worse! Dark rites," he explained, lowering his voice. "Definitely not for honest folk." As a child he'd hidden down there from Cutrath's gang a few times, but only as a last resort.

"Just stories to scare children?"

"More, I think. I've seen . . . sort of . . . shadow-shapes moving. Stay away!" That was where he was to meet Ingeld, the one place in the whole palace where they would certainly not find drunken revelers.

He led her out to the courtyards to meet more people. They joined a group at table and ate a meal. Soon after that, Ingeld materialized like a red and gold haystack beside them.

"Fabia, I must show off my gorgeous daughter-in-law-elect to some people. Benard, have you spoken to Thod?"

"Not yet."

"Do so." She whisked Fabia away into the mob.

◆

Thod was wearing a green and orange cloak with a wreath of yellow flowers, which he was probably flaunting before his friends down on the lowest
level. But Sugthar the potter was sure to be at the guild heads' table, and
Benard should ask him first anyway.

Sugthar was a wizened little man, burdened with too many children and
too many unsold pots. His wife was much larger than he, with an ugly mouth
and bitter, suspicious eyes. They were chatting with Sagrif the seal maker.

Benard tapped the potter's shoulder and knelt down behind him to open
negotiations. "Master, I wish to make you a gift."

The potter's wife said, "It is wrong to talk of trade at a feast."

"A gift of ten measures of best-quality silver."

"Eh?" barked the seal maker from the far side. "Who's that?" Like his
father and grandfather before him, Sagrif could see nothing beyond the end
of his nose, although he created miracles of art too small for anyone else to
appreciate.

"That is most wonderfully generous of you, master artist," Sugthar said.
"But what can I possibly give you in return to show you my gratitude?"

"You know my apprentice, Thod—"

"A fine lad," the potter said. His wife's mouth grew even grimmer.

"Indeed he is," Benard said. "He is eager beyond measure, most adept
and quick to learn, although I think he might be better off serving holy
Hrada than my own lady Anziel. He is greatly enamored of your daughter,
the lovely Thilia. I had in mind that you might take Thod as your apprentice
and her betrothed."

"Only ten measures of silver?" Thilia's mother barked. "Why, we have
turned down offers—"

"Be quiet!" her husband snapped, to her evident astonishment. "Your
gift is exceedingly generous, Benard! Far too generous! Of course, Thilia
will not be fourteen until next year, but she does look with favor on Thod.
He is agreeable?"

"I'm sure he will be. Haven't had time to discuss it with him. Here is the
silver. I know you are an honest man. In fact, take two more measures as a
wedding gift for them. I must rush. Please keep the arrangement quiet for a

few days. And give them both my best wishes, won't you? My thanks, master, mistress . . . twelve blessings . . ."

Leaving them openmouthed, Benard took his leave.

"Twelve measures of *silver*?" Sagrif exclaimed. "And a girl child settled? Who *was* that? I need him."

✦

Benard gave up looking for Thod. The stars moved slower than fingernails grew. Had the satrap gone looking for his wife yet? Would Ingeld be able to slip away unnoticed? Suppose Guthlag had failed to find a boat! Saltaja Hragsdor was in the palace, supposedly resting, but definitely a danger. Fabia seemed to have disappeared.

"Master Artist Benard?"

He looked up at a weary adolescent eye.

"You shouldn't grow so fast, Keev. It's unhealthy."

The page grinned. "I'm trying to give it up! Bena, I was told to tell you to go to the Bull Concourse to learn something important."

"Told by whom?"

"I was told not to say."

Benard dismissed the boy with a nod and absentmindedly crumpled the drinking beaker in his fist into a nugget while he pondered. He was not in the mood for any impromptu trysts, and no one had dropped any hints, so far as he had noticed. But the message might have come from Ingeld or Guthlag, so he decided on a cautious reconnaissance.

The great and gloomy corridor still seemed to be uninhabited. He could hear none of the give-away sounds of low-jinks in progress. He walked about a third of the way along it before a voice spoke his name from the shadows. White-draped and anonymous, a Witness of Mayn stood in an alcove between two gigantic winged bulls. She was spinning, of course.

He did not go close. "How do I know you're genuine?"

"The shapeless lump of metal in your fist was a pewter beaker until very recently. Convinced?"

"No." He slid his other hand behind his back. "How many fingers am I holding out?"

"Three. Now four."

"So you're a seer. Seers serve the satrap. I don't trust you."

"We serve unwillingly. My name is Mist."

Something about her made his skin creep. "What do you want of me?"

"To pass on a warning. Today Saltaja Hragsdor gave her brother leave to kill you."

It had come! Benard felt as if he had been slugged with a blunt plank. "And will he?"

"Oh, yes. Every time the satrap sets eyes on you, his bloodlust echoes through the palace like a scream."

"Nice imagery. What do you recommend I do about it?"

She lowered her spindle to touch the floor, then lifted it to wind the finished thread around it. "Exactly what you and your lady are already planning to do. Just make sure you don't fail."

"Snoop!" Benard turned to go, then changed his mind. "How is Hiddi?" He had horrible visions of an infuriated Horold breaking her neck.

"Hiddi is still waiting for the satrap, but he believes his wife is waiting for him and is heading for her bedchamber as fast as he can stagger. Sober, he might have a chance. As it is . . . well, if you wish to gamble, Bena, I'll bet ten oxen on Hiddi to a rabbit pelt on Horold." The Witness set her spindle turning again and began feeding it wool from her distaff.

"Thank you," Benard said. Good for Hiddi! "Twelve blessings—"

"Wait! Obviously you must flee downstream. The current will help you outrun Horold's warbeasts and it leads to more densely settled lands where fugitives can hide in a forest of people. Upstream is a dead end and you may run into Saltaja or Cutrath."

"You're hinting that Horold knows that, so we should go upstream?"

The seer chuckled. "If you believe that, then you should double-bluff him and go downstream anyway."

"Horold is cunning enough to work that out, too!" Benard said angrily, sensing mockery. "I won't tell you which way we're going!" He was planning to spin a knife and let holy Cienu decide. "The satrap'll send his host whichever way you seers tell him to!"

As he started to turn, the seer again said, "Wait!"

"What?"

"*It is known* that I am the only Witness presently in Kosord whose sight extends all the way across the river. And I am leaving."

"So?"

"So, hope that when Horold discovers your absence, he will ask 'Which way did they go?' and not 'Where are they heading?' Understand?"

She meant he should start one way and then double back. That was worth knowing. Benard nodded to the darkness. What was it about this woman that he found so repellent?

"Flankleader Guthlag," she said, "has hired *Ucr Blessed,* which is a very fast boat with a skilled crew. If you go to Sixty Ways in Tryfors and ask there for Poppy Delight, you will find friends who can help you."

"*Friends?* Friends against the Hrag gang?"

"Very much against the Hrag gang. Say Mist sent you. And may holy Cienu shower good fortune on you and your lady."

If this was a trap, why would the seer not just tell Horold what his wife and her lover were plotting? Or even tell Saltaja? Puzzled and not entirely convinced, Benard could say only, "Thank you. We'll consider your words."

thirty-two

FABIA CELEBRE

soon tired of the fat old women who formed the upper crust of Kosordian society, and they had even less interest in her. She did not know why Ingeld had dumped her on them, although she had her suspicions. When an aggrieved discussion of the outrageous price of slaves sprang up, she quietly spun a veil, as the Old One had taught her. Once she was well obscured, she backed away unseen.

She had an exploration in mind. The place Benard called the Old Ramp had beckoned her. He had implied worse danger than just amorous drunks, but she was confident she could handle those easily enough, and the uncanny held no terrors for her now.

Wheel ruts in the flagstone floor showed that the spooky corridor had once been a chariot road, and grandiose bas-reliefs suggested that it might have been the main entrance to the palace. At the bottom of the long slope she came to an unlit crypt, reeking of damp and decay. Absence of light did not trouble her, although she had brought no lamp. The only sound was a distant drip of water, whose echoes told her that this was a large, high place.

Whatever it had been in the past, now it lay buried under newer construction and was used to stash unwanted junk between its ancient brick pillars. No, more than just that. A familiar tang of mystery and the slow drip brought whispers of welcome. This was the Kosordian equivalent of the secret grotto under Skjar's Pantheon, officially ignored but secretly tolerated for the performance of chthonic rites.

She wondered how safe the roof was, for both wooden rafters and brick pillars must decay in this drippy damp. More urgently, she wondered what she would say to Saltaja if they ran into each other here. Nevertheless, her instincts said that this was Xaran's temple, so she set off to find the altar and offer prayer.

Even a Chosen need step warily through such terrain in the dark. She had not gone far—just past some decaying chariots—when a faint glow began playing around her feet. She stepped behind a spiral pillar and strengthened her veiling. Down the ramp came the Florengian hostage-Daughter, Sansya, carrying a small oil lamp in one hand and a bundle under the other arm. She paused when she reached the crypt, peering around and then moving cautiously to one side so she could not be seen from the hall above. There she put her back against the wall, but continued to hold her tiny light high, obviously afraid of the darkness.

Time dragged, but Chosen had patience.

Eventually another lamp glowed in the passageway. There was no mistaking Lady Ingeld in her spectacular red and gold robes as she swept downward, hastened by the weight of her regalia, arriving almost at a run. No one could serve two gods, so the pyromancers were not here to worship the Dark One. Why were they creeping around in crypts during a religious feast?

"What news?" Ingeld asked urgently.

"He went in and closed the door, my lady. He has been in there long enough to perform a simple act of worship . . . possibly even long enough to start considering another, my lady, except he was very drunk."

Ingeld laughed. "Praise to the appropriate god! Now help me, quickly, before . . . well, frankly, it doesn't matter if he does see me."

Fabia had understood very little of that exchange, and she watched in bewilderment as Sansya helped Ingeld shed her finery. That was not an unreasonable procedure at this time of night, for wearing all that paraphernalia would exhaust anyone, but doing so in this ill-reputed pesthole gave the action a strangely furtive air. Ingeld stripped and donned a garment from Sansya's bundle, a dark robe with a hood.

At that point, as if hearing his cue, a husky young man came running down the ramp, streaming smoke and sparks from a flaming torch. He hurled it to the weepy brick floor so he would have both arms free when Ingeld flowed into his embrace. It was a *long* embrace.

A *very* long embrace.

How revealing! Sansya was clearly embarrassed, fidgeting and trying not to stare, but Fabia sent a silent prayer of thanks to her divine mistress for showing her this little scandal. She wondered how long her scatterbrained brother had been cuckolding the satrap. This explained the sudden outburst of temper in Benard's yard this morning; only lovers would dare speak so bitterly. Absurd! Ingeld was old enough to be his mother.

"By your leave, my lady?" Sansya said quickly, when the lovers broke for air.

"Of course!" Ingeld gave her a hug. "Many thanks for your help, my dear. I leave my city in good hands."

Benard, too, gave Sansya a hug, and she went hurrying off up the ramp. The lovers smooched all over again. Even Fabia was starting to squirm. Would she ever sink into idiocy like that over a man?

Ingeld said, "Beloved, we must go. Guthlag has hired a boat. It's waiting at Candlemakers' Steps."

"I heard about the boat—*Ucr Blessed.*" Benard's low growl echoed strangely through the crypt. "A Witness who says her name is Mist is meddling in our affairs, love. She gave me some odd advice. Is 'Mist' a normal Maynist name?"

Or was Mist a committee?

"I don't recall ever hearing any Witness's name . . ."

Their voices died away up the ramp. Darkness returned to the shrine of Xaran, and the quiet drip continued to count off the ages.

Was Fabia supposed to do something with this illicit information? She could slip away from the palace and find Candlemakers' Steps easily enough, but her disappearance would betray the conspiracy to Saltaja. And what would happen to Horth? No, she must continue to bide her time. The lovers had not said whether *Ucr Blessed* would head upstream or downstream.

Fabia wished her brother good luck. She could not pray to Cienu to send it to him, but a word to Xaran would not be out of place—plus another for the mother Fabia had never known outside of dreams, but whose identity had just that day been confirmed for her by Benard's incredible art. Had the doge's wife ever been sent back to her childless home and husband, or had she met with a fatal accident, like her eldest son?

Fabia went in search of the altar that would be hidden somewhere in this holy place.

✦

The sky was blue by the time a sleepy and grumpy Fabia arrived at the riverbank in a palace chariot driven by a saturnine male Nastrarian who, typically, seemed to have forgotten how to speak. He could hardly plead the usual excuse of too much partying in the night, for a Nastrarian's idea of fun was mucking out a stable. Her jailers, Cnurg and Ern, trotted behind.

Saltaja was waiting, talking with a wolfish Werist. "This is the girl, Huntleader."

"And twelve blessings on you too, my lady!" Fabia said recklessly.

The Werist was big, surly, and had a badly scarred face. He nodded to her. "Darag Kwirarlson. At your service."

"Really at my service, or just-being-polite at my service?"

"Just-being-polite." He did not bother smiling.

Obviously this one was replacement for the late and unlamented Perag Hrothgatson. The younger Werists scowling in the background included few familiar faces, and Fabia needed no divine revelation to guess that Saltaja had reshuffled her escort so that any mutinous conspiracy must sprout again from the roots. Down on the water, the riverfolk were making ready. Judging by the squealing and squabbling, many of them had been sampling the Kosordian feast.

"I am disappointed that our host and hostess are not here to see us off," Fabia remarked airily, wondering how far away Ingeld and Benard were already, and which way they had gone.

Saltaja regarded her with a stare that would have made a shark blink, but Fabia knew by now that this was merely low-level intimidation, not necessarily implying knowledge of guilt or even suspicion, except insofar as Saltaja was permanently suspicious of everyone. It could be ignored, that stare.

Then, in one of the great shocks of Fabia's life, Horth Wigson strolled in from the shadows—bowing, smiling, offering greetings. He bussed his foster daughter.

Even the Queen of Shadows was agape. "Where did you go?" she barked.

He peered at her wonderingly. "Nowhere, my lady. I mean, I was just wandering around here in Kosord. I admit that holy Ucr is my patron god, but feasting has little appeal for a man with my fastidious digestion. I met up with various old friends instead." He beamed like some inane middle-aged child.

As his gaze wafted past Fabia, he blinked, but his eyelids were oddly out of step, so that the blink could almost be classed as a pair of winks.

She hugged him. "Wonderful to see you, Father!" He must have returned to the captivity of the river voyage solely for her sake, whatever he was up to. "Oh, Father, I wish you had been there! I met my brother Benard! He is a wonderful sculptor, and such a warm, loving young man! I am surprised that he did not come here to see me off, but I suppose it is festival time . . . I do wish I could have spent more time with him and the wonderful lady Ingeld, getting to know them . . ."

She knew quite enough about Benard Celebre already. Even a Chosen could not look after her own when he was as featherbrained as that one. She had another brother waiting at Tryfors. Perhaps he would be better.

"Go and prod those riverfolk, Huntleader," Saltaja growled. "It's time for us to leave."

Part III

Fall

thirty-three

HUNTLEADER HETH

had ruled Nardalborg for many years and initiated more Heroes for his father than he could bear to think about. Wherever the sacred rituals allowed, he had devised his own ways of doing things.

Not everything in life must be solemn ritual and blood-sweating grind. For two whole days now the runts had been allowed to rest and eat as much as they wanted—in preparation for the Fortitude Test, they had been told. Every Werist in Nardalborg was in on the leg-pull, wincing whenever the mythical ordeal was mentioned; there was much ominous shaking of heads. Some carried the warnings to absurd extremes, but the kids never caught on. After what they had been through, nothing would seem impossible. Summoned by the beat of the drums, twelve apprehensive young warriors presented themselves at the chapel door that bitter night—and gaped at the slave who opened it to admit them.

"If my lords would be so kind . . ." Heth stepped aside and bowed low. "We most humbly beg your lordships' forgiveness, but we do not have enough couches in Nardalborg. Honored lords at a real banquet recline on couches, of course, but never before has Nardalborg had a full, twelve-man flank of cadets, and I cannot recall any class where every man qualified for initiation. If your lordships will forgive stools . . ."

Flames danced in the fire pit below the terrible image of the god, but on the far side of the pit stood a table set for twelve, with silver dishes, roast meats, and fresh beer. The six flunkies waiting to serve them, clad in the sackcloth smocks and leggings worn by slaves here in the uplands, were the Nardalborg Hunt's five packleaders and the huntleader himself. As the striplings stared aghast at the sight, the packleaders erupted in guffaws; then Heth began to laugh too, and the cadets followed one by one. Relief made them howl with mirth.

All except one. Runtleader Orlad did not laugh. The glitter in his dark eyes was anger. Just because he did not see jokes? Or had he somehow learned of the extreme peril that now hung over him?

Somewhere a loose shutter was banging, and Heth made a mental note to have it fixed, but the blizzard howling outside set a fitting mood for merriment safe indoors. Snow and thunder were a killer combination, a Nardalborg speciality, but he had only himself to blame. He had scheduled this ceremony and he had never known an initiation night not be stormy. With all three mammoth trains out in a frantic dash to stockpile supplies for Caravan Six, he must just hope that the storm was only local. Half the men due to go on Six were in-house already and many more might be strung out between Tryfors and Nardalborg, camping on the moors. There was no time to lose.

Usually Heth loved inductions, because he steadfastly believed in the Heroes. He had a set speech for inductions. There would always be wars, he would explain, so there must always be warriors. The Werists were not perfect, certainly, but at their best they let extrinsics live in peace by keeping conflicts to themselves. He personally took pride in every boy he raised to manhood in the cult, and he was especially proud tonight, he would tell them, with Nardalborg gaining a full dozen warriors who would free up a dozen others to reinforce the Fist's horde on the Florengian Face. So he would say.

In truth he wasn't proud tonight. He was sick with shame at what was going to happen.

◆

The feast went well. Humbly served by their superiors, the cadets ate well, drank even better, and became stupidly raucous. Heth delivered his speech and was cheered. An ensemble of six flankleaders dressed as women dropped in to sing very badly, play pipes and drums even worse, and dance a striptease that left them wearing nothing except their collars and a total of a dozen melons. By then the audience was helpless with drunken mirth. Except the runtleader. Orlad drank mostly water and never relaxed his vigilance, as if he knew that this nonsense must presage treachery.

After the dancers had gone and the diners had eaten their fill, it was he who broke the spell. Watching him fidget, Heth was not surprised when the question came, but he saw with genuine admiration how the quiet words cut through the drunken gabble and stopped it. A born leader, that one.

"My lord? What happens next? In our training, I mean?"

"Nothing. You're done. It's over." Heth paused a moment to let the implications seep through the beer. Then he gave them another speech, and no one was drunk enough to interrupt a huntleader. "Congratulations, warriors! You know you have achieved what no men ever have. Your runtleader told me he would see you all qualified before the last caravan departed. I told him he was crazy. He has done it with days to spare and no dropouts. Yours is the honor, but you know who to thank for your success. I am going to break a host rule and promote Runt Orlad directly to flankleader."

"Fame to Orlad!" yelled Runt Waels, leaping up, beaker in hand. Another ten took up the shout and rose also, not without staggers.

Orlad sat and scowled, ever suspicious of mockery. In the silence while the others toasted his name—for even a Werist could not speak and suck on a straw at the same time—he said only, "So when do we get our collars, my lord?"

"Now. They must first be dedicated. Irig, please?"

Irig Irigson, packleader of the red, had the finest voice in the hunt. He reached into a bag he had been wearing at his hip all evening, and produced a dozen strips of shiny brass. These he took over to the god and held them high as he sang a ritual incantation. The others stood in silence until the last note reverberated away. Then he brought them over and cast them down on the table in front of Orlad.

Heth said, "Sit."

Eleven men hastily sat down. Runt Ranthr missed his stool and sprawled on the floor, but no one spared him a glance.

Orlad frowned. "What is the ritual?"

"None. You earned that collar, warrior. You won it by your own sweat and blood and no man but you has the right to hang it around your neck. The god has now blessed it. I salute you and congratulate you." Heth tried a smile, knowing it would be refused. "And I pray to holy Weru that I never meet you in battle." *That* was no lie. He heard quiet mutters of agreement from the other packleaders behind him.

The boy selected a length of brass, examined it, flexed it. He hooked a finger in the chain around his neck, snapped that away, and then glanced to Heth for guidance.

"I just bend it around?"

"Yes. I warn you, you will feel quite a jolt." The main reason Heth preferred the cadets to be drunk and lying on couches at this point was that the shock was little short of being struck by lightning, but he had no doubts that Orlad could survive it when so many lesser warriors had.

The others watched intently as the Florengian centered the metal at the back of his neck, then forced the two ends forward until they met. Weru, being also god of storms, honored each new Hero with a clap of thunder. The first one always seemed the loudest, and this time the bolt must have landed right outside the chapel. Stunned by the noise, several cadets tumbled off their stools. Orlad sprawled forward on the table, dislodging a cataract of dishes that fell unheard because every ear in the building was still ringing. Irig, still hovering at his back, had no need to catch him.

Then he reeled to his feet with one great bellow of jubilation, shaking both fists at the sky. He was pale and dazed, but those midnight eyes blazed with triumph as he fingered the seamless golden band encircling his neck. Now he had the power to make that neck thicker than a bear's or slender as the Vulture's, but the collar would always fit. He would die wearing it.

He sobered as the packleaders closed in to congratulate him. When their thumping and hugging was over, he returned Heth's handshake almost half-heartedly, as if impatient to move on to some new struggle. He did not resume his seat with the boys. Now Warrior Orlad stood with the men.

Who was to go next? The runts waited for Orlad's orders, but he was no longer runtleader and gave none. As cautious hands reached to the heap of brass, Bloodmouth said, "Can we do it all together, my lord?"

"If you wish."

They all agreed to that, although probably few of them saw as he had that this would conveniently forestall argument over who got the loudest thunder. Eleven leather collars were ripped away and eleven strips of brass bent into place simultaneously. One long crashing roll from the heavens sufficed for all of them. Only Waels and Hrothgat fell backward, and they were caught by Orlad and Packleader Ruthur respectively. The Nardalborg Hunt gained another eleven warriors.

✦

They had all risen, because that was what Orlad had done. Eighteen men in that chapel at that time of year naturally gravitated into a rough circle around the fire. *Thump! thump!* said the shutter.

Formalities followed. Heth told the new Heroes where they were assigned, so they knew what palls and sashes to obtain from the commissariat. He never sent new warriors straight off to the front, and they tried not to show relief when they heard that this rule still applied. He awarded them another day's rest before they must report in—nothing much would happen until the storm lifted. He told them where they would find girls waiting to help them celebrate.

So he came to the vital last rite of passage, their first chance to try out their warbeasts in earnest.

"As soon as the weather clears, of course, you are allowed a day to go hunting. Packleader, what did the scouts report?"

Ruthur of gold pack was a big man with a squeaky voice and a foolish braying laugh, which he used now. "A difficult choice, my lord! First, there's two herds of oribis up on Deadcold Hill."

Snerfrik's loud groan was followed by a chorus of boos from everyone else. Correction: from ten others. Orlad did not react. Oribis were good eating but as game for Werists they might as well be precooked.

"Rather chase ducks," Vargin said.

The packleader sniggered. "You want something more sporting? There's a bachelor moving in from the south."

A quick gasp was followed by bravado cheers. Ruthur brayed again.

"That's all?" Heth demanded angrily.

"Not another mouse on the moors, my lord."

With the rutting season fast approaching, a bachelor mammoth was an earthquake on legs. Every winter a few of the monsters were attracted to Nardalborg's females and had to be disposed of. They were slain with bronze-tipped spears, and Heth never sent less than thirty men for one mammoth. Only lunatics would try battleforming against something that size.

He said, "A difficult decision. If you choose the bachelor, then I'll send reinforcements with you, so it won't be your own hunt, and you'll have to use weapons. Or you can wait for something better in a sixday or two." Their pride would never let them do that. "I will allow individual choices," he added, glumly aware that not one of them would degrade himself by choosing the oribis. "Flankleader Orlad?"

"Oribi, my lord." No hesitation.

Heth discovered that he was no longer surprised at being surprised by Orlad. "Warrior Snerfrik?"

The big man stared in bewilderment at the Florengian. He looked

around the equally puzzled faces of his friends. Very hesitantly he said, "The mammoth, my lord . . . ?," so his indecision turned the statement into a question.

"Warrior Vargin?"

Vargin went through the same process. All of them did, leaving the vote at eleven mammoths and one oribi. Orlad seemed quite unworried that he alone had made the coward's choice, but he understood Heth's one-word bark—

"Why?"

He jumped to attention. "My lord is kind. Since I intend to apply for immediate transfer to Florengia I do not wish to risk an injury that might keep me from traveling on Caravan Six. My lord is kind."

He had added twist to prod. No one ever volunteered for service in Florengia anymore. But he just had, so who was the coward now?

"That explains it," Heth said grimly. "Dismissed—except for you, Flankleader."

✦

Snow swirled across the floor, smoke belched from the hearth, and then came a massive thud as the departing Werists slammed the door. While calm returned to the chapel, Heth stood staring glumly down at burning logs, ignoring the new Werist waiting at his side. He could taste vomit. For the first time since he had wrapped on his own brass—no, for the first time since Therek had tied a probationer's rope around him—Heth was tempted to disobey an order. *Thump!* said the shutter. Finally: "So you want a transfer, do you?"

"My lord is kind."

"In public, you ask."

"My lord, with respect, I did mean to apply to my packleader tomorrow."

Heth grunted. "Then my fault for asking. Let's discuss it. I want you in my hunt. You are the best. Stay and you'll be a packleader inside two years." He might advance even faster in Stralg's embattled horde if he lived long enough; promotion there was by survival more than ability. "However, if you persist in your transfer request, I cannot refuse you after what you have achieved with the runts. You have earned the right."

"My lord is kind!"

Heth glanced at him, wondering if he had just missed an actual smile. If so, it had been directed at the image of the god. Although the kid was staring fixedly ahead, he was certainly pleased. It was a possible solution—ship him out and put off Therek somehow until Caravan Six was out of reach.

"You do realize that the Vigaelian Werists in Florengia will see you as one of the enemy and the natives will count you traitor? Every time you go into battle you'll be attacked by the wrong side, or even both sides."

"It is a risk I must take."

"So you won't be put into battle. You'll be set to scouting and probably spying."

"My lord is kind. I do not speak or understand Florengian."

So he couldn't be a spy. And didn't care. This was like trying to talk a would-be suicide down off the battlements, which Heth had attempted several times, but never with success.

Twelve curses! "There is another problem. A few days ago I reported to Hostleader Therek that the runts were about to be initiated. He replied that I am to send you to Tryfors right away."

Another quick glance. The boy looked slightly puzzled, not terrified. Would he *ever* look terrified? And obviously he was not going to ask why.

"I don't know why," Heth said. "In this he was merely confirming orders he gave me in the spring, when you were sworn."

"I am very honored that the satrap takes an interest in me, my lord." The kid's voice was perhaps just a hairsbreadth less confident now. Suicidally stubborn but not quite stupid.

"He always has. They don't call him the Vulture for nothing. You do know that he lost three sons in the war? He blames the Florengian Werists for their deaths."

"The oath-breakers, my lord. I, too, despise and hate them."

Weru's balls!

Heth wanted to scream out, *He is crazy! He is my father and he is crazy! He wants to run you for the hunt!* But he couldn't say that. Therek Hragson had fought all his life for his brother, for his oaths, for the cause he believed in. He'd almost died a dozen times and always refused to quit and that was why he looked like a monster now. He was Heth's father, his mentor, his liege lord, and the words could not be spoken.

If the boy couldn't sense Therek's insanity, then there was no hope for him.

"Dismissed. We'll talk again when the weather clears."

thirty-four

CUTRATH HOROLDSON

and a much-reduced band of fellow Werists arrived at Tryfors in a driving rainstorm. He took an instant dislike to the town and familiarity only confirmed his first impression. For one thing, it was so overcrowded with Werists that there were not enough Nymphs to go round, and on his very first night he got blacklisted by both the commercial cathouses just for playing a little rough. Almost as bad, Tryfors was ruled by his crazy Uncle Vulture, who looked even more like a plucked stork dying of scurvy than he had on his last visit to Kosord. There were rumors that the next caravan might be put off until spring. Given the choice of freezing to death in the Edgelands or spending half a year with Uncle Vulture, Cutrath would ask for time to think.

He was lonely and homesick. Back in Kosord he had been the satrap's son, always able to call for the drinks. Here he was only the Fist's nephew and likely to get beaten up for it any time he went near a beer shop. His only pelf was the same pittance every other man received. He'd set out with a fortune in gold and silver sewn into his pall and lost every twist of it the first time he got laid—whatever she'd put in the beer had nearly killed him. Since his mother had predicted something of the sort while weeping farewells all over his brass collar, he was glad she was far away and would never know. Worst of all, perhaps, was the knowledge that the buddies he'd set out with from Kosord had vanished somewhere along the Wrogg. He was deeply hurt that his friends had abandoned him.

When blue pack was ordered out to Nardalborg, he was glad to see the last of Tryfors. An easy two-day jog, they said. They hadn't mentioned the slope, or the weather, or the weight of a waterlogged pall. They ignored the black clouds boiling up in the north. They took no account of what a long river voyage did to men sitting idle in a boat. They forgot that a satrap's son in training would naturally do his long-distance running with some help from a flunky driving a chariot.

Blue pack left town before dawn with everyone making nervy jokes about which body parts were most likely to freeze and fall off. Cutrath trotted along in the front row between Packleader Jarlion and Center-Flankleader Quirb, whom reassignments and desertions had left as his last remaining companions from Kosord. They both had families back there, raising dark suspicion that they had been sent along only to see Cutrath safely delivered to the Edgelands, and would then be free to go home.

At the top of the first hill, Cutrath and some others threw up. After that the stronger runners were set to help the weaker ones by caning their legs every time they faltered. That day was the longest of his life, and very nearly the last, because around noon the black clouds arrived with gale winds and blinding snow. Six men either collapsed completely or became lost in the storm. Cutrath did reach Halfway Hall alive, but he had no memory of doing so, and later could not counter taunts that he had been carried in.

Halfway Hall would have held a dozen men adequately and twenty at a pinch, but forty-three were pickles in a jar. Food and fuel ran out the next day; the blizzard did not.

The second night was worse than the first, with hunger added to the ordeal of cold and overcrowding. The refugees sat in one squalid mass and slept very little, mostly trading horror stories of Stralg's crossing fifteen years ago, while reassuring one another that the Edgelands had been made much safer now with a cleared track and overnight shelters.

"My brothers died there six years ago," Cutrath said. "We're not even into the Edgelands yet!"

Someone suggested that breakfast should be Cutrath Horoldson, and the motion carried with only one dissenting vote.

The sun came up in a clear sky, revealing a desolate world of white hills and nothing else. A sharp, undulating horizon was unnerving in itself, but the lack of a road was worse. Jarlion waded out a short distance and then came back to consult with his flankleaders.

"We can't run through the drifts," he explained. His breath smoked. "If we zigzag around them, we'll have to cover many times the distance. Nardalborg lies eastward, but I don't know exactly where. I propose waiting until the sun is higher, then returning to Tryfors. Any better suggestions?"

No one spoke up to point out that the road back was as invisible as the road forward. No one mentioned snow blindness, or the real hazard of fair-skinned Vigaelians charring on the outside while freezing on the inside. No one *seriously* suggested eating Cutrath.

♦

The first hint of rescue was a strident trumpeting in the distance. Whatever made the noise was approaching from sunward, invisible in the glare, and Jarlion drew up the pack in battle order, just in case.

They were almost certainly the famous Nardalborg mammoths, Cutrath told himself, shivering so hard that the ice in his beard crackled. There were other nasty things like catbears in the hills, but the only wildlife that could seriously harm a pack of Werists were *wild* mammoths. Whatever these were, there were a lot of them. "Kill 'em and eat 'em raw!" he muttered, and was rewarded with some approving chuckles.

The first men to make out the monstrous shapes started to swear. Flank-leaders shouted warnings against premature changing. When it became clear that the brutes carried riders, Jarlion ordered the pack to stand down.

It was not true that mammoths were big, Cutrath decided. They were enormous, and the tusked male leading them was twice that. They were hard to load because their front legs were longer than their back legs, but they could carry a dozen or so men apiece all the way to the Ice. He counted twelve females and four cubs. The five humans were all swathed in fur, but on three of them it had been dyed green. The other two wore palls as well.

When the train halted, the dozen females stopped, scratching and attending to the cubs. The male continued to move around, snuffling, but his Nastrarian mahout seemed to have him under control. The two Werists began unloading the sumpters, and Jarlion sent center flank forward to assist. The rations were only smoked meat and the sort of unleavened biscuit that would keep forever in sealed jars, but men stood around in the snow and feasted.

The Werist with the two-color pall must be Huntleader Heth himself. Jarlion bowed and gave his name with his mouth full.

"Very happy to see you, my lord."

Heth, from what could be seen of him, was a burly, square-faced man with a minimal smile. "Glad to be of help, Packleader. It was worth the ride. If there was no one here, we'd have just restocked the shelter. No others on the road?"

"None that I was told of, my lord. We lost six men on the way."

"They're dead, then. Your men can have a quick meal, and we'll give you a ride back. If you—"

"What is that *shit?*"

Cutrath Horoldson had not intended to speak so loudly, but the shock of seeing a Florengian dressed as a Werist was just too much for him.

The freak turned. "Somebody say something?" He was not especially tall; he looked very solid, but much of that must be his heavy furs. His sash and stripes said he was leader of rear flank, red pack, Nardalborg Hunt, Therek's host. There was something familiar about the broad cheekbones and deep-set dark eyes, but one Florengian looked much like another to Cutrath.

Everyone waited for Huntleader Heth to prohibit the challenge. Surprisingly, he said, "I heard something. What did you hear, Flankleader?"

"I heard somebody call me a shit, my lord." The brownie was staring very hard at the man who had.

Packleader Jarlion's glare was almost as deadly. "Warrior Cutrath, you said something?"

Cutrath's hide was still too tender from all the baiting to let him back down. "I was startled, my lord. I thought for a moment we had made contact with the enemy." That was good—no one could be punished for insulting the Florengian mutineers. He was happy to see approving grins in the background.

"You say something more?" inquired the flankleader. "You call me a traitor?"

Cutrath shrugged. If the turd wanted a fight he could have one. "A natural mistake."

"Permission granted, Orlad," Heth said. "You'll have to strip down to what he's wearing to make a fair match of it."

A mammoth wailed plaintively. Cutrath continued to chew his breakfast to show how confident he was, or at least wanted to seem. He couldn't swallow, though.

Predictably, the brownie folded. "I'll settle for an apology, my lord."

"You won't get it, dungface!" Cutrath snapped before Jarlion could issue orders. "All Florengians are cowards."

The spectators muttered encouragement and the whispered betting grew louder. He'd almost forgotten how good approval felt; it was like being home in Kosord.

"Well?" The huntleader looked madder than the freak did—his own fault for backing chocolate. "You *can't* eat that!"

"I beg leave to postpone settlement until my return, my lord."

Heth growled. "Packleader Jarlion, the satrap has summoned Flank-leader Orlad to attend him in Tryfors for a few days. I know that only his sense of duty deters him from demanding satisfaction now. Will you graciously grant a postponement until he returns?"

"If he ever dares," Cutrath remarked, and basked in the approving laughter.

Jarlion was not laughing, though. His face was florid. "My lord, the flankleader's restraint in putting duty ahead of satisfaction is commendable. I personally apologize to you now, my lord. And I swear by Weru that if Warrior Horoldson does not apologize to Flankleader Orlad when he returns, it will be because I have beaten him to death. Is that acceptable?"

Cutrath's throat tightened abruptly. They wouldn't *dare,* would they? Only slaves got beaten. Beat a *Hero?* A hostleader's son? Everyone would *laugh* at him! He'd battleform! He'd appeal to Uncle Vulture . . .

"Wait!" the Florengian snapped. "Did you say 'Horoldson'? Is he Satrap Therek's nephew, my lord?"

"He is, Weru help us."

"Then I withdraw my complaint. It would not be fitting for me to damage a close relative of my liege. I did not hear anything."

"He has shit in his ears, too," Cutrath said. He was safe now. No one was going to stand up for this worm. The laughter became a cheer as it spread through the pack. It felt nice.

"Prepare to move out, Packleader," Heth said. "Orlad, come with me."

✦

Out of earshot, he spun around, looking madder than Orlad could ever recall seeing him—lips white, breathing hard. Heth never swore, normally, but now he showed that he could do so very well. At the end of his tirade he roared, *"I stood up for you and you made a fool of me.* You shame the entire hunt!"

Puzzled, Orlad said, "I am truly sorry, my lord. I did not know who he was." Did Heth think it had been easy? After what Orlad had endured over the last two seasons, Heth could not doubt his courage.

"It doesn't *matter* who he is, you bonehead! You should have pounded him to pulp for what he said to you."

It would certainly have been a pleasure and probably not difficult. Anyone whose face was already so battered could not be much of a fighter. "My lord is kind."

"You're crazy as the Vulture himself!"

Orlad's own temper slipped. "My lord! That is an inappropriate slur on our hostleader."

Heth gaped. *"What did you say?"*

"My lord, he is one of the greatest of all Heroes! Satrap Therek has fought for a lifetime for his brother, his oaths—"

"Silence! He's crazy! Haven't you seen that yet? He wants you at Tryfors so he can kill you. He can and he will."

"Why should he do that, my lord?" Orlad was distressed to hear his own unworthy suspicions confirmed.

"You heard those men over there and what they think of your countrymen—all Florengians are oath-breakers. Therek blames you for his sons' deaths."

"I am not an oath-breaker!" If Horoldson had used *that* word, he would be a wreck by now.

"How will you prove it to a raving maniac?"

"I will obey without hesitation," Orlad said proudly, "as I swore to do. If he orders me to lay my head on the block, I will. I hope that will convince him of his error."

"You are madder than he is. Suppose he runs you for his hunt instead?"

"Then I will die. But I will not break my oath!"

Heth snorted and stalked away.

Dividing a mammoth herd was normally impossible. Fortunately, Tiny, the reigning male of third train, was elderly and tolerant and disliked the eldest of his harem, Outhouse, who was past breeding age. But he did like Oberdar, who was an extremely competent Nastrarian, so he pretended not to notice when she rode Outhouse away. Oberdar and Outhouse gave Orlad a ride down the Tryfors road to the point where snow changed to slush. They left him within sight of the river and the town.

thirty-five

BENARD CELEBRE

had never owned a sundial. He ate when he was hungry and slept when he was tired—unless he happened to be working on something interesting, in which case he forgot to eat at all and slept when he fell over. He had no idea how many days had passed since he left Kosord with Ingeld. They had gone by like swallows in fly time. He had watched the land and sky change, the trees don copper and bronze raiment and then strip naked. He had seen the harvest gathered. He spent his days just *being* with her and his nights sharing her bedroll; he would be content for the world to stay like that forever. Alas, the gods insist on change.

The idyll was over. The world had soured to uniform gray and tasseled rain clouds brushed the hills. That drab-looking town on the bluff ahead was Tryfors. Captain Bro eased *Ucr Blessed* through the maze of narrow channels and banks of shingle that were all that was left of the mighty Wrogg. The crew was helping the boat along with poles, but Benard's offers to help had been refused with the polite explanation that this was skilled work and he might put them aground.

He liked the peculiar riverfolk, with their carefree ways, their incomprehensible jabber, and monosyllabic names—Bro, Ma, Thu, and so on. They had guessed right away who Ingeld was, for Daughters were distinctive and never normally had reason to desert their sacred hearths. Since she was obviously not a new initiate leaving to take up her lifetime duties somewhere else, and since her young male companion displayed affection more extravagantly than a son would, she could only be the dynast of Kosord herself eloping with a lover. Although riverfolk were notoriously avaricious, Bro and her crew had stayed true to their agreement with Guthlag, ignoring the opportunities for blackmail or betrayal.

"We've arrived," Ingeld said. "What are you going to do now, love?" The passengers were huddled together on a thwart, shivering in voluminous cowled cloaks of oiled wool. The rain had started again.

"What do you want me to do?"

"You decide."

He eyed her skeptically around the edge of his hood. "You've ruled a great city since before I was born. Stop pretending to be a humble little peasant wife."

She chuckled contentedly. "You obviously don't know peasant wives. I love it. I have shed all my cares except Oliva on to your shoulders. For the first time in my life I have a man I can love and trust and lean on. Fear the day I start giving orders again, Master Celebre! Besides, I gave you very clear orders last night."

Those had concerned certain procedures best not discussed in public.

"I've never been responsible for anyone except myself before."

"Good practice for you."

"Rent another boat above the rapids and sail on?" Benard suggested hopefully.

"No. Oliva has had quite enough of boats."

The first time Ingeld had admitted to nausea Benard had flown into a panic and talked wildly of finding a Healer. The riverfolk had leered knowingly. Now he kept his worries to himself.

"How long before Saltaja arrives?"

"I don't know," Ingeld said. "Soon, I think. And Horold close behind her." She saw them in the campfire every night.

"I suppose you want to investigate that clue the seer gave me, whatever it was?"

"Sixty Ways. Doesn't that sound like a brothel, Packleader?"

"It does, my lady," Guthlag said.

"That would not have been my first choice for a refuge." Ingeld's eyes twinkled. "On the other hand, it may be an interesting experience. You remember the password, love?"

"No," Benard lied.

"You are to ask for Poppy Delight and say Mist sent you. And if it really is a brothel, you come straight back here, Benard Celebre!"

"That would attract suspicion. Maybe you should send the packleader instead."

A hint of Ingeld metal glinted through the meekness paint. "No," she said.

✦

Tryfors was ugly, petrified childhood nightmares. Walled cities were rare, relics of far-off days before Weru founded His cult of Heroes, or at least of almost as far-off days when savage hill tribes had not yet been brought to know the benefits of civilization. Tryfors retained only fragments of its ancient fortifications, but it still had a grim, fortresslike air. Its buildings were single-story slabs of somber gray stone, without cornices or pilasters or any other decoration, and that day all the windows were shuttered against the rain.

Werists were everywhere on the streets, but not all wore Satrap Therek's orange. Benard also saw Horold's purple, and although those men were not necessarily from Kosord itself, running into Cutrath or his friends would bring disaster. He must complete his mission quickly and leave.

He also saw many Florengians, because slaves had been cheap in Tryfors until the trade dried up. He expected them to be a ready source of information, but in practice this was not quite true. Checking that his hood hid his ears, he fell into step beside a white-haired man pushing a barrow. "Which way to Sixty Ways, brother?"

The carter rolled his eyes. "Man! That's not for the likes of us."

"Got lucky. Master pleased with me."

"Or mistress tired of you?"

"She never tires of me, man."

That won a scornful laugh. "Chickens'll all be roosting, man! Left at the grain exchange, bear right to the temple of Nula, go up the steps beside the—" And so on.

On his third attempt, Benard learned that the house he sought was near the palace and guessed that the palace was the building with the tower. That brought him close, and two more inquiries led him to a door under a crudely painted sign, not artistic but explicit. He reached for the equally explicit bronze knocker, and the door swung open.

"Enter, Master Artist Celebre," said the seer.

◆

She led him through silent corridors and several doors, down into a cellar and back up again, until he was certain they had moved into another building. Eventually they came to a small room lit only by a crackling fire and furnished with two stools, a couple of wicker hampers, and a sleeping platform much too narrow to suit the uses of Sixty Ways. The shutters were closed; several garments hung on nails. The place smelled of herbs and old lady, and now, no doubt, of wet Benard. Producing a towel from a hamper, his hostess bade him remove his cape and be seated. By the time she returned, he was steaming happily. She closed the door and handed him a beaker of a hot, spicy beverage.

"We have important business to discuss, master."

"I was told to ask for Poppy Delight."

"I am Poppy. The other is a code." She was small, slightly stooped, but alert in her movements, businesslike. She sat on the edge of a stool and folded spidery hands in her lap.

"Mist sent me," he told her featureless white veil.

"I guessed as much—sometimes even we have to rely on inference. But *it is known* that you are worried, probably hunted, that you are very deeply in love, that you are basically an honest man, and although you have no such ambition, you may make your mark on the tablets of history. I confess I knew your name only because you were pointed out to me once in Kosord. Why don't you trust Mist?"

He took a sip of wine while he considered this remarkable speech. "I'm not sure." Something about a women without a face? He did not feel the same unease with Poppy. "Because I thought that she was not being honest with me."

"Tell me, please."

He told of the seer's warning in the Bull Concourse, back in Kosord.

"Mist must be careful!" Poppy said sharply. "The division in our cult is deep and bitter. I tell you, Hand, that there are five Witnesses in Tryfors just now and all of us are Mist supporters. That did not happen by chance. We and certain others seek the overthrow of the bloodlord and all his house— are you not on our side?"

Could seers be *too* honest?

"Sides do not attract me. The war does not interest me. I will do anything in the world to defend the woman I love and our unborn child." He smiled apologetically. "That done, I would also help my sister escape forced marriage to the worm Cutrath."

"Horoldson left town two days ago for the mustering at Nardalborg. The weather upcountry is very bad, and he is now beyond my sight anyway. Who is the woman you adore so greatly? She is beyond my range."

Herded by sharp questions, Benard told how he had fled with Ingeld, how Saltaja and Fabia would soon arrive at Tryfors, and how Ingeld believed her husband to be on his way, also. Something about Witness Poppy reminded him of his deportment teacher back in the palace of Kosord—polite, gracious, and inflexible as marble. She had never failed to cuff any juvenile ear in need of cuffing.

"Things may be coming to a head at last," this other old lady mused, "if both Saltaja Hragsdor and Horold Hragson are coming here, to Therek. Or may not be. Opportunities for good or evil are equally manifest. I fear Saltaja more than either of her brothers, and a gathering of all three of them is a baleful development. I shall be happy when Mist arrives and takes charge."

None of which meant anything, but Benard's suspicions had been softened by wine and warmth. A seer would be an invaluable ally. "I, too, have a brother in these parts, I am told."

"Who calls himself Orlad Orladson. *It is known* that he lives in Nardalborg, three menzils from here, and has just completed his Werist training."

In Benard's sketchy memories, Orlando was permanently a stocky, curly-haired little tyke who laughed a lot. "The curse of the Dark One on whoever did that to him. Would he betray me if I approached him?"

The seer sat very still in the firelight as if watching things far off. Eventually she sighed. "We do not prophesy. The satrap has summoned him here to kill him."

"What! Why?" Was wife-stealing a family trait? "Can you warn him?"

"No. We never advise. Therek is insane. His dementia oppresses me even at this distance. Go and fetch your pyromancer and her warrior, Hand. I will give them sanctuary until Mist arrives."

"You are kind, Witness, although hiding from Werists in a brothel does seem a little foolhardy."

If seers smiled, they did so unseen. "You are not in the brothel now. Since ancient days the Witnesses have maintained secret lodges all over Vigaelia. Extrinsics are very rarely admitted, for any reason whatsoever."

Cuff! That would teach Benard not to waste his humor on a Maynist.

thirty-six

FABIA CELEBRE

fell in love with Tryfors at first sight. It was not inspiringly beautiful, but *anywhere* must be better than the endless trek up the Wrogg that had taken such a huge bite out of her life. Morning frost still sparkled on the shingle and her breath steamed as she walked down *Mora*'s gangplank, for yesterday's rain had yielded to a sky of dazzling blue. Here the river had become many little rivers, each with its own collection of boats. The cataracts upstream were the same brilliant white as the hills beyond—that was *snow* up there and possibly she would be walking on that soon. Tryfors was a gray sprawl on a mesa above the floodplain, and her future husband might be waiting for her up there; he was certainly not in the reception party on the pebbles.

There was no reception party. No trumpets, no honor guard. Saltaja had truculently insisted on camping one last unnecessary night just a couple of hours downstream from the city so she could send word ahead to proclaim her coming, as if she doubted her brother's ability to cope with unexpected visitors. Not trusting one runner, she had sent two, some time apart. Had neither arrived? Or had the message been ignored?

Scar-faced Huntleader Darag trod close on Fabia's heels. Saltaja and Horth were disembarking from *Blue Ibis*. Other vessels were loading or unloading or being careened, wagons and slave gangs were at work, but the latest arrivals were being ignored.

"Gods save us, my lady," Fabia said brightly. "We appear to be a little early."

Saltaja's answer was a glare. The protracted voyage had aged her. Her pallid face seemed more elongated than ever, although it was still not that of a woman in her sixties. Her black robes had faded to gray, and in some elusive way so had she. That did not mean she was any less dangerous, though; perhaps even more so.

She snarled at Darag. "More desertions, Huntleader?"

"I warned you Heroes would not be used as flunkies." The wolfish Darag was not the obsequious and unlamented Perag, but even Darag would not have spoken to Saltaja like that when they set out from Kosord. Then he had been in command of five boats and forty-eight men. But one day *Beloved of Hrada* had lost contact with the other craft, taking a dozen Werists with her, and three days later *Nurtgata* and *Redwing* had vanished with another sixteen.

As Horth had waspishly pointed out to Fabia, if Stralg's sister could lose half her escort, then the overall desertion rate in the Heroes must be enormous. Where were the deserters going and what might they do in future? Had they found some way of evading the Witnesses' notice, or were the Witnesses no longer answering the satraps' questions?

"That must be snow up there," Horth said, beaming guilelessly. "Does that make the passes more difficult, do you suppose?"

Since the desertions, the remaining Werists had become sullen and resentful, while Saltaja and Darag snapped at each other in open contempt. In a sort of reverse mockery, Horth had become exaggeratedly polite to them and fatuously cheerful—soaked bedrolls kept snakes away, he would explain, and dysentery was highly beneficial, nature's cleansing. Fabia suspected he had helped the defections along. If so, it was odd that he had not contrived an escape for the two of them at the same time, but she trusted him to have good reasons.

"This must be the harbor master approaching," he added. "Collecting anchorage. Perhaps you might hire one of his helpers to carry word to your honored brother, my lady?"

The scrawny old official hobbling in their direction was being escorted by three adolescent boys carrying staffs, doubtless a guard against unruly riverfolk resentful of the satrap's taxes.

"Gods preserve us!" Fabia exclaimed. "It won't matter which one you choose, will it?" The youths appeared to be identical triplets.

"That won't be necessary." Darag pointed to two chariots descending the long hill from the town.

The sailors referred the harbor master to Saltaja, who angrily referred him to Darag, and an argument developed over payment. By the time it was settled, the onagers and cars were scrunching across the shingle toward them. Fabia could relax again, because one driver was too old to be Cutrath Horoldson and the other wore a huntleader's green sash. Both wore trousers and long-sleeved jerkins under their palls—unlike Darag's men, who owned nothing but palls, now thoroughly waterlogged.

The newcomers reined in nearby, not venturing to descend and leave the onagers unattended. The young officer cheerfully saluting was gaunt, tall even for a Werist, clean-shaven, and young to have reached such rank. His face would have enhanced maidens' dreams had it not at some point lost an engagement with a set of claws that had left four scarlet scars running from just below his eyes to his jawline, twisting his mouth into a jagged line. He reminded Fabia a little of Cnurg, who had been her personal guard and one of the very few in the escort she could tolerate. Cnurg had disappeared in the second exodus.

"Lady Saltaja? Huntleader Fellard Lokison at your service. Welcome to Tryfors, you and your companions."

"Where is the satrap?" Saltaja demanded. "Is this the best reception he can offer?"

"We are short of men just now." Fellard contemplated Darag, each waiting for the other to salute first. When it became clear that neither would—"You are foolhardy not to dress your men better in this climate, Huntleader. Ah! The lady Fabia?" He beamed at Fabia, flashing battlements of ivory. "I have the inestimable honor to be Fellard Lokison, huntleader of the Fist's Own, but you can call me Fellard."

"I would not dream of being so disrespectful."

"Your fiancé has left town—how's that for news, Fabia?"

"How's this for a smile, Fellard?" She gave him her biggest.

His smile was cute, too, in spite of his misshapen lip, and he accompanied it with a faint hint of a nod and wink. "We can drive you ladies to the palace. Men have to walk, I'm afraid."

Saltaja turned to Darag. "Huntleader, make sure Wigson comes with you."

Seizing her chance, Fabia took four long steps and accepted a hand up. Lokison slapped the team and the chariot whirled away in a clamor of shingle. He grinned down at her.

"I am honored, Fabia."

"My pleasure, Fellard." What a joy it was to be free of the Queen of Shadows for a while! "You have made a dangerous enemy," Fabia said as they started up the hill.

"Saltaja? Bah! Their day is over, her and her brothers. Stralg's losing the war, Therek's crazier than a loon in a jug." Fellard leered at her again, paying no attention to his driving. "You really want to marry Cutrath Horoldson?"

"I may have no choice." Fabia suppressed an image of Horth with a noose around his neck.

"He's a slug." Fellard's arm nudged hers again. Like Verk's. Did large young men in chariots always crowd their passengers like this? Skjar seemed very far away now.

"Compared to who?"

"Anyone."

"How long ago did he leave?"

"Three days. The caravan is not due to leave yet; you can still catch him at Nardalborg. Or I could help you escape."

Badmouthing the Hrag family was understandable, but open offers of treason were not.

"What are you suggesting?"

"Hide out in my bedroom. I'll smuggle food in for you and keep you warm at night."

Outrageous! She wondered why she laughed. "No, that sounds much worse."

"I can't tell you how many women have tried it and raved about it."

"I'm sure you won't."

"Wit as well as beauty? The woman lacks nothing."

"Except freedom."

As the chariot left the hill and entered into a wide street between stone buildings, Lokison switched mood. "Crossing the Edge is a horrible ordeal, mistress. The war news is very bad. A lot of people think Stralg will be driven out of Florengia by spring."

That possibility would need some thought. "Why are the roofs so steep?"

"To shed snow."

"Of course. Did the satrap order you to snub his sister?"

"Not exa-a-a-ctly. When he heard she was coming he cursed until the rafters smoked, roared at me to prepare a kennel for the . . . er, lady, and stormed off to sulk in his nest."

"And a Hero puts duty before danger, of course. What nest?"

"See that high tower? That's the Vulture's Nest. Mad old Therek is up there right now, watching you. He has eyes like an eagle and much less compassion. Try not to stare when you meet him."

Fabia was amazed. "You insult your liege and slight his sister. Won't the seers betray you to him?"

"Only if he asks the right question, and Therek wouldn't care anyhow. I'm not plotting treason."

"You really think the House of Hrag is close to falling?"

"Must come soon," Fellard said. "I'm the Vulture's third in command and every night I dream of his head on a tray."

✦

There was a sense of wrongness about the palace, which was a stone labyrinth grimmer than a tomb. If anyone brought a flower into those dismal halls, Fabia decided, it would crumble to dust. The occupants seemed to be mostly scowling Werists, guarding almost every stair and doorway.

Even the women's quarters were utterly without cheer, sourly dank and dusty, as if they had not been aired in a generation. There she found a half-dozen maids, confused and frightened, who soon admitted that they normally worked in the laundry. They had been drafted to attend the noble visitors, although they had no training, nor any idea of where anything was.

By the time Saltaja stalked in, Fabia had organized the girls enough to get fires set in all the hearths. She was lolling in an almost hot bath, inspecting clothes being held up for her approval.

"These," Saltaja proclaimed in her magnificent voice, "are my quarters. You will be shown to yours. Remember that my brother has a seer to help him. You cannot escape!"

"What —and miss my own wedding?" Fabia said sweetly. She was confident that Horth was up to something, although he had refused to say what. She had less faith in the mysterious and well-named Mist, who might or might not be around somewhere.

✦

The day grew only worse for Saltaja and consequently more entertaining for Fabia. Demands for the satrap were met with the excuse that he was busy. Demands for food produced some tasteless gruel from the slave cellars; there would be meat later when the Heroes were fed. Even Darag could not be found. If he still had Saltaja's pelf bag, he might be halfway home to Kosord by now, trailing a white wake.

Saltaja arose, terrible as a black sun. "I am going to see the satrap."

Fabia looked interested. "Yes, my lady?"

"And you will come with me."

Saltaja knew her way around the palace. Four times Werist guards tried to block her, then flinched and let her pass—armed men twice her size and a third her age. That might be a useful technique to learn, Fabia thought, but it was a dangerously obvious use of chthonic power.

When they reached a stone staircase, steep and narrow, Saltaja motioned for Fabia to go first. The treads were worn, uneven, and poorly lit. Suspecting that her own abilities were being tested, Fabia was careful to stumble a few times, but she kept up a pace that soon had the older woman puffing. The stair curved continuously, periodically passing narrow window slits on the right and closed doors on the left.

The door at the top stood ajar. Fabia pushed it wide and walked into the Vulture's Nest, which was larger than she had expected, a circular room with many windows, bright with sunlight but also windy and cold, for all the shutters stood wide. It was just as unkempt and neglected as the rest of the palace—rugs and mats littering the sleeping platform in the center; discarded clothes, clay tablets, and wine bottles scattered around the floor among disordered stools and tables. There were two men there.

Or one man and a thing.

"Who are you?" it cried in a warbling, high-pitched voice. Then, "Oh, it's you!," as Fabia recoiled and was pushed aside by Saltaja.

Upright, the Vulture would have been grotesquely tall, but he was bent at the hips until he was almost horizontal, his leathery head thrust forward on a bizarrely elongated, leathery neck. He wore a brass collar and a dirty orange pall. With his hands behind his back, he came strutting forward, glaring at the visitors with sunken yellow eyes. He moved like a barnyard rooster, lifting each clawed foot high. *Click . . . click . . .*

"Yes, it's me!" Saltaja advanced two steps to meet him.

He stopped. For a moment they glared at each other. Therek backed off first, jerking his head away. He unfolded a ropy arm to point a taloned finger.

"Who's she?"

Belatedly recalling Fellard's advice not to stare, Fabia lowered herself in a deep curtsy. He detoured around Saltaja to approach her. She found herself gazing at scrawny bare legs, perhaps the strangest part of him—thighs of normal length, shins and feet grossly extended. He stood on long, scaly toes, and each heel bore a deadly spur.

"Fabia Celebre," Saltaja said. "Daughter of the doge of Celebre and future wife of Cutrath Horoldson. Where is he?"

"Don't grovel. Up!" croaked the monster. "Pretty!" Beaming toothlessly, he touched Fabia's cheek with a talon just to see her flinch. "Celebre, you said? Well! Holy Cienu is playing tricks again! Right, Leorth?" Cackling, he swung his head around to peer across the room.

Fabia had vaguely registered the other man as slumped on a stool and gazing out a window. Now he looked around, casually. He was a young Werist, his sash a flankleader's blue. "It would seem so, my lord." Still taking his time, he rose, stretched, and only then began to stroll over.

"Where is Horoldson?" Saltaja repeated.

"The maggot? You want to see?" Therek demanded of Fabia. "I'll show you where. Here." Gripping her arm in scaly fingers, he moved her around the room toward an easterly window. Smiling, Leorth stepped aside to let them past, but not quite far enough, as if he intended to rub against her. She managed to avoid him, squirming in the satrap's harsh grasp.

The tower room stood high above the sawtooth roofs of the town, looking out over rolling, snowy moors, painfully bright under an indigo sky. To the northwest they opened up to display the winding Wrogg and its endless plains, with faraway storms as lines of white froth on the landscape.

"There, child, up there?" Therek cackled again, pointing east. "No, you can't see Nardalborg from here. Even I can't see Nardalborg from here. But that's where he is, behind those hills. If it wasn't for the hills, I could see Halfway Hall. You couldn't. That's where your dear betrothed was last night, or else he froze to death." He uttered his absurd laugh again. "I couldn't see him, not even me. I saw a mammoth this morning."

"Release her!" Shouldering Leorth aside, Saltaja strode over. "Call the boy back here. I want to see the girl married and bedded before they leave."

"No time." Her brother tossed his nightmare head and stalked away. *Click . . . click . . .* "Caravan's late already. Send her up there. She can be married at Nardalborg. Or just bedded, mm?" He released a shrill bray. "Imagine the oaf can manage that much."

Saltaja was smoldering dangerously. "Very well. We'll leave first thing in the morning—you, me, your Witness, the girl—"

"Not tomorrow!" He swung around in a squeal of splintering wood. "Not safe tomorrow, right Leorth, mm?"

"My lord is kind," the flankleader murmured—softly, but as if he meant it. He gave Fabia a shy, satisfied smile. He, too, had yellow eyes, but if the satrap was a human bird the boy was a cat.

"Moving the herds," Therek said. At least, that was what Fabia thought he said. His lack of teeth made him whistle.

"Not *all* the herds, my lord," Leorth corrected, still amused.

"Not quite all. She can go the next day. Leorth's going to be leading the last contingent for Six. Caravan Six. His flank and the men you brought, if they're any good. Leorth's good, aren't you, lad? Tell them why you're eager to go over the Edge."

Golden eyes turned to Saltaja. "Revenge, my lady." His voice was low and husky. "Both my brothers were killed by Florengian turncoats. Those traitors swore loyalty to the bloodlord and then betrayed their oaths." Still he smiled.

Therek cackled. "Can't trust Florengians!"

"Indeed not, my lord."

Their private joke was clearly riling Saltaja. "What are you up to? Why are you skulking up here?"

"Watching!" said her brother. "Been watching half the day, haven't we, Leorth?" Cackle. "Seer says he's coming. Saw the mammoth and sent for the seer. Sent for Leorth. Been watching the road."

"*Who's* coming?"

The raptor eyes turned on Fabia. "Cienu likes his little jokes. Celebre, mm?"

Then Fabia guessed who was coming. Although holy Cienu was usually thought of as god of wine and jollity, He was also god of odd coincidences.

✦

For a long time Fabia stood and shivered by a window, staring out at the snowy hills. Saltaja and Therek conversed in low tones beside another, on the downwind side so that their words were inaudible. Leorth sat hunched on a stool, endlessly stropping a dagger on his sandal while keeping a fixed stare on Fabia.

A boy walked in. She had known what to expect, and yet a Werist with brown Florengian arms and legs and face was a considerable shock. He wore his hair and beard trimmed close, in whorls of black stubble, and his limbs bore random white marks that puzzled her until she realized they were old scars. He had Benard's deep-set eyes and wide cheekbones, and although he lacked the massive shoulders, he was still impressively solid. He looked very young.

He bowed low to the satrap with a lack of revulsion that showed they had met before, but he ignored Saltaja, so he certainly did not know who she was. He did not even glance at Fabia, no doubt assuming she was a servant.

"Ah, Warrior Orlad!"

"Flankleader Orlad," Leorth murmured.

"Flankleader!?" Therek reared up—towering over everyone else even though he was still far from vertical—then sank back into his usual stoop. "So? At ease. What happened to blue pack?"

The youth straightened. "They are safe, my lord, except for six unaccounted for. They had two cold nights in the shelter, but we delivered food to them this morning and they were going to proceed to Nardalborg on mammoths."

"I saw. Good . . . good . . . This is Leorth. He and his flank will be joining Caravan Six."

Orlad nodded respectfully to the Vigaelian, who smiled without rising from his stool.

"I envy him, my lord! I have applied for transfer, but Huntleader Heth is still considering my request."

"Six has too many flankleaders already."

"I would be happy to revert to warrior. I am most eager to serve under your noble brother, my lord."

For a moment the satrap seemed to hood his deadly yellow eyes. "Of course, of course . . . You would say that, of course."

Pause.

Orlad glanced around warily. Even if his air of juvenile eagerness was genuine, he could not be naive enough to miss the reek of conspiracy filling the room—Saltaja studying him in inscrutable silence, Therek smiling at Leorth, Leorth smiling back, Fabia being ignored.

"You summoned me, my lord?"

"Er . . . Yes, of course I did. I wanted you to meet your sister."

"I did not know I had a sister." Orlad stared accusingly at Fabia as if that situation were her fault.

"I did not know I had any brothers." She walked over to him with hands outstretched. "And then I discovered I had three. My name is Fabia Celebre."

He ignored her hands, looking her up and down without expression. "Who are the other two?"

"Dantio, the eldest, is dead. Benard is an artist in Kosord, a very good one." She had not minded being reunited with Benard under the acute gaze of Ingeld Narsdor, but she much resented Saltaja's snaky stare now. "You are Orlando Celebre."

"No! I am Orlad Orladson! Why are you here?"

His manner made everything seem her fault. It peeved her and yet she sensed terrible hurt behind it. She wanted to hug him until his ribs ached, as Benard had hugged her, and she suspected he would hurl her to the ground if she tried. The world was forbidden to touch Flankleader Orlad.

"How much do you know of our family?"

"Nothing and I don't want to."

Fabia knew this must be harder on him than it was on her. She had been prepared and he had not. He was on show before his lord. Flames of pain flickered behind his eyes.

"Even that name," he said bitterly. "*Celebre!* To be called after the traitor's city!"

"The what?"

"You didn't know? The vile Cavotti was a Celebrian."

Cavotti must be one of the Florengian partisans. "So are you, Brother. Our father is the doge."

"What's that?"

"The ruler, elected for life. He's old now, and ailing."

"Let him die. He gave up without a fight."

"He did fight! His army was wiped out. When he dies, the elders will choose one of us to succeed him. I am going back to Florengia. I am to marry Cutrath Horoldson and—"

"*Who?*"

"You know him?"

Orlad glanced quickly at Saltaja; then at Therek, who was leering gleefully; then at Leorth's feline smirk; then back to Fabia. "To be chosen to marry into the noble house of Hrag is a far greater honor than your ancestry justifies. Try to be a worthy wife to him." He turned to Therek. "In Celebre succession goes in the female line, my lord?"

Saltaja said grimly, "It will this time."

He must have felt that they were coming at him from all sides. "My lady? I have not had the honor . . ."

"Saltaja Hragsdor."

He bowed again. "A very great honor."

"Perhaps." As usual, her face was inscrutable. "Do you speak Florengian?"

"Not at all, my lady."

Therek said, "You did fifteen years ago."

"Then I have forgotten it," Orlad said stubbornly. "I am Vigaelian—by adoption, true, but proud of it."

"Have you need or wish to talk further with your sister?"

"No, my lady . . . Except to command her to be as true to your noble house as I will always be."

Therek muttered, "Quite, quite, quite . . ." Then he spread his lips and gums in a predatory gape that was possibly intended as a smile. "I think you should go on Caravan Six. You can keep your sister company . . . when her husband doesn't need her! You tell the huntleader I ordered it. Such touching fidelity should be rewarded, shouldn't it, Leorth?"

"My lord is kind!" Orlad exclaimed.

"Expect Leorth can make room for you in left flank, can't you, Leorth? Find him a billet for the night."

"We don't need Fabia here any longer," his sister said. "I want her locked up and well guarded. Not harmed as long as she behaves."

"See to that, Leorth."

"Guarded on pain of death!" Saltaja snapped.

"Yes, yes, yes," her brother said. "On pain of death, you hear, Leorth?"

"On pain of death, my lord." The warrior returned the hostleader's grin.

"Good, good. I wish you an interesting journey home tomorrow, Flank-leader Orlad."

thirty-seven

SALTAJA HRAGSDOR

waited until the youngsters had left, and then said, "You are crazy, truly crazy. That boy worships you."

Therek swung around, flushing. "You can't trust Florengians! He'll break his oaths as soon as he gets the chance!"

"You were not exactly encouraging him to stay loyal."

"Stay *loyal*? They slew all three of my sons!" He stalked across to the far side of the room, as far from her as he could get.

She sighed and wandered closer to the bell rope. Of the four sons of Hrag, Therek had been the hardest to mold. Left to his own devices, Therek would probably have grown up to be a reasonable farmer, but she and Hrag had shaped him into the son his father wanted, and in some ways Therek had become the deadliest fighter of them all. He was no strategist, but even Stralg, for all his brilliance and ruthlessness, had never matched Therek at suicidal close combat. He had always been unstable, of course—how else could he have been?—and now age and deformity were bringing insanity oozing closer to the surface.

"They slew three of mine, too, but Orlad wasn't there." The Celebre boy had been impressive. She would send him home instead of his sister if he knew any Florengian, but a doge who couldn't speak the language would be useless. Besides, the drastic Shaping needed to make him biddable would turn his wits to mush. "I haven't seen Cutrath for a couple of years. Has he improved any?"

"*Erch!* Poisonous little mama's brat! He's the sort who turns up dead of a broken neck after a party—if the Florengians don't get him in his first battle, his buddies will."

In Saltaja's opinion, Cutrath's problem had been his father, not his mother. "What d'you think of the Celebre girl?"

"Like to suck on her melons. What am I supposed to think of her?"

"She's a Chosen."

The satrap brayed like an onager. "*What!?* You're joking!"

"I'm not quite certain. If she is, she's good." Extraordinarily good for her age. Perag's death, those blatant desertions—bad things happening, but not so many that they might not be mere chance. The hussy had been too clever to try anything against Saltaja directly.

"Can't you tell?" Therek's tone implied, *If you can't who can?*

"Not for certain. We can test her tomorrow."

"How?" He eyed her suspiciously.

"Have you any real brute Werists, the type who have no scruples at all and look it?"

He chuckled. "Several dozen."

"We'll send the ugliest into her cell with orders to rape her. If he can, then she's clear." If he couldn't, then Saltaja would sit down with Fabia and explain the facts of life—and death—including how to Shape Cutrath into something useful. Having another Chosen in the Family again would be a big help.

"That's your nephew's betrothed you're discussing."

"He needn't know." Saltaja's wandering had brought her to the window beside the bell rope.

"Anyway, it's four!" Therek said. "Not three, four." He stalked farther away from her.

"Four what?"

"Sons. You've been missing your mail. *Deeply* sorry to tell you that Huntleader Kwirarl has died." His toothless sneer could not have looked less sympathetic.

Kwirarl Eideson, her youngest! For a moment she was speechless, dazzled by memories of his smile, his laugh, and racked by a sense of betrayal. *Mother of Death, You test Your servant hard!* After all the oceans of blood she had spilled to honor the Old One, it seemed unfair that she should lose so many of her own children so young. *It was not for me, Mother, it was for the Family! A dynasty needs heirs, and You have taken too many!*

She drummed her fists on the window ledge. *Oh, Kwirarl, Kwirarl!* None of the sons she had given Eide had made warriors to compare with the sons of Hrag, partly because Eide was not Hrag and partly because she'd had to Shape them without Hrag's help. Kwirarl had turned out the best of her second brood, probably because Eide was not his father. Gone?

"Died how?"

"It was back in the spring sometime. Stralg just said he was ambushed while on patrol. If the rebels took him alive, it would have been long and nasty."

She shuddered. Bad, bad news, ever since she left Skjar! First Horold, then Therek. Now Kwirarl. On the way home she would have to waste time in Kosord repairing Horold, and Therek had deteriorated enormously since she had last seen him. She wondered how much useful life he had left in him, really. Perhaps she could use him as an exhibit while teaching Fabia the finer points of Shaping. In a moment she would look and see how bad the problem was.

"I need a couple of bodyguards."

"Pretty ones, of course." He sneered. "You still hanker after the pretty ones?"

"I want two who came here with me, Ern Jungrson and Brarag Braragson. Send for them." It was true that they were strikingly good-looking kids, but these days she chose pretty ones only out of habit and because it amused her to let people think she had a weakness. She had not bothered with sex for years, although she was probably capable of bearing children, even yet. "And a seer. I want to ask about these desertions."

Therek wasn't mad enough to shut himself off completely in this aerie; he kept heralds on duty in the room below. "Pull on that rope," he growled.

"You pull it." She turned to stare out the window.

Eyeing her warily, he came just close enough to reach it, but that was close enough to put him within range of her Dominance. As he was about to back away again, she took control, keeping it gentle so he did not feel her touch. He stayed where he was.

A boy came scampering up the stairs, doubling over in a bow almost before he stopped moving. "My lord?"

Therek warbled, "I want Warrior, er . . ."

"Flankleader Ern Jungrson," Saltaja said, "and Warrior Brarag Braragson."

"I want them *now!*" Therek shrilled. "And the seer. If there's any delay, I'll have you all whipped again."

The boy vanished, yelling for assistance.

Saltaja went to Therek and gripped his face between her hands, pulling his head down to her level. She froze him, and the terror in his eyes glazed over in trance.

Once his mind had been as familiar to her as his face, but what she found in there now appalled her. Ruin!—like a house sliding into a swamp, an earthquake-shattered city . . . walls cracked and tumbled, pillars leaning, fungoid weeds everywhere. Wrong, all of it; wrong! Indefinable things moved in the darker corners. The mangled state of Horold's wits had shocked her, but this was much worse. With shudders of distaste she began exploring and defining.

She prodded with a mental finger at a conspicuous suppurating abscess. "Speak."

"*Oath-breakers!*" he mumbled. Of course, the notorious Florengian mutineers . . . The sinister dark murk must be Hrag. She touched that. "*Father . . .*" The purple color over here, she recalled, was herself, even more baleful than Hrag, shrouded in fear. The boys had all established much the same image of her, varying only in detail. The throbbing red sore she established as Orlad Celebre. She moved on to peer in the smaller interstices, the personal niches and crevices of what had once been a glittering set of wits. These three faint, flickering blotches? She triggered them one at a time and Therek spoke the names of his dead sons: *"Nars . . . Hrag . . . Stralg . . ."*

No one else; no women anywhere, so far as she could see. Like Stralg, Therek had never formed attachments; would even a Nymph accept such a gargoyle now?

All wrong, all warped. She would need at least a thirty to sort this mess into some semblance of order, and then how long would it last? She couldn't even think of starting now, not up here, so high above cold earth. She was about to withdraw when she sensed a squirm, a brief twitch of avoidance. Here? No, here? There was something big, well obscured. The fear increased, pulsing darkly. She had to pry past walls, veils, barricades . . . gently, or she would break things . . . "Who?"

Therek mumbled and slobbered.

Harder, then. *"Who?"*

Emotion burned in polychrome agony: "Heth."

That was a man's name. Karvak had been the chaser of boys, not Therek. She backed out until she was staring at the outside of his head once again, still clutching it. Drool hung from his lips. At some deep level he was struggling against the trance.

"Tell me who Heth is!" She used Dominance.

He moaned. "Heth . . . Hethson . . ."

A bastard. So! She was annoyed that Therek had managed to keep a nephew secret from her, but it might not be too late to use him, depending on the kid's age. Shaping worked best on blood relatives. Xaran knew she was running out of those! The Heth boy could be no less promising material than Cutrath Horoldson. Tomorrow, when she got Therek down on ground level and began work on him, she would find out who and where this byblow was, and how old.

"When I release you, you will forget everything that has happened since the boy left." She stepped back.

He jumped, pouted at her, and stalked off in a sulk, no doubt wondering what had caused that dizzy spell.

Saltaja found a stool and slumped down on it. Mother, she was tired! A day or two on the water did no harm, but that interminable voyage from Skjar had wearied her to the bone. Day in, day out, she missed the power of the cold earth. Sixty years ago she'd have thought nothing of it. She was growing old at last. Her control of events was slipping.

She saw now, in retrospect, that she had been too greedy. Twenty years ago, the Family had controlled the entire Vigaelian Face, with only sporadic rebellion left to quash—a hegemony unheard-of in all history. She should have been content with that, but she had let Stralg convince her that the horde would turn on itself if it had no external enemies to fight. She had let him invade Florengia. He had brought it to heel so easily that he had even started dreaming of expanding to the Ashurbian Face.

Ten years ago the Family had ruled two Faces, a sixth of the world, and Hrag's sons had bred another generation of warriors to hold the greatest inheritance Dodec had ever seen. Then Cavotti's mutiny had thrown cold reality in their faces.

And now? . . . Now she might have to abandon Florengia and bring the survivors home to pacify Vigaelia. There were so few of Hrag's line left! Saltaja did not fear the dead, the least dangerous of people. She cared nothing for wraiths or ghosts or walking corpses, even if they existed, which she sometimes doubted. Yet she suspected that Hrag might be an exception, that even the Ancient One was not strong enough to hold him. Still, sometimes, she dreamed of the old monster—laughing at her, usually, and sending evil against his own seed so that they could not keep what he had dreamed of owning. But those were only dreams.

There was still hope. If the Celebre girl could Shape the pathetic Cutrath into a useful tool, that would help, and this Heth boy might help too, if he was old enough.

"What other news from Stralg?" she asked.

Therek swung his vulture head around to peer across at her. "He never tells me much. Nothing good. Nothing good that I believe, anyway. He's talking of fortifying Celebre, using it as his base."

Fortifying? Mother preserve! "Since when does a Werist fortify?"

"When he's outnumbered two sixty to one!" the satrap screeched. "The brownie Werists multiply like roaches but the extrinsics are worse! Werists fortify against extrinsics. That's why I built Nardalborg, you mad old hag."

Was Stralg failing, too, like his brothers? She could demand to have his letters read to her, but the real news was waiting for her back in Skjar, all ancient now. Winter coming, the passes closing. Perhaps the news in the spring would be a Florengian horde arriving with Stralg's head on a pole.

Boots scuffed on the steps and Brarag burst in, sweaty and gasping from his run. He bowed low in the doorway. "My lord is kind!"

"At ease, lad." Therek whistled a laugh as if that were funny under the circumstances. "Inform your packleader that you have been appointed attaché to my sister."

Brarag straightened up and eyed her apprehensively. "My lady?"

Smiling, Saltaja walked over until she was within range. He was certainly the prettiest of the troop that had accompanied her from Skjar, all young and dewy. She applied Dominance, with all the power she could muster this far above the ground: "You will guard me with your life."

His blue-blue eyes glazed. "I will guard you with my life."

She released him. He blinked uncertainly.

"Er . . . great honor, my lady. To be your guard." He was lying as he had never lied in his life before. His lies stank up the room.

"My pleasure. Wait for me downstairs. I'll be down shortly . . . Check on Fabia Celebre for me. She's locked up. Make sure she is well secured. Tell her guards: If she escapes I'll see they hang by their balls for a thirty."

Brarag grinned. "My lady is kind!"

She affected surprise. "You think that's a kindness? By the Twelve, you have strange ideas of fun, Flankleader. What else do you enjoy?"

His astonished flush glowed through his stubble as he spluttered an apology, trying to explain that he had never intended . . . She was amused. If she ever were tempted to try sex again, Brarag would do nicely to start with. "Be off with you!" she said, and he ran.

Therek was plastered back against the wall like a great snake, staring at her in deathly horror. He always reacted like that when she let him watch her using power, and she always wiped his memory later, as she would do today before she left.

"Is that what you did to us?" he croaked. "Me and the rest?"

"No. I never did that to you, or the others."

"You swear?" His voice quavered.

"I swear by holy Xaran," she said, just to watch him gibber more. "It doesn't last, honestly. I reinforce it every few days and release them after a thirty or so. They come to no harm."

This was true, so far as it went. Dominance was trivial compared with Shaping, but in large doses it destroyed much faster. Ern and Brarag would likely survive, whereas her maid, Guitha, was almost useless now, after less than a year. Although Perag had lasted much longer than most, he had been insane at the end. She would soon have ordered him to kill himself, had the Celebre girl not saved her the trouble.

Saltaja shuffled back to her stool to wait for Ern and the seer. Kwirarl, Kwirarl! Her baby . . . Tonight she would offer blood to the Old One and pray for a change of fortune.

A Witness entered and closed the door behind her. Without proceeding any farther, or acknowledging either the satrap or his sister, she raised her distaff and began spinning. She was tall, thin, and probably young, for the long climb had not left her short of breath.

"Ask her," Saltaja said, "where my escort went. Half the Heroes who left Kosord with me never reached Tryfors. Where are they?"

Therek continued to cower against the wall, as if intent on staying as far from Saltaja as he physically could. "Answer, Witness."

"They were never within my range," the seer said.

"What is the Wisdom on them?"

"Answer."

"That I cannot know yet." Her spindle continued to twirl hypnotically.

"Many sixty others bound here last year did not arrive either. Do you know where *any* of them went?"

Prompted again by Therek, the seer said, "Yes. I can list them for you, but it will take a pot-boiling or so."

Aha! Information at last! "Where are *most* of them?" Saltaja demanded eagerly.

Therek bade her answer.

"Most of them have arrived at the rebel camp near Nuthervale."

Therek came off the wall. "Rebels!? What rebels?"

"*It is known* that the rebels assembled near Nuthervale refer to themselves as the New Dawn."

Therek strode closer to the seer—but still not near his sister. "How many? Who is their leader?"

"*It is known* that he is Hordeleader Arbanerik Kranson. The latest total known to me is sixteen sixty, four dozen, and three, but that was three thirties ago."

"Arbanerik! I know him. Lost an arm in Florengia. He came home through here a year or two ago." Therek was practically foaming. "Traitor! Oath-breaker!"

Saltaja was calculating how fast she could get a letter to Eide, back in Skjar, and whether he could be trusted to handle the matter. Perhaps she should send Horold to help him. She would never have thought to look for the rebel nest anywhere near Nuthervale. This Arbanerik must be stamped out before he grew any stronger.

thirty-eight

FABIA CELEBRE

was close to panic. Her room was not a dungeon, just the next best thing to it. The door was solid timber and she could hear the voices of guards outside when she put her ear to the keyhole. She had a dusty blanket but no sleeping platform, a water jug but no lamp, the remains of her evening meal, and a slop bucket. She cursed herself for waiting too long, for ignoring the dread reality of her position. All Horth's wealth could not help her now.

The window was large enough to squeeze through. Granted, it looked down on a busy street, but it was little more than head high and the drop would not be impossible. The traffic would surely end after sunset. The only problem with the window was a pair of stout bronze bars set firmly in the stonework, and she had no answer to those.

If the Old One granted her Chosen some power that let them break out of jail, Fabia did not know what it was or how to invoke it. Saltaja would know, and also know how to counter it. Ominously, this room had a timber floor, so Fabia was cut off from the cold earth, and could detect only a very faint trace of the Mother's power welling up through the stone windowsill.

Hustling a reluctant maiden into matrimony would be child's play for Saltaja Hragsdor, who had ruled Vigaelia no-holds-barred for so long. She would force Fabia's compliance at the wedding by threatening Horth, and would no doubt dispose of him later somewhere in the Edgelands. Verk and the rest of Father's swordsmen were half a Face away and useless against Werists. The deluded Orlad was completely on Saltaja's side. Benard was either a fugitive or a corpse by now. Even if he were here and available, Master

Artist Benard could never be of any practical use. The mysterious Mist had not been heard from since before Kosord. It seemed certain: two days from now, three at the outside, Fabia was going to find herself married to the despised Cutrath, whose mother, even, never praised him.

Darkness fell. Street noise dwindled to occasional passing voices. Too frightened to undress, Fabia curled up in her blanket. Somehow she must have worried herself asleep, because she began to dream that someone was throwing rocks at the shutter. Eventually the noise irritated her so much that she woke up to complain.

Plink!

She scrambled loose from the blankets and almost fell headlong in her rush to reach the window. She hauled the flap open and looked down. Florengian faces did not show up well in the dark.

"Get dressed," Benard whispered. "I'll catch you."

She was dressed already, but she needed a moment to catch her breath. How had Benard come here, how had he found her? Could he be an illusion, a Saltaja trick? Saltaja might be watching ... Veil! Even as she fumbled to find her shoes, Fabia hastily spun a web of darkness around herself—not so much that Benard would not be able to see her, but enough to blur her to any distant watcher. She leaned out of the window. "Ready."

Benard ignored her, staring along the street, keeping watch. She threw her shoes at him and he jumped. Then he reached up, gripped, and hauled; she slid over the sill like a fish and tumbled into his arms. He didn't even stagger.

He hugged her and kissed her cheek. He wrapped a dark woolen cloak around her against the night chill. "Shoes ... Don't run. Walk as if you owned the place."

As they strolled off, his arm was a bar of bronze around her, wonderfully comforting. The street was deserted under the stars. Oh, the stars! Skjar or even Kyrn never saw such skies.

"You are so welcome!" she said, fighting back tears of relief. "Where have you been all my life? I'm just realizing what I missed all these years as an only child. I met Orlad! Is there any hope of rescuing Horth? Where are we going? When did you get here?"

"Yesterday. Horth is free, the seers said."

"But how did you know where I was?"

"Mist told me the right window."

"So Mist is . . . Wait a minute! *There were bars on that window!*"

Even sculptor muscles could never have removed those bars. Besides, the sill had been smooth, unmarred by broken stone or metal stubs.

"There were," her brother agreed vaguely. "Ugly things! I just thought it would look more beautiful without them."

thirty-nine

HERO ORLAD

dimly remembered Tryfors from his childhood. It had shrunk. His most vivid memories were the daily fights and nothing had changed there, except that now his opponents would be Werists. Nardalborg had learned not to challenge him, but this place festered with Heroes measuring him up for impairment: *Brownie brother? Can't have that in the cult.* They took their lead from Hostleader Therek, no doubt.

Therek had been lying. Why would Cutrath Horoldson have left town if his betrothed was here? If Therek had known she was coming, why hadn't he kept Cutrath here, instead of just summoning Orlad?

Heth's warning sawed away at the back of his mind: *He blames you for his sons' deaths. He wants you at Tryfors so he can kill you.* Not in person, obviously. Everyone knew the Vulture's battleforming days were over. But Leorth, now . . . gracious, considerate, hospitable Leorth? *Charming* Leorth.

Leorth found the visitor a berth in the barracks and took him along to the mess for chow—much too spicy, not as good as Nardalborg's—and there introduced him to many people, including every member of his flank. Beer and wine flowed, but Orlad drank very little but water at the best of times. Leorth and his friends knew something they weren't sharing. They persisted in addressing him as "Brother Orlad" and he would trust none of them as far as he could throw a mammoth. A *bull* mammoth.

Leorth was what they called a preener, one who acted his warbeast all the time, as if he couldn't leave it alone. That was bad tactics, because any fool could see that Leorth would go cat, and there were ways of dealing with cats. Young Werists were versatile and should avoid settling upon a single battleform for as long as possible, Heth said, because the predictable die first.

While the west still burned in scarlet, stars poured into the black eastern sky. Slaves hurried around the mess, lighting lamps. Orlad lingered at table with Leorth and half his flank; the others had gone on duty.

"Eaten enough?" The flankleader stretched languidly.

"Too much."

"Anyone feel like tickling a little swansdown?"

"Get in before the rush!" said big Merkurtu, who was obviously the leader's henchman and doer-of-heavy-stuff in the flank.

Orlad had been expecting this. For years he had promised himself that he would hold back on women until he'd won his brass, and now he had done that. That same night he'd learned of his summons to Tryfors, and the fit was perfect, for here there would be anonymity and a wider choice. He had not counted on a group party for his first outing, but that would allow him to take his time and see how it was done. Tonight was going to be *it!* He had three copper twists on a pelf string under his pall.

The others were engaged in a highly technical argument as to whether a man should go for Nymph first and commercial women after, or the other way around. Pros and cons were presented.

Leorth settled it. "Sixty Ways is just down the road. We'll drop our loads there first and then travel light." The flankleader had spoken. Everyone rose. With no visible signal given, the flank closed in around Orlad as it escorted him out of the mess.

✦

The room in Sixty Ways was dim, too large for its three little oil lamps, and furnished only with rugs and cushions. Leorth had negotiated hospitality for eight Werists in return for a gift of four coppers—taken from his own pelf string, much to everyone's surprise and approval. They would be of no use to him in the Edgelands, he explained, without saying where they had come from. Some men hailed and claimed old friends; the rest soon found suitable companions, and everyone settled down to cuddle.

"I think Florengian men are wonderfully sexy!" Orlad's partner announced, cuddling close. He thought she was one of the youngest, although it was impossible to be sure in this light. She was certainly wonderfully plump and soft; and smelled nice. She held a beaker to his mouth. "What's your name, Hero?"

He tasted the wine; it was sweetened with honey. "Orlad."

She sniggered and explored his mouth with a fingertip. "You don't have pointed teeth!" She leaned close to whisper. "Do you have fur?"

He knew that humor was not his strong point. "What's your name?"

She took a sip from the same beaker, regarding him with huge dark pupils. "Musky."

He doubted that was her real name, but he did like her scent. He established that her thigh felt as smooth as it looked. He learned that kissing involved more than just touching lips. He was both alarmed and reassured by the urgency developing under his pall. Clearly, he didn't need to worry that anything down there would not perform as required. Very soon Musky established this also, while leaning on him to lick up some wine she had accidentally spilled on his chest.

"Darling, you brought me a present, didn't you?" she murmured in his ear.

He muttered something while his hands explored her breasts.

"Lover man, why don't we go and get started?" She rose and he went with her. Other couples were already disappearing out the door. He was glad that there would be no public performances, because his previous idea of holding back to watch no longer seemed necessary or even possible.

"Mmm," he said.

Entwined, they followed a dim corridor lined along one side with poky cubicles, even dimmer. Some were emitting whispers or sniggers, some were empty, but Musky clearly had a specific destination in mind. Her arm was around his waist inside his pall, which was starting to unravel, seemingly of its own accord.

She opened a door and guided him into a larger, brighter room, heavily scented and obviously intended for grander clients than mere front-fang Werists. To his left was the largest sleeping platform he had ever seen, to his right a hearth with a crackling fire, plus a table bearing a wine jar and beakers. Directly opposite, beside a second door, stood a Witness in white robes, head and face concealed by a white cloth. She was spinning with distaff and spindle.

"Twelve blessings, Flankleader Orlad," she said.

He kept a firm grip on Musky. "Let's find somewhere else."

"No, listen to her."

"I will leave if you wish," the seer said, "but I warn you that the wine in that jug is drugged. The woman knows it."

Musky broke free and shut the door. " 'Fraid she's right, darling. I was warned not to drink any." She sauntered over to the table and sniffed at the wine. "I can't tell."

"I have said it is, so it is. The meal they fed you was highly spiced, to make you thirsty. Don't worry, the wine won't kill you, just make you ill."

Orlad's romantic dreams had turned to burning fury already. "Who? Why?"

The shrouded woman shrugged. "The satrap ordered it. He did not say why. After a night of cramps and vomiting you may not fight as well in the ambush tomorrow, but I doubt that was the real intention. Because he would not want to spoil the show. Spite, perhaps, or just to keep you from slipping away before first light. He does want to watch."

"I don't believe you." But he must believe her. Even the skeptical Heth said seers never spoke false.

"You have a triangular scar on your right hip, claw marks under your navel, and your left nipple is missing. Before you went to the mess you hid four coppers under the sleeping rug in your billet. Do I speak true?"

He wanted to scream and smash something. "Ambush? What ambush? It's another joke, must be."

Her flat, emotionless voice never changed. "Leorth was given very specific orders. The herds have been removed from the hillside known as the King's Grass, which you cannot avoid if you head for Nardalborg. The flank is to run you down and kill you there, where the satrap has a clear view from his tower."

"No!" But Heth had warned him of his danger, and he trusted Heth even more than he trusted a Witness. "What can I do?" he whispered. "How can I convince my lord that I am true to him?"

"I offer no advice on that." The Witness touched her spindle to the floor and pulled it up to wind the new thread around it. "I can call in people who wish to help you, but I must have your word that you will not betray them or reveal what is spoken in this room."

"My word?" Orlad said bitterly. "If my liege lord cannot trust my oaths after I have worked so hard and long to be able to serve him, why should you believe a casual promise?" He felt nauseated.

"Because I will know if you are lying."

The hardest part of fighting was thinking clearly. So he had been told often enough. So life had taught him. But to stay calm in the face of cold-blooded treachery was something else. Everything he had worked for—shattered! Seer or not, he could not believe that. He tried to consider his options and could think of none. Needing time to think, he said, "I promise."

The seer said, "Fetch them."

Musky sauntered over to the other door and went out, leaving it open. The Witness set the spindle turning again. Orlad leaned back miserably against the door he had come in by. Tonight was not working out as he had hoped.

In walked the girl who claimed to be his sister. She was supposed to be locked up, so there was a conspiracy afoot, and the seer was not loyal to the satrap, as she was supposed to be. But that was absurd! The Witnesses were always loyal to Stralg and his hostleaders, and now they said Therek had ordered the ambush. Orlad was the best—Heth had said so! Why would Therek want to kill his best new Hero?

Maybe he didn't want to! Maybe this was just another test, a test to find out if a Florengian really could be trusted. After all, Therek could *change* his orders before morning! Orlad was required to prove his loyalty by betraying his supposed sister. The only oath binding on a Werist was the oath he had sworn to Weru, and the light of Weru in his case had been Satrap Therek. It was a loyalty test.

Having worked that out, he felt much better.

The girl came to him. "Oh, Orlad! I am sorry!"

He folded his arms. "For what?"

"Sorry for you, of course." She shook her head, frowned. "I know how terrible you must feel. I want to help you."

"Do you really? Well, seer? Who is lying now?"

"No one. She is sorry for you and frightened by your anger."

"She is really my sister?"

"She is. I did not lie to you about the ambush."

Then they were mocking him. They must be mocking him. Who would not laugh at a warrior betrayed by his lord?

A man had followed her in and closed the door. He was about Orlad's height, clean-shaven, with black hair hanging below his shoulders—enviable shoulders and a thick chest to match. He, too, approached, but the girl held out a hand to stop him.

"He doesn't like emotional greetings. Orlad, meet our brother, Benard."

"You're an *artist*? You look more like a woodcutter to me."

The newcomer blinked a few times. He smiled, starry-eyed. "You have grown, too, Little One."

"Amazing."

"It is wonderful to see you again. I wish we could have met in happier circumstances."

"Sit, all of you." The Witness remained standing, twirling. The newcomers obediently sat on the edge of the platform. Orlad stayed where he was.

"You still have doubts," the seer said. "Will you confirm for the others that you promise not to repeat what is said here, Flankleader?"

"I promise. But stop prying in my mind!"

"I cannot read thoughts. I can smell mood and emotion. You are naturally very troubled and unsettled. However . . . quickly, because time is short. This is the story as it is told. I can testify personally to a few parts of it, but to save time I will not specify which. *It is known:* When Celebre fell, the doge yielded his four children as hostages—"

"Don't be too quick to condemn him, Orlad," the girl said. "He saved his people from massacre. He saw this as his duty and paid a terrible price for it. That is not cowardice. That is high courage."

"Depends who's judging." Weru accepted no excuse for failure. All that ever mattered was winning.

"You boys were brought here, to Vigaelia," the Witness continued. "You were left with Therek, Benard went to Horold in Kosord, and Dantio to Saltaja herself, in Skjar. Fabia followed later, in the care of a wet nurse, Paola Apicella. They were sent to Satrap Karvak, in Jat-Nogul. The next year, rebels sacked the city and the nurse escaped in the confusion, taking the child. She made her way to Skjar and married a wealthy merchant. Fabia grew up knowing nothing of her past. Apicella was later murdered on Saltaja's orders."

"How old was . . . were the boys?" Orlad asked. *Some* of this might be true.

"Eleven, eight, and you were three. I assume you remember little or nothing of those days. Benard was nurtured by Horold's wife, lady Ingeld, who encouraged him to develop his artistic talents."

"*Must* you keep up that accursed spinning?"

"It is part of our mystery. We seek to gather myriad events into a single history; spinning aids us in this."

"You're telling stories just now, not 'gathering events.' "

"While talking with you, I am also watching Leorth and his flank.

When they have finished their business they will come looking for you. I told you time is short."

"What did happen to Dantio?" Benard asked. "I never heard."

The seer sighed. "He was old enough to try fighting back, but too young to understand the extent of his danger. He kept running away. Saltaja warned him that he'd pay for it. She prides herself on never making a vain threat. Eventually she raised the punishment so high that it killed him. Was he brave or just stupid, my lord Werist?"

Before Orlad could rise to the bait, the chunky artist said, "So here we are! Fifteen years later, the survivors reunited. The gods are not without mercy."

Orlad looked at the two firelit faces and the shrouded Witness. "And this doge-king is dead?" The eldest son was dead. An artist would never make a ruler. But a Werist could. *If,* temptation whispered, *your liege lord has betrayed your trust, then your oath to him is void and you owe loyalty to no man, only Weru. Better a Hero to rule than a woman.* He rejected the thought. That was part of the test, to see if he could be bribed.

"It has been reported that the doge is close to death," said the seer. "It was also reported that the Vigaelian horde is falling back on Celebre. All such news is out of date, but I have more recent information than Saltaja or Therek do."

"How can that be?" Orlad asked, with a sudden return of anger. Mention of the war had jabbed like a fingernail in the tattered wounds of his loyalty. He could *not* cheer for the Florengian oath-breakers! Therek was just pretending, testing. "And who are you, that you betray the bloodlord you are sworn to aid?"

"My name is Mist. Do you know how Stralg won the aid of the Maynists?"

"I don't care," Orlad shouted. "The treaty was sworn in the names of gods!"

"He tortured one hundred and fifty helpless women and five equally helpless men to death. He was quite prepared to do the same to all the rest of the cult. How does even a Werist justify that?"

"Please let's not bicker," the girl said. "Orlad, what do you want to do? If you try to go home tomorrow as you have been ordered, then Leorth will kill you. Will you set out for Nardalborg tonight and hope to be safe there, or will you seek out another life?"

"There is no other life. You are not going to marry Horoldson?"

She screwed up her face in exaggerated disgust. "I hope not."

"I almost broke his neck this morning until I found out who he was." Orlad wished he had; then the satrap would have had good reason to kill him and he wouldn't feel this terrible sense of betrayal. "How did you escape from the dungeons?" Looking down at the unlined face, the shiny hair, he realized how little he knew about women. Musky had been *a lot* older than this alleged sister of his.

"I had help." She smiled at the artist beside her.

More treason! Yet Orlad could not imagine that bovine lump letting a songbird out of its cage, let alone rescuing a prisoner from the satrap's palace.

He said, "So what will you do now? You and your brother? You are going to sneak over the Edge to Florengia and steal back our city? Two against the Fist?"

She flushed at his mockery. The artist was ignoring both of them, scowling at the seer as if he disliked her as much as Orlad did.

"I don't know," the girl admitted. "The most urgent problem is yours, Orlad. What can you do? If Mist can find you safe refuge, is that what you want?"

What sort of a name was *Mist?* Who were all these people that he must trust them before his liege lord? "Witness, what is your interest in me? Why warn me of this supposed plot?"

She set her spindle going yet again. "Our blessing includes more than just seeing, Flankleader. We are interested in you because you have potential to transform the world. I do not prophesy that you will do so, I merely affirm that you may have the opportunity, just as a sharp sword has power to kill but may never see battle. We call it 'seasoning' or 'flavor.' All of you are seasoners and so was Dantio, although four in one family is unprecedented. So if fame is your ambition, you may well succeed. At the moment, Orlando, you are also *important,* which is not the same thing. Importance is not uncommon and usually short-lived. A paid assassin may seem important, but the person who paid him is more likely to have flavor. Because you are currently important, you were visible to my sight this morning before you even reached King's Grass, far outside my normal range. Your coming mattered!"

Orlad did not feel important. "Why are you betraying the satrap's plans to me? Tell me why he should *want* to kill me?"

"Because he is insane. Because he and all the children of Hrag are evil. Tell me why you support them, why you want to fight for Stralg against your own people."

"I want to fight against false Werists," he shouted. "Traitors who broke their oaths! Extrinsics have nothing to fear if they stay out of our road and do as they are told."

"How will you distinguish the oath-breakers?" the seer asked. "A few dozen Florengian youths swore loyalty and then reneged, led by Marno Cavotti, but they are almost all dead now. They trained many sixty-sixty others to succeed them and those men are as true to the vows they made as you want to be to yours. How will you—"

Red anger propelled Orlad one step forward. The girl jumped up and squealed, "No!" Even the artist lurched to his feet, as if mere bulk could stop a Hero.

"Killing me will solve nothing," the seer said, but her voice was squeaky. She had stopped spinning at last.

"I will fight the Florengians because I am true to the Fist!" If they would just *let* him, just *trust* him!

"Why?" the seer asked. "Stralg has murdered and pillaged and shattered your homeland. Do you know why? You know what started the war?"

"What does it matter? If they had submitted to the rule of the Heroes as they should, they would not have been hurt."

"Tell him, Bena."

"Tell him what?" the artist growled, still frowning.

"Tell him why Stralg invaded the Florengian Face."

Muscleman shrugged. "Because he had too many men. In his struggle to conquer Vigaelia he'd built the cult up too big. With no one left to fight, they'd just start fighting one another. So he took half of them over the Edge to get them killed off."

Orlad laughed. "He told you this, I suppose?"

"He told his sister-in-law," Benard said absently. "She told me." He turned to stare again at the seer.

"Don't believe you."

No one answered. Somehow the mood of the room had changed.

"Stop that!" the Witness shouted, raising her distaff threateningly.

"Stop what?" Benard took a step toward her, looking puzzled.

"*Stop it!*" she shrieked.

"I know you!"

"No you don't! How could you?" She tried to strike at him with her distaff.

Parrying the blow easily, he reached out and ripped away her veil.

Forty

BENARD CELEBRE

had sensed something wrong about Witness Mist when they first met in the Bull Concourse in Kosord. The feeling had returned this morning, even stronger, when they met again here in Tryfors. It had been growing on him all day. At last he sent a prayer to Anziel that She let him see through the veil, and he had discovered a maddeningly familiar face. So he unmasked her . . .

Him.

He thought for a heart-stopping moment that he was face-to-face with holy Eriander—Eriander as he had shown Her in Ingeld's mural and Hiddi's idol. The coloring was wrong, of course, and the ghastly cropped ears; he had caught the straight nose, the wavy hair, and the pointed chin very well. But the real horror was the hideous de-sexing mutilation.

"I thought you were dead!" He had modeled the god as a youth of indeterminate sex, but the features were those of his older brother—who should not look like that now, nor sound like that, either. "Oh, Dantio, Dantio! What did they do to you? And what have I just done to you?"

Heartsick, Benard grabbed the Witness in both arms and hugged him as tight as he could. Dantio gasped, tried to break loose, then submitted to the inevitable, hard-put even to breathe in a grip so ferocious.

"How very touching!" said the Werist. "What exactly *is* that?"

"Don't you sneer, you stupid thug!" Fabia yelled. "Dantio? Really?"

Benard let go and stared at him. Dantio nodded. His eyes were tight shut, his mouth twisted in a rictus of pain. He spun around and hid his face against the wall.

Benard thought, *Brute, callous brute! How could I have been so insanely cruel?*

It seemed an age before the seer spoke, in a whisper choked with emotion. "Yes, really. You can guess what they did to me, Benard."

Beardless, sexless features, treble voice. Benard glanced at his other brother, the brute killer, and thought, *I was the lucky one.*

Dantio said, "There are other eunuchs in the . . . in the cult . . . We don't make them, but we take them in."

Fabia went to put her arms around him. "I thought you witnessed that Dantio died?"

"I did," the seer told the plaster. "I was going to tell you, truly I was. I wanted to get this all settled first."

Shamefaced, Benard scooped up the veil he had dropped, offered it. Dantio took it without looking around and covered his head again.

"I do think," Orlad sneered, "my duty requires me to warn my liege lord that the Celebre hostages are loose and dangerous. They may even gang up on him! An artist, a girl, and a gelding! He will be terrified."

Fists clenched, Benard strode over. "Shut your foul face!"

"Or *what,* brother?" Orlad said softly, eyes gleaming.

Caution cooled Benard's rage. Any Werist thug would relish a brawl after an emotional beating like the one Dantio had just administered. This young monster had obviously fought his share and more in the past; dangerous in many ways now, he should be placated. But Benard was too disgusted to try.

"You should have fought sooner, Hero."

"Meaning what, Hand?"

"Meaning that what they did to Dantio is no worse than what they did to you. You didn't fight the foe, you joined him! You believed his lies and adopted his vile ways. You betrayed Florengia."

The kid flushed. "Hold your tongue, artist, or I'll strangle you with it. At least he must have come by his wounds honorably. You're a human puffball, not fighting on either side, blowing in the wind. From now on remember to address me as 'my lord.' I won't warn you again." He stepped over to the table and peered in the wine jug. "Hey, No-balls, how much of this sewage would make me spew just a little?"

Dantio turned, anonymous again. "Impossible to say. Just one mouthful might. Don't go back, Orlad! Please don't go back! They really mean to kill you tomorrow."

Without a word, the Werist splashed some wine into a beaker and raised it in a toast. "To holy Demeter, Who witnesses all oaths!" He tossed it back.

"Not bad!" He paused with his hand on the latch and seemed to reflect. "I gave you my word, so I won't report your nasty little treason. I am not an oath-breaker."

"Don't go!" Fabia said.

"Please don't go!" Benard said.

The warrior scowled. "Speaking to me?"

"My lord, if it makes you happy. Please don't go, my lord. We are your family and we want you. Siblings may bicker among themselves, but they help one another."

"You can be chief pallbearer." Orlad walked out, closing the door quietly.

Fabia hugged Dantio again. "What's he planning?"

"Gods know. He doesn't. He's wildly unstable."

"Hardly surprising!" Benard slumped down on the platform edge and put his head in his hands. "He ought to go after Therek and wring his neck."

"He's misguided," the seer said, "not evil. Doing what he's been brought up to respect. Except now they won't let him."

"And tomorrow?" Fabia asked.

"Tomorrow?" Dantio sighed. "He didn't drink very much of the wine. If he has to, he will die to prove his loyalty. But Flankleader Leorth may find he has quite a fight on his paws. Orlad has nothing in the world to value except his prowess as a Hero. He'll be no easy victim." The return of anonymity seemed to have restored Dantio's confidence. He retrieved his distaff and spindle from the floor. "Please forgive my exhibition earlier. I didn't expect so much pity."

Benard did not think he had felt pity, not at first. Repugnance, more like—deliberate mutilation of the human body was a desecration of everything he held holy. He glanced at Fabia, and saw his own guilt reflected. He said, "Brother . . . I am truly sorry. I should not have unmasked you."

"No, I should have told you who I was . . . am. I was planning to, just not yet. It was stupid of me to wait."

"Who did it—Saltaja?"

"Not personally. Her orders."

"But all the seers—even you—said you were dead. Even Saltaja believed you."

"No. We never report that Dantio *is dead,* only that Dantio *died.* I did die. It is a long and sad story, not for telling now."

"I knew Mist was one of the riverfolk," Fabia said. "But I only considered the women. A Florengian, a man, a slave. No wonder I didn't spot you!"

"It can be handy at times," the seer said in a voice dry enough to empty the Wrogg. "We must make plans. Please, both of you . . . will you keep my secret a little longer? Exposing me may confuse the issues we must discuss."

Benard and Fabia said "Of course!" together. He added, "Family secret!," and she said, "Where is Horth?"

"He's here." Dantio chuckled shakily. "Ucr is just a little slower than Anziel at opening jails." He held the door for Fabia. "Bena—those window bars you . . . your goddess . . . removed for you—would She put them back, too?"

"She might. Why?"

"Just to upset Saltaja. Petty of me, I'm afraid."

Benard thought about it. "The building must look very unbalanced without them. I can ask."

Forty-one

INGELD NARSDOR,

truant light of Veslih on Kosord, self-exiled dynast of that city, runaway wife of its satrap, and cradle-robbing mistress of Master Artist Celebre, was indulging herself by munching yet another peach, her fourth since she had refused the evening meal. Just to be ashore again was pure delight. To be under a roof, dry and snug before a crackling fire, and with someone new to talk to, was unimaginable heaven. Her hostess on the other side of the hearth, Witness Poppy, was probably the light of Mayn on Tryfors, although no one had said so and she clearly deferred—like everyone in this curious secret warren—to Witness Mist, who had arrived that morning and was presently elsewhere. Ingeld did not particularly care where, except that Benard had gone with her and might therefore be in danger. She did not know how many of the dozen or so residents of the refuge were Witnesses. All of them, veiled or unveiled, were friendly, courteous people. She had always thought of seers as vile snoops and sneaks, Stralg lackeys, without seriously considering that they might hate their servitude.

"Matters came to a head this spring," Poppy said. She rarely directed her words to her listener, but rather turned her head at random as if she studied events unfolding far beyond the walls. The timbre of her voice confirmed that she was old, but clearly her mind was sharp as a thorn. "The previous Eldest died, although the news has not long reached us in Tryfors. It was she, Witness Raven, who had made the compact with Stralg, years ago. I would not reveal more, but since you are suddenly caught up in hectic events, you deserve to understand the source of your danger."

The source of Ingeld's danger was her insane love for Benard, absurd though it was in a woman her age. "I shall not betray your confidence."

"The cult has long been divided over our support of Stralg. Most were content to obey the Eldest's dictum that we must wait for his death, which cannot now be long in coming. Then the infamous compact would also die and set us free. Mist's faction argues that the greatest power behind Stralg is not Weru, who may be very terrible but is still one of the Twelve. They hold to the opinion that Saltaja Hragsdor is a Chosen of the Foul One."

Poppy's lecture was interrupted by an ear-destroying roar, which could have been the sound of a felled forest giant parting from its stump, but was in fact merely a reminder that Packleader Guthlag lay stretched out on the sleeping platform. He had celebrated his disembarkation with several bowls of beer and in at least one of the Sixty Ways available next door.

"She is my sister-in-law," Ingeld said, "and that would not surprise me at all. But surely you can tell?"

"Never with certainty," Poppy told the fireplace. "Much of her life is hidden from us, but we cannot prove that this is the Ancient One's doing. Also, the powers of chthonians seem to vary."

"They live long lives?"

"There are records of some doing so. Since we can rarely identify them, those that we can may be exceptions."

Ingeld said cautiously, "In my experience Saltaja has always seemed much cleverer than any of her brothers, and I've met all of them. She may well be the genius behind the bloodlord."

"Did you ever meet Hrag?"

"No. I met all his children, but he himself was never mentioned."

"It is curious," the old lady said, nodding, "that we can find no record of his death, but the present Eldest, like her predecessor, refuses to listen to arguments not based on proven fact."

"Mist is the chief of the rebels?"

Poppy allowed herself a discreet chuckle. "There can be no rebellion when the Eldest's authority is absolute and no secrets are hidden from her. She is aware of our discontent and ignores it, although we represent a majority of our order. Mist is best described as our most outspoken spokesman for our views. We maintain that the evidence linking the Hrag family to the Old One is strong enough to nullify the treaty, while recognizing that revocation by us will undoubtedly engender drastic retaliation from the Werists."

"Their revenge may be very terrible," Ingeld agreed. She bent to toss her peach pit in the fire and flinched as an image of Horold flashed out at her. She threw the pit at it. How long until he caught her? She savored every moment of her freedom with Benard, knowing how brief it must be. She lay awake at nights listening to his soft breathing, feeling the heat of his body, worrying over the inevitable vengeance bearing down on them.

"We are about to have company," the seer said before the door opened behind her—nobody knocked on doors in the lodge. A small, middle-aged man walked in and peered around nervously. The door closed behind his back.

The seer did not turn. "Welcome, Master Wigson. I seldom need a name, but when I do I am Poppy. My lady, this is Horth Wigson, Fabia's foster father . . . Lady Ingeld, Daughter of Veslih, dynast of Kosord."

"I am indeed honored!" He bowed to each in turn.

Ingeld was surprised. She understood that Horth Wigson was one of the wealthiest men on the Vigaelian Face, if not *the* wealthiest, and had built his fortune entirely with his wits. This newcomer seemed impossibly insignificant. He had a head like an inverted pear which would barely come up to her shoulder if she stood, and he tapered downward from there, stooped and wizened. True, she would not expect a merchant to be built like a Werist— or a sculptor—but surely there should be a flash of razor intelligence lurking in unfathomably calculating eyes? This man's eyes were as banal as boiled wrens' eggs.

"I understand that you have just been rescued from the satrap's cells, Master Wigson," she said. "I congratulate you on your escape."

"Oh, er, thank you, my lady."

"Fabia has also been released and is here in the lodge."

"So I am told." Wigson blinked like a bewildered owl.

"We have very effective friends here."

Poppy sniffed pettishly. "The Witnesses had nothing to do with Master Wigson's departure from the palace dungeons. He organized that himself. We merely intercepted him on the street and offered to bring him to a safe place to meet with Fabia."

"I am doubly impressed, Ucrist!" Ingeld said. "I understood you arrived in Tryfors only this morning and were thrown in jail right away."

He should not have had time to organize anything on such short notice, let alone a jailbreak. He did not explain. In the absence of a vacant seat, he perforce remained standing, hands clasped in front of him like a child reciting lessons.

Guthlag released another stupendous snore.

"He set it up when he was in Kosord," Poppy said. "His accomplices there sent a fast boat ahead of him to enlist the help of our local harbor master, who tailors the seamy underside of Tryfors. Wigson made himself known by an agreed signal on the strand this morning, and later the harbor master bribed the night guards to release him. He also provided Horth with several curious items not readily available in the bazaar, didn't he, Master Wigson?"

"Indeed he did, Witness." Horth smiled shyly, showing no surprise or alarm at having his secrets thus exposed, which was evidence of commendable control, if not necessarily razor intelligence.

Ingeld did not inquire what those curious items might be. "And how do you propose to remain at large when the satrap discovers your absence?"

"My plans were still, er, fluid, my lady. I had originally hoped that Frena and I could escape tonight by boat. Alas, whereas I was merely in the town jail, I discovered that she was being held in the palace proper, guarded by Werists. Polytheists can be bribed, Heroes cannot. I was balked. Naturally, I was overjoyed to learn that she had already been, um . . . sprung." His wishy-washy smile faded on and off. "So I cannot answer your question, my lady. I do not know what is going on."

"You are not the only one, although I expect our hostess can tell us?"

"In good time," Poppy snapped. "Fabia is on her way here. She has been meeting with the youngest of her brothers, who has proved to be a very stubborn young man."

"You amaze me. Benard has a head of solid brass."

Wigson cleared his throat. "Frena herself can be quite determined at times."

On cue, Fabia burst in the door and hurled herself at him. "Father! Oh, you're safe! I was so worried!"

And so on. She was taller than he was and certainly louder. No doubt she had the makings of a charming young lady, if she could just be taken in hand by someone with suitable knowledge and skill ... plus a strong arm and a switch. Someone like Ingeld herself. About three years should do it.

"It is known that you met lady Ingeld in Kosord," Poppy said.

"I did have that honor." Fabia bobbed to Ingeld.

"Then why," the seer persisted, "are you not surprised to meet her here, so far from home? Did Benard mention her to you?"

"After what I have seen tonight, I shall never be surprised by anything. Here he is!"

Benard shambled in, reacting to the sight of Ingeld by turning on his goofiest grin. It was less convincing than usual. He was upset by something—so much so that he was trying to hide his feelings, for once.

"No luck with Orlando?" she asked.

"Like making soup with live cats." Scowling, he flopped down on the floor beside her stool. "It's horrible, what they've done to him. He's become a death-before-dishonor fanatic!"

"I know someone who was prepared to die for his art."

"No, you don't." He leaned back against her leg. In Ingeld's wildest nightmares she could never imagine Horold sitting at her feet like this. Moving to pat his shoulder in motherly fashion, she was annoyed to discover that her hand held a half-eaten peach. The empty basket he had just pushed aside had contained at least a dozen when it arrived. They were small, but why did Oliva have this mad craving for peaches?

Ingeld moved the fruit to her other hand and stroked the nape of Benard's neck. She felt the tension knots there, despite his pretense of calm, and wished she were alone with him so she could knead them away. Never in her life had she been a clinging vine. It was as if her departure from her city had changed her into another person altogether—not necessarily one she approved of, just one she was insanely happy to be, at least for now. Love!

A Witness tall enough to be Mist entered and closed the door. The little room was now very crowded. Fabia, lacking a proper seat, pouted and perched on the edge of the sleeping platform beside the rumbling Guthlag. Wigson clasped his hands behind his back again. The newcomer remained standing where she was.

328   Dave Duncan

"I am Mist. You all know one another. I suggest we pool our resources, because cooperation will help all our causes. Let us begin by stating our aims, to make sure they do not conflict. The Witnesses—those in our faction—wish to hasten the downfall of the Fist and all he stands for. Lady Ingeld?"

Ingeld decided she hated all masked women. "Benard and I seek a comfortable hiding place where we may live in peace. I have left my husband. Holy Veslih warns that he is following me."

"Satrap Horold is unlikely to find you without the aid of seers, so you must favor our revolution. Master Wigson, what do you seek?"

The little man shrugged. "Happiness . . ." He paused as if waiting for someone to protest that he was a Ucrist, then smiled and added, "for Frena. With respect, lady Ingeld, my foster daughter does not wish to marry your noble son."

"No offense taken." It would be harder to imagine a less promising match than those two.

He bowed. "On the other hand, if she is entitled to succeed to the throne of a great city, then I should be very selfish if I did not do everything in my power to assist her achieve this goal."

The girl smirked, no doubt contemplating the prospect of Celebre without Cutrath.

Poppy uttered a snort almost as loud as Guthlag's snores, apparently indicating disbelief. "Does that explain why your purchases from the harbor master included a packet of marsh calabar seeds?"

Ingeld suspected that the old lady's obvious dislike of Horth stemmed from frustrated nosiness. If Veslih and Xaran could block the seers' sight, it was a reasonable assumption that Ucr could.

"Not a fatal dose," the merchant retorted blandly.

"Physic may have unpredictable effects in the Edgelands."

"Just what is marsh whatever-you-said?" asked Benard from the floor.

"A medicinal herb. In excess it causes a severe loss of muscle tone, which can last for half a year or longer. Crossing the Edge is a severe test of endurance. Furthermore, in males, calabar may cause prolonged penile disfunction."

Horth, Ingeld was pleased to see, was carefully not looking in her direction. She would just hate for him to catch her eye and drop dead. She would strangle him later.

Minx Fabia smirked shamelessly.

Poppy continued her interrogation. "In your private conversation with the harbor master, you questioned him at length about Varakats."

"Varakats?" Horth repeated vaguely. "There is nothing illegal in discussing Varakats, is there? A very beautiful mountain, I am told. My eyes are not what they used to be." Most people when threatened turned either very red or very pale. This little man remained unruffled, maintaining his mousy pose—which the seer obviously thought concealed a rat.

"That depends on what is discussed. You also asked about High Timber. You were trying to lay a false trail to mislead us Witnesses and hence divert Satrap Therek tomorrow."

"I wish you two would speak a language I understand," Benard grumbled.

Horth inclined his head to the Witness, deferring to her.

"There are two passes over the Edge," she said. "The Nardalborg Pass is the closer, and the kings of Tryfors taxed trade on it, although there was never much. When Stralg was preparing to move a horde to Florengia, many years ago, he naturally chose the pass nearer the city, where he could billet his men, and it is now a Werist highway, much improved. The other pass has been officially forgotten, but traders still use it. Master Wigson and his accomplices have been running a huge smuggling industry over it for years."

"You do not trade in slaves, I hope?" Benard demanded.

"Slaves can tell tales, Hand." Wigson at last protested against Poppy's inquisition, although still in the same mild tones: "Are you seeking to blackmail me, Witness? I fail to see what relevance Varakats has to this meeting."

"What relevance did it have to you, tonight? You discovered you could not release Fabia from captivity and it was unlikely you could even pass her the calabar and other nasty devices you had collected for her. So you were going to run away to High Timber. You hoped that the satrap's men would follow your trail and discover the rebel threat. That would distract Therek thoroughly, and delay the caravan's departure until after the winter. This was a massive betrayal of your friends."

"That is unfair!" Fabia shouted. "Horth was kidnapped, too, as a hostage for my good behavior. I would have been very happy if he had escaped. That would not have increased my danger in any way; it would have helped me. How long do you think Saltaja was going to keep him alive once she sent me off over the pass, anyway?"

Poppy sniffed. "I understand his desire to escape. I cannot stomach his betrayal of Varakats and High Timber."

"You do me wrong, Witness," Wigson said, still speaking softly. "I was investigating options. Learning that the Varakats Pass is still open, I was contemplating the possibility of hiring a party of dissident Werists from High Timber and sending them over the Edge to rescue Frena on the far side."

Benard jumped as if an idea had just hit the inside of skull. He whipped around to look up at Ingeld with delight—Horold would never think to look for her in Florengia! At times she was unhappily reminded how young her lover was. What matter if she was pregnant and there was a war raging on the far side of the pass? She smiled and nodded.

Mist intervened with a chuckle. "I think that's enough. We all play for the same team. If we Maynists try to withdraw our support of the Fist, his men will retaliate with violence. The Eldest could announce a date when we should all remove our veils and vanish. We would have to abandon the Ivory Cloisters and generations of labor on the Wisdom—but it could be done. Our new Eldest, LeAmber, follows her predecessor in refusing to issue the command, and no one else has authority to do so. If we dissidents provoke the split, we shall bring down the Werists' wrath on all our sisters who remain on duty. Tryfors may seem a strange place to launch a revolution . . . You disagree, Master Wigson!"

"I can think of counterarguments."

"Such as?"

The trader smiled. "Fords, passes, crossroads—these are all strategic places. I know you seers can read a sealed tablet, so I assume you monitor Stralg's correspondence on its way through here. Then you lecture me on betrayal?"

Again Mist laughed, breaking the tension. "Leave ethics for another day! It has taken Saltaja an amazingly long time to appreciate that, where once Stralg could promise the Heroes glory and loot, the trip over the Edge has now become a one-way road to the Old One's cold embrace. The new initiates were duped as boys and are doomed as young men. They cannot shed their collars, but they can seek out a leader who offers better hope than that. His name is Arbanerik Kranson. His horde is called New Dawn, and is camped at High Timber, not far from here. Saltaja would give both arms for that information!

"We are not required to volunteer information to Stralg's agents, and over the years most of us have become extremely skilled at deceiving without actually lying. However, when Saltaja read Stralg's first dispatches this spring, she decided to make a personal tour of inspection—escorting Fabia was incidental—and that decision was a critical turning point, what we refer to as a 'weft.' We sensed it like a clap of thunder. The journey opened her eyes to the fact that the numbers did not add up, that at least a third of the reinforcements being sent to aid the bloodlord were never reaching Nardalborg.

"Even at Kosord we still managed to hide the details from her, but after that her own guards began deserting. This afternoon she had Therek summon a seer. I knew the moment had come, so I answered the call, and I *lied*. I told her that the New Dawn rebels were mustering at Nuthervale and I grossly understated their number. I gave False Witness, and for that I shall be expelled from the mystery. I broke my most sacred oath, but I feel no shame or guilt."

Ingeld said, "In my opinion it is long overdue. Without the seers' complicity, Stralg and his hateful gang would have all died years ago."

"So it wasn't Father!" Fabia said. "When the Werists disappeared on the way here? It wasn't Father helping, it was you!"

Mist chuckled. "It was the riverfolk. They receive a bounty for every willing deserter delivered to High Timber. We need not discuss where that silver comes from—agreed, Master Wigson?"

"Um? No." Horth seemed to be preoccupied in studying Fabia.

Benard grunted. "I always thought Witnesses *couldn't* lie."

"Oh, we can sin as well as you can. We can only do it once, though."

An uncomfortable silence settled on the room. Everyone there except Fabia was a henotheist, sworn to a mystery, and they were all breaking faith. Ingeld herself had broken her vows—in spirit if not in word—when she had invited Benard to father her child and then fled the city with him. Benard was neglecting his art, Guthlag had broken faith with his lord, and perhaps Horth Wigson was breaking oaths to Ucr by pursuing Fabia's happiness instead of simply amassing wealth. Now the seers, too!

At last Ingeld said, "Have you consulted a Speaker? Holy Demern does allow certain oaths to be set aside—those made under duress, for example, or those that conflict with earlier vows."

"I can quote holy law to better effect than that," Mist said curtly. "That does not matter now. Tomorrow, the satrap will learn that his prisoners have vanished. He will summon his seer again. Do you think he would believe another denial?"

"So the revolution has begun?" Benard said.

Ingeld could feel the knots in his shoulders tighten even more.

Mist said, "It begins tomorrow."

"No more seers," Benard said, "but . . . Flankleader?"

"Hand?" The old Werist still seemed fast asleep, flat as a puddle, but he had not snored in some time, Ingeld realized, and only Benard had noticed.

"Fabia and Master Wigson have escaped from the satrap's cells. How long will it take his warbeasts to track them to this room?"

Still the old man did not open his eyes. "Ever drop a raw egg off'na table, so it broke on the floor?"

"Yes."

" 'Bout that long."

Benard looked around. "I've lived with this problem all my life," he said apologetically.

"We did think of that, Bena," said Mist. "But now you have the Witnesses on your side, which makes a difference. Poppy and I are currently keeping watch on the palace and all is calm. It's highly unlikely that the prisoners' absence will be noted before morning, but we're all going to head down to the river very shortly, just in case. We'll wait there for dawn, unless the tocsin sounds, in which case we'll sail at once. Even Werists can't follow a scent over running water—right, my lord?"

"Right," Guthlag said, opening his eyes and yawning.

"So tomorrow the satrap will find no seers in Tryfors. All of them will be heading inward along the Wrogg, spreading the word, and by the time the Eldest hears the news, it will be too late. She can anathematize us, but she will probably be too busy evacuating Bergashamm. Since we cannot continue to shield you here in Tryfors, I suggest that you and your lady accompany us."

Benard looked around to seek Ingeld's approval.

"What of my son?" she asked, trying not to show her anger. She had no love left for the brute Horold had become, but she had no love for treachery either, and news of a secret rebel army poised to strike appalled her. She feared for Cutrath, the Fist's nephew, innocently standing in its path. "Is there to be yet another civil war? Tell us what this illegal host at High Timber is planning. I would think any rebels' first logical move would be to seize Nardalborg and block the pass, to trap Stralg on the Florengian Face. What of Benard's brother?"

Mist sighed. "Orlad is as good as dead. I gave him as much warning as I dared, but his long-awaited initiation day had a black dawn, and he cannot bear it. Your son, my lady, will I think be much more valuable to the rebels as a hostage to be used against your husband than he will as a dead body. I realize that this is small comfort, but it is the best I have to offer. Tomorrow I propose to take word of our revolt to High Timber myself, but I cannot predict what Hordeleader Arbanerik will choose to do. I invite you all to come with me."

She offered no alternative, Ingeld noted. They were all conspirators now. It was death-to-traitors time.

Benard had apparently not seen that, or else he was astonishingly willing to trust this faceless seer. "Of course we will. And you, Fabia?"

"Certainly. You agree, Father?"

"Possibly. Why don't you introduce me to your other brother, Frena?"

Benard's shoulders went hard as marble.

"He calls himself Mist now," the trader continued, "but on the river he was Urth, and long ago was he not Dantio?"

When no one corrected him, it was Ingeld herself who said, "Praise the gods! Praise holy Veslih, who cherishes families! All four of you?" It was a long time since she had felt such a pain of joy in her throat.

The reunion was tainted. When the seer removed his veil, he revealed a youthful Florengian face, but his features were no more masculine than his voice. "How did you work that out, Master Ucrist Wigson?"

"It was fairly obvious, Master Witness Celebre," Horth said with his usual diffidence. "From what 'Mist' just told us, 'she' had been in Kosord and even Skjar at the same time we had. Then 'she' arrived in Tryfors on the same day we did, so I knew that 'she' had traveled with us in our convoy. After that it was merely a process of elimination. When none of the riverfolk I remembered fit, I was left with their Florengian slaves, and I recalled that one of them, Urth, had a treble voice and no beard, so obviously had been castrated in boyhood and was therefore no prisoner of war. He was Mist's size. In age he would match the 'deceased' Dantio, and . . . Well, I do know your sister very well, Witness, and when she came in here she was bursting with some secret. Although she was pleased to have her brother Benard back again, she was much more interested in you." Wigson's eyes were still as bland as wren's eggs.

"It is wonderful to have you back from the dead!" Fabia said.

"It is wonderful to be able to greet my sister and brother without deception." Dantio shook his head sadly. "This is the day I have dreamed of since our parting, fifteen years ago. I have worked for it unceasingly. Today I return and the family is complete again. Today we are reunited at last. But tomorrow we lose Orlad."

Forty-two

HERO ORLAD

soon discovered that the seer had not been lying, at least about the wine. Before left flank reached Eriander's temple, its out-of-town guest fell on his knees in the gutter, thus provoking much mirthful comment on overindulgence. He was still puking when they carried him back to the barracks, and by then the cramps had started. Orlad was faking some of it, but he was in enough real pain and distress to know that the conspirators had been dangerously over-generous with the drug. Had the seer not warned him, they might have seen their planned entertainment ruined by the premature death of the star attraction. They left him on his rug with a bucket and went away laughing to continue the evening's program. Confident that there would be listeners in nearby cubicles, Orlad continued his playacting, and he kept it up much of the night, even after the others returned. Why should they sleep when he couldn't? The effects of the poison wore off, but he was starting to believe that he was going to die on the morrow.

Praise the Lord of Battle, who alone decides!

♦

On the morrow, it rained.

At first light Orlad rose, dressed, and repeated the Heroes' morning prayer. The final words took on a significance he had never truly appreciated before: *Today I will win or die.*

Guests were always given the cubicles farthest from the door, where the traffic was lightest, but there were times when that seemed a very sinister courtesy. He tiptoed the length of the barracks and went out as quietly as he could. It was only then that he discovered the glorious mercy of Weru—a steady drizzle falling from a gray murk almost low enough to touch, a total absence of wind. Heroes did not kneel to thank their god, they raised both fists to the heavens, and Orlad barely restrained a scream of joy as he did so. He could not hope to win, but now he could make a fight of it. First score to him!

There would be food in the mess, but his stomach roiled at the thought. He trotted across the yard to the trough, rinsed his mouth, filled his canteen, and splashed water over a face already soaked. Rain! Oh, great god of battle!

"Orlad!" Flankleader Leorth came stumbling out of the dormitory wearing his brass collar and nothing else. He looked up at the sky in horror.

"Thought I'd make an early start!" Orlad yelled. Stealth could not help him now. "Fine day for a run." Recalling that it was polite to give thanks for hospitality, he added, "May holy Veslih reward you as you deserve."

He headed for the gate.

"Wait!" Leorth came running to intercept him, wincing as his bare feet impacted the pebbles. "No, no! I'm sure the Vulture won't expect you to travel on a day like this. There will be snow on—"

"My lord commands and I obey."

"But after your gripe last night—"

Orlad spun to face him. "Shouldn't have said 'early' start. Meant 'head' start."

Leorth's guilt flamed red above his flaxen beard. "What do you mean?"

"I mean that I intend to make a fight of it. You I will send to Weru to announce my coming. And your precious Vulture can flap on his nest all he wants."

Something genuinely catlike showed in Leorth's eyes. "Would you prefer to make it single combat?"

"Not after that wine, thank you." Orlad was being unfair in condemning unfairness, because fairness was no part of the code. The road to victory need not be straight, Heth said.

"Then I wish you an interesting journey." Smile.

"I wish you good hunting and an early death." Sneer.

Orlad trotted out the gate.

Now he believed.

✦

He jogged on cobbled streets between buildings of stone, ran on a muddy track lined by poor-folk shacks, and dropped back to a walk as he reached the vegetable plots and orchards beyond the town. Already the Vulture's Nest was fading into the grayness behind him. He wondered if anyone had yet dared waken the satrap to break the bad news.

The trail wound interminably through a maze of tiny, stony plots, but the harvest was in and the leaves all shed, leaving a drab, waterlogged landscape that offered no hiding places. He had seen no empty mats in the barracks, and no one had slipped out before he did, so he could assume that the ambush could not be set up yet . . . unless Leorth's flank was to have help, which seemed unlikely. Twelve against one should be adequate.

Seers never lied, but that Dantio creature bent truth like a sailor tying knots—going around dressed as a woman, flaunting a distaff! Wasn't that lying? Of course, he wasn't actually a man, either. Gelding was the most fucking horrible thing to do to a kid, and artist Benard's blasphemy in comparing it to Werist training should have cost him half his teeth. Forget him. Forget all three of them. Families were for children. Orlad Orladson would live or die alone.

Tactics?

A backward glance revealed nothing moving among the stark black trees and tumbledown stone dykes. Yet his prints in the mud were clear enough. The skin on his back crawled at the thought of pursuit. Wind and rain would make tracking harder, but there wasn't really enough of either yet to throw warbeasts off the scent. The worst thing he could possibly do was panic, although only an utter madman could stay calm with twelve warbeasts on his track. Breath recovered, he moved up to a trot again.

Soon he neared the end of the farmland, where even Tryforian farmers gave up. Ahead of him lay more orchards, then pasture rising steadily until mist became fog and fog turned to cloud. This slope overlooking the town and offering prime grazing, which some old-time ruler had claimed for his own, could only be the King's Grass. Today the killing field.

Tactics?

Know your enemy.

Leorth liked being feline and feline meant ambush. Almost certainly this would be his first human kill, so he would want to do the deed himself. In order to let the satrap watch, he would have planned to set up his trap close by the trail, having spread the rest of his flank around King's Grass to make certain the victim did not escape. The wine had been poisoned so the killers would have time in the morning to take up position—nothing slowed a man like a night of vomiting and belly cramps.

But Orlad had been forewarned, thanks to brother-sister Dantio. Leorth would have to go dog, meaning running the quarry to exhaustion. It would be a straight chase, and holy Weru had sent this glorious mist and drizzle to deny Therek the pleasure of watching.

Orlad reached the last scabby trees. Boulders of all sizes lay scattered over the King's Grass, everything from nasty cobbles for breaking ankles to monoliths the size of small houses, but he recalled that there was a denser boulder field near the crest of the first rise. That would certainly have been where Leorth had planned to lie in wait, still within the satrap's view. Conversely, the pursuers must go through there, too, so it would be the best place for the quarry to make his last stand and ambush the frustrated ambushers.

Orlad had no reason to carry a waterlogged pall now. Pausing to shed it, he heard a low complaint, which he traced to a solitary mouflon tethered to a last, isolated tree some distance uphill to his left. If he had still doubted the eunuch's warning, that poor bleating beast would have convinced him. The herds had been removed in case they distracted the hunt, but a light snack had been left there to reward the returning victors. His murder had been carefully catered.

As he kicked off his sandals, he scanned the slope below him. The town itself was completely invisible, but he guessed that the hunt had started by now. Let the game begin!

He began to lope, angling into the wind. Up ahead a clammy breeze dragged filmy draperies of rain across the hillside. It would carry his scent back to the hunt, but even that might be turned to his advantage.

As his breathing and heartbeat increased, he summoned the power of his god and changed. Not very much yet, although enough to hurt like the rack. He stretched his legs, hardened his feet, and increased his chest capacity while trying to leave his head alone, although his thinking was bound to be cramped as his muscles became greedier for all available blood. Now he swung along with a six-foot stride on legs coated with dense black fur like moleskin. Hairiness came naturally because it gave protection, and hair color was conserved. Vigaelian warbeasts were flaxen or golden, rarely bronze, so there would be no trouble telling the players apart in this match.

The world, too, had changed—losing color, gaining relict scents of the herds that had grazed there only yesterday, of herders and their dogs. He remembered to angle upwind. His breath came in gales, his hooves beat rhythmically on the turf, and he rejoiced in his strength. Speed was exhilarating. No, he was not a victim being hunted down. He was a warrior leading his foes into a trap, and although he had no hope of dining on that victory-feast mouflon, he would make sure that some of them did not live to enjoy it either.

He must not let left flank catch him before, er . . . wherever it was he was going . . . rocks. Rocks? Rocks all around him now. He had reached the rocks. He stopped and drove himself through the agony of retroforming, which was always worse than the original change. Rain seemed colder coursing down smooth skin.

Now he could think, while gasping for air. He was just inside the boulder field, but there was still enough grass there to make walking on human feet possible. Who was the hunter now? If he could manage to make his first few kills in silence, he might take quite a toll on the enemy. His best option was to move downwind inside the cover and hope the enemy would follow his trail, letting him catch their scent. It was a sign of his desperation that he was reduced to hoping that his opponents would be utterly stupid.

As he scrambled up on a rock to look back, something moved behind him, in the corner of his eye, something still human and vulnerable. *The seer had misled him!* He was up against more than just rear flank, and he had run right into a trap. Roaring fury, he flashed through a change even as he leaped, claws out and fangs bared to rip open the prey's throat.

The prey screamed something . . . human words . . .

Orlad managed to retract his claws, but no Werist could have retroformed fast enough to complete that leap in human form. The prey went flat on his back with Orlad's fangs at his neck. Eyeball-to-eyeball . . . Familiar scent. Without conscious effort or awareness of pain, Orlad finished retroforming.

"Waels!"

Face white as chalk around his bloody birthmark, the victim stared up at his deadly assailant. He made a choking noise.

"That was close," Orlad said. Too appallingly close! He had very nearly torn out the throat of his . . . his former classmate.

"You're safe!" Waels whispered. "Oh, Orlad! We were so worried!"

"Who's 'we'?"

"Me, then." The disfigured mouth twisted in a smile. "My lord is kind?"

"Looks like attempted rape," remarked a familiar voice above them.

Those large hairy legs belonged to Snerfrik. Orlad sprang to his feet and confirmed this. Vargin was emerging from behind a boulder. But both of them were wearing palls striped in orange, green, and red. And so was Waels. Orange for Therek's host, green for the Nardalborg Hunt, yes. But red pack? Their sashes were standard warrior brown, but the knots were at their backs, out of sight.

Waels had been assigned to blue pack, left flank; Vargin and Snerfrik to gold pack, right flank. And there stood Ranthr, who had been red pack, right flank, but his sash was tied at his back, too.

Red pack, *rear* flank, was to be Orlad's own, as soon as Huntleader Heth assigned him warriors. Could he trust what his eyes were telling him?

"Weru's balls!" he roared. "What are you all doing here?"

Snerfrik laughed. "We got called for first hunt, and old Heth—"

Orlad was about to do battle. "Report, warrior!"

Big Snerfrik jerked to attention. "My lord is kind. The huntleader summoned us for our first hunt, my lord, but when we mustered, he had us change palls. I mean, he reassigned us all to your flank. Temporary assignment. He ordered us to make sure our leader returned safely."

Waels clambered to his feet, moving gingerly. "He also said you might find us better game than oribis."

"And we saw a *black* warbeast coming," Hrothgat explained from the top of a large monolith.

Orlad hurled a fast prayer at Weru: *May Your servant Heth Hethson gain glorious and immortal memory among Your Heroes!*

"Well?" Waels said, rubbing his back. His eyes shone fiery bright. "Did you find any game worth our attention, *my lord?*"

Orlad distrusted that gleeful smile, but there were too many other things going on to worry about it now. "Did you break anything, warrior?"

"My lord is kind. A shoulder blade, three ribs, and possibly my neck."

All of which he could heal in battleform. The rest of rear pack were visible now, emerging from behind, or on top of, boulders. A leader might take some pride in the fact that they were all still paired with the buddies he had assigned them back in the spring.

"I'm being hunted. Anyone in sight yet, Hrothgat?"

"Four . . . no, five. Ah, seven. Warbeasts of various types, my lord. Well spread out. Coming at a slow trot. Eight."

"There should be twelve in all. They intend to kill me. Anyone want out?"

Eleven heads shook. "No," they said, or, "No, my lord." Eleven sets of teeth showed.

Oh, Weru! Last night family, and today friends. *Friends?* He didn't know how to deal with family and friends. All his life he'd been alone. He must find time to think about these things later.

"Then spread out." He pointed both ways along the length of the boulder train. "Take cover and wait as long as you can. When you're spotted, attack, otherwise hold off until the ruckus starts, and then join in. Any questions?"

"Prisoners?" asked Waels, always the spokesman.

"No."

All those teeth flashed again.

"My lord is kind," they said. What else could they say? Those who lived would have a memorable first hunt to relate. What a pity satrap Therek would not be able to watch!

Orlad might not die after all—might even win a victory. Dear, wonderful Huntleader Heth! But how many *friends* was he leading to their deaths? He shivered violently—fight now, think later.

"Rear flank—strip!"

◆

Orlad hurried downwind through the rocks with Waels at his heels. "I feel catty," he said over his shoulder, thinking of Leorth.

Waels laughed as if this was a tremendous game. "Beef for me, then. Just point where you want me." Soft-spoken Bloodmouth was ever an ocean of surprises; his amusement seemed genuine.

Orlad found a suitable monolith, climbable on one side and vertical on the other, high enough to give him a view. He raced up the slope, and by the time he reached the top he was down on all fours, grinding bones and joints, sprouting dark fur. The pain took his mind off a horrible hollow feeling in his gut. He had fought often enough, but not this sort of fight.

Extrinsics often wondered—but were rarely foolish enough to ask—how warriors told friend from foe in battleform, when appearance was useless and speech limited at best, usually impossible. The answer was that men living together for an extended period and eating the same food acquired their own group scent. A pack knew its own and was expected to recognize the other packs in its hunt. Larger units had to resort to artificial markers—paint sometimes, but not all warbeasts could distinguish colors. Strong-smelling herbs worked better. Even so, there were many tales of friend mauling friend in the heat of battle.

With odds of twelve to one and permission to accept all necessary casualties, Flankleader Leorth must be feeling very confident as he closed in on the boulder train. He need no longer worry about driving the subject out into the open to die, because the mist had blocked the satrap's view. He could guess why Orlad had headed upwind and he was certainly not going to lead his flank into that nightmare maze and then turn downwind. With only one man opposing him, he did not start by seizing the high points, as he should have done. Indeed he almost made a game of it, spreading his men out to enter the boulder field in line abreast.

Unaware that the entire former Nardalborg runt class was in there also, every pair caught what they thought was Orlad's scent and tracked it back, straight into the labyrinth.

Shivering with bloodlust, Orlad watched from his perch as they came. He was in full cat-form now, with the addition of a pair of dagger fangs, a useful variant old Gzurg had told him about. Had he been thinking at human rate, he might have been amazed at his opponents' folly, but all he knew was that the nearest of them, slinking in on all fours practically under his aerie, was white and feline. Close to its tail lumbered a great yellow bear-thing on two legs—standard practice being to pair speed with strength. They could as easily be Leorth and Merkurtu as any others. They were heading to pass below Orlad on his left. Remembering his buddy waiting below, he forced his tail to stop twitching and point right, so that Waels could circle around that way, keeping out of sight. So far, this was just standard training.

For almost sixty heartbeats, Leorth's flank prowled through the rocks, looking for one warrior. Battle broke out everywhere simultaneously—hunter encountering quarry, quarry pouncing on hunter—just as the cat below Orlad decided to jump up on this convenient rock. Raising its tawny eyes, it saw a panther looking down. Orlad screamed to warn Waels as he sprang, but his voice was just one in the uproar. Three Tryforians broke from cover, four Nardalborgians raced out after them, and a free-for-all developed in the open.

Orlad's opponent, already rearing back to leap upward, was bowled over by the darker warbeast. Each immediately tried to disembowel the other with rear claws. Yes, the white cat was Leorth. Although he was underneath, he had a momentary advantage because he could bring his forepaws around to rip Orlad's back while his own was unreachable. He tucked in his head to try for a throat bite and Orlad drove a tusk deep into his left eye.

Even that blow would not kill a warbeast outright, but it did throw Leorth into convulsions. Freed from his grasp, Orlad was able to do a thorough job of ripping his neck open.

He rose from the bloody, twitching corpse to look for his mate, and heard the struggle before he dodged around the boulder and saw it. The bear-creature was still upright, roaring as it tried to hug Waels to death. Waels had gone badger—squat and thick and solid—and fortunately had managed to keep his front paws inside the deadly embrace; so far he was resisting the crushing pressure that would otherwise collapse him. The bear was visibly shrinking in height as it moved bulk into its arms; Waels's neck was growing steadily longer as he tried for its throat with his teeth.

Waels was in trouble, but Orlad would have helped him even if he had been winning. Claws extended, he went up the enemy's back as if it were a tree. The bear-thing screamed and dropped its victim. It reeled back in an effort to smash this new tormentor into the rock behind it. Orlad sawed at its neck with his tusks. Waels hit the ground, rolled, and then went for its groin and belly, front paws flailing in a blur of knife-sharp claws. It screamed again and crumpled in a scarlet flood. The winners savaged it until they were certain it was dead. That was all.

Silence had returned. Hero battles never lasted long.

The tang of blood in his mouth warned Orlad that he was ravenous. He needed meat, raw meat for preference. There was meat there. Forbidden meat. Must not. Bad example.

He was so overwhelmed by the excitement of the battle and the smell of blood that he needed a moment to realize that there was a blazing agony in his back and some of the blood must be his own. Fortunately, he had made his hide loose enough that Leorth's claws had slid before they could dig deep; although the gashes ran the full width of his back, they were mostly superficial.

Heal first, retroform second. He twisted around and managed to lick the lowermost cuts—which helped little with healing, but felt good. Another large and slobbery tongue joined in. *Bloodmouth* was an entirely appropriate name now for this gory monster with the familiar scent. He wagged his stumpy tail, but that was just Waels being consciously funny.

Orlad managed a purr.

Not just the healing. Something else wrong . . . yes, a leader must not lie around letting his wounds be licked. He struggled up on all fours and headed for the King's Grass, still in battleform, spine very stiff. Waels shivered and yelped and became a man on hands and feet. He rose and came to walk alongside, chattering human noises that the Orlad beast did not understand.

Death smells led him to many-many bodies on the grass. Most were warbeasts, but a few had tried to change back as they died and those looked much worse—half-human monsters, fur alternating with livid corpse-pallor, all streaked watery crimson by the rain. Their brass collars, which had been golden bright only minutes before, were tarnished now to a dingy brown. Two-legged people were dragging out more dead.

Orlad drew a deep breath and retroformed. The world of smell and sound dimmed; vision and thought surged back. But it *really* hurt, and he would have to go through it again because he wasn't properly healed yet. He turned a shriek of agony into a brave attempt at a victory howl.

"All right?" he asked Waels. "Anything broken?"

His buddy was one big walking bruise, but he was grinning. "Not anymore."

Thirteen corpses. Plus the two he and Waels had killed. "Who did we lose?"

"Caedaw and Vargin," Snerfrik said glumly. He was sitting on a rock and gingerly flexing his right arm, which looked well chewed but mostly healed already.

"Ranthr, Charnarth," Hrothgat added. "My lord is kind . . . one got away."

That was bad news, although the massacre could not stay secret long. "Eleven for four? This is a great victory, men!" Anything better than fifty-fifty was good in the Heroes' eyes when the initial odds had been roughly even. "We have done well, for cubs."

"My lord is kind," Waels said, staring into the fog. "You didn't see any cattle on your way up here, did you, lord? I could eat a mammoth."

"I could eat *anything*," Namberson muttered.

Judging by the corpses, so could some members of the flank. It happened, and a wise leader pretended not to notice unless the offense was flagrant.

Now what? The leader must decide. First the mouflon, to dull the insane craving for meat. And then, according to the rules, Orlad should report the unfortunate incident to Satrap Therek. That ought to end the matter, because self-defense was an unalienable right within the order. Resisting arrest was never a crime. But who had ambushed whom? And if Orlad Orladson expected a fair judgment from Therek Hragson, he was still as crazy as he had been yesterday at this time.

He would have to lead his troop back to Nardalborg and rely on Heth to shield the others from the satrap's wrath. He doubted very much that even

Heth could shelter the hated Florengian, though. Would he let Orlad sneak away and head out over the pass ahead of Caravan Six? A solitary crossing would be quite a feat for any man, even a Hero, and he would need the proper clothes, and rations for the first leg, to get him as far as the cache at First Ice. Would Heth let him attempt it? No. Orlad could not even ask him. Therek would send a seer to find out how the criminal had escaped and then loose his murderous rage on Heth.

Leadership was less easy than expected.

He must send the others back to Nardalborg while he . . . He what?

He needed time to think.

"I have to battleform again and heal my back. Snerfrik, you'd better come with me and finish that arm. Waels, you are in charge. Get the men dressed. There's a mouflon tethered near the road, down where the trees begin. Try not to let anyone . . . Listen!"

Even puny human hearing could distinguish hooves, squealing axle, and cracking whip, all coming fast. Someone was driving a team brutally up the hill. That made no sense. The survivor could not have reached the town yet. Even if he had, the response would be Werists in force, not a chariot. The fugitive might have missed a driver in the mist and failed to pass a warning, but who would be driving a chariot up a moorland road the way this one was moving? If he was only some extrinsic attending to his own business, he might go past the battlefield without noticing. If he saw the bodies and tried to go back to Tryfors, he would have to be stopped before he could raise the alarm.

Perhaps his team might be persuaded to bolt in the wrong direction? No, the chariot was already too close for Orlad to position men behind it. He realized with a shameful, un-Heroic dismay that he might have to order a murder in a couple of minutes.

A faint shadow of onagers and car congealed out of the gray murk, going by on the left, probably not close enough to see the watchers. But the sole occupant was tall as no man was tall. Therek Hragson had not wanted to be cheated out of his entertainment, an entertainment that had already cost the lives of Ranthr, Charnarth, Vargin, Caedaw, Leorth, and ten others.

"Kill him!" Orlad screamed, and battleformed.

✦

He ought to have died on the spot. Every one of his companions had sworn his oath to Therek Hragson as the light of Weru, so the satrap had claim on their loyalty before all mortals on Dodec. Orlad had not worked that out ahead of time and his warbeast couldn't. He knew nothing then but hate. Unaware even of the healing gashes in his back, he streaked.

Therek saw the black cat coming like the hand of death and knew who it must be. No doubt he congratulated himself on his good judgment in foreseeing the faithlessness of Florengians. He turned his car on one wheel and laid into the onagers without mercy, steering them down the steepest grade he could find. Having scented the pursuing carnivore, they needed no encouragement, and for a few frantic minutes they managed to stay ahead of the warbeast.

The hillside was steep. Given a clear stretch of turf, the terrified onagers might even have held on to their lead long enough to reach the town, where Therek could have found aid. But there were rocks. The little ones he ignored. The boulders he had to dodge, whereas Orlad simply hurdled them, black death inexorably gaining on its prey.

He was closing the gap, but a middle-size rock ended the chase. Chariots were not meant to be driven like that. A wheel shattered into a cloud of fragments. The car spun full circle around its long axis, hurling the satrap out like a shot from a sling, while snapping shaft and yoke and hopelessly entangling the onagers in the traces. The axle splintered into tinder, sending the other wheel careering off down the hill. Rig and team crumpled together on the grass.

Having the choice of hitting the ground as an elderly man of fragile build or of battleforming in midair, Therek naturally chose to battleform. His pall flew free. His appearance changed little—his talons grew larger, his mouth expanded into a true hooked beak—but from that moment he was a dead man, for he could never go back. No matter; as the greatest fighter of his generation, he would acquit himself gloriously, sending his foes ahead to proclaim his arrival in the halls of Weru. This he prepared to do.

He landed nimbly enough on needle-tipped toes while Orlad ripped turf in a mad effort to change direction, find footing, and launch himself in attack. As he left the ground Therek swung on one foot and lashed out with the murderous spur on his heel. Driven by the full power of his five-foot leg, that scythe could slice a man open like a soft fruit. Alas, time takes its toll. A third his age, Orlad twisted in midair and caught the leg in his teeth as it went by him. Bones crackled like bacon rinds.

Orlad hit the ground full-length and bounced upright, spinning to face his foe. Therek fell headlong on the turf and was buried under a screaming heap of warbeasts.

✦

"I wanted him," Orlad said petulantly, scowling at the remains—which covered an impressive expanse of ground.

"Greedy!" Bloodmouth muttered. "Must learn to share."

"There's a piece for everyone," Hrothgat countered, grinning. "Er, what's the rest of the host going to say, lord?"

Ah, Weru! Left flank had come hunting in battleform, clear evidence of naked aggression, so their deaths could be forgiven, but liege lord and brother to the bloodlord was the wrong game in any man's bag. Heth could not save them now. Eight men had just become outlaws.

"My lord is hungry?"

Orlad recoiled as Snerfrik thrust a steaming mass of gory meat at him. Then he saw it had hide on one side and must be onager, not satrap, so he snatched it and began tearing it with runty human teeth, every lump sliding down his throat as purest joy. Soon all the naked, soaked men around him were doing the same, laughing and growling, rubbing gore on one another's faces in childish joy at being winners, being blooded Werists, just being alive. Their wounds were already healed to old white scars.

Their leader could not laugh. The score was twelve for four now, but the monster they had unleashed would not stop feeding soon. Even if Stralg tried to appoint a new hostleader, his decision could not arrive until spring and the matter would not wait that long. There were currently only three huntleaders in Therek's Host—Heth, Karrthin, and Fellard—and the vote would tie at one apiece. That was the Heroes' way. There would be war.

The danger was extreme. Extrinsic outlaws could be arrested, imprisoned, tried, and executed, but not Werists—what jail would hold them? Anxious to demonstrate loyalty, the three hunts would compete for the honor of running down the renegades and dismembering them.

Meanwhile seven men were waiting for their new lord to issue orders. Beyond sending them back up the hill for their palls and sandals, Orlad had not a useful idea in his head.

He had several useless ones. If Fellard and Karrthin suspected that Heth was behind the assassination and his whole hunt was lurking in ambush . . . so leave the dead men's Nardalborg palls as a clue? . . . perhaps so obvious a clue that the Tryfors men would suspect a trap . . . the only thing that could throw warbeasts off the scent was running water . . .

Where to run, where to hide? Before Stralg unified the Face, dozens of cities would have been happy to hire a small band of Werists, no questions asked, but now the only independents were brigands. Must they sink to that? Orlad knew no world except Nardalborg, a staging post and stronghold. Tryfors was a trivial little town, yet last night even Tryfors had shown him how naive he was. He needed help, but no one would help an outlaw. Dantio could become Mist or Mist Dantio just by changing his clothes, but a Werist's collar was there till death. With his call to battle, Orlad had sent four friends to their deaths—he'd also accepted the other seven's loyalty, and to betray their trust would be to sin as Therek had sinned. Having no lord but Weru, he was now a hordeleader. He wanted to scream.

"Another chariot coming?" Namberson muttered. Eyes turned downwind, downhill.

Yes, coming fast, too. *Please, holy Weru, no more killing today!* This one was heading straight for them and no extrinsic driver could locate them in this obscuring drizzle. As it became visible, the driver veered aside to keep his onagers upwind from the blood—no passenger, just one man wearing a shabby leather cloak, whose hood framed a brown face and hid his ears. Eyes and teeth shone as he reined in, showing no fear of this mob of blood-streaked killers feasting at the scene of their crime. He did not disembark.

Orlad regarded the smile with distrust. "What do you want?"

"To help."

"Why?"

"Why?" Dantio's laugh showed amusement, not alarm. "Because I'm your brother, you big ruffian. Families stand together, don't you know that?"

The brother combinations Orlad had known at Nardalborg had taught him that a fight with one was liable to become crowded very quickly, but this was different. "You don't know me."

The bizarrely boyish face smiled in triumph. "Yes I do. I held your hands when you were learning to walk. And even if you weren't my brother, I'd want to help you for what you just did. That!" The seer pointed to the mangled remains of Satrap Therek. *"Down with the House of Hrag!* You just changed the world—I said you were a seasoner, didn't I?"

"What sort of help?"

"Save-your-neck help. We're all fugitives now—you and me and Fabia and Bena. We've all got to get out of here smartly."

"Can't leave my men."

"Of course not! Where are you planning to lead them? Go back to Huntleader Heth and apologize for killing his father? Oh, you didn't know that? None of you knew? Well, it's true." He laughed shrilly. "My lords, you have chosen yourself a worthy leader. I'd say so even if I weren't his brother. It only takes one snowflake to start an avalanche. I think Orlad is that snowflake and the avalanche is moving. All your lives you will boast that you fought with Orlad at King's Grass!"

Munching Werists stared back coldly at this high-pitched curiosity. If their flankleader vouched for him, fine. If he didn't, still fine. The dead could not testify.

Orlad was confused by too many unfamiliar emotions. Dantio's strangely gentle face sent disturbing signals, yet he had no choice but to trust the seer. "What are you offering?"

"The others have gone on ahead by boat. I stayed behind to enjoy the palace's reaction when Fabia's disappearance was reported . . . and to see how you fared, Brother." The smile returned. "A very welcome surprise! Now I'm on my way to meet them at the mouth of the Little Stony. It's not far. I expect you can run."

Waels was Tryfors-born. "Bloodmouth?"

"Easily, lord. Won't even need to battleform, unless my lord wishes it."

The seer said, "Know the reedy inlet just downstream from the ferry dock, Hero?"

Waels said, "Yes."

"I am going to meet the boat there."

Orlad looked over his horde and they were all grinning with relief. "We'll give you a fair start and try not to eat you when we catch you." He had no choice. "So we escape by boat. Where to?"

Still the Witness smiled. "I can't answer for Benard and everyone else, but Fabia and I are planning to go home. We have business to attend to."

"Go," Orlad said.

Dantio drove off into the mist. For a while they could hear him yodeling a joyful song. It faded into the mist and wind.

"Where's 'home,' my lord?" Narg asked around a mouthful of raw onager.

"Celebre, on the Florengian Face. Our father is a sort of king there. He's either dying or already dead."

"Aha!" That was Waels, but others were leering also. "And who will succeed him?"

"Dunno. Some old fogies get to choose—it could be me, or one of my brothers, or—"

Snerfrik's stentorian bellow was louder than anyone else's. *"Then we'll help them decide! Won't we, lads?"*

The flank roared its approval. That enthusiastic show of loyalty gave Orlad a rush of emotion that almost choked him. Struggling not to show it, he shrugged. "Eat up, then."

A eunuch, a girl, an artist—and a *Werist?* What sort of contest was that? May the best man win!

This story will be concluded in *Mother of Lies,* in the city of Celebre.